FULL MOUNTIE

AINSLEY BOOTH

SADIE HALLER

BOOTH HALLER BOOKS

COPYRIGHT

Ainsley Booth & Sadie Haller, 2017

For Megan Linden, who called Lachlan as her book boyfriend while we were still writing the first book—we did our best to make him worth the wait

ABOUT THIS BOOK

Lachlan:
365 days I've wanted Beth beneath me, begging for release. One long, angst-filled year we've circled each other, keeping things strictly professional.
But I've also got shit in my past that complicates relationships.
And I should know better than to hope secrets can stay buried.

Hugh:
A year? Try ten. A decade ago, I let Lachlan walk away because deep down, I knew he needed something else.
As soon as I laid eyes on her, I understood what I was up against: he loves Beth. Looks at her in a way he'd never look at me.
I get it.
Curvy, smart, and bossy? I just might love her, too.

Beth:
Two men. Two first dates.
Two first kisses…
But this doesn't feel like a love triangle.
Oh no. It's much more complicated than that. I'm not complain-

ing. I'm game for anything. I just have one rule: we don't tell anyone.

SECURITY BRIEFING:
* Warning: there are no limits to these Mounties' willingness to please
* Never underestimate the strength of a woman
* Sometimes the past can come back and bite you...if you're lucky
* Top-secret clearance means three doesn't need to be a crowd

GLOSSARY

Canadianisms

Mountie - an RCMP officer (see below)
Riding - voting district
Toque - wool winter hat, handy at the hockey arena even in summer

Acronyms

RCMP - Royal Mounted Canadian Police
PM - Prime Minister
MP - Member of Parliament
PMO - Prime Minister's Office (like the West Wing for the American President, where most of his staff works)

FOREWORD

This book is a work of fiction, spun from our filthy imaginations. Some of the places and events happening in the background may seem familiar, but we promise any similarities to real people are entirely coincidental.

For purposes of keeping this story focused on a very complicated romance between three people, we've taken some serious liberties with the office of the prime minister, the structure of the RCMP, policing practices in general, and office administration. Our apologies to executive assistants everywhere. In exchange for our flights of fancy, we promise a delicious happy-ever-after ending for three characters we've fallen head over heels in love with.

If this is your first Frisky Beavers book, same note goes for the political stuff. It's simplified for storytelling purposes. And please note that while each book stands alone as a romance, this book does contain spoilers for what has happened in *Prime Minister* and *Dr. Bad Boy.*

Curious about our entire series?
Visit our website at www.friskybeavers.com

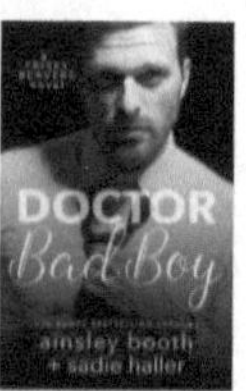

1

———————

LACHLAN

May

Torture is working side-by-side with the woman you adore—and can't touch.

It's a gorgeous spring afternoon in Ottawa, and outside Centre Block on Parliament Hill, flowers are blooming and people are milling around, waiting for the prime minister's arrival.

As his chief of security, I give that go-ahead. This final sweep of the event site should be my only consideration at the moment. I shouldn't be thinking about Beth.

But I know exactly where she is, and have from the second I stepped outside. After a year, the way she affects me shouldn't be a surprise anymore. And yet I still find myself wondering why my head is spinning, why my core pulls tight...then she smiles and there's no mystery at all.

Most days, we work within arm's reach of each other. Close enough for me to memorize the elegant line of her neck, the curve of her cheekbones, the way her hazel eyes glitter differently in every light.

Definitely close enough for me to know better than to indulge a crush fueled by lusty desires, because that very closeness is exactly why she's off-limits.

Beth Evans quietly and efficiently runs the prime minister's world. She's his executive assistant, his calm and steady gatekeeper.

I. Can't. Touch. Her.

I'm not the kind of guy Beth deserves. I'm complicated and kinky. And even her tentative, curious explorations over the last year have been adorably vanilla.

The one time she got a real glimpse at my depravity, she was horrified.

Not that she stayed horrified, though. That would have been easier to handle. If anything, the chemistry between us has ratcheted up lately.

I still can't touch her.

And I want to with every aching part of my soul.

Now I search for her, as I always do, and unerringly, I find her in seconds. She pauses her conversation and looks up, as if she can feel my gaze.

Moments like this burn at me. If only... But there's no way to finish that statement.

Then the tension ebbs as she takes a deep breath and returns to her task at hand, but it doesn't take her long to wrap it up. I watch her the whole time as she walks across from where she'd been chatting with the catering manager. She gives me a cool, professional smile. "Good to go?"

I return the exact same expression, but where she looks right at me, I can't bring myself to hold her sharp gaze. I have to look just above her head. "Yep."

"Lachlan..."

"Not now."

"No, you don't get to tell me that." She sighs as my radio crackles. "Or maybe you do. Saved by the bell."

She's been trying to talk to me for two days now about something personal, and I've been dodging her, because...

Well, because I'm a fucking idiot, mostly. But the shit between us is complicated, and two months ago it got even more complicated when Hugh Evans slammed back into my life.

"After the party," I tell her, my heart sinking. I'm pretty sure she's met a new guy. There's a lightness to her step that's been missing over the last year.

It's a good thing.

Beth deserves all good things.

But it makes me want to crawl into a bottle of scotch and die.

Today, of all days. Today marks one year since we met, one year since Gavin was elected in a stunning upset, a come-from-behind victory that catapulted Beth from an ordinary Hill staffer to the Keeper of the PM's Everything. One year since I walked into a meeting with the brand-new PM and his staff. I fell in love, head-over-fucking-stupid-heels with the sharp-eyed, smart-mouthed brunette with the legs that go on for miles.

It's also been one year since I made myself promise I'd never act on those feelings.

"Sure, after the party," she says, lightly touching my forearm.

I lock down the part of my brain that thinks about Beth non-stop. The part that wants to turn in to that touch, let her fingers sizzle my skin.

The next ninety minutes tick by exactly as expected. Gavin pulls out a two-four of beer for those who don't want champagne. A cheer goes up for that, yet another example of how he knows how to read a crowd just right.

They have good reason to celebrate. This is a government nobody thought would be formed. The underdog prime minister and his merry men. In the past year, Gavin Strong has proved himself a confident international diplomat and a caring national leader.

And personally, a good friend.

As soon as he says a final thanks and heads inside, members of my team with him, I allow my gaze to snap back to Beth.

She's hopped onto a table to sit, her legs swinging gently as she leans back on one hand. After a long winter of tights, tall boots, long skirts, and heavy wool pants, the dirty dog part of me is fucking pleased to see her in flirty summer dresses again. Ottawa winters are too damn long when all one gets is lusting from afar.

Today's dress is floaty and soft looking, a couple of layers of flower print fabric over a slip of silk against her skin. Earlier she had a blazer on over it, but she's taken that off now, and has it bunched up in the hand that's leaning on the table.

In the other hand, there's a nearly-empty champagne flute.

She's talking to Gavin's chief of staff, Stewart Rochard, and as she nods her head along to the conversation, her short, dark hair swings around her face in a sharp bob.

Not long enough to wrap around my fist, but the perfect length for her to role-play a sexually adventurous flapper girl.

Not that I've had any speakeasy fantasies about Beth or anything. Ha. I don't kid myself. When she sets her glass down and shimmies off the table and saunters towards me, I let myself go there, just for a second.

And then, as always, I lock it down.

I nod when she stops in front of me.

"Done being the guy in charge?" she asks lightly.

"For now. Do you want to get a cup of coffee?" Technically I'm still on duty, but I'm not on Gavin's personal guard at the moment, and I can walk across the street with Beth.

She parts her lips, then stops and shakes her head. "Not today."

"Of course."

"I do…"

"It's okay." This is another reason why I haven't asked her out. Because we can't even coordinate going out for coffee and we work together every single day in a high-level way. Things getting awkward between us is not an option.

"Actually, I have a date," she says, her eyebrows tugging in ever-so-slightly as she holds my gaze. "That's what I wanted to tell you."

A date. It's a punch to the gut that I deserve, and one I saw coming. I manage to make a guttural sound of acknowledgement, but nothing else comes out.

"I'm hoping it won't be awkward." Her voice is smooth, practiced. How did we end up in this place, where she's had to rehearse how to tell me that she's seeing someone else?

Let me take you out instead, I want to say, but it's too late. I had my chance. Three hundred and sixty-five of them. "Not awkward at all. You don't need to tell me about your private life, either. I mean, I'm happy for you. But—"

"It's just that it's—" She stops and glances behind me.

I realize who her date is with before I turn around. I can feel Hugh's smug grin penetrating my back, and when I do glance back, there it is—but even though his expression is entirely meant to set my brain on fire, and it does, his gaze is locked on Beth like she's the only person in the world he can see.

I know that feeling well.

She's hypnotic.

There's only one other person that has ever made me feel anything close to what I feel for Beth. And it's entirely because of how explosive—and disastrous—my affair with Hugh was ten years ago that I can't allow myself to go there with Beth.

Hugh doesn't share my concern about mixing business and pleasure, though.

He never has.

Didn't care that he burned me a decade ago.

Doesn't care now that he's playing with fire again.

Fucking Hugh. Tall, dark, and arrogant. He's a sexual pyromaniac, and since I've refused to even talk to him outside of work, he's turned to Beth.

I grind my teeth, but I can't make a scene. Not here.

"Ready to go?" he asks her, and she brushes past me, her fingers sweeping across my arm just below where I've rolled up my shirt sleeves.

"Definitely." She casts one last, quick glance back at me. "See you tomorrow, Lachlan."

I cross my arms as I give her a curt nod, and I watch them head across the lawn towards Spark Street.

I can't follow them.

I won't follow them.

My radio crackles to life.

Fucking hell. The reality is, if I had half a chance to sneak along behind and spy on their date, I probably would.

I rub my hand across the muscles of my forearm before I press the talk button. I can still feel her touch there. But duty calls. "This is Ross, go ahead."

2

HUGH

I UNBUTTON my suit jacket and loosen my tie as we navigate around the tourists taking pictures in front of Parliament. Heading out after work was Beth's idea—and it took me long enough to get her to say yes that I wasn't going to argue.

"Where are we heading?" she asks as we stop at the street that separates Parliament Hill from the rest of downtown Ottawa.

"There's a cocktail bar a few blocks from here I've heard good things about."

Her face lights up. "Intermezzo? I've been meaning to go there!"

I know she has. I saw her reading a newspaper article about it a few days ago, and when she agreed to go out with me, the first thing I did was call and reserve a booth.

There's nothing I like more than a first date. The potential is huge, and the expectations are low. Let's be honest—most people think first dates are utter shit.

Then I come along.

It's cocky to say that I give a good first date, but I'm cocky— and first dates aren't the only thing I'm good at giving.

First dates are foreplay.

I've spent my entire adult life in unapologetic pursuit of giving good foreplay. Flirting, first dates, second dates, second base, third base—a personal favourite—I love everything about the build-up towards sex.

There's a lot you can learn about a sexual partner through foreplay. How they like to flirt and talk and touch is all good intel when it comes to finally getting them naked and in your bed.

And that's what this date is all about—getting Beth Evans naked. Not tonight—foreplay takes time—but soon. My bed, her bed, Lachlan's desk when he's away…I'm easy about where we eventually fuck.

But seducing a woman like Beth is a long game. For a bunch of reasons, like she deserves to be wooed, and her standards are justifiably high. But the most important reason is she's clearly in love with Lachlan.

Sure, I should probably feel bad about poaching her, but I don't. Just because she's got a flame for Lachlan doesn't mean I can't treat her right while she's waiting for him to unfuck himself and his precious feelings.

As we wait for the streetlight to turn green, I brush my arm against hers. Light, casual touches are important on first dates. They say, if all goes well, I'll be happy to hold your hand, but I'm not going to be pushy about it.

They're also an excellent test of chemistry.

And every time I touch Beth—when I reach across her desk to borrow a pen that just happens to be in her hands, when I drop my arm if we're walking next to each other, or nudge her shoulder—there's a warm sizzle under my skin.

This one's magic, the sizzle says.

Beth plays her cards close to her chest. I have no idea if she feels the sizzle too. If she doesn't yet, that's okay. It can take time to figure out that connection. Sometimes it needs coaxing. And if it doesn't work out, that's okay, too.

There are plenty of fish in the sea, although none of them are quite as pretty as Beth.

There's something about her—like she gives zero fucks about shit that doesn't matter, but when something is important to her, she's all in with her entire heart. She loves her job, that much is clear, and right now that's where all of her focus lies.

Over the last two months, I've learned: she doesn't have a boyfriend; her last relationship was serious, but they didn't live together; it ended because he was a dick about her job getting more complicated when her boss became the prime minister; and she knows she's better off without that guy.

All of that is good stuff.

I've also learned a lot about her and Lachlan.

None of which is good stuff, not really. Not because they shouldn't end up together—they probably should, although I'm not magnanimous enough to want that for them.

No, I want them for myself. Choosing would be impossible, but Lachlan's made the choice for me. He's not interested in me right now and he's throwing up all the barriers between him and Beth.

Right now, taking Beth out for a drink and then dinner? I'm practically doing a public service.

THE BAR IS EVERYTHING I'd hoped it would be and more. We're seated in an intimate booth near the back, and our bartender is a hot young guy who flirts just enough to get a good tip, but reads my body language and gets that we're on a date.

Beth orders a glass of Prosecco. "I had champagne at the party. I should probably stick to wine if I want to keep my faculties about me."

I grin. "Now what fun is there in that?"

She laughs, a full-bodied throaty sound that sends a healthy surge of blood to my groin. "You're dangerous."

"I can be."

She gives me a long, perusing look. "Good."

"It's been a while since I've been a bad influence on someone, though."

"You think I'm a good girl?"

"Oh, I hope not." I get another laugh there and she leans back against the booth. The bartender returns with our drinks, bubbly wine for her and rye on the rocks for me. I watch as she murmurs her thanks, her lips curving in a sexy smile.

I lift my drink once we're alone again. "To a little break from work and reality."

She tips her glass against mine. "Yes, please. It's been far too long."

"All work and no play?"

"Exactly." She presses her lips together, and I know what she's going to say next. "It's not that I don't love my job—"

I reach across the table to touch her hand. "Beth, I don't think anyone in the country loves their job more than you do. But it's okay to say it's been a long year."

She groans and nods at the same time. "Such a long year."

I take a sip of my drink and watch her over the rim of the glass. She's very good at schooling her features. I don't want her to have to do that around me. So I watch, and wait, and eventually she finds my gaze. "What?"

"Tell me about it."

"No."

"Yes, please."

She laughs. "I don't think that's great first date conversation."

"No?" I shift a bit closer to her around the small, circular table in our booth. Not crowding, just getting more friendly. "I'd wager the most important thing to test on a first date is how good a listener someone is."

Her eyebrows bob up for a second, then settle back into place. A momentary flash of surprise. "Maybe about other things, but work is so ordinary."

"Again, there's nothing ordinary about your job. But let's say there was. Let's say you worked as an office manager or a nurse or a hairdresser. Or a cop." I point to myself. "Where every day is the same old thing, over and over again. You don't think I want to date someone who's willing to listen to boring?"

She tips her head to the side, thinking about that. "Good point."

"Tell me about the most boring part of your job."

"When Gavin's gone, it's deathly quiet," she says immediately. "I'm still not used to that. It was never like that when he was just an MP. But now so much of what he does either travels with him, or is handled in the PMO across the street." She gestures in the general direction of Langevin Block, the office building across from Parliament Hill where most of the PM's staff have office space. It's a select few that work in Centre Block.

"I hadn't thought about it like that." I frown. I've only been a part of the prime minister's security detail for two months, but in that time we've been away from Ottawa an awful lot. And for the most part, Beth stays behind. "I'm sorry."

She waves it off. "It's fine. It's insane the rest of the time."

"I've seen some of that."

She snorts. "Like the last-minute schedule upheavals?"

"And the million phone calls you make, ever so sweetly, to resolve conflicts with seeming ease."

"That's my superpower." She winks, but I like that she knows it, even if she's teasing.

"It is." I lean over, and we're close enough for our arms to touch. "I like it a lot."

She glances sideways at me. "Yeah?"

I hold her gaze as it grows warm. "Yeah."

She shifts closer, closing the gap between us. Her arm presses against mine—again with the sizzle—and she looks out of the booth, a smile playing on her lips as she searches for the bartender. "Maybe we could have another drink before dinner?"

Most definitely.

WE END up walking to the restaurant, where we take our time over three slow, amazing courses of food before winding our way back to Parliament Hill. Hours have passed since we left on our date, and I didn't drink anything over dinner because I knew I wanted to drive her home.

She skipped wine with dinner, too. Because faculties and first dates.

Smart, and sexy.

The walk back is charged with electricity. Our conversation flows, interspersed with laughter and more and more brushing touches of hands and arms. Glances sideways that make us smile. I finally take her hand a few blocks from the Hill and the conversation fades in a good way.

My pulse is thumping as we slowly drift around to the priority parking lot for the RCMP detail.

Yeah, I really like first dates.

And tonight is right up there as the best first date I've ever had. Only one other rivals it, and that one probably doesn't count because the guy I was with didn't realize it was a date.

But he doesn't get to intrude on this moment. Right now, all I can see is Beth. We stop beside my car. I rest my hand in the small of her back as I reach past her and open the passenger door.

At the bar, I'd caught the faintest whiff of vanilla and brown sugar, and now I get another hit of it, a heady mix that I get to breathe in and in and in because she doesn't move to get into the car. Instead, she turns towards me and lightly touches my jacket with her free hand. "I'm glad we did this," she says softly.

I brush my fingers over her cheek, then I touch her hair for the first time. It's glossy and smooth, the dark brown strands sliding over my fingers. I want to muss her up. I want to see what she looks like after a night of sex, lips swollen and hair wild.

I settle for the briefest of kisses, a light brush of my lips against hers that feels anything but simple. She makes a little noise in the back of her throat, and I run my fingers down her neck, over her shoulder, and along her bare arm.

She shivers, and I kiss her again before picking up her hand and pressing my lips to her knuckles, too.

"Let me take you home," I say. I mean it however she wants me to mean it.

She sways towards me. "I want to be smart about this," she whispers, twisting her hand out of mine and pressing her fingers against my chest, this time inside my jacket.

She doesn't need to spell out how complicated her feelings are. I draw her in close, wrapping her in a hug that she leans right into. God, she feels perfect in my arms—soft and sweet and strong at the same time. "You know what I think we should do?" I murmur against her hair. "Go on a second date. Talk more. Kiss some more. And not worry too much about anything else."

She inhales slowly, her ribcage expanding under my touch, then she lets it out. Slow. Steady. Thinking.

I didn't want him to intrude on this date, but maybe that was impossible to avoid. I squeeze her tight. "Do you want to talk about Lachlan?"

She laughs. "God, no."

"I'm not trying to stake some kind of claim here. We're not going to be two bucks fighting over you." I ease up my hug, and she leans back far enough to look at me, her eyes searching my face. Did that surprise her? "I'm not the jealous type. If anything, I usually get dinged for being a little too Mr. Free Love."

"An interesting thing to advertise at the end of a first date," she says, a hint of laughter drifting back into her voice.

"But maybe the right thing to tell you?"

She smiles. "Maybe. Yes. I'm not in a good place to get serious right now." She hesitates, and I hear the unspoken, *but if I were, I'd have thought it would be with Lachlan, the stubborn and confusing jackass.*

"Let me drive you home." I change the offer to make it clear I'm good with whatever she wants. "And we can talk about what we want to do for our second date."

She directs me to her apartment, a short drive away, and I park just down the street.

This time, she's the one who takes *my* hand as we step onto the sidewalk. She lives in a tall apartment building with decent security, so we stop in front of the passcode-protected entrance.

She doesn't punch in her access code right away. She doesn't let go of my hand, either.

Fuck me. "I want to kiss you again," I admit, my voice a bit rough.

She bites her lip and smiles. "Good?"

I laugh and pull her close, both of my hands sliding into her hair. This one isn't going to be chaste, not after that saucy little display.

Her lips part for me and I get my first taste of her for real. So fucking good. Sweet and bright, like the sun at high noon, and just as far away. I chase her, curling my tongue around hers, and she welcomes my exploration. It's playful and hot, a flash of what she'll be like in bed.

Will be. Definitely betting on that happening now. She'll want to be on top. There will be lots of laughter, and teasing.

I move my hands down her body, forming the shape of her through her soft sundress. My fingers tighten on her hips, and the urge to walk her back, to press her up against the bricks is almost overwhelming.

But her dress feels delicate, silky, and ruining a date's outfit is bad etiquette. So I turn us around and press my own back against the wall as I spread my legs, urging her into the space between them.

She comes so eagerly it makes my cock pulse with anticipation.

Down boy, we're not doing more than this tonight.

But soon. I can't wait to get inside her.

She presses in closer, nestling my growing erection against the soft swell of her belly. "I wish we'd done this sooner," she whispers, kissing my jaw.

I close my eyes and try to do some advanced algebra. Her breath on my skin is dangerous. "We're doing it now, and that's all that matters."

But that's a simplification of the situation, a fact that's rammed home when I open my eyes and over the top of her head, I see the outline of a familiar body leaning against a car in the shadows across the street.

What the fuck?

I tense, and Beth shifts against me.

How long has Lachlan been watching us?

And even as my brain churns in outrage, something else kicks in deep in my gut. I weave my fingers into her hair again and tug her head back.

This time my kiss is more deliberately seductive. I'm doubling down on what I want to prove—to both of them. I want to cement her desire for a second date. And I want there to be zero fucking doubt on Lachlan's part that he's missing out.

I don't want to be a dick—well, maybe I do—but there's something else about knowing Lachlan's watching, too. Something hot and uncomfortable—but mostly just plain *hot*.

We both like women. We both like men, too—maybe me more than him, but we definitely liked each other at one point.

But this? We've never performed for each other. I've never

kissed a woman in front of him. Now I am, and it's a woman he's not just interested in, but probably a woman he's stupidly in love with, not that he'll allow himself to go there.

That should be a cruel thought.

It doesn't feel mean, though. And the way Beth is surrendering to me, pliant and gorgeous, it doesn't feel like my kiss has been lacking in any way on the receiving end.

I forget that we're being watched. Or I stop caring, because she's soft and warm and she's got her hands inside my jacket, so all that's between us is my dress shirt and the soft fabric covering her breasts, and my brain goes primal.

Woman. Breasts. Mine. Get naked.

It's Beth who finally ends the kiss, slowly and sweetly.

"Goodnight." She presses her hand against my chest. Message clear—thanks for the smoking hot kiss, but you can't come up tonight.

I want to. Fuck, I want to so much it hurts. And the way she swayed against me, pressing herself against my cock, I know there's a part of her that wants me to as well.

And if Lachlan weren't across the street, probably steaming mad by now, I'd want to walk her upstairs just to make sure she got into her apartment safely.

But I have no doubt that when I walk away, he's going to do that instead.

Maybe that's the way this needs to go.

I burn hot under the collar at the thought of him finishing what I've started here. Him tasting, touching, taking the soft wetness I've caused between her legs.

I'm going to go home, that burn aching at me the whole way. I kiss her again, lightly this time. "I can't wait to do this again."

She touches her fingertips to my jaw and makes a sweet little sound before taking a deep breath. "Same here. Thank you."

Stepping back, I watch as she punches in her code and the apartment door unlocks. I take a few more steps down the path as she turns around, her skirt swinging around those stunning legs.

When I drag my gaze back to her face, she's watching me, her lips curled into a smile.

I wonder how long it'll take Lachlan to make his presence known to her.

Fuck.

3

BETH

As I walk into the lobby of my building, I turn my head for a final glimpse of Hugh through the glass doors.

He gives me a warm, fuzzy feeling inside I haven't had in a long time. Hugh, of all people. I watch as he disappears from sight.

But the warmth he's filled me with vanishes as I catch sight of Lachlan standing across the street, hands in his pockets, staring towards my building.

My heart starts pounding. Spying on me like a…like… I have no words, but a hell of a lot of feelings. The gall of him. I turn away and hit the button for the elevator.

The intercom for the main door is buzzing away by the time I let myself into my condo.

I should ignore it, but I can't.

We need to have this out and it's probably better for it to happen here, where it's private. Things have been strained in the office enough as it is.

I pick up the phone and hit the intercom button.

"Yes?"

He hesitates, not that he needs to say anything. I know exactly who it is. "It's Lachlan. Can I come up?"

I don't bother to respond, I just buzz him in. He's never been here, but I don't doubt for a moment he knows everything about where I live.

It doesn't take long for his knock to come at the door.

He's looking rough. His suit is rumpled, and a day's worth of scruff covers his normally clean-shaven face. Seeing him with his mask dropped like this really shouldn't make me wet, but it does. He does, always.

That doesn't stop me from being angry with him, though.

"Come in," I bite out as I open the door wider, allowing him through before I close and lock it.

I turn to face him, hands on my hips. I don't bother offering a seat. I don't plan for him to be here any longer than it takes for me to give him the sharp side of my tongue.

"If you're here about me going on a date with Hugh, you can just—"

"I was here to make sure you got home safely."

"You don't trust a member of your own security team?"

"With you? I don't trust anyone."

I swallow a scream, because that is beyond frustrating. I tamp it down and try to let it out in a long, slow exhale. It half works and I groan.

He steps towards me and reaches out, setting his hands on my shoulders. He crouches slightly so our eyes are level. "Beth, he's using you for sex."

Yesterday, I would have welcomed the feel of Lachlan's hands on my bare skin, but now…

Now, it just fuels my anger.

"Well, it's about time somebody did." *Because it's not like I haven't given you enough chances over the past year.*

His eyes flare at that. Yeah, jerkface. I'm going to talk about sex if you storm into my apartment after the hottest makeout session ever. Deal. But I don't say that out loud.

He curses under his breath, and his fingers tighten on my upper arms before he lets me go. He looks to the ceiling as he drags his fingers through his hair, and I immediately miss his warmth.

"Damn it, Beth, I'm just trying keep you from getting hurt."

"The PM is the only person you need to keep from getting hurt. I can take care of myself."

"I'm not saying you can't. But, I know Hugh—"

I hold up my hand. I don't want to hear his overprotective nonsense. They worked together a decade earlier. From the fiery clash they had when Hugh first showed up in Ottawa, I'd gleaned they didn't always see eye-to-eye. But in the end, Lachlan hadn't objected to Hugh's posting to Gavin's security detail. And over the last two months they'd been nothing but professional to each other. "It's been ten years. I can't imagine either of you are the same men now as you were back then."

"Some things never change, no matter how much time passes."

"That may be, but I'm capable of coming to my own conclusions about a man. And I think you're underestimating how open Hugh is about the kind of man he is—and isn't."

Lachlan's eyes flare wide. "What did he tell you?"

Interesting reaction. Now I want to know what Lachlan knows. I almost laugh, but he doesn't see anything funny about this situation, so I'm not going to push any more of his buttons tonight. I take a deep breath. "He told me he's not looking for anything serious. So you can—"

"You deserve serious."

"I want fun. And besides, how am I supposed to find someone to get serious about when you keep cock-blocking me?"

"That's—" He cuts himself off. A muscle twitching in his

cheek is the only reaction I get. It's probably the only one he can't control.

What, he doesn't like me accusing him cock-blocking?

Well, I don't like anything about this. And frankly, if he's going to be this difficult, I don't know why I'm holding back. He came to me. He got in my face about this, and now I'm going to blast him right back.

I jam my finger into his chest. "You know what? If Hugh wants to use me for sex, that's *just fine*. He can use me like that any time he wants."

"Beth…"

"And you really should know that it didn't feel like he was using me when he kissed me." I drop my voice. "It felt good. *He* felt good."

He groans deep in his throat. I jab my finger at him again, but my hand is shaking now, and it skips off the hard planes of his broad chest. He grabs my wrist, holding me still.

"You can't tell me who to kiss," I whisper, my voice cracking.

"I know." His voice is equally ragged, but he's not shaking at all. He's tense all over. Tense and big and suddenly, right up against me. His mouth crushes against mine, the kiss demanding and primal, and before I can stop myself I'm kissing him back.

It's messy and confusing. It's also probably wrong, but oh my God, Lachlan is kissing me. It's totally different from Hugh's kiss.

But it feels just as right.

Before I can stop it, I'm dragged into the feelings of it, the hunger and bite, the desperate need zinging between us.

A kiss a year in the making.

A kiss that should have happened for a hundred other reasons, not insane jealousy. But I don't care, I'll take this however I can get it.

And before I can get enough, it's a kiss that ends with a curse.

Lachlan drags himself back, and I find myself following him. *No.* He shakes his head and I skid to a halt.

No, no, no, I want to scream at him, but he's backing away just as fast as he came at me.

I watch, regret building inside me so fast it hurts, as he lurches backwards and turns, letting himself out of my apartment without a word of explanation or apology or even rejection.

Nothing.

Communication has never been his strong suit, but this kind of takes the fucking cake.

Men.

Two kisses in one night.

Two men who couldn't be more different. Now what the hell do I do?

4

———

LACHLAN

EVERYTHING I'VE DONE—WELL, everything I haven't done—in the last year would point to me being a coward.

I'm not.

The first thing I do when I arrive at Centre Block the next morning is head to the PM's office. Beth is already at her desk.

Her eyes go wide with surprise when she sees me stalk through the doorway.

I give her a terse smile. "Morning."

That's all I can say right now, and we both know it.

Her lips part. Fuck me, now I know what they taste like, and I want another hungry go at her more than anything else in the world. I'm not a coward, but I am weak. I let my gaze linger on her mouth until she purses her lips disapprovingly. Then I jerk my eyes back up to meet hers.

Right. The whole point of me marching in here was to show that what happened last night didn't affect our working relation-ship. Or, I hope, our friendship, but that might be wishful thinking.

I've already reviewed Gavin's schedule for the day, so I know he's got a few minutes before his morning briefing, and I have a

23

message that he needs to talk to me at some point today. I'm just not sure if now is a good time, and Beth holds that magic bit of information. "Can I steal five minutes with him?"

She tips her head to the side and gives me a wary look. "Depends what it's about."

It's not about firing a certain member of my security staff who also got to kiss Beth last night. I get hot under the collar again. Yeah. Very weak. I'm both pissed and turned on.

"It's about his wedding," I say through gritted teeth.

"Ah!" Her entire expression lightens, like she's grateful we're able to move past last night, too. "Right. I have a note here from the hotel for you…" She reaches across her desk and grabs a light purple file folder. She hands it over, her eyes now twinkling, and relief washes over me.

"Purple?"

She nods pertly. "*Lavender* is the wedding colour. So I bought special file folders for the occasion."

"You're enjoying this." A reluctant smile tugs at my mouth. God, I want to say so much more. Tell her how confused I am, how wrong I know it was to kiss her when she's decided to date Hugh.

I don't think he's going to be good enough for her, but she's right—she can handle herself and she's going into whatever it is with him with her eyes wide open.

"You wearing the wedding coordinator tiara?" She blinks up at me innocently. "What's not enjoyable about that?"

"I'm coordinating logistics from a security perspective."

She nods sagely. "For sure. I think today's topic is whether or not they need an east coast food item on the menu since they have B.C. salmon and Alberta beef."

Fuck me. I take a deep breath. "What time is the conference call with the actual wedding coordinators in Squamish?"

She beams. "Noon. So you've got lots of time to talk to both Gavin and Ellie about this and round up some ideas."

"This wasn't what I was expecting this to be about."

Another nod. "I know. When Gavin said he needed someone to handle this, though…"

"You didn't want to do it?" I regret the words the second they're out of my mouth.

She doesn't have a big reaction. She doesn't need to. Beth is a master at subtle shade. She'd never make a scene outside the prime minister's office, so she knows how to smoothly and politely shut people down.

She reaches for a pen, one with a clicky top, and flicks her thumb against the button. "You'd best go in," she says, no longer looking at me. "He's expecting you."

"Beth…"

Her hair is neatly tucked behind her ears this morning, smooth and shiny. She reaches up and pretends to tuck one side again. Then she straightens the lapels on her jacket. She's wearing a suit today, pants and jacket over a buttoned-down men's-style shirt. Like she knew she'd need armour today. Maybe she couldn't have anticipated I'd come in here and make a jackass suggestion about her being a woman and more wedding-interested, but after last night, I've definitely shown my hand, and it's not welcome.

She wasn't wrong. She'd needed that armour because I'd trounced all over the perfectly acceptable boundaries she'd worked so hard to construct.

"I'm sorry," I say quietly, leaning in. "That was stupid of me."

She glances up at me, and her glittering hazel eyes soften. "Maybe you had other things on your mind and forgot not to be sexist," she whispers.

She'd never make a scene. But she wouldn't pull her punches if she knew they'd land silently.

"I definitely had other things on my mind," I admit. "But that's no excuse."

"We should talk about those other things." She presses her lips together. "At some point."

Before I can answer her, Gavin swings the door to his office open. "Beth, do you know—oh, Lachlan. Good, you're here. Come on in. I can't believe how many questions keep flying back at me about this thing."

I clear my throat. "This thing? Your wedding is a big deal."

"Getting married is a big deal. The wedding is what it is because of who I am."

"Fair enough." I grab the purple file folder and follow him into his office. I've always liked this space. Wood-panelled and with secret doors, it's big enough to hold his daily briefings with the senior staff, but also comfortable enough to talk, just the two of us.

He sits behind his desk and grabs his travel mug of coffee. "Okay, so you get the deal, right?"

"About the food?" I flip the folder open. "Beth gave me a bit of a rundown, but I'll need to follow-up…maybe with the protocol people? And your communication staff?"

He grimaces. "I'd really rather avoid pulling too many staffers onto this. You need to be liaising with them for security stuff, so I know pushing back on menu details is way outside your area of expertise, but…"

Ah. I get it. "You don't want to be accused of using your staff to plan a personal event."

"I don't want to *use* my staff to plan a personal event." He gives me a wry look. "Although avoiding the appearance of impropriety is always good, too. Just…talk to the wedding people. Find out how many more of these types of questions there are going to be, and do I need to privately hire a wedding coordinator at this end."

"Beth says that's my role."

He laughs. "Well, if she said it, it must be true. You know who's really in charge."

For a second, I think about telling him everything. We have a unique relationship, and if there's one thing I'm sure of, it's that Gavin wouldn't judge the complicated dynamics I've got going on with Beth and Hugh.

But in exactly the same way as the PM can't use his staff to plan his wedding, it would be beyond inappropriate for me to use my boss as a personal kink and relationship counsellor.

"Okay, I'm on it. I'll talk about security concerns often enough to make the call legitimately within my purview, and get a clearer picture on why they seem so over-their-heads on planning a VIP wedding."

"Perfect." He takes another sip of coffee. "Missed you at pick-up this morning. I thought we might talk about this on the drive."

"I had a late night last night, so I switched the schedule."

"Hot date?" He gives me a hard look.

Hot something. "It's complicated."

His face tightens into the now very familiar *don't-break-Beth's-heart* look. Okay, so maybe he wouldn't be an objective relationship counsellor after all. "You should come over for a beer soon."

I can't refuse, but I can fight dirty. "I'll bring all the wedding details with me."

He groans, then laughs. "Well played. Actually, it would be good to go over everything together. Ellie's been really chill about all the planning, but we're getting close now, so...yes. Good idea."

There's a knock at the door. My cue to leave.

His staff file in as I rise, and we exchange a quick handshake while the conversation shifts around me to topics that are more befitting the prime minister. A new trade deal with the European Union and an upcoming First Ministers Meeting with the provincial leaders.

AFTER I CHECK in with my teams, I go over the material sent from the wedding venue. I quickly realize that the problem lies with the bride and groom not answering some basic questions. Well, that's easily enough fixed.

I head over to the University of Ottawa where Gavin's fiancée, Ellie, is a PhD candidate.

I find her in her cramped office, reading what looks like an academic journal. I knock on the door frame.

She jumps, and I laugh. "Sorry to interrupt."

She sets the journal down and waves me in. "No, it's fine. I may have dozed off there. What's up?"

"I sent you an email..."

She winced. "I've been ignoring the internet today."

"No worries." I hold up the purple—*lavender*—file folder. It makes me think of Beth, and therefore it's actually my favourite thing about today, complicated shit aside. "I've been designated the unofficial wedding coordinator for this end, and I've got some quick questions for you."

"I'm sorry." She drops her head into her hands. "It's just that one wedding thing leads to a hundred other wedding things, and suddenly entire days get consumed with the stuff. So we've kind of been dodging it."

"At least you recognize that," I tease as I fold myself into the wooden chair across from her desk. It's terribly uncomfortable, and I tell her as much.

She winks. "It keeps student visits short."

"That's evil." I clear my throat and open the file folder. "Now. Your wedding is happening in less than two months, and the menu hasn't been finalized." I hand over a piece of paper that I've scrawled all over. "I'm not a foodie, exactly, but from the options they suggest, this is what I think would work best for you and your guests."

She scans down the page, nodding. When she reaches my favourite suggestion, she starts giggling. She glances up at me.

"Fanny Bay oysters?"

"It's important to have food from across the country," I say with a straight face.

"Oh, Lachlan. You do get us, don't you?" She gives me a warm look.

"I try."

She grabs a pen. "My only addition to this would be that I'd like more of the cheese to come from Quebec, s'il vous plait."

"Consider it done."

FROM THE UNIVERSITY, I head to the protocol office where I unofficially ask some advice from their staff. Their recommendation is for the PM to ask the Ethics Commissioner to review the wedding plans. Oh, he's going to hate that.

So instead of talking to him about it again, I head to the Ethics Commissioner's office myself, where I make an appointment to return the next day.

I don't get back to my office at Parliament until dinner time. The PM has already left for his official residence at 24 Sussex Drive, so I review the day's reports. Then I call over to the residence and speak to the constable on duty, who confirms the PM and Ellie are in for the night.

"They've ordered pizza for dinner," he adds, and I laugh.

"Of course they did. I could go for some pizza myself. Thanks." I hang up and rock back in my chair.

From the doorway, someone clears his throat.

I sit up and open my eyes.

Hugh is leaning against the doorframe. "Evening."

I nod. "Just finished reading the reports. Easy day today."

He nods too, then glances behind him.

I grit my teeth.

That doesn't stop him. Once he's checked that nobody else is around, he goes straight for the kill. "So I went on a date with Beth yesterday."

"I'm aware. I was there when you whisked her off."

He glares right back. "And you were there when I returned her safely home again."

Ah. So he'd seen me. Fine. "You can't blame me for being worried."

"Afraid of what I'd do to her?"

Heat slams into me at that thought. Hugh doing Beth is stuff of my darkest fantasies. "We're not doing this."

He laughs quietly under his breath. "Did you get a goodnight kiss last night, too? Are you all full of complicated feelings?"

I get to my feet. "Jesus Christ. You still don't have any fucking boundaries, do you?"

"There was a time when you enjoyed that about me."

I round my desk, ready to do battle. "And that had consequences, didn't it? Leave Beth alone."

"That's not your call to make."

"No, it's hers, but you haven't given her all the relevant information, have you?"

His jaw tightens and his eyes flash as he squares right up to me. Oh, I've struck a nerve. His voice goes silky. "What exactly do you think I should tell her before a first date?"

Silence pulses between us.

He moves in closer. "Does she know how much you like to be on your knees?"

My mouth goes dry and my pulse hammers at the base of my throat.

"Does she know how rock solid you get grinding against a muscular ass?"

I shove him hard in the chest, pushing him back. "Shut up."

"Still in the closet?"

"Not exactly."

"What does that mean?"

It means that aside from group stuff, I haven't been with another man since him. I'm not giving him that much power over me. "She knows I'm pretty fluid in what I like. She knows about my kinks. Who I like to fuck isn't something we've discussed because *I respect her.*"

"You don't think I respect her?"

"I think you're using her. So, no."

"You've got it wrong." He steps closer again, his chest brushing mine. He's two inches shorter than me, which compared to how delicate Beth is feels like nothing. Everything lines up. Chests. Mouths.

Cocks.

He's growing hard even as I yell at him. I'm not immune to the tension between us, either.

"I don't think I do," I say quietly, my voice coarse. "This is exactly what I'm talking about. You shouldn't play with Beth's feelings when…"

"Say it."

"Fuck you."

"Any time. My door is always open for you." He sets his hands on my hips and sweet fucking mercy, that feels so good. My knees practically wobble as desire stabs through me. Every inch of him is solid. Thick. The first time we kissed, it was like a boxing match on steroids. There are things I can do to Hugh—and things he can do to me—that just don't work with a woman.

Beth.

Her name whispering in my mind is like a splash of ice water.

"Come on," he whispers. "Gimme your mouth."

"No."

"Lachlan…"

Fucking hell. "Not now." No, that's not what I meant to say. I should say, no, never, but I know deep down the word never won't cross my lips when it comes to Hugh.

5

BETH

BY FRIDAY, I've made up my mind that not only do Lachlan and I need to have an adult conversation, we should probably do it sooner rather than later.

Pretending that everything is fine at work isn't going to cut it. I spent most of last night tossing and turning, my bed sheet twisted around my sweat-slicked limbs as I slipped in and out of filthy dreams featuring both Hugh and Lachlan.

Hugh, at least, I can handle. He passed through my office earlier today and gave me a dirty wink, but other than a quick good-morning text, that's been our only contact. He seems to have picked up on the fact I need a bit of time to figure out what I want, and I'm grateful for that.

Lachlan…I can't handle him, at all. I could, until Hugh showed up. I can see now that the unraveling started then. Hugh lit a long-burning fuse, and now two months on, Lachlan's getting pretty close to exploding.

Unfortunately, after our brief conversation about the PM's wedding, I don't see him again. So late Friday afternoon, I open an email window, and then promptly close it.

It would be the height of stupidity to send this message using a government email address. Or really any email address from inside this building.

Instead, I grab a blank piece of paper and a pen.

Lachlan,

From the day we've met, there's been something special between us. I know I can trust you to be a good friend, right? And good friends talk about their problems. Talk *out* their problems.
I don't want there to be any secrets or confusion between us. I'd like to see you this weekend. You are welcome to come to my place, or we can meet for coffee. I think we need to talk, and I hope you agree.

Beth

I read it over, then I scrawl my personal phone number and email address at the bottom of the page. I could call a page to take it to him, but he'll freak out if anyone else's hands have been on it. Hell, he's going to freak out enough if he knows I'm the only one who's seen it. So I carefully fold it up, then wrap it in another piece of paper to ensure the message can't be read though the envelope I seal it in.

Then I grab an intern to sit in my seat until I get back, and head for Lachlan's office.

Most of the time, he works at a desk nearby, preferring to be on Gavin's personal detail as much as possible. And sometimes he works out of the guardhouse at 24 Sussex. But he also has a formal office deep in the basement of Centre Block, where his files are kept and he meets with his officers when he needs private space.

My heels click on the stone stairs as I make my way down there, echoing in the quiet of a Friday afternoon in May on the

Hill. Everyone who could get away—either to their local constituency or head off on a long weekend—did. It's the first really nice weekend, a precursor to the always too-short summer.

Nobody is around.

My heart rate picks up at the idea of finding him alone in his office. I'd give him the letter and maybe we'd get that coffee now.

But when I arrive at his door, it's closed. I know he's not done for the day, so I slide the envelope under the door. I can send him a cryptic email letting him know I dropped something off.

I turn to head back upstairs, and collide with a hard wall of muscle.

"Whoa, what's the rush?" Hugh slides his hands up my arms, and even through my blazer, my skin remembers his touch.

I sway into his body before remembering where we are—then I take a big step back. "No rush." I take a deep breath. "I was heading back upstairs. I just dropped something off for Lachlan. Have you seen him?"

Hugh shakes his head. "Not in the last hour." He points to the staircase. "We can walk and talk if you want."

I give him a grateful smile. I'm not looking to hide anything from Lachlan, but I don't want to goad him, either.

I want us all to be mature adults about whatever this is, and Lachlan finding me in Hugh's arms outside his office would be a shitty start to turning over a new leaf.

"So other than saying good morning," he murmurs as we climb the stairs together. "We haven't talked. But I've been thinking about you."

I give him a genuine smile. "I've been thinking about you, too."

"Terribly inappropriate thoughts, I hope."

"Of course."

He laughs. "Good. Maybe we should talk about that second date, then."

"We should." I hesitate. "But maybe next week? I've..." I trail off, but then I think better of being vague. No. They work together. They have a history of conflict. I want everything to be as on the table as possible. "Honestly? I need to talk to Lachlan this weekend. I promise that doesn't affect how much I want to see you again."

To my surprise, he doesn't even blink. "Yeah, of course. I was actually thinking about trying to get together with him this weekend, too."

"Yeah?" For some reason, that makes me feel better. Maybe their history isn't as hostile as I think it is. "Good. Maybe next week we can compare notes on how to handle him."

He touches my arm, and I stop on the next step. He gives me a serious look. "I can't lie to Lachlan, though."

"No." I press my lips together. "Neither can I. I don't want to hurt him. But…he's overreacting. We're grown-ups, and who we kiss is nobody's business. It doesn't mean anything other than I want to kiss you." I look at his lips. I want to kiss him right now, but that can't happen. "So don't let him get under your skin."

Before he can respond, a couple of House staffers enter the stairwell, and I wave goodbye.

6

LACHLAN

THE DOORBELL RINGS about twenty minutes after I arrive home from work and I groan.

Of course, someone would have to show up right after my shower. I've finished towelling off, but I'm still naked. I slip into a pair of sweatpants, not bothering with underwear because whoever it is won't be staying.

Between the letter from Beth and the shit day I've had, I'm in no mood to socialize. All I want to do is grab a beer from the fridge and veg out in front of the television.

Or maybe think about her note and what it means.

My irritation at being disturbed on my down-time is amplified when I open the front door to Hugh standing there holding a large pizza box.

He's still wearing his work clothes. I instantly regret my decision to skip the boxer briefs. If he's here longer than the time it takes to slam the door in his face, my dick will be at serious risk of pitching a tent in my sweats. It should be illegal how good he looks in a suit.

I scowl. "What are you doing here?"

He shoots me a slow, easy grin. The one that ten years ago

would've had me dropping to my knees and devouring him whole.

"I brought your favourite." He says as he opens the pizza box with a flourish.

I am not surprised when I see the ham and pineapple toppings. That had been Hugh's favourite, not mine. And considering the pizza joint in Moose Lake didn't offer pizzas topped with sundried tomato, artichoke hearts, olives, prosciutto, and feta cheese, I had seen no point in letting Hugh believe any differently.

Still don't. That's hardly the biggest problem we have. "I ask again, why are you here?"

He gestures to the pizza, but his eyes stay glued on my face. "I couldn't ignore the craving any longer. And I'm pretty sure you're hungry, too." I ignore the double entendre, but when his tongue pokes out and slides across his upper lip as his gaze wanders down my body, all I can think about his how good that tongue used to feel on my skin.

I don't react.

But I don't slam the door shut either, and that speaks volumes about my choice.

Hugh tries another tack. He's always got another angle. "If it makes a difference, Beth knows I'm here, and she's good with it."

I'm surprised by his words and I don't *want* to believe him, but even though Hugh is the kind of guy to say whatever it takes to get in someone's pants, it won't be a lie. "She does?"

He nods, all serious now. "She said she wanted to talk to you this weekend, too."

Ah. So she knows he's here to talk. That's not exactly the same thing as showing up with a pizza as a pretense for a quick and dirty fuck.

On the other hand, she's gone out of her way to underline that she's a grown up. We're all grown ups. Hell, I've seen an

NHL player play with her on the St. Andrew's Cross in Max's basement.

It's not the same thing and you know it.

No. It's not. But tomorrow I'll tell her everything and we'll see where the chips fall.

I should make him leave, I really should…but I'm tired of fighting against the decade-old unfinished business between us, so I open the door wider and gesture for him to enter.

"Have a seat and I'll go grab us a couple of beers."

I'm feeling way too vulnerable in front of him topless, so I detour to my bedroom to grab a t-shirt.

When I return to the living room, Hugh's jacket and tie are lying across the back of the sofa where he's reclining—his shirt half undone and his bare feet propped up on the ottoman.

Fuck.

"Feel free to make yourself at home." I let the sarcasm drip from my lips as I place a bottle of beer on the coffee table in front of him.

He slides a slow appraising look over me. "You needn't have bothered with a shirt on my account."

Ignoring his jab, I grab a slice of pizza and the remote before dropping into the armchair—because the sofa isn't big enough for both of us.

I turn the television on and flip to TSN before chucking the remote back on the table. Sports recaps are just the thing to help me ignore the big, sexy suit-wearing elephant in the room.

After a minute, Hugh leans forward, and instead of grabbing another slice of pizza or his beer, he snags the remote and hits the power button.

I don't react on the outside.

On the inside, I'm sliding back ten years. To bossy commands that would yank me out of a pissed-off, post-work funk and get me hard as a rock.

"Beth came to a holiday play party organized by a friend of mine," I finally say. I stare straight ahead at the dark television.

"Do you want to talk about Beth tonight?"

That gets my attention. I turn and give him a hard look. "Always."

Something moves in his eyes. Regret, maybe. Understanding, definitely. "She's gorgeous. And smart. And funny."

"Yes."

"And lonely."

Fuck me. "Yeah."

"You need to treat her better."

"I know."

He gets up and crosses to stand in front of me. "What are you going to do about that?"

"That's what I was thinking about when you interrupted me." Fucking hell. I don't want to think about this right now. I don't want to think about how I've let her down, or how I can't handle Hugh properly, or—

"Maybe you need to stop thinking, and start doing." From anyone else, it would sound like a line.

From Hugh, it is a line, but it works.

I roll my head back and look at him through heavy, hooded eyes as he unbuttons his shirt the rest of the way and peels it off, baring his torso.

In theory, this would be a chest I could have seen a dozen times already this year.

In practice, I've avoided working out with my team since he's arrived, because this view undoes me every single time.

I still remember the first time I saw him naked—in the only gym in Moose Lake. I'd invited him to workout with me, and when he stripped down afterward and walked into the shower, I'd died a little inside.

He hadn't been the first guy I'd been attracted to. He wasn't the first guy I'd fooled around with.

But he was the first man I'd wanted with my entire being.

He was a lot of other firsts, too.

Some onlys.

Now as his eight-pack ripples in front of me, decorated with a few new tattoos, I die all over again.

Thinking time is definitely over.

Whatever Hugh wants, Hugh is going to get, at least for tonight. I lick my lips.

"Tell me what to do."

7

HUGH

OH, that's tempting. If anyone needs a firm hand, it's Lachlan. He's wound so fucking tight. But we're not in a good place for that kind of strict power exchange right now. Probably not any kind, but I'm not a play-it-safe kind of guy.

I kick his feet wide, making space for me to get closer.

The groan I get in return is magical.

I give him a dirty half-grin. "Take off your shirt. Let me see you shiver for me."

He grabs the hem and peels it up his body, tossing it to the side. He's beautiful. Big and broad, hard planes of muscle running flat across his body. A familiar line of hair running down his lower abs, thicker now than a decade ago. His muscles are different, too. He's bulkier, harder, but not as cut as he once was. Not as lean through the chest, but those narrow hips are still carved from granite.

My cock flexes, thickening in reaction to a sight I've been deprived of for far too long.

Lachlan's gaze drops, and I know he can see the bulge in the front of my dress pants.

"Touch me," I tell him, my voice low. Smooth.

He's so fucking eager. His hands shoot out, one landing on my thigh, the other going straight for the goods. Ah, fuck yeah. I grow against his fingers, throbbing under his touch. He traces my length through my pants, up and then down again. He cups my balls and I rock up onto my toes, flexing my thighs to give him more space.

We need more space. More skin. More than however long he'll give me until he kicks me out because he regrets this.

Fuck, we shouldn't be doing this if he'll regret it.

But I won't.

And maybe I can make it good enough that he won't, either.

His hands go to my belt, then he pauses. I die a little inside, but his fingers tighten as he glances up at me. "Do we need a condom for this?"

Relief pulses through me. I shake my head. I wouldn't put him at risk. "Haven't been with anyone since I cleared my physical for the transfer."

The hungry grin he gives me is a dirty promise I have no doubt now that he'll keep. Deftly, he gets my pants open and they fall down my thighs. I step out of them, then sway my hips toward him again. He leans in, his breath ghosts against my skin. Yes, yes, more. I don't wait for him to do it. I shove my boxer briefs down my hips, and my dick bobs out, hard and heavy.

His hand wraps around me and his mouth, wet and hungry, covers the tip. Yeah, fucking eager. And perfect.

I growl as he swallows me deep. Not all the way to the root, but right to his fingers and that's good enough. I tangle my hand in his hair and start to control his movements a little. Force him to slow it down, and hold me at the entrance to his throat when his lips are wide around my base. Ease him off when he's greedily swallowing more of my flesh, making him moan a little from the denial.

But it doesn't take him long to give in to me and let me set the pace. Long, slow strokes in and out of his mouth, with a pulsing hold at either end. His hands start on my hips, but as I fuck his mouth, he curves his fingers under the elastic of my briefs and finds the curve of my ass. I flex against his touch there, and he makes a helpless sound for me.

"Yeah, baby. Missed my ass, didn't you?"

He growls around my cock, and I grin. I want to go dancing with him. We never got a chance to do that. We danced, just the two of us, drunk and horny, but it would be so much better in a club. Pulsing lights, grinding bodies.

I'm getting close now. That little tingle at the base of my spine pushes me to thrust faster, chasing my release.

I hold his face tight against me as I come harder than I have in longer than I care to remember.

I'm still twitching as I pull out of his mouth. I drop to my knees and drag him to the edge of the chair. He's a big beast of a man, but so am I, and I'll manhandle him wherever and whenever I want. Right now, I want to taste myself on his lips. I stroke my hands up his chest and squeeze his shoulders, holding him in place as I kiss him.

Our first kiss this year was angry. This is decidedly not. I just came like a fucking champ down his throat and he lapped it up like a hungry alley cat. Now he kisses me like he's starving for this, too, and I need to hold him steady. *Oh, Lachlan.* How long has he deprived himself? Need vibrates off him.

"Did I not teach you anything?" I ask gently as I push him back, my hand flat against his chest.

He licks his lips. "About what?"

"You can't be a monk. It's not healthy."

"Not everyone can be the hedonist that you are."

I roll my eyes. "You should try it. You're a powder keg about to go off." I hook my fingers into his waistband. "Although going off is exactly what I want you to do now."

He groans and rolls his head back against the chair as I slowly fist him. His cock is a thing of a beauty.

"I haven't been a monk."

"Tell me…" I slide my thumb over the head of his cock. I lean in and breathe in his scent. I want to know all his secrets. "Tell me everything. And I'll reward you for each story."

He bucks his hips, driving his cock through my fist, but I dodge my head out of the way. He's only going to get my mouth one way, and that's by opening up.

I squeeze him tighter by way of warning. "What was the last dirty thing you did?"

"Can't tell you. That's a matter of national security."

I jerk my attention to his face. "Really?"

His cheeks flame. "Yeah."

"With the PM?"

His eyes go wide. "Not just…" He tries to slide his hips back onto the chair, but I've got a firm grasp on him. He's not going anywhere. "Uh…"

"Tell me."

"You…" He struggles around his tongue. I want to laugh at him, but his concern is legit.

"I won't tell anyone."

"Beth knows." He licks his lips. "And that's it. Uh… the PM asked me to help him with Ellie. Lend some hands, so to speak."

Fuck, that's delicious. "I'm going to jack off to that later."

He glares at me. "It wasn't like whatever you're imagining."

"Ah. You were just being helpful? Mr. Kinky Helper Man? That doesn't count. What was the last dirty thing you did for *you*?"

His blush deepens. "I don't remember."

"That's shameful."

"And yet I told you anyway, so…" He nods towards his dick.

He's not wrong. It's not what I asked for, exactly, but it was honest and open. I lick him with a broad, flat tongue. His taste is heady and still familiar after all these years. I suck just the head into my mouth and pull what I can get from from his slit onto my tongue.

Fuck, my dick is chubbing up again. I want to jack his legs up to his knees and drill him so hard, but that would be too much for tonight.

One thing at a time.

"Tell me something else," I whisper, my breath brushing against his cock. "Tell me what you would do if you weren't so duty bound. If I ordered you to be a hedonist for a night."

"Ahh…" He swallows his cry and pumps his hips into my mouth. I'm not going to even pretend that I'll deprive him of this. I'll keep sucking because I love the taste of him. But I'm not going to change it up or add a hand or fingers until he fesses up.

He's not coming until I get something truly filthy in return.

We all have them. Dirty, disgusting wants.

What's the point of a fantasy if it's not utterly awful to say out loud? There's nothing mind-blowing about that which you can voice without wanting to die a little on the inside.

I wonder if Lachlan wants a dirty threesome of his own. I picture us dancing at a club. Taking someone home. More than one person.

Lots of bodies.

I want Lachlan in a pile of sweaty limbs. Mouths and hands all over him.

But that's my fantasy, and right now, this minute, I want him to admit to his.

I slide back, giving the head a quick little flutter with the tip of my tongue while I use the V between my thumb and index finger to trap his sack up against the base of his cock.

His frustrated groan goes straight to my dick.

"Come on, Lachlan—I know you want to come. And all it'll take is one dirty little fantasy. How hard can it be for you to share that with me when I've been balls-deep inside your body?"

I lock my gaze with his and flick the tip of my tongue back and forth over that sensitive spot where the head of his cock meets the shaft, occasionally swiping up to lick away a drop of pre-come.

As soon as he starts bucking his hips, I squeeze a little with my hand and pull my head back. "What's so hard about one little confession? Who am I going to tell?"

He shakes his head, and I loosen my grip on his cock slightly and go back to teasing him with my tongue until he's close again.

I could keep this up all night. And he knows it. I've done it before, and he didn't love it. He took it because that's what I wanted. Now he's taking it because he's not ready to give me what I want. Not yet, but he's close.

After two more trips to the edge, he finally gives in. His face, his body in that moment where he submits entirely to me—it's beautiful.

"Tell me."

He squeezes his eyes shut and balls his hands into fists. "I… want to see what it's like…to…um…get topped by a woman." Flopping against the back of the chair, he lets out a big rush of air.

"Well done." Reaching up, I grab him by the back of the neck and pull him forward. I take his mouth hard, my tongue pressing deep. I'm proud of him for opening up, making himself vulnerable to me. His submission was hard won tonight, and now it's time for me to reward him for his bravery.

Releasing his lips, I lower my head and tease that spot that makes him crazy before taking his cock deep into my mouth. I love the way he moans when I take him into my throat. I slide back up his shaft, swirl my tongue around the head, then straight back down. Another long trip up, a swirl of the tongue and then I let loose.

Tightening my grip at the base of his cock, I slide up and down his shaft hard and fast, varying the depth. Sometimes shallow, sometimes all the way down.

It's not long before his breaths come faster and his hips start jerking.

He spurts hard against the back of my throat, and I swallow every drop. Even after he stops pulsing and slips out of my mouth, I stay on my knees for him, my head pressed against the hard flat of his belly.

But it's not for him at all. It's for me.

I don't want to step away from him. I don't want to watch him shut down and send me away. So I stay right where I am until my heartbeat returns to normal. Then I stand up without looking at him.

"There's probably a baseball game on," I say, not giving him space to tell me no. "Let's finish our pizza."

8

BETH

SATURDAY MORNING BRINGS another good morning text, but this time it's not from Hugh.

Lachlan: I got your letter.

Okay, it's not the warmest first-thing-in-the-morning text. It also is missing two critical words.

Beth: Good morning to you, too.
Lachlan: That's what I meant to say.
Beth: I knew that.
Lachlan: Ha. I'm free later, by the way.
Beth: Okay. Good. Do you want to get coffee?

He takes a few minutes to reply. It wasn't that challenging a question, really, although when he answers, I realize he was probably struggling over what he really wanted to say.

Lachlan: Maybe your place would be better.

I punch my fist into the air. Yes. Good. No, better than good. Exce-fucking-llent.

Beth: After dinner? Around seven?
Lachlan: See you then.

IF I THOUGHT his coming over was a sign of wavering principle, though, I'd have been wrong.

He sets a clear tone for the evening as soon as he walks in the door. "I shouldn't have kissed you."

"I disagree." Three days later, that kiss is still zinging through me. How could that be a mistake? Except he'd dropped me like a hot potato.

His gaze drops to my mouth. He wants to do it again, and I agree. He should. But he doesn't want to, as well, and I don't do complicated and reluctant.

If I did complicated and reluctant, I've have dragged Lachlan into a storage closet months ago.

"Okay, so you shouldn't have kissed me. Fine." I step back. "But that doesn't feel like the end of the conversation to me."

He shakes his head. "It's not."

"Then come on in."

I give him the most cursory of tours that he missed on his first visit—"This is the living room, that's the kitchen, have a seat on the couch." He does as instructed as I cross to my bookshelf that doubles as a bar.

I don't really have any stiff drinks, but I have some maple whiskey liqueur that will do a decent job of dousing any embarrassment. I pour two glasses, an ounce or so in each. If he doesn't want one, I'll have two.

He takes it and tosses half back immediately.

I don't know if that should make me feel better, but it does.

But that relief quickly disappears when he levels a serious look at me and cuts right to the chase. "Hugh and I have a history."

"I know you worked together…" But I let that hang out there, because I'm starting to figure out it's gotta be more complicated than that. "Did you…I mean, was it like with you and Gavin and Ellie?"

Lachlan goes pale beneath his tan. Yeah, I went straight to the thing we just don't talk about.

He had a threesome with our boss. I had the misfortune of overhearing about it when Gavin and Ellie had a fight.

Ellie told me…details. Unnecessary details, because I don't have any kind of claim on Lachlan, but enough to know it wasn't really about him.

"No, nothing like that," he says quietly. "But I guess I owe you more of an explanation about that incident, too."

"You don't owe me anything." I take a swallow of my own drink. "I just want to clear the air between us so we can move forward."

"As friends."

"As whatever we both want," I say firmly. I haven't ruled out the idea of more kissing.

Now that I've brought up the threesome, I wouldn't rule that out, either, although that would require them liking each other enough to be in the same room for sex. Although there is a certain chemistry between them that is…spectacular. Just highly explosive.

"That day with Gavin and Ellie…that was just the one time. And it wasn't much more than what you've seen at Max's house." Now he's blushing.

"I've seen a lot there," I murmur. "Not that you've let me do much of it myself."

"Those hockey players don't know what they're doing."

"And you do?" I wave my hand. "No, don't answer that. I think we've gone off in a weird direction."

He gives me a long, confusing look. "Maybe we need to go there. It's just that I'm way out of practice on this. It's easy to suggest to others, to help others with, but actually pretty hard to negotiate for myself."

That's more sharing in a couple of sentences than he's done in the last year. I move closer, but I still don't sit next to him. I pace back and forth, slowly, as I sip my drink and process what he's telling me. To the best of my knowledge, Lachlan hasn't dated in a while. He may have had sex here or there, but where I thought I was observing a tightly wound up guy all these months, I was just really seeing a monk-by-choice.

Why did he make that choice? "So…what is this between us, then? Some kind of kink thing that I don't understand yet?"

"No. Maybe. I don't know. I know that I look at you and I want you, but I've got this other stuff in my past that confuses that in a big way."

"Like what?"

"My history with Hugh."

It hits me like a ton of bricks. He'd already said that, more than once, but I'd mis-filed it. "Oh."

He's got a *history* with Hugh. All the while I was lusting after him. But I won't feel like a fool. No. There's nothing wrong with being attracted to someone.

Or two someones. Even if they maybe really want each other. I lick my lips and try to be cool. "So you're gay?"

He lets out a strangled laugh. "No."

"Are you…" I trail off. I don't want to play a game here, some fishing expedition for information that might not be any of my business. "I didn't even think you like Hugh."

He laughs.

I don't see how it's funny. "You glower and snarl and act like you hate him."

"Yeah. Sometimes I think I do."

Ah. "So you like him and you don't like him. That's positively high school."

He rolls his head from one side to the other and I hear a quiet pop. I ignore all the complicated stuff that remains unsaid and put my glass down, then move around the back of my sofa to stand behind him.

I put my hands on his shoulders and make a shushing sound when he protests. "Let me. You're...tense."

He laughs. "That's an understatement."

"Mmm. You're welcome to talk about that if you want."

A sigh is the only answer I get at first. That's okay. *If you want* is what I said and I mean it. I tug his jacket off and smooth my hands over his shirt-covered muscles.

He finally speaks, low and quiet. "This isn't how I pictured any of this going. You and me, I mean."

Regret rolls over in my tummy, because maybe if we'd acted sooner, if I'd opened my mouth and issued an invite last fall, over the winter...

But I didn't. And maybe that was for a reason.

Plus this is *Lachlan*. No matter what, I think I love him. I want to be his friend. His face is the first one I look for each morning and the last I seek out before heading home at night.

I roll my thumb along a knot in one of his neck muscles. He has more than most men, it's hard to name them all. And I tell myself to hold my tongue, but that's a total fail. "Yeah. Me, too."

I swear he growls under his breath, but he holds still as I work my fingers from his neck down to his shoulders and back again. He rolls his head, stretching his neck out, and I let my fingertips glide onto the bare stretch of skin above his shirt collar.

Smooth, warm, and taut, his skin stretches tight over flexing tendon and muscle. He doesn't move, so I let myself explore further, to the sharp edge of his hair cut, short and cropped in the back, fading up to a bit longer on top.

Precise, just like the man himself.

Controlled.

Whatever history they share, Hugh's arrival has thrown Lachlan for a loop. I should step back and let them sort that out.

Instead I play with his hairline and let myself imagine touching him in a more intimate way. Exploring more skin than the few inches above his collar.

Hearing that tight, reserved grunt because I'm taking him deep into my mouth and he's throwing his head back—

Lachlan's hand closes around my wrist and I freeze.

"Come here," he says quietly, tugging me around the sofa. His long arm doesn't let me go, not even for a second, and my pulse is pounding by the time I settle next to him again.

9

LACHLAN

SHE CURLS up beside me on the couch and I gently stroke my thumb over the back of her hand as I gather my thoughts.

I need to get this right.

"Hugh came to my house last night," I finally say. *And our history became something quite present tense again.* Hard to say that out loud.

"He told me he was planning to get together with you this weekend." She says it without any sign of irritation or jealousy, and some of the guilt I've been carrying slips away. Maybe they've been doing a better job of sharing than I have.

Although I wouldn't put it past Hugh to mislead her a bit. Innocently so, I'm sure he'd think.

"We didn't just eat pizza." My gut churns as I prepare for her reaction to my almost confession. She deserves honesty, but I don't know how much detail to get into. "I want to be up front with you about what happened."

Her eyes go wide, but at the same time, the corners of her lips tug up a little, and then a lot. She leans in, her smile broad and her eyes soft. "Lachlan, it's fine. I don't need the particulars."

I search her face. She's heard what I've said tonight and she's not blinking. Not wavering. She's still right beside me, leaning in. Even though I still feel like I owe her an explanation, I take her at her word because I've waited too long for another taste of her.

Turning more fully towards her, I cup her cheek in my hand and I brush my lips over hers.

She opens for me and I lick my way into her mouth. She tastes like the liqueur we've both been drinking. Right now, maple might be my new favourite flavour.

As I slide my fingers through her silky tresses, I deepen the kiss...but not as deep as I want to go. She deserves sweet and gentle, and I want to be the one to give it to her.

She twists her body, sliding her leg over mine until she's straddling me, a welcome, soft weight in my lap that feels just right.

Her mouth is demanding as she rubs herself up and down my jean-clad cock. It's an exquisite torture, but this isn't about my pleasure. Not tonight. Beth's enthusiasm is a precious gift I intend to reward, handsomely—but there's that damn voice in my head reminding me we need to talk.

Tangling my fingers in her hair, I hold her in place as I ease away from her. "Beautiful, I want you more than my next breath, but I don't want to fuck this up by taking things so far you'll end up with regrets."

She presses her fingers to my lips and gives me a no-nonsense look that makes my dick throb. "I've been waiting a long time for you. Don't hold back. I want it all."

Then she'll have it, damn it. Skimming my fingers beneath the hem of her shirt, I pull it up and off.

I release the front clasp of her bra and slide it down her arms, exposing the most glorious pair of breasts I think I've ever seen. I lean forward and suck a nipple into my mouth as I cup her other breast.

She resumes her maddening grind in my lap, rubbing herself

harder and faster. If I let her go on much longer, I'm going to come in my jeans.

Grabbing her by the hips, I hold Beth tight to my body and rise from the sofa. I don't bother to ask where her bedroom is— the options tend to be limited in apartments like this, and I'm right. I find it on the first guess.

I lay her on the bed and immediately turn my attention to getting her all the way naked. Her jeans are a bit on the snug side, so it takes a little effort for me to shimmy them down her legs. But damn, is it ever worth it.

Live, naked Beth exceeds my fantasies by many orders of magnitude, and I take a moment to appreciate the view.

I pull my recently-added emergency in-case-of-Beth condom from my wallet and toss it on the bed before stripping down.

She smiles at me, slow and sultry. An invitation she doesn't need to issue twice. Taking hold of her ankles, I ease them apart and kneel in the space between.

She's wet and glistening. I stroke my fingers irreverently over her outer lips, where her soft skin meets delicate curls. She shivers as I stroke her, parting her folds so I can find more of that slippery wetness.

"Tell me what you like," I say, my voice catching. I can't wait to taste her, but I don't want to rush, either.

"That feels good." She takes a deep breath as I delve deeper, gathering moisture with the tip of my finger and swirling it up to her clit.

"Oh, you like that, too," I murmur. She's responsive, quivering as I rub on either side, finding all the spots I should explore with my tongue.

"More," she breathes, and that's my cue. I lean in and follow the same path with my mouth, outside first, then in, starting lower, where she's wet for me, and so fucking delicious.

Then higher, where I need to be more gentle, because her clit is throbbing now, hard and eager but oh so sensitive.

Back and forth I go, in lazy figure eights until she starts lifting her hips to meet my tongue, my mouth, and then I kiss her deeper. I fuck her with my tongue and suck her clit into my mouth, but I don't let her have either of those long enough to get herself off on my face.

There's plenty of time for that in the future. Beth can ride me whenever she wants. I'm already addicted to the taste of her. But I want more tonight. I ease off and she protests, so I dive back in, playfully this time.

I love the way she squirms and tries to push my head down when I tease her clit with the tip of my tongue. All restless and desperate. I should make her come, but I want her all on edge when I finally take her.

"Lachlan, *please*." She sounds desperate. Perfect.

I pull back far enough to see her face and she bangs her head against the pillow as she lets out a frustrated growl.

"Please, what?" I ask. I know what she wants, but I need to hear it. Both for my ego, and my overactive sense of responsibility that wants her enthusiastic consent to my cock in her pussy.

"Please don't make me wait any longer. Get up here."

Close enough.

I lean in for a final taste of her before slowly kissing my way up her body. So many sensitive places that make her squirm and giggle, and I linger in each newly discovered spot. The crease where her thigh meets her body—I'm fascinated that she only reacts on the one side. The nip of her waist—both sides.

By the time I reach her breasts, she's writhing beneath me. I circle one nipple with my tongue as I tease the other with a finger. Her hips rock and I latch onto her and suck hard while I glide my hand down to her pussy. I dip a finger in and out, coating it in her cream.

I press my finger to her lips. "See how good you taste." She licks and sucks at my finger, and my heart hammers in my chest.

The look in her eyes nearly takes me apart as she swallows eagerly. I want to bury myself hard and deep inside her body, her soul.

Instead, I pull back, taking a moment to put on the condom and slow down.

Because this is Beth. The woman I've been wanting since the first moment I saw her. The woman who's made me ache to be right here every single day for the past year. And this is my chance to show her how I feel.

Lowering myself over her, I reach down and position myself at her entrance, then, I hook my arm under her knee, easing it up and to the side—opening her as wide as possible. Our gazes lock, and Beth's lips form a silent O as I press into her, inch by inch.

She's snug and soft, warm and welcoming. Sinking into her body is disorientingly good, but after the first few strokes I gain the control I need to stretch out her pleasure. Our pleasure. I never want this to end.

Before long, she's trying to tip her hips upward, but with her legs spread like this, she's my perfect prisoner. "You want more?" I ask her as I slide into her heat again. "Tell me what you need."

"Just this. It's so good," she breathes.

"Deeper?"

"Yeah. Sure." She rocks her hips again, a helpless little pulse because she has almost no range of motion and I won't be rushed.

On my next thrust, I flex my hips, burying myself in her body. As she takes the last of me, her breath hitches and I lean down and gently kiss her mouth.

She's hot and tight, and now, she's mine. It takes every bit of my restraint not to tell her that out loud. *Mine.*

Angling myself so I slide over her g-spot, I pump my hips at a nice, leisurely pace as I hold her gaze. And on the down-strokes, I grind against her clit. I watch her eyes light up, then get heavy. I like both reactions and I push her buttons again to zig zag her between them.

We can't undo a year of distance. I can't make up for three hundred and sixty-five nights of empty beds. But I can make tonight worth the wait.

I can give her so much pleasure she'll be sore in all the right places.

As I move us together, she gives up trying to meet my thrusts, and instead of rocking her lower body, she stretches her arms over her head and writhes beneath me, brushing her nipples against my chest.

I kiss her again. *I know what you're doing*, I think, but I don't say it. Instead I release her leg and take her hands in mine, pressing her back against the bed. Her eyes darken as she tugs against my hold, and her lips curve into an ecstatic smile.

"No rushing," I tease her as I swivel my hips, easing my cock partway out of her. She groans and tosses her head as she tries to chase the shallow strokes. Her legs crawl up my torso, urging me deeper again, and when I finally give in she gasps and presses her face into my forearm.

Inside, she clenches around me, too. Every part of her body is responding to me, and that's so fucking heady.

That we're doing this is still unreal.

I breathe her name to ground myself, and she turns her face again, looking right at me. "Yes," she says. Simple as that.

I say it again. "Beth."

"Yes. Lachlan, yes." She arches her back, surging under me, and I release her hands, dropping my forearms to the bed. Caging her in but letting her move, too. Letting her suck me into the whirlwind of arousal. Fuck control. Fuck patience.

My thrusts grow wild and frantic as she grinds up against me. Her hands cup my shoulders, my neck, and she pulls me down, until we're plastered together.

I realize I'm shaking as I buck into her, my thrusts starting and stopping deep inside her, more a rutting than anything else.

Her teeth graze my shoulder, then her tongue follows, a slow lick that makes my balls pull tight.

"Do that again," I growl hoarsely, and she does, squeezing me inside her at the same time, and a stream of profanity slides out of my mouth. "Need you to come with me. Fuck, I need you…"

"So close," she whispers, her breath hot against my skin. "Harder."

I blindly reach for her leg with one hand, going back to the position we started in, and she cries out. Yeah, that's the stuff. Each stroke drags another gorgeous shout from her mouth, so I stick with powerful thrusts of my hips. My own release begins to churn, and there's not much I can do about that. But even if I spill into her before she comes, I'm not stopping. I'll get her there. I'll fuck her forever if she wants.

She clings to me, her voice sweet and husky in my ear as I drive into her. "There, yes. Oh, Lachlan. I'm going to…"

And through some blessed luck I don't fucking deserve, she gets there just before I do. She tightens up in my arms, shivering and clutching as an orgasm rockets through her. Her face contorts delicately, her mouth parting, her eyes squeezing tight, and it's all so gorgeous, so private and erotic, watching her come undone, that I lose myself.

I thrust hard one last time, holding my engorged cock deep inside her. No release has ever felt this good. My thighs throb, my arms ache, and I'm coated in a thin sheen of sweat.

I should probably get off her. Even as I think that, I press my hips against hers. My cock is sensitive and softening, but she still feels amazing.

"Am I heavy?" I finally ask.

"Mmm." She laughs lightly. "Yeah. I like it, though."

With a sigh, I roll to the side. I need to get rid of the condom. "That was…incredible."

She makes a contented sound. "It's been a while, and I don't want you to get a swollen ego or anything, but that was quite exceptional. I'm not sure it's ever been that good."

"No worries on my ego. You get all the credit for making that special." I stretch out and she does the same, but on her stomach. I look at her sideways and reach out to lazily touch her hair. "And it's been a while for me, too."

She doesn't say anything, and I stroke my fingertips over the elegant line of her neck and around the delicate muscles in her shoulders. When I stop at the top of her spine, she twists her head to look at me. "What?"

"I want to tell you about what I did with Gavin and Ellie."

She smiles ruefully. "Right now?"

"Yeah." It might not make sense, except in my head, and I want to get this out. "It wasn't about sex. That's what I want you to know." She doesn't move. I trace my fingers down her spine. "Not like this. This is intimate and special and nothing like what I did with them. What I did for them. That was kink. That was service."

She nods, a small little movement. "Okay."

"It's just—"

She turns and presses her fingers to my mouth. "I said okay."

"I won't do it again. They wouldn't ask me to, but I'd say no if they did."

Another bob of her head, but this one comes with a bite of her lip. "I don't think I want more explanation there. I'll get past it."

My turn to slowly nod. I don't want to turn this into some kind of confessional beyond making sure we're on the same page. "We're going to find our own way here."

She leans in and brushes her lips against mine. "I'm figuring that out," she says, her breath sweet and hot as she gives me a loose, sleepy smile. "None of this has been like what I expected. I'm sure whatever comes next will be strange and wonderful, too."

HUGH

Beth: Can we have lunch?
Beth: Today?
**Beth: I could introduce you to the poutine at ESD if you
haven't tried it yet…**

WHEN I WAKE up to three texts from Beth, back-to-back-to-back
at five in the morning, there's only one response.

**Hugh: Would you rather grab breakfast? I don't have to be on
duty until seven.**
Beth: Okay.

Twenty minutes later, I meet her at Elgin Street Diner, which
I've heard of but have not yet experienced. She's already halfway
through a cup of coffee when I arrive.

She gives me a nervous smile, and I lean down and brush a
kiss against her cheek. "Good morning, beautiful."

"Morning."

"Couldn't sleep?" I slide in across the booth from her and grab the menu. Apparently I can get poutine as a breakfast side. Perfect.

"Not really."

I put the menu down and give her my undivided attention. "Want to tell me about it?"

She opens her mouth, then closes it and shakes her head.

I give her a gentle but disbelieving smile. "Then why did you text me?"

"I wanted to have lunch."

"Hmm. Okay. Why don't we say what's on our mind together. Count of three?"

"Hugh…"

"Three…two…one." I look at her evenly. "I slept—"

"—with Lachlan." Her eyes go wide. "Wait, when?"

"Friday night."

"Ah." She licks her lips. "He kind of told me about that. Not the details, but…"

"Do you want the details?" I'm ruthless about this, but fuck it. Secrets between lovers are fucked up, and I still want to be Beth's lover. Until they tell me they're exclusive and I can take my perverted ways and buzz off, I'm all in with both of them.

Pink spots bloom in her cheeks, but she doesn't look away. "Maybe not here."

"Where were you planning on taking me for lunch?" I arch one eyebrow. "We're the only people in here right now. The waitress can't hear us."

Her hand shakes as she picks up her coffee cup. "Right."

"So that's a no?"

She shakes her head. "No." Her chest rises and falls raggedly. "Oh, this isn't how I thought this would go."

"Tell me what you want to hear."

"I don't want to be a problem between you and Lachlan."

She doesn't get it. "That's not a concern." It's up to him to tell her how he feels, but between the dirty fuck-buddy connection that I have with him and his un-dying love for her, Beth isn't the one to worry about messing things up. "If anything, I should be apologizing to you."

Her blush deepens. "I...I don't know if I should admit this, but I don't have a problem with you guys fooling around."

My eyebrow goes up again. "Fooling around? We're not in high school."

"Right. I mean...everything. Anything. I think...whatever makes Lachlan happy. I don't have a claim on him."

"Do you want one?"

"I..."

My pulse has picked up, and I know I'm pushing her now, but this is everything. "What do you mean, whatever makes Lachlan happy?"

She shrugs. "I don't honestly know. But when I think about him and you, I don't get jealous. You said you're not a jealous person either, so maybe...for now..."

She trails off as the waitress realizes we're not looking the menus and approaches. We both order the special and I ask for coffee.

When we're alone again, I lean back and spread my arm wide across the back of my side of the booth. I'm about to tread on dangerous ground, but that's what I do. "Do you get jealous at the thought of him with anyone else?"

She glances away. Yes.

I wait until she warily lifts her gaze back to my face. "Beth, don't confuse being attracted to both of us with not being jealous."

She frowns. "Well, it feels different."

"Until the bloom falls off the rose of dating two men." I raise my hands. "I just want you to go into this with eyes wide open."

I hadn't meant that as a test, but if I had, she'd have passed it with flying colours. She doesn't even blink. "Into what?"

Into what, indeed. That was the million dollar question. "Honestly? I don't know. But I have some ideas…"

11

LACHLAN

I can't pretend I wasn't worried about how work would go after the weekend of Hugh and Beth and me and holy shit, but as Monday unfolds, those fears prove to be unfounded.

If anything, Hugh is more professional today than he has been in the last two months. No dirty looks, no mostly-innocent slips of the tongue that I know are anything but.

Mid-morning, he checks in with me as I hand off the PM to his team for a trip across the road to Langevin Block, where the bulk of the PMO staff work, and his expression is cool and all business.

Maybe I should have blown him sooner.

Beth doesn't wear a mask quite as well as Hugh does, but she's completely professional, too, even if her smiles are warmer and her eyes follow me more than usual.

I like that. A lot.

At noon I have another wedding conference call, and when I get off that, Gavin's back and his itinerary for the week has changed. Now we need to send an advance team to Winnipeg as well as Regina for the cross-country trip he's taking next week. It takes most of the afternoon to confirm the details from the travel office. Flights for my officers not traveling on the PM's plane, extra hotel rooms, and a local RCMP liaison officer to get the ball rolling before they arrive.

Once all of that is done, Beth likes to be copied on the confirmation. It ticks a box on a master list she keeps. I could email her, but...

I take the stairs two at a time.

She's doing her end-of-the-day routine when I arrive. Clearing everything off her desk, one project at a time. Carefully locking away anything sensitive, and slotting papers that staffers might need overnight if something comes up—like Gavin's daily schedule printout, a call sheet of critical phone numbers, letterhead and envelopes—into the designated spaces. The red folder for the chief of staff's team, blue for communications, green for special projects. She re-arranges the pens that, over the course of the day, have gotten stuck in the wrong cups, then grabs a cloth and gives her computer a quick wipe down.

Watching her do something so ordinary shouldn't affect me, but I love the care she takes to make things right.

She finally finishes what she's doing, and without looking over at me, says, "Are you just going to lurk there?"

"No."

She gives me a sideways glance. "Good." Then she smiles, and that's everything.

My chest swells. "Everything is organized for the advanced party to go to Winnipeg on Thursday."

She nods. "Good."

"I could have told you that in an email."

Another smile. "I'm glad you didn't."

"Do you have dinner plans?"

Her eyes flare in surprise. "No."

"Was that too forward?" I move closer, suddenly feeling too big and oversized for the refined space. For her.

A slow, gentle shake of her head. "Not at all. Feel free to be as forward as you want with me."

"I want to take you out for dinner." Hugh got to do that. It's only fair. But I keep that to myself.

"I want to go home and change first."

"I could pick you up at seven?" I think of where I want to take her. "And dress casually. Jeans would be fine."

FOR THE LAST YEAR, I've spent more hours on duty than most supervisors do. I've taken my role as Gavin's chief of security seriously—and when he started seeing Ellie, that effort doubled because she didn't ask for any of the extra exposure dating him brought down upon her.

But I sign out tonight without a second thought. There are good protocols in place and I've got my phone on me.

And more importantly, Beth is worth it. I'd lost sight of that, but I see it clearly now, and I want to make up for lost time.

I head home and shower and shave again, then change into jeans and a long-sleeved t-shirt. I grab a jacket, too, but it's warm enough I won't need it.

Beth is ready to go when I get to her place. She followed my advice and put on jeans, which she's paired with a funky pair of heels and a bright red floaty tank top under a cardigan.

She's got bright red lipstick on, too. That's new. And irresistible. I draw her close and brush my lips against hers, sliding my tongue against the seam of her mouth. Asking—no, begging—for entrance.

She opens for me with a happy little sigh and I kiss her thoroughly, until she's soft in my arms and my head is buzzing.

And when I let her go, her lipstick is still intact. Miracles.

"Ready to go?" I ask.

She grabs a small purse off the hall table and flicks it open. I don't miss that she's got a condom in there—I think she angled the purse towards me on purpose—and the buzzing gets louder. She double checks the contents and then snaps it shut and gives me a big grin. "Yep."

Tease.

I take her to a pub I like, that's got a big west-facing patio enclosed in wrought-iron gates, now hung with blooming flower baskets. The sun is low on the horizon, but still warm. We sit with our backs to it, on adjacent sides of a small, square table. Close enough for me to take her hand, but on enough of an angle to each other I can see her face as we talk.

"This place is nice," she says, looking around.

"They've got my kind of food, and it's always good and fast."

"What do you recommend?"

"The sweet potato fries are great. The burger's good. They always do a really nice soup, that's different every day. Everything, really."

She looks at the specials on the outdoor chalkboard. "Soup. Yes, I want that."

We order half-pints of beer to go with our dinner, and then I take her hand like I've wanted to since we arrived. "So."

An amused look settles on her face. "Yes. So."

"This weekend was interesting."

"Are you freaking out?" She squeezes my fingers.

"A little." I shift in my chair and lean toward her. "But I'm more interested in making up for lost time."

"I like the sound of that." She presses those perfect red lips together and smiles like she's got a secret. I'm sure she's got many, and I want to discover all of them. "But I don't want to rush, either."

"Oh?" I don't know how I feel about that.

"I want to explore what we have between us, don't get me wrong." She drags her gaze all over me and her smile grows. "Explore everything. But after a year of wanting each other, I think there's a risk of swinging too quickly into something serious."

"You want to keep things casual." I *really* don't know how I feel about that.

"I want…" She takes a deep breath. "Casual? I don't know if that's the right word. Nothing about this weekend felt casual. It felt intense and crazy and wonderful. It felt good, exactly as it was."

"Okay. I don't think I'm following."

She hesitates a beat. "I had breakfast with Hugh today. And I might have dinner with him tomorrow or Wednesday."

Ah. I nod slowly. "And…"

She shrugs her delicate shoulders. "And if you wanted to have dinner with him, that would be fine, too."

Unbidden, my ass flexes and my thighs tighten up. My jeans get tight as I think about what she's saying. "You want to date other people still."

This pause is long and everything in the background fades away. I swear I don't breathe again until she shakes her head. "I want to date Hugh. And you. Nobody else."

I exhale in a fast rush. "I can handle that."

I'll more than handle it. If she wants to take things slow because she's enjoying Hugh's company, that's fine. I'd be a hypocrite if I didn't get his appeal.

But I can be a dirty bastard, too. Not as filthy as my ex-lover, but…I've got game. If that's what she's looking for, then game on.

Hugh's a great guy.

Hot and kind and loyal.

But if there's a competition for her heart, I'll not only fight, I'll win.

And in the meantime…if Hugh shows up with pizza again…

She watches me react, her gaze turning liquid and hot. Jesus. I'm not sure she knows what she's playing with here, exactly, but I have zero doubt in my mind that she's having fun.

We eat while the sun sets, then she starts yawning. I know I'm being selfish when I invite her back to my place, but I want her in my bed.

She shakes her head. "Then you'll need to drive me home later. Better if you come up for a few hours when you drop me off."

A few hours. I want to drag her back to my place and keep her in bed all night. I want to sleep wrapped around her, my cock inside her. "Okay. But I don't mind driving you home, later or first thing in the morning."

Next time, I'll remember to suggest she packs a bag with work clothes.

"It's just…I was up early today. It's been a long day." She slides her fingers through mine and tugs me close. "I'd be happy to have you tuck me in, though."

I frown. "Why were you up early? Did something happen?"

She gives me an enigmatic smile. "Nothing work related."

"Are you okay?"

She presses into me. "More than okay."

"Then let's get you home." I lower my voice. "And into bed."

12

———

BETH

Tuesday morning, I wake up—thankfully at my usual time of half past six and not the panicked four in the morning of the day before—and there are two text messages waiting for me.

Hugh: Good morning, beautiful. How was your night last night?

Lachlan: Dinner was amazing. After dinner was...even more so. We should do it again later this week.

I read them both a dozen times over.

Then I get out of bed and dance my way into the bathroom. Once I've showered and my hair is dried, I take my phone into my closet and text Hugh back.

Beth: I had dinner with Lachlan last night. Want to hear about it?

He calls me back immediately. "Tell me everything."

"Not everything," I say with a smile. "Surely you don't want to hear about how he kissed me when he picked me up…"

"Every dirty detail." He laughs. "Or whatever you're comfortable with. I often forget that other people have different boundaries than me."

"I think I like your boundaries."

"What are you doing right now?"

"I'm getting dressed for work. You?"

"At work already. I'm at 24 Sussex today."

"Quiet day."

"Very. I'm all alone in the guardhouse. What are you wearing?"

"At the moment?" I look down at my naked body. "Nothing."

AFTER A DELIGHTFUL WAKE-ME-UP round of phone foreplay with Hugh, I finally get dressed. I send Lachlan a quick text, too, once I arrive at work. He's swamped, and we decide on dinner Friday for sure, and maybe sooner if he can squeeze it in.

I finally sit down at my desk just as Gavin's wrapping up his daily briefing with his senior team. When he started as the PM, I made sure I was here for those, too, but after two months of me routinely working twelve and fourteen hour days, Gavin put his foot down. Now I try to be at my desk at half past seven or quarter to eight, and I'm pretty good at leaving before six most nights. It's still more hours than I've ever worked in the past, but I don't want to miss anything.

In a small way, I'm a part of making history. I take that seriously.

But it's not all work and no play. Mid-morning, I'm distracted from work again. Not by a sexy man, or another sexy man, but by an email from Violet Roberts, Gavin's best friend's new wife.

From: Violet Roberts
To: Beth Evans

Sasha and I have convinced Ellie to let us throw her a wedding shower, so I'm hoping you might have time to meet for lunch or dinner this week so I can sweetly talk you into helping us plan it? It's going to be a tea at the Chateau Laurier. First Sunday in June. And could I ask you to put together a list of women from Gavin's side to invite?

I take a quick look at my calendar. Since Gavin's trying to cram a lot in to the week before he leaves on his trip out west, lunch is out.

From: Beth Evans
To: Violet Roberts

How about dinner either tonight or tomorrow? Lunch is hard this week, but totally open next week.
That sounds lovely, by the way. Exactly her speed and style.

We settle on dinner tonight, because Violet wants to nail everything down. Efficient and orderly—I can't fault her for that.

The rest of my day speeds by, and at six, I wave goodnight to the security guards and leave Centre Block behind me.

I hadn't seen Lachlan all day, but now as I walk down the path towards the central business district—and Violet's law office, just two short blocks away—I see Lachlan's big, broad form walking swiftly toward me.

I wave, and stop, waiting for him.

"Hello," he says with a smile. He's ditched his suit jacket at some point. He's in fitted trousers and a dress shirt, but the sleeves are rolled up and his top button is undone.

He looks completely fuckable and I'm very, very sorry I agreed to dinner plans. "Hey yourself."

"Where are you off to?"

"Dinner with Violet. Wedding shower planning."

"Ah." His grin broadens. "Need my tiara?"

A laugh bubbles up from deep in my belly. "I'll borrow it, but you're getting it back."

"Good deal."

I regretfully point towards Spark Street. "I gotta go."

He points back in the direction of work. "Yeah, me too. Someone's called in sick, so I'm covering an overnight shift tonight."

Bummer. No late night booty call for me from the forearms I'm gazing at lovingly. "Good luck with that."

"Have a nice dinner." He gives me one more smile, then he's gone.

I rub my chest. Oy. That man makes me feel things on top of things.

13

HUGH

I'm on the schedule to work at 24 Sussex all week. I don't mind these shifts—they're quiet and it's a good chance to get to know the other RCMP officers I'm working with.

But this week, of all weeks? It means no lunch encounters with Beth, and little-to-no run-ins with Lachlan.

I live for run-ins with Lachlan, so this seems terribly unfair on a totally irrational level.

Except Wednesday morning when I show up to work, there's the chief of security, every last inch of him, slouched in the guardhouse watching the security videos.

We're not alone. There's a constable filling out an end-of-shift report at the desk. So I don't say anything, but when Lachlan spins around in his chair and gives me a look, I notice.

"Morning."

He yawns. "Indeed."

"You were here all night?" He'd worked yesterday, too.

"Malcolm called in sick. I'm heading home now that you're here. John will do the shift handover." He rubs his eyes. "I've got my phone on me, but seriously, don't call me about anything until I've gotten at least a few hours sleep—not unless the residence is on fire or something. I'm on again tonight and tomorrow night."

"Are you still going on the junket out west?"

He nods. "Even if Malcolm is still out sick, we've got two more officers back from holidays by Saturday. It'll work out."

And in a pinch, he could pull staff from RCMP headquarters or the Ottawa police department. I've done the supervisor and scheduling thing a few times, in both small town detachments and big cities. It's never easy and it always falls on you to fill in the gaps.

"We've got it covered here." I move closer. Nothing a colleague wouldn't do. I clap him on the shoulder and squeeze. "Go to bed."

His muscle rolls beneath my hand. He doesn't move, but he does turn and look at me, amusement and something else, something tighter, playing across his face. "Thanks, boss."

I chuckle. Then I squeeze harder. "Give us a call if you need anything later."

He doesn't call. I wasn't expecting him to, not really. I've been at work all day—his work, too—so he can hardly call me up and ask me to bring him another pizza.

But he brings takeout with him at the end of the day shift, and enough for me to stay and share.

That gives me an idea.

So the next morning, when he drags his sorry ass home, I'm sitting on his front step with breakfast.

Thursday is the start of a couple days off for me. I'm pretty sure he's only got a few hours of down time now, so I'm not going to stay long.

"What are you doing here?" He stops in front of me, his feet wide.

I lift the bag of food. "Brought you some egg sandwiches. Thought I could help you unwind."

He flicks his gaze over me. To the bag. Back to my face. Then he holds out his hand—not for the bag, but for me. I seize his hand in mine and he hauls me up, right into his body. "Yeah. Okay."

He pushes past me and unlocks the front door. The last time I was here, he pointed me into the living room and told me to sit.

Today he doesn't say anything at all. I follow him past the living room and down a narrow central hallway into the kitchen at the back of the house. It's newly renovated, handsome and clean. Spartan. A lot like Lachlan.

He points to the coffee machine on the counter. "You want a cup?"

"I brought some." I set the bag on the counter and open it up. Inside are two travel mugs, a smaller bag of breakfast sandwiches, and a couple oranges.

"'Kay." The single syllable utterance is hard to read.

"Hey, is this a problem?"

He turns and glares at me. "Would it matter if it were?"

"Well…" It depends whether or not I'd believe him for real if he said yes. Lachlan's conservative definition of a problem doesn't always align with mine. "I don't want you to be uncomfortable."

He laughs. "That's such a fucking lie. You love it when I'm uncomfortable. You like nothing more than making me blush."

"That's different." I grin at him. He's not wrong.

He moves closer, bumping right into me. Hello. I twist, bracing my hands against the counter. He leans against me and groans. "We need to talk about how we're going to do this. I don't like surprises."

"I know," I whisper. "But I do."

"This can't affect work."

"I get that."

"I know you do. I'm just repeating the rules out loud for my benefit as much as yours."

Rules. I love rules. I love breaking them, too, but it's just as much fun to get super fucking creative inside the bounds he sets out.

I cup the side of his neck, my thumb sliding around the front, right above his clavicle.

He freezes.

I bump against his chest, giving him a split-second warning before I spin us around, so he's the one pinned against the counter and I'm the one in charge of the kiss.

Because yes, we're fucking kissing.

It's been too long.

Ten years, then two months. Now it's been a week and I need him.

I hold him tight as he tenses, but there's nothing hesitant about the way his mouth opens for me. How eager his tongue is, or the moan I swallow.

He's got a hint of regrowth that scratches at me as I kiss him, and I drag my hand up to cup his face. Granite jaw covered in scruff. Damn. I want him to leave beard burn on my thighs.

Maybe not today. Maybe when he gets back.

"I want to kiss you," I say against his mouth.

"You are." His lips are soft now, and as he smiles against me, I feel him slide right into this. His dick swells, pressing into me.

"I mean in general. In private, but not just one-offs. I want you."

"I invited you in, didn't I?" He reaches around to cup my ass, pulling our erections together. I'm wearing jeans and he's got heavy khakis on. The thick layers of fabric add to the effort it takes to frot, and making Lachlan work for what he wants has always pleased me.

"Okay. What else?"

"I can't remember." He drops his head to my shoulder. "Fuck."

"Yeah, I want to do that, too. But not now. You're tired."

He grinds against me, making my dick wet. "Not that tired."

"Mmm." I slide my hand over the back of his head, where the hair is too short to grab on to, but he gets the idea. He lifts his head enough for our mouths to slide together again, and I start to rub against him as we kiss, lazy and dirty.

He spreads his legs wide and pulls me between them, until there's no space between our bodies and we're reduced to the hard, pulsing need to just get off.

This is familiar. Even after a decade, I remember the shape of Lachlan's body against mine, the press of his dick and desperate pull inside me to get closer, closer, closer. His hands tighten against the hard curve of my ass as I flex and grind against him. Up and down, my hips move, fluid and slick and totally focused on the mission—getting Lachlan off. Making him shiver and shake as his balls draw tight, as his orgasm starts to coil deep inside him, and he wants to fight it, but he can't.

I bite his lower lip as he gasps and slams his hips against mine. "Shit, fuck, damn."

God, I want to ride it out with him, but I don't have a change of clothes here. "So good, watching you come," I whisper, kissing the corner of his mouth as he shudders in my arms. "Fucking hot."

"You didn't." He tries and fails to focus his glassy eyes on me. Tired boy.

"I'm good." I kiss him again. "You'll owe me when you get back from out west."

"On my knees," he whispers, then drops his head to my shoulder and drags in a ragged breath. "I need to go get changed. Don't go anywhere."

I pat his ass as he heads out of the room. He doesn't go far. It looks like his bedroom is across the hall. I watch through the half-shut door as he pulls off his clothes and throws them in a hamper, then he disappears and the shower turns on.

I turn to the breakfast I brought, and grab one of the coffees.

Fucking hell. Pressing my hand to my still swollen cock, I try to think of drill routines. That doesn't work. I just see Lachlan half-dressed in our red serge.

Paperwork makes me think of Beth.

Mmm. Beth. Right. I don't need to wait until Lachlan gets back to have some fun.

I cross my legs at my ankles and take a long, slow sip of coffee.

1 4

LACHLAN

I TAKE A THREE-MINUTE SHOWER, then pull on a clean pair of sweats and rejoin Hugh in the kitchen.

He hands me a coffee.

"Thanks."

"My pleasure." He gives me a dirty grin as he takes a sip from his own cup, and I feel my cheeks heat up.

Then I yawn.

He shoves a sandwich in my hand and I gesture to the table. We sit and eat, and don't talk. It's perfect.

When I'm done, I sit back and watch him finish eating. He sees me looking at him, but he doesn't say anything at first. Like, *look your fill, Mr. Ross. Get hooked on the big, bad Hugh.*

He quietly gathers up our garbage and disposes of the wrappers, then rinses out the travel mugs. I don't miss that he leaves them on my dish rack to dry.

I stand, too, and I yawn again. These all-nighters. I can't do them as easily now as I could when I was younger.

He points across the hall. "Is your bed through there?"

"You're not tucking me in."

"Why not?"

"Because I…" I lick my lips. Because I tuck Beth in. Because I don't need him to take care of me. What we have is different. He's not going to like any of those answers. So instead I pull him against me and put his hands on my bare torso. "Because I'll see you out, and kiss you goodbye properly," I whisper before I nip at his lower lip.

"You're a chicken, you know that?"

"Yeah. There's a difference between reticence and being a coward, and I'm not sure where chicken falls on the scale, but sure." I kiss him hard on the mouth. "Now get out of my house so I can get some sleep."

He pats my cheek and shakes his head, but he makes for the front door. I follow and watch him saunter down the drive.

From the kitchen, I hear my phone vibrate.

I close and lock the door, then go to find it. I've just received a text message from Beth.

Beth: Are we still on for dinner tomorrow before you fly out west? A little birdie named Gavin mentioned that you had to pull another overnight shift last night.

Lachlan: Wild horses couldn't keep me away. Where do you want to go?

Beth: How about you come over to my place? I can make spaghetti.

THE NEXT NIGHT I clock out of work at six on the nose. I'll need to be at the airport at nine, and I'm already packed, so I've got three hours, and they're all hers.

I stop and pick up a bottle of wine and a bouquet of flowers on my way.

I've arrived at her apartment just a minute after she does, she explains after giving me a quick kiss. She's still in her work clothes. She excuses herself into her bedroom and comes back a few minutes later in yoga pants and a t-shirt that has an over-sized watercolour flower on it.

"You look good enough to eat." *Again,* I think to myself, picking her up and swinging her onto her kitchen counter.

She laughs and leans into me, her arms wrapping around my neck. "You've confused me with my unforgettable spaghetti sauce," she whispers.

I'm not confused at all, but maybe I'll save Beth for dessert. Right now I settle for a kiss, long and slow, one that leaves us both panting a little. She's so responsive, I just can't get enough of her.

"I'm an idiot for waiting so long to do this," I admit when I hug her again, my mouth next to her ear, my words quiet.

She doesn't say anything, she just squeezes me back. Then she slides off the counter and leads me around the kitchen, getting me to help her as she pulls together a quick dinner. The sauce is already made and frozen in individual servings. She pulls out two packets, then does an exaggerated look up and down my body and grabs a third from the freezer.

Smart girl.

She throws the freezer bags into a hot water bath to start them thawing as she directs me to fill a pot with water. Then she rifles through her fridge. "Do we need a salad on the side?"

"I'm easy either way."

She pulls out a clamshell of baby spinach. "Can I just add this to the sauce instead?"

I crowd against her and take the spinach. "You can do what-ever you want."

She leans back against the counter and raises her eyebrows. "That's dangerous."

And she says it like we're not just talking about food. Not just talking about fucking, either.

"I know." Fuck, do I know. But I'm spinning pretty hard out of control for her now, and I'm finding it hard to care.

She presses her hand against my chest and looks up at me, her eyes full of concern. "You'll tell me, right? If this is all too crazy?"

No. There's not a chance in hell I'll tell her that. No matter what, I'm in now. "It's not crazy at all. It's…" I think about Hugh in my kitchen yesterday morning. I pull her close. "This feels right. Exactly as we're doing it."

Right, completely out of control…those two things can co-exist for me. They have before.

And then it all went sideways pretty spectacularly.

Yeah, well I'm a decade older and at least a modicum wiser now.

And when she gives me a wink, I'm reminded that she's more than capable of drawing her own boundaries. "It feels right for you, too?"

She nods definitively. "Yep. Now put the pasta on."

Okay, then.

I measure out a larger portion of spaghetti for myself and a smaller one for her, double-checking before I slide the noodles into the boiling water. She gives me a hip bump as she nudges me out of the way so she can add some salt, then she sets a timer for eight minutes.

I find a corkscrew and open the wine, and while we wait for the sauce to heat up and the noodles to cook, we share a drink.

It all feels delightfully domestic. It's been ages since I've done this with a lover. Friends, yes. Group munches. Gavin and Ellie a few times.

"Do you want Parmesan on yours?" She moves around me to the fridge. Her hand stays on my hip as she pulls the door open and grabs a chunk of cheese neatly wrapped in plastic and bearing a sticker from the cheese shop at Byward Market. "I dashed over at lunch and picked this up."

"That sounds great."

"There's a rasp in that drawer there—" She points with the block of cheese. "Can you grab it?"

Once our dinner is plated up and we've done a quick tidy, we eat at the table. I tell her about the overnight shifts at 24 Sussex, which morphs into a bit of a history lesson about the time someone broke in and a previous prime minister's wife had to defend herself with an Inuit carving.

"I think I heard about that," Beth says, shaking her head. "How scary!"

"I think it probably happened when you were in high school."

She winks. "Right, because you're so much older than me."

The eight years between us doesn't feel like much now. "I was young at the time. I was…" I trail off, trying to figure out how old I'd been. "In university, I think."

That twists into a conversation about school, but Beth isn't very forthcoming. She went to college in Fredericton, near where she grew up, she shares that much, but quickly slides the conversation back to our respective moves to Ottawa.

"So you're fully bilingual?" I've heard her speak French, and she slides back and forth with ease, but my own French is hard-fought, and it's difficult to know sometimes.

She shrugs. "Yes, but…" I give her a *don't-brush-this-off* look and she laughs. "Yes. I am." She takes a sip of wine. "It was really my mother's doing. She enrolled me in the immersion stream of school from the beginning. In hindsight, I should thank her for that, although I'm not using it as she'd like me to."

"What would she rather you be doing?" That doesn't make any sense.

She waves her hand dismissively. "Ah. Well. My mom is a whole other conversation. She's an artist, and sees the world through a very special, totally impractical lens."

"Gotcha."

"How about your family?"

"The complete opposite of that. My dad was a city cop in

Guelph, my mom is a nurse. Now he's retired and coaches hockey, and she goes to work to avoid him." Ah, my parents. I shake my head.

She laughs. "Yep. That's different. Do you go home often?"

"Nah. Once a year or so. We don't have a lot in common."

She curves one eyebrow up in obvious disbelief. "He's a cop and he plays hockey."

Shit, I walked right into that. I swirl my wine around in my glass. "Those aren't enough to make up for the fact that his son is bisexual."

Her face falls. "Oh. Oh, Lachlan. I'm sorry."

I shrug. "Old news now. We just don't talk about it."

"Your mom…?" Her eyebrows draw together. "Surely she…"

I shake my head. Surely nothing. "She'd rather not talk about it, either."

And we haven't needed to. It's not like I'm a dating machine. But old wounds run deep. That's not what I want to think about now, though.

"This is delicious." I change the subject in a firm way. "That's smart, to make the sauce up in advance. I'd eat way less takeout if I did that."

"What do you cook?"

"I'll make stew sometimes. I can fry a mean egg. Steak and salad."

"Mmm." Her eyes light up. "Make me a steak sometimes."

"As soon as I get back." I tell her about my back deck and the new barbeque I treated myself to at an end of summer sale last year.

When we finish eating, she stretches her arms above her head and rolls her neck. Her breasts bounce under her t-shirt and my blood starts to hum. I'm ready for dessert, definitely. I add more wine to her glass. "I'll do the dishes."

I don't give her a chance to argue. I take our plates and quickly rinse them off, then fill the sink with soapy water. She doesn't have a drying rack out, so I find a towel and dry them off.

She's followed me into the kitchen, and now is watching from the doorway to her small galley. I like her watching me. I like being in her space and feeling at home. I take my time putting the plates and cutlery away, finding where the pots go. Then I grab a cloth and start to wipe the counters.

Her hand comes down on mine and she sets her wine glass on the counter. "Stop teasing me," she whispers.

"Doing the dishes?" I grin as she slides her body between me and the counter. "That counts as foreplay?"

"And I think you know it." She presses up onto her toes and I take her mouth. She tastes like wine and warm desire. It doesn't take much for that heat to ratchet up, for her to lift her leg and urge me to pick her up.

I brought a condom with me, but over dinner I decided not to use it. Like Hugh did for me, I'm going to do for her—give her something to think about while I'm away.

"When I get back, we're going to have an entire night together," I tell her, my voice rough as I trace the curves of her body. "All night. My place. I'll cook for you, and I want you to sleep over."

Yes. I want that so much it hurts. Heat pulses deep inside me at the thought of her in my bed.

"That sounds amazing." Her breath catches as I rub my thumbs under the waistband of her pants, and ease them down her hips. Underneath, she's wearing pink cotton underwear, and those can go, too.

I don't take her shirt off. I like the flower. Instead, I cup her breasts through the material, rubbing and tugging on her nipples until she's squirming against me. Then I finally ease the fabric up, baring her flesh for my mouth. I lift her up and sit her on the counter. She gasps at the coolness of the granite beneath her.

"Shhh," I say before kissing her.

She groans as I move my way down her neck, then to her nipples. I cover one peak with my mouth, then the other. She's so soft, her tits overflow my hands. And she squirms perfectly when I roll my tongue across her skin. Here, and lower.

I ease her back, getting her to lean against her hands, and I lift her legs so her feet rest right on the edge of the counter.

So she's wide open for me. On display.

"I've missed you," I say.

"Me, or my…"

"Beautiful pussy? Shhh. I'm reacquainting myself with your perfection." I wink at her before stepping back so I've got enough room to brace my forearms on either side of her hips. I lean in, kissing the smooth, sweet skin of her inner thighs.

Her legs fall away, revealing more of her perfect pinkness, and I breathe her in. Gorgeous. My first taste is light, encouraging her to swell for me, but I have no self-control, and at the first lick against her slick skin, I lose my mind a little.

She's the perfect mix of sweetness and musk, and tasting her again is like coming home. A familiar hit of a private drug. Something to hold us both. And there's another element to my desperate need to consume her.

I want her on me, in me, as I fly away from Ottawa.

She obliges, lifting her hips. Offering herself to me. I take. I gorge. I spear two fingers into her snug pussy and fuck her with my hand as she writhes under my tongue, because one way or another, I need to feel that clutch of her heat around me.

Her inner walls clamp down on my fingers as she tenses up, her clit hard and throbbing against my tongue. I suck her over that peak of pleasure and she explodes into an orgasm I can feel everywhere she's touching me.

Each trembling shudder gives me more to lap up, and I continue to lick her until she slumps back, pleased and worn out.

When I push myself up, she reaches for my belt, but I wave her off. "That was just for you."

Her eyebrows hit the roof. "This is the point where the sex-drunk girl recklessly proposes marriage to the perfect man."

I laugh. "That would be dangerous, because I'd probably accept."

She sits up and grabs the front of my shirt, pulling me close so she can kiss me. She licks my lips and into my mouth, whimpering as she tastes herself on my skin. "Don't be a martyr. Let me do something for you," she whispers.

"I gotta go. Rain check."

She smiles softly. "Okay."

"And…" I'm not going to send her running into Hugh's arms. But… "Don't miss me too much."

Her eyes sharpen as she watches my face. Still a lot unsaid there, but now's not the time. "I won't be lonely."

I exhale roughly and nod. "Good."

"While Lachlan's away, the mice will play…" she whispers.

Oh, Jesus. That makes my dick twitch. How does she know what to say? "Have fun."

"I will."

I'M fifteen minutes late getting to the air field. I park in the reserved spaces and jog through the small terminal. I arrive at the prime minister's plane at the same time as his car pulls up, followed by another armoured sedan carrying some of my security team.

Gavin gives me a surprised look as I approach. "Running behind schedule?"

"Something like that." I wait for him to climb the stairs into the plane, then I follow him. There are four of us accompanying him on this trip. Another two are on the advance party already in Winnipeg.

We take our seats and get comfortable. Our scheduled departure is at ten, so we've got about half an hour. "You know, really, you're a bit early."

He gives me a bland look. "So you always cut it this close and I just don't notice?"

"No." I clear my throat. "Extenuating circumstances tonight."

His expression shifts from bland to wary. "Do I want to know?"

I'm not sure. There's a fine line here. But the last thing I want is for him to have a problem with this later on. Better to be upfront, but with limited disclosure. "Beth and I had dinner."

Beneath us, the plane shakes as a cargo door is closed. One of my officers in the set of seats behind Gavin starts watching a playback of tonight's playoff game.

The prime minister just looks at me. Finally he sighs and reaches for his briefcase. "It's about time," he mutters under his breath.

And that's thankfully the end of that conversation.

15

BETH

I SLEEP in on Saturday morning. It took me ages to finally drop off. I tossed and turned and smiled and longed, and it was well after midnight—and after Lachlan texted that they'd landed in Winnipeg—that I finally gave in to the sandman.

When I get up, I do laundry from the week and think about going swimming at the YWCA. Thinking about it is as far as I get, though, because after lunch I get a text from Ellie Montague.

I didn't even realize Ellie had my phone number.

Ellie: Hey! It's Ellie.
Beth: LOL what's up?
Ellie: I was wondering if you'd be free to get coffee today.

Ellie and I have a weird relationship. I like her, and I want to be friends with her, but…she had a threesome with Lachlan. At a time when he was refusing to acknowledge the zing between us.

Jerk. Lachlan, not Ellie. That wasn't her fault. And now I understand that wasn't about sex for him, but kink and service, but *still…*

No. Gah, it's not healthy to hang on to even that little bit of resentment.

Beth: Of course. I'm free now, and later. No plans.
Ellie: Does three work?

She names a small, independent coffee shop in the east end, and I confirm I'll be there. When I arrive a few minutes early, she's already there, two RCMP officers in tow. Thankfully, neither of them are Hugh.

We order iced coffees and take a seat next to the window. One advantage of going out with bodyguards—they scope the most private seats, and then save them for you while you get your drinks.

She gets right to the point. "I want to plan a baby shower for Max and Violet."

Of course she does. And she's right to want to, but holy moly, it's celebration shower central with these women.

I don't think anyone is going to throw me a yay-you're-dating-two-guys-at-once-and-they're-both-smoking-hot shower, although that's totally party-worthy. I don't point that out. My dirty dating life is…well, dirty, and therefore, secret.

Instead I pull out my phone. "Just tell me what to do and where to go."

We talk about dates—after the wedding, but not too much later, because we don't want to get too close to her due date. Location—Ellie wants to have it at 24 Sussex, which I think is a great idea. It's where Max and Violet got married, in an understated, private ceremony.

Guest list. "Definitely co-ed," I say. "A wedding shower makes sense to be just for the bride, but Max is totally psyched about this baby."

The last time he came by to see Gavin, he sat at my desk and showed me sonogram pictures for fifteen minutes. Violet's growing a super-cute alien inside her.

"Agreed. And maybe just friends, we don't need to extend the list too much beyond that. The same circle they invited to their wedding?"

I nod. "Do you want to have it catered? Just a cake?"

She taps her pen against her lips. "Maybe we could do a breakfast type thing? Brunch?"

"Oh, I like that." I give her a short-list of caterers I like for breakfast events, and I take on the task of getting a separate cake made, then we call the planning a success and tuck our notes away.

"So…" She swivels her straw through her iced coffee. "Now that we've taken care of the baby shower stuff…" She gives me a positively gleeful look. "Gavin told me."

I rack my brain. What did I miss? "Told you what?"

"You know." She wiggles in her seat. "About dinner."

"The wedding dinner?"

She laughs. "No. Your dinner. Last night. With Lachlan."

My mouth drops open as my pulse pounds in my neck. Oh. Heat tries to swarm up my face and I hurriedly take a sip of my drink. Nope. Not enough iced coffee in the world to compensate for this.

A stricken look falls over her face. "Was it not good?"

"Oh, God." Did I say that out loud? "Ellie, please stop." And that. I'm officially no longer in control of my face or mouth, and both are usually well within my control.

She bites her lower lip and nods.

Then she waits.

And waits.

My mind slides from emotion to reaction and back again. Confusion, because why would Lachlan tell Gavin *anything?* Embarrassment, too. Now there would be pressure. But there was already pressure. I know Gavin thinks Lachlan should ask me out. But I swear, threesomes aside, Gavin has some stupidly traditional ideas of men and women and dating and relationships.

I don't need my boss thinking about my dating life.

Especially when he only knows half of it, and the whole of it is way too complicated to satisfy whatever expectations he might have for "good enough for Beth."

I puff out my cheeks as I exhale. "Okay. So here's the thing…" I take another rough breath. I'm way overreacting, but hey, if Ellie wants to be friends, here's her chance. "I wish Lachlan hadn't told Gavin that, to be honest. We've had a couple of dates, and they've been amazing, but this just amps up the pressure in a big way." I hesitate and take another sip of my coffee. "And we're not exactly exclusive yet."

That's fudging the truth a bit. We've had a conversation that definitely narrowed the scope of who else we'll date—to a list with a single other name on it. The same name for both of us, although I don't know that Lachlan and Hugh would call whatever they do together dating.

Ellie's eyes brighten. "Well, that makes total sense. I'm so sorry. I was just really excited for you. Both of you."

"Just don't get your heart set on a happy ever after ending for us. I adore Lachlan, but we've both got a lot going on that takes precedent over a relationship."

"Famous last words," she mumbled as she tried to innocently hide behind her coffee.

Ha. If she only knew the rest of the story. Over my dead body.

I TEXT Lachlan as soon as I leave the coffee shop.

Beth: You told Gavin that we're dating?
Lachlan: I didn't use that word.

Beth: I just had coffee with Ellie. The telephone game definitely translated it into her being super excited that we're finally together.
Lachlan: To be fair, I'm also super excited that we're finally together.

He's totally missing the point. Are we "finally together"? And where does that leave me and Hugh? Lachlan and Hugh? Hugh in general, the deliciously dirty man?

Beth: Can you please call me when you get a free moment?

He calls five minutes later. "Hey."
"Hi."
He sighs. "So you're not happy. I'm sorry."
"I thought our first fight might be about jealousy or something. Not…spilled secrets."
"I'm sorry. Really, truly sorry. I didn't think we needed to keep dinner a secret." He sounds hurt.
"When you get back, maybe we need to have a clearer conversation about what we share and what we don't."
He makes a frustrated sound. "I don't think you want to share anything."
He's not wrong. "Is that a problem?"
"Ottawa's a small city. What if someone sees us together?"
"And what if someone sees me with Hugh?" Silence is the only response. "Should we tell the PM that I'm seeing two of his security detail?"
Lachlan swears under his breath. "I didn't think of that."
"I know. And I don't want to harp on it. But…"
"I understand now. And I'll talk to Hugh. Apologize to him."
I roll my eyes. "We don't need to make a big deal out of this. I don't think he'll care. Just be more careful going forward."

"Okay." He sighs. "So now is probably not the time to tell you I miss you, eh?"

I smile. "Any time is good for that. Just don't tell anyone else that you miss me."

Even when I'm grumpy, I'm counting down the days until he returns.

16

BETH

IT's the Monday after Lachlan left with Gavin for the prairies, and the morning just keeps dragging.

When Gavin is away, I get time to catch up on the less important tasks around the office, but those also tend to be the most boring.

Hugh struts into the office just as I'm putting the finishing touches to a report on softwood lumber. It's one of those tasks that has been perpetually pushed down the priority list, but suddenly becomes pressing.

Gavin has a meeting next month with Jack Benton, a guy he knows from his labour union days. Jack's like a real-life lumberjack billionaire. He made his money modernizing the family's lumber business, then diversified in a big way. He owns an NHL team now, among other things. But he still looks like he just chopped down a tree. Right down to the beard and trademark plaid wool shirt collection that he wears instead of suits half the time. I bet he even keeps a chainsaw in the back of his pickup.

Great. Now I have that Monty Python song ringing in my ears.

I click save on my file, then look up from my computer to see Hugh smiling at me.

"Hey, Beth. Any chance you could squeeze in a coffee break this morning?"

For Hugh? Always. "Sure, just let me arrange for someone to cover for me."

He walks over to the security team's desk and sits in what I think of as Lachlan's chair while I make the call. By the time the intern arrives a few minutes later, I'm ready to go.

"It's a beautiful day, so I thought we'd grab coffee from the cafeteria, and take a short walk," Hugh says as we head down the corridor.

"Sounds good to me."

After we get our coffee, we walk out the front doors. The grounds are a little crowded—people likely looking to get themselves a selfie with the prime minister. They're all out of luck. Sometimes I think there should be a flag flying when he's around —kind of like the queen has on her palaces to say she's in residence.

I'm really not in the mood to deal with all these people.

"Let's walk around to the river," I suggest as I point to the left.

"Great idea." Hugh places his hand at the small of my back and guides me through the crowd.

Once we settle on a quiet bench, I ask how his morning is going. Normal small talk.

He's having none of it. "My morning's going just fine. Talk to me about the play party you went to."

It takes my brain a second to catch up. Whoa.

"What's with the jump-shift?" Apparently, his idea of appropriate coffee break conversation and mine are different.

Hugh just grins.

"What exactly are you looking for me to say?"

"Pretend you're telling a friend about it. Make me feel like I was there with you."

There is no way he's getting a bedtime story and I tell him that.

He's undeterred. "Don't you think this is good information for me to have?"

Maybe. "Fine. I'll answer three questions. So choose them wisely," I say as I give him my best no-nonsense look.

He, in turn, gives me a look I can only assume is meant to resemble puppy-dog eyes. It fails, and I have a hard time maintaining my stony face and not laughing. Although he's amusing me, so maybe they do work in their own way.

"Only three questions. I can work with that. Here we go, first question. What's the kinkiest thing you did at the party?"

Of course, that would be his first question. I'm sure he's walked the length and breadth of the wild-side, so the kinkiest thing I did at the party—which also happens to be my kinkiest thing ever—is going to be sadly disappointing for him.

"Getting flogged on the Saint Andrew's Cross."

I watch his face for any kind of reaction, but he gives me nothing. No clue that I even got the vocabulary right. I'm pretty sure I did.

"Next question. What did you like watching the most?"

No follow-up. I had thought he would at least want to know if I liked it. Or if I was naked. But I limited him to three questions, and apparently he's going to use them to cover a lot of ground.

I waffle back and forth over my answer. Do I tell him what I really liked watching the most, or do I tell him what I liked the most that would be considered a little more conventional, and possibly more…socially acceptable?

I know he wouldn't be shocked by the content of my real answer…but I worry that it could affect the way he sees me.

Unvarnished honesty wins out. "So, there was this couple. Two guys, actually. And, well…the way things were between them was really different from the other couples. It was more intense, raw...seriously hot." I force myself to hold my chin up and push past my embarrassment.

Hugh nods slowly, saying nothing.

His continued silence makes me uncomfortable. Is he judging me? I regret agreeing to respond to his curiosity at all and I just want this over and done with.

"Last question?" I try to push him along.

"I'm thinking. I want it to be a good one."

I take a sip of my coffee and wait.

"Okay, last question." He pauses a moment, then his gaze locks on mine. "What was Lachlan like at the party?"

Oh. Probably fitting that he lands here. A broad swath of questions, ending with our mutual obsession over the stoic giant with the quietly kinky side. My heart beats faster as I think back to that night. "He was totally in control. He was the dungeon something...minder... master...monitor. That's it. Dungeon monitor. He was in charge, making sure everyone played safely. He took his job very seriously, too. Lachlan monitored Brandon —he's a hockey player who offered to give me taste of what a flogger feels like—the entire time he had me on the Saint Andrew's Cross."

Hugh's eyes light up, and I decide to give him more. Suddenly I want to tell him a lot about that night, and I understand why he asked.

"Then after Brandon did that taking care of me thing, Lachlan took him aside...to give him some pointers, maybe? I don't know."

The corners of Hugh's mouth tug up a little, and I wonder what it is he finds amusing, because for me, it was hot as hell. Lachlan's intensity was anyway. The Brandon part, I could happily leave.

"After that, Lachlan stuck fairly close by, and radiated a pretty strong keep-away vibe." He totally spent the rest of the evening cock-blocking me—and in hind sight, that was extra jerky, because he was holding out on me. We could have been having the most explosive sex of my life all this time.

Hugh nods...like he knows something. "Sounds like a good time was had by most."

I shrug, then look at my watch. There's a lot I want to tell him —about how I was fascinated, but not turned on that night, not as much as I am now thinking back to Lachlan's role in it. And how I want Hugh to open up, too.

How annoyed I am at his close-to-his-chest approach to this conversation.

But we've been gone over thirty minutes and while the seniority of my position affords me some flexibility, especially when Gavin's away, I'm always careful not to abuse the privilege. Also, it's a good escape from the discomfort of this conversation. "I need to get back to the office."

"Yeah, me too."

The walk back is brisk. Hugh escorts me to my desk, and loiters for a few minutes after the intern leaves.

I give him a look, and he smiles right back. At some point soon, we'll have to have a more comprehensive conversation about secrets. I hate them.

Something tells me he won't care. He'll try to convince me that they're fun.

Finally he gets up. "Okay, I'm leaving now." Moving in behind me, he bends low. "Tomorrow I want you come to work in a skirt, no underwear," he whispers, his breath ghosting over the shell of my ear.

What? Where did that order come from? What part of his inquisition-style coffee date lead him to think I could just be commanded to leave my underwear at home?

I stare straight ahead and continue typing like I hadn't heard him. But the thought of doing something so illicit because Hugh tells me to sends a tingle up my spine, among other places. It also scares the hell out of me. What if I get hit by a bus and my skirt rides up and the whole world discovers that the Prime Minister's assistant doesn't wear panties to work and all the sordid details wind up all over the news?

"Beth?"

I nod. "I heard you."

He waits until he's out by the elevators to chuckle, but I hear him anyway. And I start mentally flipping through my closet to figure out what I can wear.

THE NEXT AFTERNOON, he shows up at my desk ostensibly to check on a scheduling thing, but I know it's really to check on the skirt and underwear thing and, as it turns out, to arrange a dinner date.

"Tomorrow night?"

"Yes."

"Your place." He glances down at my skirt. "We can discuss how today went."

On Wednesday night, he arrives promptly at seven with dinner.

Tipping my chin up with his fingers, he touches his lips to mine and I open for him. He only gives me a small taste of his tongue before he ends the kiss.

He always leaves me wanting more. So much more.

I take the bag of food from him and lead the way to the kitchen.

He takes a glass of wine that I offer, then gives me a stern look. "So I didn't expect you to play dirty yesterday."

"What are you talking about?" I grin at him. "I did as you asked. I'm surprised you didn't demand proof."

"I assumed asking you to flash me at work would cross some hard limits for you."

He's not wrong. "Thank you."

"Although it would be a good punishment for wearing such a school-marm-esque skirt."

Ah. I blush. "Well, it was kind of windy yesterday…"

And yes, I'd chosen the longest skirt in my closet. But underneath, I'd been completely bare, all day. For him. "Then you should have been more clear in your instructions. You said skirt, I wore a skirt. If you had something more specific in mind, you should have said so." I don't tell him that I'm not wearing any underwear beneath my skirt right now. It's my little secret.

One I hope he discovers on his own, and he likely will, because today's skirt isn't school-marm-esque at all.

He clears his throat and gives me a look. Firm and bossy. "There's a distinct difference between spirit and letter of the law. I expect you to adhere to both."

I want to push back against that, but there's something really sexy about Hugh taking charge this way. "Because you'll be issuing more edicts like this going forward?"

"Yes."

I hesitate, then smile. "Okay. Good to know."

He laughs. "Let's eat."

DINNER PASSES QUICKLY, with the conversation light and easy, but there's a frisson of anticipation skittering around us. After, we take our wine to the living room, and I sit on the sofa. Hugh settles down right beside me—so close, our legs touch almost the whole way down.

He doesn't beat around the bush. He brushes his fingertips against the back of my neck and leans in, his voice low and totally sexy. "Slide your skirt up."

I'm still not sure how I feel about being bossed around, but he gives me this look, and all I can think is, how high? That was the plan, after all. Show him how good I can be at following orders. When I want to, of course.

I inch my skirt upwards, stopping halfway up my thighs.

"Higher, I want to see what you have on under there."

My belly flutters. He's about to discover my secret—a lot sooner than I intended.

I slide my skirt up until it's bunched at the top of my thighs, framing the trim curls covering my mound.

He strokes his other hand up my bare leg. "Mmmm, tell me… is this how you dressed for work this morning, or did you change when you got home?"

Confession time.

"I didn't change a thing when I got home."

It had been a delicious and dangerous secret I held close to my chest all day. I have no idea why I did it.

"Your skirt's much shorter today than yesterday."

I suck in a ragged breath. "Yes."

"Very brave of you. Spread your legs."

Holy shit. The timbre of his voice coupled with that look makes me forget any reservations I had.

I slide my legs apart and he slips to the floor and kneels between my knees.

His hands slide up the inside of my thighs, making me quiver.

I feel so exposed and vulnerable, but when he licks his lips, I also feel desirable…and that totally wins.

He leans in and takes a long, slow swipe at my pussy with his tongue.

Right. He can be bossy all he wants. I close my eyes and tip my head back, giving in to the delicious sensations. He takes his time with oral, just like he does with everything else. Hugh Evans gives spectacular head, and I don't even need to tell him where I want him to linger.

He's reading my body like a book. No, like a conductor, and I'm sheet music. Not only is he familiar with all the notes, but he's bending them a little, making the music new and fabulous and something I want to experience again.

And again.

Oh, yes. Hugh can…conduct…my pussy any time he wants. My hands ball into fists against the couch as he licks around my clit, up and over, teasing on either side before the next swirl of his tongue. Left and right, rub rub rub. Then down and in, fucking into me a bit, but he's not one of those guys who thinks his tongue replaces a dick.

No, he knows exactly what his tongue is good for. Being dexterous and nimble. Flicking and licking, sucking and pulling. Okay, that's his whole mouth, those last two bits, and *that's* so good, too.

I'm rocking my hips now, can't help it, and his name keeps spilling off my lips. "Hugh…"

He growls at that and nips at my inner thigh. "Fucking right. Gonna come for me?"

"Yes."

"Good."

He gets his fingers involved now, stroking my labia up and down as he licks me again, and as my slick arousal spreads, he moves in, sliding a finger into me, then two.

I ride his hand all the way to a tight, hot climax, and he holds me there, on that peak, pulling at my clit until I beg him to stop. And even then, he keeps kissing my thighs until I stop trembling.

He crawls back onto the couch and holds out his arm. I have other plans, though.

I nip and kiss my way down his body, but he stops me as I start unfastening the button of his jeans.

"We'll get there soon enough, but that's not on the menu tonight."

I pout a little and he gives me that look again.

"There are going to be times, like tonight, where I'm in charge and call the shots."

I have to be the luckiest woman on the planet—I have not one, but two men eager to go down on me, and they both have zero expectation that I return the favour. On one level, I appreciate their selflessness, but on another, I feel a little deprived. "I like doing it."

"Doing *it?*" He grins. "Doing what?"

"Sucking cock," I say, the words barely louder than a whisper. "I want to suck your cock, Hugh."

He groans. "Come up here, beautiful."

I scramble up his body, because he wants to call the shots and he made me scream his name, so whatever, that's fine.

He takes my hand and cups his erection with my fingers. "Soon I'll have your mouth, those perfect lips, stretched wide around my *cock*, as you say. I love hearing that." He leans in and kisses me. "But I want to take things slow."

I give him a little frown. "Why?"

He shrugs. "Reasons." He squeezes my hand around his erection, showing me what he wants. "Yeah, just like that. We've got all summer long to get dirty together. This is perfect for tonight. Just like that. Ah."

"Let me give you a hand job," I say, leaning back a bit as I straddle his thighs. God, from this position, it would be so easy to pull his cock out of his jeans and sink onto him. Danger.

"Next time."

"You're killing me," but I smile at him. "Are you always this bossy?"

"Not always but sometimes I like to be."

"Are you bossy with Lachlan?"

He grins. "Yeah."

"Like this?"

"No. Bossier."

That's crazy hot. I shiver. "Lucky him."

His eyes are liquid swirls as he searches my face. "You could try it sometime. He'd be game for you to top him."

I wouldn't even know where to start.

Hugh licks his lips, then stretches out. "I can show you some things."

"Yeah?"

"Sure."

"I'd like that," I whisper.

1 7

HUGH

It takes every bit of my self-restraint not to call Beth up Thursday night and suggest we work our way through a box of condoms.

Every second since I left her place Wednesday, I've been cursing myself for not taking what she was obviously offering. When she perched herself on my lap, legs spread, and wanted to stroke my cock?

I just about came in my pants from how fucking sexy that was.

But the fact that Lachlan's out of town looms large in my mind.

We've got a long weekend coming up. I'm seeing Beth tomorrow night, before he returns. Then he'll have some time with her, and hopefully me, too.

The only way this triangle works is if we take our time.

And our Beth wants to learn about kink, too.

Good lord, that opens up a world of possibilities.

Before I can go any further with that, I need to find a way to talk to Lachlan about us, and her.

Talking has never been our strong suit.

That's going to have to change.

In the meantime, my mind is free to get as pervy as it wants.

What if Beth really gets into kink? I'd love to see her take control. The idea of her topping Lachlan takes over. I undo my pants and reach for my hardening cock as I envision Lachlan on his knees, naked in front of us.

Maybe she jerks him off slowly.

Maybe she wants to see me fuck him.

We could do those things at the same time.

I lube up my hand and close it into a loose fist at the tip of my cock, then push my way into the tight space, imagining I'm breaching Lachlan's ass for the first time in a decade.

How good his groans would sound.

How tight he would be.

Fuck. I pump my hips, pushing into my hand. Imagining I'm kneeling behind him and Beth is moving around us, whispering dirty instructions she probably doesn't even know yet in real life.

Rim jobs.

Double penetration.

Edging.

God, I'd love to see her take him right to the edge, until his cock is drooling come. Twitching everywhere and helpless under her control.

I fuck my hand harder.

Fuck Lachlan harder. Ram his ass and bend over him as Beth croons for us both to come.

When I come, it's hard and fast and makes me see stars.

My hand is covered in jizz, I'm breathing hard, and all I can thing about right now how much I want that to be real.

I pull out my phone and send them both a text.

Hugh: Thinking of you.

LACHLAN

In general, a water main break is not a good thing.

There's no *good* reason for me to happy about a flood at the community centre Gavin's afternoon event was going to be held in.

There are two very bad reasons, though, and their names are Beth and Hugh. If we leave for Ottawa sooner than later, I might get to see one of them tonight, and it's been a long and lonely week.

We've just left our lunch event at the University of Edmonton, and a local staffer is next to me in the front seat, trying to figure out on her phone what the new plan is.

I glance at Gavin in the rear view mirror. He looks tired, but I won't use that. I will *not* suggest we do a quick meet and greet outside the community centre and then get out of the repair team's way.

I will not—

Gavin leans forward. "Aline, what do you think about just stopping at the community centre real quick, doing a meet and greet, and then getting out of their hair?"

On the inside, I do an epic fist pump. On the outside, I keep my mouth shut and my face passive.

She finishes her text message and nods. "Yeah. That should be fine. The church parking lot across the way is pretty big. We can't use their basement, it's too small, so…yeah. Okay. It looks like that's the new plan. Thirty-minute stop there sound good?"

It sounds fucking amazing.

I TEXT Beth from the Edmonton air field, but I keep it vague and about Gavin. I hope she can read between the lines because she'd also have received the schedule update from the local staffer, so the only reason I'm telling her, too, is because I'm coming home to her.

In the air, I try to compose an email, but I'm not good at the subterfuge of a secret love affair. This not-telling-anyone thing can't last long, I'm not going to make it.

When we land, I head straight home. I call her from my driveway. There's no answer. It's eight-thirty at night. Maybe she's gone out for the night and left her phone at home.

I send her another text.

Lachlan: Back in the province. Give me a call when you're free.

That's innocent enough. I get out of the car as I dial Hugh's number.

He answers on the first ring. "Hey. You guys landed? Heard the return got bumped up by a few hours."

"Yep. Just getting home now." I put my key in the lock and turn. "You want to come over?"

He doesn't answer right away. I push the door open and flip

on the lights. There's something extra still about a house that hasn't moved in a week. "I would, man, but…"

Fuck. I know what he's going to say. I finish his sentence for him. "You're seeing Beth tonight?"

Another hesitation. "Yeah."

Right. "Disregard me, then. Maybe I'll see you tomorrow." I hang up before he can say anything else.

My bag slips off my shoulder and bangs against my arm as it tumbles to the ground. I give a half-hearted attempt to catch it as it slides past my fingers, but they're loose and useless.

Fuck.

I stare at the duffle bag.

Maybe she's in the shower right now, getting ready for their date. Water sluicing down her body. Between her tits. Slick bubbles, steam.

I get half-hard thinking about it, even as a weird, uncomfortable anger burns beneath my collar.

Hugh arriving at her door. Giving her a dirty look.

Now I'm all the way hard.

Fuck.

I kick my duffle bag and it sails all the way down the hall, landing in front of my bedroom door.

Empty, quiet house.

Fuck.

He'd kiss her. Right there at the door, as she giggled in his arms. His lips soft, his jaw covered in stubble. Rough scratching kisses.

My phone vibrates in my pocket.

Fuck off, Hugh.

This is the awkward reality of what we're doing. It's fine. I'll go jerk off furiously in the shower and get the fuck over it.

The vibrating stops, then starts again. This time a text message.

It would be torture to look at it, but I can't help myself.

I pull my phone from my pocket. A missed call, and a text message, both from the same person.

Beth: Want to come over tonight?

19

____

BETH

HUGH ARRIVES a few minutes after I send Lachlan the text invitation.

"He isn't answering his phone," I say as I open the door. My voice cracks.

"Shit." He pulls me in close and strokes his hand over my hair as I bury my face in his chest. "I shouldn't have told him I was coming over."

I shake my head. "No lying. We can't do that."

"We could go over to his house. Stage an intervention."

I laugh weakly. "Yeah?"

"Sure. We'll point out he can't have it both ways. Crack an egg and tell him that's his brain on jealousy."

My laugh gets stronger and I step back. I'm still shaking my head, though. "He's not really jealous. Well, maybe he is, but that's not his primary reaction. That's…social conditioning, maybe. Or maybe he just had a really long day and can't deal. Let's not push him just yet. Give him a night to sleep it off and worry about it tomorrow."

I lace my fingers through Hugh's and tug him into the kitchen.

"You want a glass of wine?"

He grins. "Am I invited to sleep over?"

"Ooh, forward. I like it." I tap my chin, mock thinking about it, and wink at him. "Maybe."

"Then yes, please."

I empty the remainder of the bottle that we opened on Wednesday into two glasses and hand him one. "To big, dumb Mounties who forget they like it both ways."

"We're talking about Lachlan, right?" He leans in and taps his glass to mine. "Cheers."

I take a big sip and set my glass down. "Yes. Lachlan." I growl under my breath and Hugh gives me an amused look.

I reach for my glass, but a heavy knock at the door interrupts me. I exchange a glance with Hugh before hurrying to answer.

On the other side is Lachlan.

His eyes are bright and his lips are set into a firm line.

Without a word, he stalks in and cups my face in his hands, crushing his mouth to mine.

Oh.

His tongue sweeps past my lips, claiming me in a ruthless, brutish way that—heaven help me—is totally hot.

I open for him, pliant even as my heart pounds in my chest. His kiss fills an emptiness inside me. *I've missed you*, I try to show him.

I should be thinking about the other man in my apartment. About boundaries and asking first before you just take things.

But he's taking with such...ferocity. Such perfect, demanding confidence. My body responds without hesitation because when it comes to Lachlan staking a claim on me, it's open season. No limits.

And yet somewhere behind me, there's Hugh.

This is so complicated, and I didn't want to do complicated, but I want this. I want Lachlan. And I want Hugh.

And, if it's not asking too much, I want them both to be okay with that.

He kisses me until I feel full and floaty, and when he finally stops, he still holds my face against his, his thumb rubbing my cheek as we breathe hard together.

My head spins as he lifts his gaze and stares past me. "There," he growls at Hugh. "Now we're even."

I stagger back against the wall, bracing my hands wide to keep from falling over. "Even? For what?"

Hugh laughs. At least he's not offended. I give him a confused look. "He's talking about our first kiss, beautiful."

Our first kiss.

Outside my apartment, just downstairs. When Lachlan watched from across the street…

I glance back and forth between the two of them, then narrow my gaze at Hugh. "You knew he was there? When you were kissing me?"

I don't know how I feel about that.

Hugh shrugged. He's looking at Lachlan now, and a different kind of zinging is happening. "Yeah."

I glare at him. Okay, the kissing good-times buzz is wearing off fast. "Well, that was mean."

I want them to both be okay with the kissing, but we need to discuss it first. Enough of this brutish assumption, no matter how deliciously hot it is.

Hugh seems to think otherwise. "Nah. He liked it."

I swivel my head toward Lachlan. A muscle twitches in his cheek.

"Is that true?" Now the buzz is coming back. Warmer, and in my chest this time. I press my hand there and do another look at both of them. But we just need to clear up one more thing before I get too excited. "Wait… Am I some kind of pawn here?"

Lachlan jerks his head toward me, his eyes wide and filled with alarm. "No."

I hold his gaze. The pieces are falling into place. "You like kissing me, then?"

He gives me a tense smile. "God, yes."

"And you like watching me kiss Hugh…?"

He nods. Still tense.

"And you like kissing him, too…"

This time he freezes, but yes, another nod.

I lick my lips. "So I think…we're not even yet."

"What do you mean?"

Hugh's behind him, and out of focus because my eyes are locked on Lachlan's face, but I'm pretty sure—no, completely sure—that this will be okay with him. "I haven't seen you kiss Hugh yet. And I want to."

"What?"

Big, dumb Mountie. Oh, how I adore him. I move closer and press against him. His hands settle on my hips, and I lean into him, pushing him off-balance. Making him take a step back. His grip on me tightens, but I push him again, smiling up at him now.

I nudge him until he bumps into Hugh, who's moved into his path.

Then I push up onto my toes and brush my mouth against his. "Please," I whisper. "Show me. Get me as hot as you got that night. Drive me a little crazy."

"What are you doing?" He spears his hands into my hair. Against my belly, I feel how hard he's getting right now. With Hugh pressed against his back and me against his front, and I want…I want… Holy moly, do I want.

I want things I can't even name yet.

20

HUGH

She's fucking insane.

She's also a glorious little genius. She twisted Lachlan's comment about being even right back on him, and now he's sandwiched between us.

Where I've wanted him for weeks, if I'm being honest. But this is more than I could allow myself to hope for.

And I can feel how tense Lachlan is. Every muscle tightly coiled, ready to burst away from the embrace between his lovers.

But Beth is persuasive. And sexy as hell. Over his shoulder, I watch her face. It's all there. How much she wants to see us together. Fuck me, I don't think she realizes what she's asking for, but I'm game. I'll drag them both to her bed and make them mine, over and over again.

Just when I think it's not going to work, I feel Lachlan submit to her—and that's a fucking jolt to my cock. His body relaxes, and he shifts back and forth on his feet, rubbing against her. And against me, too.

I stand there and take it. My hands hang loose at my sides.

When Lachlan's fingers brush mine, his right hand reaching back and finding me blindly, I'm not sure it's deliberate at first.

He still has his gaze locked on Beth, but with his second touch, he hooks my hand and tugs me around his body. As I move, not giving him an inch of space, he squeezes my hand, his knuckles rubbing against my erection. And when I get to Beth, he switches hands and pulls me right against her back.

Now she's in the middle, and Lachlan finally looks at me again.

"You heard her," he says roughly. "You up for some show and tell?"

Beth turns halfway towards me, turning us into a tight triangle of fascination, voyeurism, and terrible ideas.

Doesn't change the fact that yeah, I'm fucking up for it. I slide my left hand over her back, and my right hand up his flexing biceps and onto his shoulder.

His mouth is red and swollen from kissing her. His lips part, glinting wet as his tongue swipes against the inside of his lower lip. Will he taste like Beth?

His hand fists in my shirt, pulling me in, and his eyes do that glassy, horny thing they usually do when we're about to kiss.

This isn't our first rodeo.

It's just the first time—ever—we've had an audience.

I guess he's done processing that fact in his head, because he closes the distance between us smoothly and fits his lips against mine, a hard, familiar press of his mouth.

He draws me in, sucking on my lower lip as he lines up our bodies in that way he likes. We're not flush against each other because we're holding on to Beth, too, but our hips are locked on my right and he releases his hold on my shirt to find my ass and curve his fingers around the right cheek.

I deepen the kiss, cupping and squeezing the back of his neck until he groans in my mouth. If we were alone, I'd be shoving him to his knees right now.

Shit, maybe I should do that. I curl my tongue around his,

twisting the kiss in a dirty direction. Full of filthy promises I'm not sure I can keep tonight.

Filthy teases are just as good.

And maybe…

I ease us apart and pull Beth between us, giving her to him again. He doesn't hesitate, bending his knees so he can wrap himself around her.

I watch them kiss and trace my hands in lazy circles on her hips. I could fuck her like this, while they made out. I could push them down on her couch, on the floor, and slide my cock all over their bodies. Into her, into him.

I inch my fingers up, finding the bare skin at her waist. Higher, just a little bit. Her belly trembles under my touch.

Jesus. I weave one hand into her hair and tug her away from kissing the big guy. "I know he's tasty," I say quietly when she whimpers. "But I gotta ask…how much more do you want?"

She spins around, her eyes closed, and shamelessly rubs her ass against Lachlan's bulge. My hands land on her ribcage and I stroke upward, teasing the bottom of her breasts.

"Beth. You need to tell us."

"Shhh," she whispers, still not opening her eyes. "Just kiss me."

I can't not give in to that. I mirror how Lachlan had kissed her, gentle hands and plundering tongue, and she writhes against me until he moves in closer and eliminates any space for her to shift between us.

His hands replace mine on her torso. I feel him cupping her breasts, then rubbing his way down her body and playing with the waistband of her pants.

Fuck.

I press closer, fitting myself against her, Lachlan's fingers now rubbing both of our bellies. Hers soft, mine hard. There's twice as much sizzle when they're both touching me.

Beth whimpers into my mouth.

"You feel it too?" I nip at her lower lip. "Feel what you do to me? Both of you…"

"I want more," she whispers.

Not specific, really. But Lachlan doesn't seem to care. He slides his hands lower, into the front of her pants.

I could combust just from watching him do this.

We need to get more comfortable. I ease away from her, but before I can suggest the couch, the floor, the bed….anything, Lachlan's got his hand between her legs and I'm frozen, watching as she slides into bliss for him.

He doesn't get her all the way off, he just winds her up, and when he lifts his hand again, it's glistening.

I step closer again and grab his wrist as he goes to lick them clean.

"Let me," I growl.

"She's delicious," he says, his arm stiff. Not giving in.

"I know, I've had a taste." I grin at him and squeeze his wrist, reminding him how much I like to get my own way. I suck her juices off his fingers, pulling them into my mouth longer and harder than is strictly needed to taste her. I bet he's so hard it hurts. Maybe Beth should be the one who goes down on her knees. "While you were gone, in fact."

Her eyes go wide as she looks up at me. "Hugh."

He ignores her. "What else did you do?"

She swipes at me, but I dance out of the way. "That was enough." I wink at her. "That was amazing."

He ducks his head and whispers something against the curve of her ear. She listens as she watches me with naked arousal written on her face, then slowly shakes her head. "Not yet."

Need punches hard in my gut. I know what he just asked her. And no, not yet.

He lifts his head and locks his gaze on my face. The roll of emotions there is like a one-two punch. He's relieved I haven't fucked her yet. Like dick-in-pussy is some magic claim. I've fucked with her mind and made her scream my name. She's mine just as much as his.

But his eyes are liquid pools of want, too, and I know it's not simple. He's selfish about her. I can't blame him too much for that—he'd convinced himself she was off-limits.

When she—and maybe I—pushed him to admit what he wanted, then he really *wanted*. He's desperate to claim her.

And it's not like I'm looking for the same thing.

He can be as possessive as he wants. It won't change what we do. No. The look on Beth's face promises that much.

I begin to unbutton my shirt. Her eyes follow the trail of my fingers. When I get to my belt, she pulls away from Lachlan and moves to help me. I don't look at him. I don't need to. I know he'll be right behind her.

21

LACHLAN

My brain is firing in a million directions.

Misfiring, really.

The two people I've wanted more than anything else in the world—at different times, for different reasons, but still...*these two people*—are touching each other. For me. In front of me. Beth's hands are on Hugh, and he's moving her towards the couch. She does a backward side-step around an end table and they share a private laugh about something I can't hear because blood is rushing, pounding in my ears.

His shirt is off now and she leans in, brushing her lips over his chest. Maybe one of his tattoos. I could give her a tour of his ink —what's old, what's new. I know the story behind most of the designs.

I know what his skin tastes like. My mouth waters as I follow them, circling around so I'm behind Beth again. I've learned the delicate taste of her skin, too.

She glances at me over her shoulder, her eyes full to the brim with questions. *Is this okay? Is this hot? Do you want to join?*

Yes, yes, hell yes.

I can feel Hugh looking at me, too. His questions as loud as day. *Where'd your jealousy go? Want to get your head on straight before you hurt her?*

We need to talk. In the back of my head, a bunch of stuff is pinging around. Polyamorous guidelines, how to have healthy open relationships…and none of it is coming out of my mouth.

Instead, when I finally part my lips, a guttural plea slides out. "Kiss again." I clear my throat. "I didn't…couldn't see…last time." Need pounds through me. It turns my blood into fire and stretches my jeans tight. My hands swing loose at my sides, itching to grab them both.

I grab myself instead. First my hips, planting my hands hard there. But as Hugh threads his fingers into Beth's hair and holds her still so he can take her mouth, I give in to my deep, dark perverted side, and cup my cock through my jeans. It's so hard it hurts, and just that touch alone is enough to crowd any thoughts about right and wrong and rules and common sense out of my head.

Their kiss is intimate and private, but I don't feel excluded. I move closer, shifting around them again so I can watch from the side. Seeing their lips brush back and forth…flashes of tongue and teeth, cheeks tugging back into unconscious smiles as they parry back and forth…that's the hottest thing I've ever seen.

"Mmm," Beth whimpers. I lean in. I don't want to miss a single sound she makes. "I need…"

"I know," Hugh murmurs.

He's so gentle with her. I can't get over the difference. Where's the man who holds me down and takes what he wants?

He kisses her again. "He's right behind you."

Me. She's talking about me, and he knows it. That's heady. He turns her around and gives her a nudge, pushing her into my arms.

We fall into one another, kissing and clawing at each other's clothes until we're both stripped down on top, just like Hugh.

Her breasts overflow my hands as Hugh unhooks her bra, then his hands bump into mine.

He cups her from behind, freeing my fingers to tug and play with her nipples until her eyes are glassy and her head is thrown back against Hugh's shoulder.

We've never shared a woman before, but I know we're going to tonight. All the parts are moving in that direction, click click click, like a tumbler lock. Insert Beth and the pins slide effortlessly into place.

I duck my head, but I'm too big, too tall to worship her breasts while I'm standing. I move to fall to my knees, but Hugh clamps a hand around my biceps and stops me. "Hang on," he rasps. He sounds just as affected as I am, but when I meet his gaze, his eyes are sharper than mine feel. "We need to be sure we're all on the same page. This wasn't the plan for tonight."

"Plans change." I flex my arm against his grip. He doesn't let go, and that makes my cock ache. I soften my expression and give him a slow smile. "Come on. I know I charged in here like a bull in a china shop, but it's been a long week. I've missed you both."

Between us, Beth's breath hitches. I shift my attention back to her. *Mine.*

"I missed you more than I expected," I say softly as I stroke my fingertips up her chest, along the delicate line of her neck, and up to her mouth. "And I wanted to see you tonight. Mission accomplished. No more grumpiness."

Her lips part and I trace the soft, pink lushness. Her tongue slides out and licks at my fingers.

I glance at Hugh, snug behind her, watching our every move. "See? We're all good."

He brings his lips to Beth's ear. "Is that true, beautiful? Are you *all good*?"

"I'm definitely good," she whispers back. Heat zings through me as her eyes darken and her lips part further. I slide my thumb over her tongue and she closes her mouth around it, sucking gently.

Hugh chuckles darkly. "Then let's move this to the bedroom."

I pick Beth up.

"Put me down, I can walk."

Hugh chuckles. "How about you show Lachlan what a good girl you can be?"

She snorts, but stops insisting I let her go.

Hugh pulls up short as we enter her room. "Jesus, that's a small bed," he growls, and I wonder what dirty choreography he's already working on.

"We made it work," I mutter. I fucking know better, but it slipped out because Hugh's dickishness has been rubbing off on me.

He turns slowly and raises one eyebrow. "Reminding me that you've had more of a taste of our Beth than I have?"

Our Beth. I like the sound of that. I wink at him. "Just saying, don't let the bed cramp your style."

"Oh, I won't." His hands go to his belt. "Beth, what do you want to see us do together?"

"Uhm…" She kicks her legs and I set her down. She twists between us, her cheeks pink. "What are my options?"

A dirty slideshow of all the ways Hugh has fucked me flashes through my mind. Heat swirls low in my gut as he sinks his teeth into his lower lip. How much do I want him to say?

Fuck it.

"Do you have lube?" I ask her. I know she's got a drawer full of condoms, but I don't remember anything slippery in there.

Her eyes light up. "Yeah."

I feel turned inside out as I glance back at Hugh. "Then pretty much anything you could imagine is on the table."

I was a jerk to him earlier. Jealous for no reason, and possessive of a woman who most definitely wants to be shared by us equally. This is my way of saying I'm sorry. *Fuck me into next week.*

She takes my hand and swings our arms back and forth as she gives me a once-over, up and down. "Do you...bottom?" Fuck, the way her blush darkens as she asks that reminds me of her curiosity at Max's holiday play party. She's pretty vanilla, but damn open to trying things. Now she nods, confident in her assessment. "You must. There's no way Hugh bottoms."

He coughs as an unexpected laugh shakes his entire body. "Usually not. But not never."

"Oh?" She spins around, letting my fingers slide free of her hand as she reaches for him. "Really? That's...awesome."

He grins. "Have you ever fucked a man, Beth?"

She makes an adorable little squeaking sound. "You don't mean just being on top, do you?"

He shakes his head and tugs her in close, kissing her deeply before he whispers against her mouth, "No, but that's a gorgeous picture to put in my head. You want to ride Lachlan tonight?"

She nods. "And you, too."

"Good." He kisses her nose. "But first I think Lachlan owes me something." He looks over at me. "On your knees."

"Do you want to put that in the form of a polite question?"

He grins. "No."

Cocky fucker. I don't go to him. I drop where I am, ignoring the achy pinch as my jeans pull even tighter against my cock. I rest my hands on my knees, spread wide, and give him an almost defiant look. Almost, because we both know it's a sham. Inside, I'm a liquid puddle of desire.

He takes Beth's hand, bringing her with him as he steps between my legs.

I return his smirk as I pull his thick, beautiful erection out. He's already wet at the tip, and I don't hesitate to lick up that pearly pre-come. His taste explodes in my mouth, and I suck up every last drop before I swallow more of his heavy length.

He doesn't draw this out. Now that we're in it, I recognize what this is. He wants to come, hard and fast, so his head is clear and he can be bossy. I relax my mouth and my throat, letting him take over, and he thrusts into me, using me like the willing hole I am. He's not rough about it. Holding back, maybe, although I like this just as well. I can taste him as he pumps in and out of my mouth, getting harder and tense as he gets closer.

But Beth has other plans. She doesn't know that Hugh just wants to get off, clearly, because she slides to her knees beside me and reaches between us, circling his cock with her hand.

Hugh slides his hand over my head, stilling me. I can feel a tremor run through his body. He was close, and he's stopping for her.

"May I?" she asks as I ease back. I turn my head, and she's right there. My heart pounds in my chest as she gives me an eager smile. "Maybe we can do it together?"

Above us, Hugh grunts his approval of that plan. I smirk up at him. "You'd like that, wouldn't you?"

"Suck my cock," he growls. "One of you, both of you. I'll even put up with little kitten licks if Beth needs some time—"

She opens wide and leans in, tossing her hair back as she takes a good few inches into her mouth. Her lips close tight around him and her eyelids drift shut as she bobs her head.

So. Fucking. Pretty.

I touch her reverently as she finds a rhythm. I trace her jaw, her neck, her spine. She's poised, even on her knees. I don't think I'm ever this graceful during sex. I get all distracted by how fucking good it feels, and sometimes how bad in a terribly good way. I like that messy place, and dive into it head first.

I can't imagine anything about Beth ever being messy.

She shivers as she pulls off, her hand still stroking him. She glances at me. "Your turn."

She doesn't move her hand.

I swallow him greedily, right to where her fingers are, and each time my lips brush her skin, I get a jolt deep in my belly.

"This is so hot," she whispers, leaning closer. "My turn."

We go back and forth, Beth calling each switch, until Hugh's hips are thrusting roughly. Normally...but this isn't normal. And he's being a fucking gentleman.

"He needs to come," I finally tell her as she tries to rub his tip against my mouth. I open my lips, but I don't let her put him in my mouth again. "Either let him take control or jerk him off."

"I'm right here," Hugh mutters, and we all dissolve into reckless, wild laughter.

I clap his denim-covered thigh. "Right. What would you like, boss?"

He touches both of our faces, gazing down at us like a bemused overlord. Pretty accurate, really. His expression tightens into a hard lust I recognize. "I want inside Beth."

He helps her up first, and I reach for her waistband. "May I?"

She twists around so she's facing me and nods.

I strip her bare, slowly and carefully, and I kiss each part of her body as I expose it.

"I like watching Lachlan on his knees for you," Hugh murmurs to Beth.

"I can hear you."

He chuckles. "Good. Gives you a taste of what I'm thinking comes next."

I groan and press my face into Beth's bare thigh. She pats my head. "It'll be okay," she says with a giggle.

He's turning her into a cruel queen.

I love it.

With a shudder, I sit back on my heels. My thighs ache, my cock is dying for relief, but I'm filled with so much intense pleasure, too. "Are you going to make me sit here and watch?"

Hugh steps back and strips out of his own clothes, then tugs

Beth towards the bed. They tumble together onto the blanket, and for a second, I die a little inside. My eyelids slam shut—no, you can't make me watch this—but then they peel themselves open again because fuck it, I want to watch anyway.

And Hugh's holding his hand out for me. *Get over here, you idiot*, his face says.

I stumble as I get up. Beth meets me at the edge of the bed and tries to help me with my jeans, but they're too fucking tight. I gasp out loud when I finally free my cock, but then they're pulling me onto the bed, Beth on top of me, Hugh beside me, and the agonizing need to come is forgotten as bliss takes over again.

Hugh kisses me first, as Beth nuzzles my neck. Then it's her mouth I'm tasting, sweet and warm, as Hugh goes hunting for condoms.

"Wrong drawer," Beth tells him, giggling before burying her face in my chest.

There's more swearing and laughing and so much touching I want to die from the pleasure of it.

"Ready?" I ask her. I don't know why we're whispering now, but it feels right. Like if we're too loud, we might wake ourselves up.

I stroke her with eager fingers as Hugh sheaths himself. He catches my attention and gestures for me to help her straddle him, her back to him.

"Up you get, beautiful," I say, and she follows my instructions. I kneel between Hugh's legs, my own cock throbbing in front of me, and I guide her onto him. I watch, holding my breath, as she finds her balance, her body stretching and arching as she rises into the air. Then she sinks, one slow inch, then another. He's big and she's deliciously snug, I know this already for myself. But her gorgeous pussy stretches for him, and as she groans, he pushes up. I know how good that feels, too, thrusting into her wet, tight heat.

"God, you feel so fucking good," Hugh says, his voice straining, his body coiled with tension. "I was a saint to wait this long." He slaps his hand lightly on her hip. "Ride me."

She blinks her eyes open and stares at me as she flexes her legs, rising up his cock, then down again. Slowly at first. In control. And then faster, as Hugh spurs her on. Not one to be passive, he's moving beneath her, and at first she keeps her balance, but as they fuck, she starts to lose her composure inch by sexy inch. Her limbs start to shake. Her skin flushes, then pebbles, her nipples the hardest peaks I've ever seen.

I lean in, unable to resist her breasts. They feel swollen and heavy in my hands, lush and perfect, and I groan as I pull first one tip into my mouth, then the other. My cock hangs heavy between my legs, the crown hypersensitive as it brushes against my thigh. I *can* resist the urge to stroke myself. I'll wait for whatever comes next.

Her hands land on my shoulders, lightly, then heavier as Hugh begins to pound into her. I suck harder, wanting to get her there before he does, although it's not a fucking race. We're doing this together. All three of us.

She's holding on to me for dear life now, her fingers digging in to my shoulder as Hugh holds her in place and grinds against her, pulling the sexiest moans from her perfect little mouth. "Ah, yes. Ohhh, God. Right there. More. More, more… Yes."

"Touch yourself. Show Lachlan how to get you off," Hugh growls. I reach between her legs and find her hand already there, rolling over her clit. I wrap my arms around her instead, holding her as she shudders, as her teeth sink into my shoulder and Hugh shouts that he's found his own release.

Then he eases her up and off him, and we're tumbling to the side. I can't let go of her, but he's on it. He gets me a condom, taking his dirty time getting it on me, and then he lifts her thigh on top of mine and guides us together.

The fucker found lube, too. He slicks me up, then Beth moans. "What…oh, God."

"You okay?" I ask her quietly, and she refocuses her gaze on me.

"Oh, yeah." She gives me a weak grin, the gasps. "Fuck, that's cold!"

Hugh laughs. "You're all swollen and Lachlan needs relief."

"I can wait," I say, my voice breaking.

"No." She shakes her head, her breath hot against my lips as she shifts against me, rubbing her wet pussy against my cock. "I want you now."

Hugh hisses as he slides in behind her. He gives me a devilish smile. "See? She wants you now, Lachlan. Take her."

Fuck. Fuck, fuck... I lock my gaze on Beth and flex my hips, driving into her. She's tighter than before. Swollen. Fuck. I should give her time to recover.

But she feels so good.

And there's literally a demon on her shoulder whispering to her that she should clench down on me, milk my come. He's evil.

He's beautiful.

I swear under my breath as I find a rocking hip movement Beth likes. Her eyes go dreamy as Hugh reaches around her, clasping his hand on my waist. I let myself imagine him inside her, too, buried in her ass.

How good we could make that for her.

How amazing it would be to feel him inside her, to rub back and forth through her body.

To pour ourselves into her and leave her marked in every possible way.

Mine.

Her lips brush my mouth, her tongue wet and inquisitive as we twist together, tighter, higher. We kiss again, deep and dirty, until we feel like one. And when her orgasm begins to spiral, I feel it inside myself, too. She pulls me with her, calling me to chase her up, up, up...

The release, when it comes, is blinding bliss. Beth trembles in my arms, her sounds sweet and breathless as I pound into her, a ruthless last surge toward climax.

As we tumble again, gravity and reality reclaiming us from that place, Hugh catches us.

Mine.

And this time, I mean them both.

2 2

BETH

I DON'T THINK I fully fell asleep, but at some point I wake up, so I must have dozed off. I can hear the shower running, and Hugh's missing from my bed. Lachlan, however, is right behind me, and when I try to roll over to see if he's still asleep, I nearly push him right off.

"Whoa," he says sleepily, grabbing my headboard with one hand as the other arm wraps around my waist. "Your bed is too small. Next time we do this at my place."

My heart leaps. "Next time?"

"Don't you want to have us together again?" He rubs his nose against my cheek, breathing me in. That's hot as hell. "There's so much we still haven't done."

That's even hotter. I scoot back a bit so I can see him better. At some point we need to have a conversation about all this stuff, without touching and getting distracted by how good it feels when our bodies slide together. "Yeah, I want to. If you want to...?"

He gives me a happy grin and rolls onto his back, his erection bobbing into the air, hard and ready. He wraps his fingers around it and leisurely strokes himself. "I do."

Hugh walks in, slinging a towel around his narrow, inked waist. He must have caught that last exchange because he gives Lachlan a surprised look. "Look at Mr. Responsibility taking a walk on the wild side."

Lachlan lets go of his cock long enough to flip Hugh the bird. "Your hedonistic ways are rubbing off on me. Come join us."

Hugh drops the towel and sits at the foot of the bed. Erect cocks everywhere. I can't decide where to look next. "You were both asleep when I went to shower."

I wiggle my fingers at him, inviting him closer. "We're awake now. Should we make the most of our second winds?"

He rises on his knees, and for the first time I realize something very familiar is on his body. A compass inked below his waistline.

I twist my head around and look at Lachlan's hip, then back to Hugh. "You have the same tattoo."

"Yeah."

"Did you get them at the same time?" I trace Lachlan's version. Inside the compass are pine trees, tall and spindly.

Lachlan clears his throat. "Yeah."

"Do they have any special meaning?"

Neither of them answer, so I look back at Hugh.

He glances past me toward Lachlan. "Nah." He shrugs. "Just something we did."

I don't buy it for a second. Their feelings for each other are big. Maybe bigger than either of them realize. But getting matching tattoos? Did the artist not say, *hey, this is really sweet, how long have you two been together?*

Maybe not in Moose Lake.

I roll onto my right side, so I'm facing Lachlan, and there's just enough room for Hugh to fit in behind me. I change the subject because I want more sex and feelings are complicated. "Did you hear him say next time we're doing this at his place?" I ask Hugh, but my gaze stays locked on Lachlan.

If the tattoo question bothered him, he's not showing it. He's all loose and happy, a big mountain of muscles perched on the edge of my bed.

Hugh kisses my neck. "That's an excellent plan. And a very generous invitation. You should thank him with your mouth on his cock."

Lachlan moans as I twist down his body, my hair dusting the ridges of his abs.

I circle his erection with my fingers and hover above him, licking my lips.

Hugh crowds in behind me, his arms wrapping around my body. He cups my breasts in his hands and tugs on both nipples, sending electric pulses into my core. "You get him off, and I'll make sure you follow."

Deal. I lower my mouth, soft and wet, and swallow the thick crown of Lachlan's cock into my mouth. He's big enough I have to tell myself to relax as I take him deeper. Big enough to make me panic and make me wet at the same time.

I squirm back, finding Hugh's erection with my bottom as I find a good bobbing rhythm with my mouth.

"Do you want us both in you, beautiful?" Hugh strokes his fingertips around my nipples before tugging again. "Lachlan in your mouth and me in your pussy?"

"She might be sore," Lachlan mutters.

I shake my head and mumbled that I'm fine, but it probably sounds like gibberish since I've got a mouth full of Lachlan.

Hugh rocks against me. "I can be gentle with our Beth."

No need. I arch my back, practically begging him to take me, and he doesn't miss the blatant invitation. He disappears for a second, then returns with the crinkle of a condom wrapper. Yes, thank you, sex gods.

I'm not sure what I did to deserve this, I think as I rise up fully onto all fours. As Lachlan takes over playing with my breasts and

Hugh strokes my sex from behind, making sure that I'm ready for him. I'm totally ready.

Sort of ready. Getting fucked while giving a blowjob takes some coordination, it turns out. But after the first two thrusts, I realize Hugh is being gentle for another reason—so we can match speeds. He pushes into me as I swallow Lachlan deep, then pulls back so I can take a breath. In, down, out, back. And the whole time, Lachlan's got a careful hand on me, making sure I don't lose my balance. But it's not mechanical at all. It's…poetic. Like a strange dance, where they're both partnering me. Strange, but natural. I don't need to think about the blow job. It's just happening. Same with how Hugh is fucking me. There's too much going on to worry about if I feel good, if I'm moving the right way.

I'm just moving. He's moving me, Lachlan's moving me, and we're all gliding faster and faster, spinning and twirling towards a crescendo that should be dirty and messy and maybe it will be. Maybe. But it's beautiful, too.

Hugh shifts his legs between mine, pushing my thighs wider, and inside he finds a new spot to rub. A magic spot that dulls my awareness of anything else, that steals my breath and makes me rock back against him, harder, harder harder, because I want more of that spot. More of his cock, right there, rubbing just so.

"More," I moan, and I realize I've slipped off Lachlan's erection. It's bobbing in front of me, wet and painfully hard, but he just slides his hand over it as I lick my lips and reach for him.

"It's okay," he whispers.

"Noo…." I lunge forward, because it's not.

Behind me, Hugh fucks me harder. "She wants us both," he growls. "Take her mouth. She's close, I can feel her hot little cunt clutching at me."

Lachlan swears under his breath and scrambles to his knees, getting right in front of me. He rubs his cock against my lower lip and I tip my head up, welcoming him back into my mouth.

Hugh squeezes my hips as he resumes those deep thrusts that caused me to derail. Lachlan follows with a shallower pulse, but I suck him in, wanting everything. I don't care if I choke or gag, I want every last inch of him.

I want them both deep inside me. At the same time. I want to have them as they've had each other, I want to have them *together*, because there's something…oh, God, something…

But there's something *else*, too. An orgasm gathering steam, building fast and furiously inside me.

And I can't control it, because I've given myself over entirely to them, to be this bridge so we can all have what we want together. The three of us. Three lovers.

I feel taut. Strung out between two men. And now my climax is charging hard, loud and raging, and I'm tighter still. Hugh is filling me to the point of an aching stretch with each heavy rock of his hips. He's massaging that spot inside, that I've decided to call the oh-my-fucking-God spot.

Right there, I think, and he gets the telepathic hint, because he doesn't miss a beat. And each time he hits it, I swallow Lachlan deeper, until he's tapping my shoulder in warning.

I don't need it. I swallow his quick spurts of hot come down my throat, then he eases out and holds me as Hugh pushes me over the edge, make me cry out both of their names. And some swear words, I think.

One thing is sure, though. I'm grinning like an idiot when we collapse in a heap diagonally across my bed.

"The OMFG-Spot," I say under my breath, giggling softly.

"What's that?"

"A magical new thing inside me that Hugh discovered. It's like the G-spot on cocaine. I assume. I've never done cocaine."

"Sounds more like ecstasy than coke," Hugh mutters from face down in the blanket.

Lachlan laughs and pulls me close. "Ignore the guy that did some time undercover. The OMFG-spot, eh?"

"It's magical," I say with a happy smile.

"You're magical," he says quietly. "And the weekend has just begun."

"Should we come up for air at some point?"

He shrugs. "We should just come."

"So the non-stop sex isn't a bad thing?"

They both start laughing at the same time.

"I guess if I ask a silly question…"

Hugh climbs on top of me. "It's not silly, beautiful. Do you want us to court you? Take you dancing?"

I don't know how that would even work.

Lachlan nuzzles in behind me. "Let's worry about that once we've exhausted the combined force of three very healthy libidos."

I nod. That's an excellent plan. But we will have to worry about it at some point.

HUGH

WHEN WE FINALLY DISENTANGLE OUR sweaty limbs late on Saturday afternoon, and Beth throws a broad hint that she might go to the gym, Lachlan and I hit the road, but we don't stay apart for long. Before we leave, he reminds her he wanted to grill her a steak and she agrees to come over to his place for dinner.

The bigger bed was a draw, too.

Four hours later, she shows up. He meets her at the door, then waves her into the kitchen where I'm on salad prep duty.

"Long time no see," she says as she wiggles in between me and the counter, distracting me from the task of chopping vegetables. I feed her a chunk of red pepper and she makes a delightfully content hum.

I kiss her nose, and Lachlan snorts from across the room where he's prepping steaks for the grill. "What?"

He waves his tongs at me. "You're being adorable."

He looks strangely pleased at this, but that doesn't stop me from teasing him. "Do you want me to be adorable with you, too?"

All I get is another snort as he pushes his way out the back door to the deck.

"Do you want wine?" I ask Beth as I pick her up and put her on the counter. She spreads her legs and I step right up against her and give her a deeper, hungry, not-at-all-adorable kiss.

She's breathless when I finally let her answer. "Sure. Red, if he's got that."

"We stopped and picked up both." I pour her a glass, then finish making the Greek salad per Lachlan's directions. He's left olives and feta cheese out, too. I point to them. "How do you feel about olives?"

She wrinkles her nose. "Not my favourite, but I can pick around them."

"Cheese?"

"Yes. All of it. Extra cheese. That's what motivates me through a workout, the promise of creamy, salty…" She trails off as her cheeks flood red. "Cheese."

"Uh huh."

"You're terrible," she whispers.

"Definitely. It's my best trait."

She takes a long, slow sip of wine as she looks me over. "You've got lots of awesome traits. Dirty is just one."

It's the only one that makes people stick around for any length of time. "You want to go sit outside?"

She gives me a delicate frown before nodding. She didn't miss my change of subject. "Sure."

I help her down, then stick the salad bowl in the fridge before grabbing the wine and Lachlan's glass, too.

On the deck, I deliver the chef his drink and a quick, hard kiss before settling in one of the two Muskoka chairs in the corner. Beth curls up in my lap, and I play with her hair as Lachlan asks her about her workout. Apparently he's been giving her gruff exercise tips for a year.

"You haven't taken her to the gym on the Hill?"

He shoots me a silencing look and Beth squirms in my lap. Ah, I've stepped in it.

Fuck it, I don't care. "What?"

He sighs and grabs his wine.

Beth kisses my jaw. "Leave him alone. He's prickly."

"You're way too kind to him."

She laughs under her breath. "I promise I wasn't before. But it doesn't matter now." She turns her attention to Lachlan and they share a long, meaningful look. "Right?"

He nods gruffly. "Right."

"We're living in the moment," she says lightly, taking a sip of wine. "Enjoying a long weekend together. That's all that matters."

Living in the moment is usually my motto. Apparently all it takes to shatter that is one pokey comment from Lachlan about me being soft with Beth.

"What else do you want to enjoy tonight?" I run my fingers up her neck and into her hairline where it makes her shiver.

She taps her index finger against the sweet swell of her lower lip. "Should we see what sort of kinky toys Lachlan's hidden around his house?"

I didn't see that coming, and neither did Lachlan. The tongs clatter against the barbeque and we both swivel our heads toward the man of the house. He's not blushing, exactly, but he's affected.

"You do have stuff here, don't you?" I flex my thighs, suddenly restless to play.

He clears his throat. "Yeah. Some."

I look at her. "What are you thinking?"

She takes another sip of her wine as she takes in both of us. Her eyes are dancing. "What do *you* like to do, Hugh?"

I tug on the silky strands of her dark hair and think about that question. "That shifts depending who I'm with. I'm always domi-nant, though. You've gotten a taste of that." Lachlan makes a wounded noise from by the grill and I wave my glass at him. "Settle down. I didn't do anything inappropriate."

He stretches to the full extent of his impressive height and gives me a solid glare. I see how he's a good dungeon monitor.

"Maybe we should talk about this over dinner. Lay out some really clear boundaries."

"Boundaries are so hot," I say dryly and Beth pokes me in the chest. "Okay, fine." I rub my fingers against her scalp and she rolls her head into the touch. "Up you get, beautiful. I'll go set the table and we can talk like grown ups."

He's right, of course. I'd followed Beth's lead and kept our relationship vanilla so far, but if we intend to seriously add in some kink, we'd need to know a lot more about each other to make it work.

Three way kink.

The possibilities are exhilarating.

As I set the salad in the middle of the table, I catch a glimpse through the window of Beth leaning into Lachlan's side. He kisses the top of her head. It's sweet.

Protective.

They look good together. His arm slides around her waist, pulling her in tight and her head tips up, her face lighting up as he makes her laugh.

I shove away the discomfort in my chest. This is fine. This is better than fine, because once this is all over, they might find a way to hang on to that—and no matter what, I'd want that for them. A forever kind of happiness, nothing that burns too bright or too hot. Something stable and warm.

Grown up.

Beth comes in first, carrying the wine bottle and their two glasses. Lachlan follows with the steaks.

She waves the bottle. "Who wants a refill?"

I shake my head. "Not if we're going to play."

Lachlan sets the meat platter down and reaches for me, his grin big and broad. "Now who's being Mr. Responsibility?"

"You like that?"

He bumps against me, leaning in for a kiss. "Yeah."

"Excellent. My seduction plan is working."

When we break apart, Beth's eyes are big and she's squirming. I tug her close. "And I think you liked *that*, didn't you?"

"Yes," she breathes before I cover her mouth with mine.

It's total hyperbole that I now taste like him, but it feels that way, like each kiss we share gets more complicated and layered as we do this dance around the triangle we're playing with. The way she kisses me after I kiss him is…hungrier. Dirtier.

I cup her cheek and hold her against me for a moment when we stop. "Okay. Time to eat."

She drags in a ragged breath, and slides past me into a chair Lachlan's holding for her.

The steak is a perfect medium rare and I comment as much.

Lachlan grins. "Remember that guy in Moose Lake…what was his name, John? Tom? The one who kept insisting we needed to do a big steak night?"

"The one who always bowed out of poker night halfway through because he didn't want to buy in another twenty bucks."

"Yeah." He turns to Beth. "This guy talked up his new grill like it was a muscle car. So we all bought steaks and beer and went to his place one night. And the asshole turns them to lumps of coal."

She groans. "What a waste."

I nod. "Yeah. And on constable salaries, too. And that wasn't even the worst of it."

Lachlan puts his fork down and claps his hand against his leg, howling. "That's right!"

I make a face. "The fucker pulled out a bottle of ketchup and tried to pretend that would make them better."

Beth giggles. "Oh, God. Actually…" She presses her lips together for a second. "I shouldn't say anything. It's mean."

"Mean?" I spread my arms wide. "Bring it on."

She holds up a finger. "You're sworn to secrecy."

"Definitely."

"When Gavin was in Washington last month… President Best

did the same thing. Well-done, dipped in ketchup. A filet mignon."

"No." I'm horrified.

Lachlan coughs. "No comment."

Beth rolls her eyes. "We're going to talk about nipple clamps next, but we can't gossip about world leaders? The German Chancellor is picky about her toast."

"Toast isn't the measure of a man. Or a woman," he hastily adds, and Beth winks. He laughs. "And I don't have any nipple clamps."

She pouts.

"Disappointed?" I ask.

She grins. "Only because I wanted to use them on you."

"That's not my kink," I say smoothly. "Is it yours?"

"No." She says it swiftly, instinctively. "Oh! Look at that. I don't think I like nipple clamps. Unless Lachlan…"

He waves his hand in the air. "I'm good. Feel free to pinch me, but fingers only. I like the human touch."

"Okay." She holds his gaze then, the heat ramping up quickly, and holy hell, yeah, I want to see that. I want to tell her what to do, how to hurt Lachlan just enough to make him squirm. How to boss him and tease him and make him moan. "What else?"

"I…" He laughs under his breath and slides a quick glance my way. "Hugh was my first experience with someone really dominating me. He's got a special touch. I haven't explored that since our…"

Affair? Fuckfest? Clusterfuck of unspoken feelings? All of the above, really. I throw him a bone. We're having fun this weekend, nothing else. "Since Moose Lake?"

"Yeah." He shifts on his chair. "It opened my eyes to a whole new level of kink. I'd played a bit before, but nothing like that. When I moved to Alberta, I got more involved in the world. For almost a year, I just went to social things. Fully clothed. Didn't find anyone…" This time he doesn't leave me hanging. He looks me right in the eyes. "I didn't find anyone who yanked my chain the way you did. So I started to explore other things. Figured out I like service. Which is kind of obvious in hindsight." He laughs gently. "Kink often is."

"Service." Beth's brain is going a mile a minute. "So whatever we want?" She gestures at me, then back at herself. "That'll make you happy?"

"Well, I like that. But there's a lot more to it. Service topping isn't the same thing as playing inside an intimate relationship. I don't want to top Hugh." I snort, and he laughs. "See? And he wouldn't like that, either. But I could top you."

Her eyes go wide. "Do you want to?"

He shrugs. "If it pleases you."

Her gaze is unsure, but the flush in her lips, the change in her breathing...I think she'd like that.

Lachlan's paying attention, too. He leans in. "It's important to me that people's first times be safe."

"Like at the holiday party?" Beth asks.

I shove a piece of steak in my mouth to keep from pointing out that this whole *just having fun* thing would be a hell of a lot easier if we didn't have bucket loads of history between us.

Lachlan carefully nods. "Yeah. I wanted to make sure that was safe for you."

She lifts her chin. "You kind of spoiled the vibe."

I almost choke, and I grab my napkin. Shit.

Lachlan doesn't blink, though. "No. That's what it's often like."

"Oh." A frown tugs her eyebrows together. "Then maybe flogging isn't my thing."

Ha. I doubt that very much. I wait for Lachlan to say what I'm thinking, but he stays quiet.

Fine. I cross my arms and lean back. "I think what we need to do is undo some of the assumptions you've got about kink."

She snaps her attention to me. Her eyes are bright. Eager and ready to be corrected. My dick responds accordingly.

"Like what?" She sets down her cutlery and laces her fingers together.

"Domination and submission doesn't need to be adversarial. In fact, it rarely is."

"But you and Lachlan…"

I grin. "Yeah."

"You snap at each other."

"And it makes our dicks hard." I get up and round the table. I smooth my hand over the nape of her neck and take her wine glass, setting it aside before I lean in and brush my lips against the curve of her ear. "But you are to be treasured. Completely different."

She inhales shakily. "I'm not good at letting go of control."

"We'll take it slow."

"Maybe I'm a top."

I doubt that very much. "Even Dommes need to learn how to bottom. Let's take it one experience at a time until you figure out what you like and what you don't."

"What if…" She's looking across the table at Lachlan, but I'm right behind her. I can feel the nervous tremor run through her body. "What if we don't like the same things?"

Lachlan's hand curls into a fist. "We will."

I settle my hands on her shoulders. "We know we've got some decent chemistry, right?"

She dissolves into relieved laughter. "Right. Yes."

"So now we just need to find out if you like being spanked, too."

She gasps. "No."

"I gotta tell you. When you say no, that makes me want to do filthy things to you."

She twists her head around and glares at me. "Pervert."

"Guilty as charged." I kiss her full on the mouth. "Finish your dinner. And give Lachlan your olives, he loves them."

Lachlan raises one eyebrow and gives Beth a concerned look. "You don't like olives?"

"They're not my favourite thing. But I can eat around them, no problem."

He shakes his head. "We can leave them out next time. I should have asked. Is there anything else you don't like?"

"Besides nipple clamps," I interject, teasing her.

"I really don't think I'm into pain," she mutters.

"I don't like liquorice," he continues mildly, ignoring how I'm trying to steer the conversation back to sex. But seriously, who wants to talk about food preferences when we could talk about banging preferences instead?

"Oh, so it's fine not to like liquorice but we can't mock someone for eating steak with ketchup," she says not-at-all-innocently.

"Beth..."

She rolls her eyes. "Yes, Lachlan?"

"Enough," I growl. I'd like to pull out my cock, now fully erect, and suggest something better to go in her mouth than backtalk and sass.

But Beth would be just as likely to give me a good nip for presuming too much. Maybe one day I can convince her to let me be in charge for an entire day, blow job manner lessons and all.

"Let's get back to the more important question at hand. How do you know you wouldn't like a spanking?"

She looks back at me. "I don't know. That's a good question."

"It wouldn't hurt if you didn't want it to. But you're right. Maybe not a spanking tonight. Maybe we'll wait until you've actually been a bad girl for that."

Okay, I'm only a halfway decent person. And I can't resist the squeak of surprised outrage. It fucking turns me on.

I catch her by the wrist when she lashes out at me with her pointy, bossy little finger. I kiss the waggling point and wink at her. "Tonight, Lachlan's going to show you the difference between being flogged for fun at a play party, and being flogged by someone who's been inside you."

"Lachlan?" Surprise rocks across her face. "Not you?"

I look over at him. He's not surprised. And he's definitely pleased.

"Yeah. Lachlan. And I'll be calling the shots. You will be doing exactly what I say. We're going to work on your trust."

"Flogging as a team building exercise?"

Yeah, it might be. We're going to need to be a team, the three of us. At least until they decide they're better off as a team of two. That'll be right around the time one of them gets a wedding invitation and needs a date.

Date.

Singular.

That leads to mate, singular. And I'm not the mating kind.

I'm the long weekend of debauchery kind, and fuck it, I'm going to be the best there ever was. "You bet your hot little ass." I point to her plate. "Eat up."

LACHLAN

I use an old hockey bag for my kink stuff. It's easily transportable, and is disguised in plain sight.

Plus, over the past ten years, I've amassed quite the collection. In the four years I was stationed in Alberta, I dove into Edmonton's kink scene as a way of finding my way post-Hugh.

I learned about ropes and cuffs. All the ways people liked to be tied up, tied down. Tied up in knots, emotionally and physically.

I learned about pain and pleasure, and started to make sense of what was so good about what I did with Hugh.

None of it touched what we had, though.

So I gave up hunting for someone to push me to my knees. I scratched my itches in other ways—through service and care.

It's been a long time coming, me using this collection of stuff in a truly intimate way.

After dinner, I pull out the hockey bag. I sift through the neatly sub-divided contents. Rope bundles, smaller bags of cuffs, some still-in-their packages one-time-use vibrators. I want the leather roll that houses my small flogger collection.

Beth crowds in beside me as I run my fingers over the

options. I want a soft, gentle toy for her tonight. Something that will warm her up as it lands on her bare skin. The right tool to move her from mildly interested to definitely hooked.

"That looks soft," she says breathlessly.

I nod. "It is. Similar weight to the one Brandon used on you at Max's. It'll feel different on your bare skin, though."

"Bare?"

"You can leave your panties on."

"What fun is there in that?" Hugh asks as he joins us. He wraps his arms around Beth and kisses her neck. "You don't need training wheels, do you?"

I give him a dark look. "Let her ease into it."

"But I want that leather caressing her everywhere," he says silkily.

She shivers.

I shrug. "Up to her. *Not* you."

"Everything is up to me," he says, completely undeterred. "You should take off your shirt, for example."

Half way to naked? That sounds like a great plan. I pull off my t-shirt and toss it onto the couch, then I grab some condoms from my travel pack—right next to my first-aid kit, because I'm a responsible kinkster—and I pocket two before handing the others to Hugh.

Then I tug Beth out of his arms and peel her out of her clothes, leaving her underwear on. She gives me a nervous look that gets my blood humming, then wiggles out of them herself.

Even better.

Once she's naked, I arrange her over the arm of the couch, bent at the hips with her legs spread enough to afford me a spectacular view of her glistening pussy.

"Find a comfortable position for your hands in front of you and keep them there. If they move, it's the same as a safeword and I'll stop."

I settle in behind her and gently drag the falls of the flogger up the back of one leg, then the other.

She lets out the cutest little whine.

"Patience."

I stroke the flogger back and forth over her ass. She squirms her hips. I pull the flogger back and start swinging in a figure eight.

The tips of the falls brush the bare skin of her ass, alternating cheeks. Left, right. Left, right. Occasionally, I drop the stroke to the tops of her thighs, then back up.

I keep it steady until she's pink and warm. Beautiful.

"That's so good," she moans, wiggling her hips back and up in the air. I can see how wet she is, her pussy juices glistening on the inside of her thighs.

"Don't come yet," I tell her roughly. "Not until I'm inside you."

She whines and presses her cunt higher in the air, damned near presenting herself to me like she's in heat.

Fucking hell. I drop the flogger and fall on my knees, burying my face between her legs.

I don't know what gets me harder—her sweet, musky scent, her glorious, unique taste, or the simple, womanly feel of her. She's soft and wet and warm, and when Hugh tells me to put on a fucking condom and fuck her already, I don't need to be told twice.

Having Beth bent over the arm of the couch was perfect for flogging, but Hugh will want to see everything as I fuck her, so I take her by the hand and lead her in front of the sofa, to the middle. I motion for her to climb up. "On your knees, facing the back."

She does as I ask, then turns her head, catching my eye before she taunts me with a wiggle of her ass.

I sink right into her, pushing balls deep as she groans. I close my eyes and count to ten, because I'm dangerously close to losing control.

But on the third thrust, she cries out, and on the fourth, she shatters.

So my sweet Beth likes being flogged.

Best fucking news all week. I speed up, making my thrusts more shallow, too, because I know she's sensitive, but there's no way I'm not coming inside her. I'm not that selfless. Not with her.

It doesn't take long for the tension of a climax to mount inside me, and as it does, I latch on hard. My brain slithers into the gutter, and my world narrows to Hugh watching me pound Beth.

Watching my ass tighten as I pulse in and out of her cunt.

Maybe jerking himself off, his hand clenched around that thick cock of his. The tip of it coated with pre-come, just as tasty as the sweet saltiness of Beth I still have on my tongue.

Come.

Cock.

Pussy.

Hot, sweet, amazing pussy. "Fuck, Beth," I growl, and she whimpers. I'm fucking her so hard she *whimpers*.

But then she begs me to come. "Give it to me, Lachlan," and the tension spikes, jacking me through the roof. My release is hard and fast, my vision darkening as I hold on to her hips and bury myself inside her, slumping forward when my right leg cramps up.

I catch myself on the back of the couch before I fall on her, and roll to the side.

Beth immediately curls up beside me, and I kiss her. Over and over again, open-mouthed and desperate.

We've both just come like fucking champs, and it's barely taken the edge off. I want to do her again.

I tug on her hair and together we glance over at Hugh. His gaze is dark and his lower lip is caught between his teeth.

"Not bad," he says slowly.

We both laugh.

She rises on shaky legs and crosses to him. I get up and head to the bathroom to get rid of the condom and get my head back in the kinky game.

When I return, she's primly kneeling between his legs.

He gives her an indulgent look. "What do you say?"

She exhales as she shakes her head. "I don't know."

"Say, *thank you, Hugh.*"

Her eyes widen. "Seriously?"

He raises both eyebrows. "Wasn't the flogging a great idea?"

She laughs as she nods. "Yes. Thank you, Hugh."

"You could be more grateful."

"Thank you very much?"

He gestures to where his erection is stretching against his jeans. His fly is open, the zipper down and the denim flapping open lewdly, but his cock is dressed to the side.

Deliberately so, I'm sure. So she'll have to reach in and get her prize.

And now her punishment for being impertinent. From the happy sigh she makes as she tugs his dick out and starts to lick him, I don't think she minds.

I check the flogger over and make sure it's clean before I put it away in the roll. That was a lot of fun. I run my fingers over two lighter, matching floggers. Maybe next time I'll show off some fancy Florentine arm work.

But for our first night of kink, this was amazing. I heft the hockey bag onto my shoulder, and Hugh snaps his fingers to get my attention.

"Where are you going with that?"

Was amazing? I grin. Maybe *is* amazing, still. "What, we aren't done?"

He shakes his head. Beth bobs lower in his lap, interrupting whatever he was going to say next. He pauses her with a quick touch of his fingers to her hair. "God, she's too good at that. No, we're just getting started. What else do you have in there?"

I swallow hard at the way his eyes rove hungrily over my chest. "Rope, cuffs…" A spreader bar, but maybe he doesn't need to know about that just yet. "What do you want?"

He glances up at the bare ceiling. "Do you have any anchor points installed?"

I point upstairs. "Yeah."

"Cuffs and rope, then." He grins. "Time to show Beth the first thing I ever did to you."

She pulls off him with a wet pop. "Oooh…."

"After you finish, beautiful." He fists his cock and taps the wet, straining head against her mouth. "Priorities."

WE HEAD UPSTAIRS, Hugh carrying two bags of ropes, Beth skipping along with the cuffs he's promised she can put on me. I've got the hockey bag, because Hugh darkly promised that nothing is off the table.

My little cottage has fantastic ten foot ceilings on the main level, but up here there are steep dormers in each room, and the maximum height even in the centre is just barely eight feet. No room for my king-sized bed or a shower I can stretch out in. So I converted half of the space downstairs into a master suite for myself, and I use these rooms only occasionally. One of them has a desk and a filing cabinet in it, although I'm just as likely to use my laptop on the couch downstairs.

And the other one is empty, except for an exercise mat, some weights in the corner, and four anchor points in the ceiling. One has a punching bag hanging from it.

The other three are where I practice rigging when I have people over.

Hugh lays out the bundles of rope, carefully sorting them. I'm not the only one who's learned more over the last decade. He obviously knows what he's doing, so I don't go into monitor mode.

I stand there, at the ready, and wait for instructions.

Hugh chooses a sturdy hemp rope, then gestures for Beth to join him in front of me. "Have you used velcro cuffs before?"

She shakes her head.

"Open them up. See how tough that is? So they're great for him to resist against." He smirks and blood rushes to my groin. He's going to torture me and I'm going to love-hate it. "Put those on his wrists. Not too tight, but don't leave extra space, either. We want him to feel safe and secure."

Another smirk. Desire skitters across my skin, lighting up all my nerve endings.

Beth slides in front of me. She's amped up. I'd like to think some of that is the residual high from the flogging and fucking, but really, this helper role—an eager mini Domme—is a perfect fit for her.

And I'm not complaining. Having her touch me as Hugh watches, his gaze hooded and hot? It's got me buzzing already.

Once Hugh checks my cuffs, he reaches up and loops the rope through the anchor point, then hooks my left hand up to the long line.

It's not until he moves across the room and grabs another bundle of rope that I realize what his plan is. He's going to string me out between two anchor points.

Jesus. My pulse speeds up, and I want to widen my stance, but I also trust that he'll take care of that for me. And it'll be a good safety lesson for Beth.

Once that rope is up, I expect him to point me to the midpoint, but instead he turns toward the hockey bag—and he grabs a crop from my collection of hitty things.

Fucker.

He's grinning when he turns around, and I don't hesitate to give him a *what the fuck is your plan, man* look.

Because seriously, a lot has changed in ten years. And he's never used a crop on me.

"Relax," he says evilly. "Where's the trust?"

"It fled as soon as you picked up that crop. Have you turned into a sadist in your old age?"

"Liar," he say softly as he crosses the room and stops right in front of me. "You still trust me."

I do, but we should just double-check we're on the same page. "What are my limits?"

"No marks. Lube and go slow for anal. Edging is cool. You like to say no and not mean it, so we'll need safewords. And your favourite part of bondage is straining against the ropes and not being able to go anywhere. That gets you so hard you start drooling come down your leg like a teenager. Did I miss anything?"

My face is so hot it must be beet red. "No. That about covers it."

"Safewords, then?"

I can't look over at Beth. I feel more naked than if I were actually nude. *You like to say no and not mean it.* Fuck me. He hasn't forgotten a single thing.

Hugh taps the crop against the inside of my denim-clad thigh. "Should we use ten codes like we used to?"

A hot rush of memory slams into me. The first time we kissed, Hugh had shoved me back against a wall. The tension had been growing for weeks and we were both pissed off.

"You want me to back off, Ross? Really? I don't think you do."

"I don't know what I fucking want, asshole, and you aren't helping."

"You want me to help you sort out your precious feelings?" He was closer, all of sudden. Right in front of me. "I'm going to kiss you now. 10-4?"

10-10. Negative. 10-3, Stop Transmitting. He was giving me an out, and all I had to do was tell him clearly this wasn't what I wanted. Instead I stared at him in stony silence. Unable to say yes, please fucking kiss me. I need that more than I need my next breath, you fucking asshole who's gotten under my skin.

But we'd used those because they were second nature to us, and a nod to that weird and wonderful start to our affair.

I shake my head. "Beth doesn't know them well enough." I lick my lips and finally look at her. "We should pick new safe words we all agree to."

"Cupcake," she offers. "Lemon drop. Ice cream."

"Now I just want dessert," I say weakly. She isn't freaking out about what Hugh said. And from the way her nipples are hard, tight little peaks, she's enjoying this idea of safewords.

What have we tumbled into?

"Maybe it should be something you don't like. Liquorice?" She leans in and brushes her lips against my cheek. "My safeword can be *olives*," she whispers. "And maybe Hugh doesn't get one because he's mean."

"I heard that," he growls. "And I get one. I like this food thing. My safe word, should I want to end a scene because Beth's a brat, will be *cabbage*."

"And we should have—"

"A caution word," Hugh says, finishing my sentence. He bounces the crop lightly up my hip and slides it between my body and Beth's. "Lachlan likes to slow me down."

She grins. "I can imagine why."

He just shrugs. "I humour it. You'll discover it's got its advantages, too. No worry about pushing him past a limit, so I don't have to hold back."

"And we both like it like that," I say quietly. Beth jerks her attention back to my face, and her expression is both curious and warm. It gives me a surge of courage I grab on to with both hands. "I've never submitted in front of someone else before. It's unnerving."

She looks at Hugh's crop, then carefully pushes it out of the way so she can plaster herself against me, her arms winding around my neck. "When are you going to figure out that I find every last inch of you, and all of your desires, incredibly sexy? Inside and out."

My heart hammers in my chest. "Same." My mouth is dry, but I ignore that. "And Hugh, too. Even with the crop."

She winks. "I especially like the crop. I can't wait to learn how to use it."

"That's a very advanced lesson," I say, my voice cracking. I'm not ready for her to try that on me. Not when I just want to toss her over my shoulder and carry her off to the nearest bed.

"Then we'll have to work up to it," she whispers. "Now can we finish tying you up so you're at our mercy?"

"Caution word," I croak out. "And any time you want to take off my pants, that would be great."

She giggles and cups my erection, straining behind my zipper. I should have taken the jeans off downstairs instead of zipping them back up again. Force of habit from play parties.

Gonna need to break myself of that. Nothing with Hugh and Beth is anything like casual kink.

"How about *cupcake* for your caution word? Not a bad thing, but not something you're going to blurt out, either."

Hugh takes my hand and strings it up on the second rope. "Beth, you're going to make an excellent top."

I groan and close my eyes as a shudder racks through me.

HUGH WARMS me up by showing Beth how he likes to use the crop to flick at my nipples, my boxer-covered ass, my bare thighs. He likes to change it up, between stroking with the cool leather and gentle flicks, so I don't know what to expect when he touches me.

"What Lachlan really wants is my touch," he says, using his

words just as effectively as the crop. To get into my head and fuck with my mind.

"And you should give it to me," I growl.

"I will." He hands the crop to Beth. "Stroke him only. No flicking."

"Got it." She grins with unabashed pleasure as she lays the keeper against my shoulder and trails it across my chest. "You look so good stretched out like this."

"Yeah?" I roll my shoulders, flexing my muscles. I'm not stretched tight between the two points. Hugh's left enough slack in the ropes for my arms to rest below my shoulders, which helps with circulation, and allows me to move a bit. Also, show off for a sexy woman.

She circles my right pec with the crop. "Do that again." Her voice is low and husky. I flex for her and she bites her lip. "Yes."

She lowers her arm and steps in, replacing the leather with her mouth on my skin. I tip my head back and groan at the pleasure of her tongue, her lips. The warmth of it, which Hugh always deprives me of for so much longer.

Except that's what he wanted—me distracted.

Because now he's behind me. He brushes his knuckles against my lower back before tugging my boxer briefs down and touching the crease between my ass cheeks.

The fucker has lube.

I gasp and rise up onto my toes, the ropes catching as I surge forward.

"Easy," he murmurs. "You'll knock Beth over."

"You sneaky jerk," I moan. My ass is clenched *shut*, like no joke.

"Did you expect anything else?"

I burn inside as I roughly shake my head.

"Down on your heels," he orders. "Beth, use the crop to show him how wide I want his feet. Same width as mine."

I refocus my gaze on her as she eagerly complies, tagging the insides of my legs, left and right, until I'm spread so far apart there's no way he's not getting inside me.

Fucking fuck fuck.

And my cock is straining at the front of my boxers like it's my birthday.

Basic rule of sex: trust your dick. When it's happy, you should be happy. But Jesus, that's easier said than done when your boyfriend is rubbing circles around your asshole and your girl-friend is grinning at you on the other side, and pretty soon you're just going to come on the spot because you haven't done this in ages and—

Beth's hand closes around my cock. She gives me a sweet smile and tightens her grip. "What did you say to me downstairs?"

"Don't come yet," I groaned. "Easier said than done."

She winks. "I know."

Hugh probes me gently, working the lube into my puckered hole until he breaches my defences. That first press inside is shocking, but it's also damn welcome. Beth doesn't miss how my cock jerks and swells as his long finger pushes deep inside me and finds my prostate. He rocks the thick pad of his finger over that spot and my legs go weak.

"Wow," she breathes, swirling her thumb over the wet head of my cock. I'm sure I'm like a fucking fire hydrant on a hot summer day, spewing pre-come right now.

Jesus. My hips rock back, seeking more contact, maybe another finger.

Instead I get Hugh's retreat, then another cold press, this one firmer. Another tool to deprive me of human touch while still driving me crazy.

A plug.

"Oh God, no, no, no…"

Hugh chuckles. "This is why we have safe words, Beth."

She giggles.

Evil, the both of them. "Fuck you, Hugh."

"I prefer it the other way around, but I'd make an exception for you." He presses more firmly and the widest part of the plug violates my ass.

My head lolls forward as I tell myself to hold fucking still and try to relax.

I succeed on being still.

The plug pops into place, and Hugh lazily slaps my ass cheek before circling around to Beth at my front. She's petting my balls like I'm her fuck toy, and tonight, maybe I am.

"What do you want to see?" He's so fucking casual while I'm stuffed and panting.

She shakes her head slowly, her eyes wide. "I don't know. Anything."

He grins and wraps his arm around her waist, getting closer so he can share the space right in front of my body. With his other hand, he unzips his fly and leisurely begins to stroke his cock.

She mimics him using my dick. Duelling hand jobs.

We've all come already tonight. That should have taken the hungry edge off and let this just be about kinky play, but damn if I don't want to chase an orgasm right now. I sway my hips forward, clenching my ass around the plug Hugh's stuffed in me, and I manage to knock cocks with him before he realizes what I'm doing.

"Lachlan," he warns.

"What?"

"No topping from the bottom."

"It feels good."

He grins. "Okay, Beth, lesson number one. Sometimes kink is about power exchange. Earning submission from your bottom. Making them wait, making them beg."

She nods, an eager pupil at the school of Professor Evans' Deranged Perversity.

He exhales roughly and steps into me, taking my cock from Beth and sliding our flesh together. "And sometimes," he mutters right against my mouth. "It's just about dirty fucking sex."

I moan as he sinks his teeth into my lower lip.

Without thinking, I reach for Beth, and my arm jerks hard against the rope. She gets the message, though, and presses into my side.

Her hand lands in the small of my back. She hesitates there, her fingers fidgeting, then she smooths her palm lower. Heat races through me as she curves her fingers over my ass. *Cupcake,* I think. Maybe. I don't know.

It's one thing for a guy—for Hugh—to work my cheeks open and lube me up.

It's another for a woman I've practically put on a pedestal to see or feel me split open.

But you gotta trust the dick.

And the dick is thumping hard as Beth explores the tense curves of my backside.

I stop breathing entirely when Hugh's mouth drifts to my neck and at the same time, Beth rolls her fingertip along the edge of my crack. Takes a stroll all the way down the cliff's edge, but never tumbles over.

And then she's shifting again, touching Hugh, and I stop thinking about what she's doing and give in to the sensations.

Hugh, stroking me hard against his own cock. Flexing and straining muscles. Mine and his. Bumping chests, then soft skin too, as he draws her between us.

A rush of air as she drops to her knees, then her mouth. No, just her tongue.

I groan and look down between our bodies.

She's licking us both. Back and forth, everywhere Hugh's hand isn't. Wet tips, swollen balls.

Hugh shifts to the side, dropping his own erection so it

swings wildly, obscenely, for a second. He fists me tight. "Suck him deep, beautiful. I want you to gag on him."

She slides her mouth over my crown, lapping and licking.

Lust hazes my vision as I watch Hugh sheath himself in a condom, then kneel behind Beth.

"Don't stop," he murmurs, and she doesn't, even as he guides her up, then settles her back on his lap slowly, filling her with his cock.

Never in my life have I seen anything as hot as Beth's wide eyed look of almost alarm as he stretches her out, followed by an undeniable smile before she swallows my cock again.

He's got his arms wrapped around her, one low across her hips, the other across her breasts, and he's moving her entire body up and down. She still doesn't miss a beat in blowing me.

My balls are heavy, full for her again, and the noble thing to do would be to hold it in until she comes first, but I'm strung up and tortured and her mouth is magic.

I don't stand a chance.

When her breath dances against the underside of my cock, I groan a plea. "Lick there. Right there."

Her tongue swipes at that sensitive spot on the bottom of the tip, where my foreskin pulls back, and I thrust my hips forward.

Another swipe, and the plug rocks inside me.

Fuck.

Fucking fuck.

"Your tongue..." I whisper, shaking now.

She licks around the head of my cock like it's an ice cream cone and the slippery pre-come flowing out of me is Madagascar vanilla. Too precious to let even a drop slide by.

Fucking fuck.

Fuck.

My brain short circuits as her hand tightens, pumping my length. The third stroke of her hand bumps my cock against her tongue, and that's it. That's the thing that will explode my mind. A few more tugs and everything's gone black, pure pleasure.

Sweet, warm mouth. Firm, nimble fingers.

Hugh's grunts behind her.

Dirty fucking sex.

With a shout, I come, shooting my first spurt into her mouth, then she strokes me again, cool air sharp against the sensitive tip.

I blink my eyes open in time to see her direct the next shot of my come onto her breasts.

Fuck.

My cock spasms in her hand and I paint her again, spurting three more times before I'm wrung out.

She wraps her hands around my thighs as Hugh carries them both over the finish line, his thumb on her clit, his mouth against her ear.

Dirty words. Dirty sex.

They gaze up at me, him knowingly, her in awe, and I have no doubt this is the rightest thing I've ever done.

2 5

BETH

LACHLAN FALLS ASLEEP FIRST, his arm growing heavy over my side as his breaths slow and even out. Hugh's in front of me. The other half of my delicious man-Beth-man sandwich. He silently touches my lips, and I kiss his fingers. *Good night,* I mouth.

He watches me for a few minutes, a happy, sex-drunk smile on his face.

But then he blinks. Once, then twice. Slow, sleepy blinks. And after a bit, his eyes don't open, and his breaths, too, grow steady.

I'm so ridiculously lucky.

I know that.

So why can't I sleep, too?

I lean back against Lachlan. He's so warm and stable. If I squint, today is a lot like how I expected being with him would be. Except Hugh wasn't in those fantasies.

And that makes my chest hurt, because…I slowly follow the shape of my new lover with my eyes. His dark stubble, his full lips. The big, thick bulk of him in front of me, hyper-masculine and all mine to devour.

He's perfect.

Funny, bossy, sexy.

Just like Lachlan's perfect in a different way. Strong, kind, sexy.

I could never choose between them.

Ugh. I clench my fist, not wanting my thoughts to go there. Not tonight. Not after this weekend. But the question has encroached, here and there. It can't really be ignored.

This perfection is fleeting.

Deep down, I always thought maybe Lachlan might be the one.

Now there are two.

Have I fucked myself over for a happy-ever-after with the only man I could ever see myself having babies with?

Hot tears threaten to fall, and I am *not* doing that now. Not between them.

My heart pounds as I carefully slide myself off the bed, then pull on one of Lachlan's t-shirts. I don't bother with underwear.

I need busy work. I need to distract myself.

In the kitchen, I poke through his fridge. He's got mushrooms and onions, so the leftover steak from tonight could be turned into the filling for meat pies. I don't even know if he likes meat pies, but whatever. My fingers shake as I pull out the ingredients. I get that going, and as I chop and stir, my pulse slows down again. *Breath, Beth.* Easier said than done, but the cooking helps.

As the gravy simmers, I wander to his pantry. He's got oatmeal, raisins, chocolate chips.

Flour. Sugar.

Butter and eggs from the fridge.

When I'm done investigating, his counters are covered in supplies and I have enough work to do for at least an hour so I don't have to worry about…whatever is on my mind.

The second tray of cookies is just going into the oven when I feel Lachlan's presence. I glance toward his bedroom just in time to see him step into the hallway and pull the door shut behind him.

He rubs the sleep out of his eyes. "Can't sleep?"

"Did I wake you?"

"That's not an answer." He pulls me close and kisses my forehead. "But no, I don't think so. Hugh rolled into me and he's a lot bigger than you. I wondered where my Beth had gone."

I shrug it off. I feel heaps better now, anyway. "Sometimes when I've got insomnia, I like to cook. And bake."

"And tonight you're doing both."

"I made you cookies."

He glances at the tray I just pulled out, now cooling on a rack. "Yum."

"You have a very well-stocked kitchen."

"I told you I like to cook."

"I think you said something like, 'I make a decent steak and a mean egg.'"

He laughs. "Those are both true statements."

"I can vouch for the steak, yeah. But I think you undersold your abilities." I sigh. "And why am I surprised? You're never one to toot your own horn."

"I don't need to brag. I just need to do." He grins down at me. "Can I help?"

I shake my head. "All done. Even the dishes. Just need to wait for twelve minutes until the last batch is ready to come out."

"Do you have a timer, or are you watching the clock?"

"Timer."

"Good." He picks me up and sets me on the counter. His body is right against mine. Hugh had me in the same position earlier, but now I'm half-naked.

I shift on the cold counter.

"Are you okay? Sore from earlier?"

I shake my head. "Not sore at all. It's cold."

"I can warm you up."

"I know you can." I lean in and kiss him. He tastes sleepy and warm, but the heat turns up quickly. It's just like the first couple of times we were together.

Hugh was right. There's no doubt about our chemistry.

I close my eyes and try not to think about Hugh. I'm kissing Lachlan. Just Lachlan right now.

"What is it?"

Damn him and his attentive ways. "Nothing." I groan. "No, not nothing." I turn my head and look in the direction of his bedroom. "I was thinking about him."

Lachlan chuckles. He clearly doesn't get why this is a problem, although the way his erection is lazily growing against my thigh, maybe it isn't one.

"Should we wake him up?"

"To make out?" He kisses my jaw. "No. How much time do we have left?"

I glance at the numbers counting down on his stove. "Nine and a half minutes."

"That's appropriate. Okay. In the morning, over pancakes, we'll talk about this with Hugh. I'll tell him how you blushed with worry at the thought of cheating on him with me in the kitchen—"

"I know it's not cheating."

"Doing *filthy* things with chocolate chip cookies and milk."

"There's no milk."

"Yet. I have plans." He kisses my chin, my lips, my nose. Delicate, laughing little kisses. "They'll be scandalous. And Hugh will love hearing about them, I promise you."

"You can't blame me for wondering. This is my first…whatever we're doing."

"Polyamorous relationship?"

"That's a mouthful."

"If we're lucky, yes."

I laugh, and it takes hold, shaking my entire body.

"See?" He rubs his nose against mine. "No big deal."

"Mmm."

"You sound unconvinced. Is this what had you up in the middle of the night?"

"I didn't actually fall asleep. You have six mini meat pies in your fridge for the week."

"Ah, Beth." He sighs. "Come on. Tell me what else is on your mind."

I tap my fingers against his chest, trying to frame it in a fair way. "You know, maybe Hugh's question before dinner wasn't completely out of line. He doesn't understand why we hadn't hooked up before. And… I still don't completely understand. And now we're doing this, and it changes everything that I thought might one day happen."

Surprise rolls over his face. I can't blame him when he looks away. There was a lot loaded in what I said.

But he asked. I cup his cheek, stopping him. He sighs as he turns back to me. "I know. You're right."

"What's changed?" I drop my hand to his chest and tap his heart. "Right here?"

A tortured look rolls over his face. "I don't know. I mean, shit, that's an awful answer, but it's the truth." He grabs my wrist and lifts my hand, pressing a rough kiss to my palm. "I never want to lie to you. Even if it's uncomfortable."

My chest is tight, but my head is clear. "It's fine." I stretch my arm out, inviting him to kiss my wrist and up to my elbow. "We'll figure it out together. Slowly."

"I am sorry it took me so long." His voice rasps in the quiet of the kitchen. "And it's not because of Hugh. I didn't think I'd ever see him again. Fuck. I'm glad he's back, though. And I'm glad he pushed us together, even if that wasn't his plan."

I glance toward the bedroom. "Maybe it was."

He shakes his head. "No." Tension pulls at the corners of his eyes. "There's a lot of history there that I don't know if he wants me to spill. None of it bad. Well, except where I treated him badly."

"No."

He nods. "I was young and stupid and falling out of a closet I didn't even know I was really in. I didn't handle our affair well. Not at the beginning, and definitely not at the end."

"In the middle?"

He laughs ruefully. "Okay. I handled it just fine in the middle. We were good together."

"But it didn't last." That hurts my chest. "I'm sorry."

He shakes his head. "Can't be sorry. I needed to find you."

"Shush."

His eyes flare bright and he cups my face, his fingers gentle but firm as he holds my head still so I can't shake it. "Don't. Don't pretend this is something casual between us. Or that because Hugh and I have a history, our relationship is deeper or more meaningful."

"Lachlan…"

He takes my hand and drags it to his chest. I can feel his heart beat, pounding faster than I expected. His gaze doesn't waver from my face. "I'm scared as shit that I'm not going to figure out the right thing to say to you before you give up on me."

Oh. "No." I lean in and press my forehead against his. "That's the right thing to say, right there."

"I want you so much," he whispers. "Every minute of every day. I've wanted you since the first minute I laid eyes on you. And I've l—"

I press my mouth against his. That's enough for tonight. I don't know if my heart can take any more. And across the hall, there's another man who's laid a claim in the same space, too.

We're too complicated for l-words.

LACHLAN

THE LONG WEEKEND comes to a hot, sticky close, and when Beth and Hugh leave my place Monday night, they need to dash through a heavy rain storm to get to their cars.

The wind and rain intensify overnight, and early in the morning on Tuesday, devastating news alerts start to ping out.

Three tornados have touched down. One in southwestern Ontario, which caused property damage but no injuries.

But in a small town just north of Kingston, two twisters have caused significant damage. Many houses destroyed, half the town population displaced, and at least six people missing.

It's one of the worst tornados in Canadian history.

I'm not politics-savvy. I'm adjacent to it, though, so I hear stuff like news cycle and response management. Shit like that grates on my nerves, because as law enforcement, it's my preference that the news and politicians stay far away from the life-or-death work of emergency response.

On the other hand, apparently jackasses on Twitter are already freaking out that Gavin hasn't made a statement.

"It would be a good idea to say something before the morning news shows are over," his communications director says.

The regional disaster response liaison, who was brought in for the morning briefing, shakes her head. "Unless it's the world's shortest statement of support for the fire department and police on the ground, there isn't much to say at the moment. Be careful that we don't promise anything we can't follow through with."

Gavin nods. "I can do that."

His communication director protests. "People want a pledge of federal dollars. They want a state of emergency to be called."

"That's a provincial call," Gavin says tersely. And he's already spoken to the premier of Ontario, who is facing pressure to *not* call it. "But we can pledge military support."

"How much will that cost?"

I don't see who asked that question—the room is packed—but Gavin's answer is exactly the one I want to hear. "It'll cost what it needs to cost. People lost their homes this morning. Probably lost loved ones and neighbours, too. If you think there's a financial cap on the federal response to that, the door is over there."

A stunned silence pauses the room for a moment, then the sound rushes back. A flurry of polite and some not-so-polite political debate points get tossed back and forth, but the parameters have been set. The prime minister wants the federal government to fix this, and as quickly as possible.

By mid-day, he's in an awful mood because his brief statement didn't go over well with his critics, and he's chomping at the bit to get down to Beaumont.

"The logistics of you showing up on the scene are nightmarish," I tell him candidly, because I pull no punches. I can't, not if I'm going to do my job properly. "Because it's not just you. It's the media train that will follow, even if you try to keep it under wraps. It's not like flying into a war zone, where we control the media access. They're camped out down there already. You show up and the perimeter that's been established will fall apart."

He glowers at me over the roast beef sandwich Beth has shoved in his hands. "A month after I was elected to the House, there was a mudslide in my riding, and I was at home. I went and helped. People liked that. It wasn't a stunt."

"You can't help with the search and rescue."

"I realize that."

"Do you? Your job here is to provide national leadership, and that unfortunately means, you can't do things like just show up in a disaster zone."

"Yeah." His frown deepens.

"Is this about something else?"

"No. Yes." He sighs. "Now's not the time. But I want to be bolder, and simpering, expected, mediocre responses that feel canned and unhelpful—even if right now there's no way for me to do anything else—it underlines how hampered I feel in this role."

Shit. That is something else. He's been the prime minister for a year, and I know it's been quite the adjustment for him. He's young and willful, accustomed to be big, brash wins.

But this is pretty far outside my wheelhouse if he's having some kind of… I glance around. Nope, only me. We're sitting in his office, having a five minute lunch together.

He gives me a rueful smile. "Right. You can't advise me on that."

"I'm flattered that you'd confide in me."

"Bah." He wipes his mouth with a napkin, then shoves it in the brown paper bag his sandwich came in. "I'm just frustrated and I can trust you. It'll be fine."

Beth knocks at the door and pokes her head in. "It's time."

And then we're off, for another round of briefings and speeches and decision making so high up, the prime minister can't do much but throw money at a problem he'd dearly love to try and fix shoulder-to-shoulder with the people on the ground.

When Gavin goes into the House of Commons for Question Period that afternoon, I head to the gym, but I'm barely ten minutes into my workout when I'm paged by security. I have a visitor, and he's been through clearance many times before, but he's not on the expected guest list for today.

Max Donovan. The prime minister's best friend, Beth's favourite person to flirt with before Hugh showed up on the scene, father-to-be with the beautiful Violet, and the man I've been dodging for a few weeks.

He's waiting outside my office when I get there.

Apparently he's committed to planning a bachelor party and no amount of me pretending that isn't on the agenda is going to make him go away.

"Lachlan, I was starting to worry you didn't like me anymore," he says with an incorrigible pout.

"I like many things about you, Max." I open my door and gesture for him to enter. "But our friendship is definitely going to be on the line if you insist on planning any kind of stag night for Gavin."

"I've been preparing for this event for twenty years. Don't rob me of the joy."

"You didn't have a bachelor party for your own wedding."

He waves his hand dismissively. "Details."

"You decorated your holiday party with dildos."

"They were festive cocks, not dildos, and that wasn't me. I gave Corinne free rein with the decorations."

Our hockey team's goalie does like to mix craft and kink, but that's not the point. "How long did you leave them up after the party?"

"We got distracted by real life stuff."

"Are they still up?"

He makes a face. "No."

"Okay, here's the deal. You and me and Gavin can do a private thing with the hockey team. *Not* in your dungeon. *Not* anything kink related. It has nothing to do with who is involved and everything to do with…" I trail off. A bunch of shit Max doesn't have security clearance for. "Anything can be recorded. Anywhere. We scan 24 Sussex constantly, but anywhere else is just too risky. Not to mention he's constantly aware of how things look."

"Then we'll bring the party to him."

"No strippers."

"Fine."

"No hookers."

"Of course."

"No women paid for any reason."

"So the pretty little clown I hired to do face painting?"

"Max."

"I got it. Beer and pizza and poker—all proceeds to charity. Is that square enough for you?"

"That sounds great."

"You know what you need, Lachlan?"

I can't wait to hear this one. "What?"

"A sweet little sub to turn that frown upside down."

Ha. I grin and point to the door. "Feel free to let yourself out."

"I'm telling you, man. You need to find a woman. You're wound way too tight."

"That's because someone interrupted my workout, the only hour of today I was going to have to myself. I got here at five, picked your best friend up at six, and I'll be eating dinner right here, too. I'm doing just fine, considering."

He gives me a curious look. "What's going on?"

Do I have *banged two people all weekend long* written on my forehead? "I just told you."

"I know, but I was mostly projecting from the last year of grumpiness. You're actually agreeable today." He snaps his fingers. "You finally got over your hang-up about Beth. Yeah? Are you two…"

"Get out."

"That's a yes." He bites his lip as he punches his fist against his hand. "I knew it. Good for you guys."

Shit. "Stop. No. Beth…" I take a deep breath. I suck at this. "She doesn't want anyone to know. We're dating. Yes. We're not making a big deal about it. And she freaked out when I mentioned to Gavin that we had dinner together. So keep it under your hat."

"Lips sealed."

He takes his leave, finally, thankfully, and I wait until the door clicks shut behind him before I groan and pitch the hockey puck stress thingy-ma-jiggy from desk across the room.

Fuck.

BETH

INSTEAD OF HEADING home after a very long, very tense day, I leap on an invitation to go shopping with Sasha Brewster, Ellie's maid of honour. Well, it's more window shopping for me, because Sasha's an honest-to-goodness socialite.

Sasha and I don't shop on the same level. We don't even shop in the same galaxy.

She seems to think we need an entire new wardrobe for the wedding weekend in British Columbia. I'm happy to watch her tear her way through Holt Renfrew and make notes.

Plus she's funny, and not at all quiet.

Also, nosy. I get a text from Lachlan, and before I can click on it, she's giving my phone a nosy Parker look. "Who's the text from?"

I stick it back in my purse without reading the message. I'm not risking her peeking over my shoulder. "A guy I'm seeing."

Her eyes narrow. "If it's not Lachlan, don't tell Ellie."

I laugh. "Why would you ask who it is if you might not like the answer?"

"Wishful thinking."

"Why does everyone care so much if we get together?"

"Oh, come on." She gives me a big, google-eyed look of disbelief. "You know."

I take a deep breath. "No. Yes. But no."

"You guys are both head over heels for each other."

"It's not that simple." I'd always known real life was more complicated than fairy tales. I'd never expected this level of complication, but still… "It's *really* not that simple."

"Was it Lachlan?" She presses her finger to her lips. "Promise I can keep a secret."

"From Ellie?"

"From everyone." Her expression is drop-dead serious now. "Honestly, you don't need to tell me. But…if you want to, I'll be a vault with it. Secret gossip is even better than regular gossip."

I weigh the pros and cons of telling her. At some point Ellie might mention it anyway. Hell, Gavin might drunkenly mention it in his wedding speech. Threaten to chuck Ellie's bouquet at Lachlan's head or something stupid like that.

Maybe I should skip the wedding.

I grit my teeth and nod. "Yes, it was Lachlan. We're…kind of dating. We're dating."

"What's the kind of part?"

"That's not exactly my secret to share."

Her eyes go wide again. "Oh."

"Oh, nothing."

"No, I think it's something." She nods slowly. "I like this. Your life is fabulously interesting."

She's not wrong. I give her a wobbly smile. "Hey, where would be a good place to buy lingerie?"

WE END up driving to a high-end boutique—of course—where the owner loves Sasha and gives her a suspiciously high discount on everything in the store.

Sasha claps like it's our lucky day, but I think I know better. When we finally collapse in the coffee shop a few doors down, me with my one bag, her with two much larger ones, I take a deep breath. "Did you arrange that somehow? The deal? Did you…help me somehow?"

She wrinkles her nose. "No. Although yes, sort of. But not like you're thinking." She leans in and lowers her voice. "Now it's your turn to keep a secret. Not even Ellie knows this. That shop? I'm her silent partner. I own 49% of it and put up the capital. So she extended my discount to you, but she does the same for Ellie. No secret blinking messages or anything like that."

"Oh!" I frown. "And Ellie's never questioned the discount?"

She laughs. "She was my roommate for ages. Me getting a discount at a store isn't an odd experience for her. Other than quite rightly pointing out how the last thing a poor little rich girl needs is a discount on satin and lace, no, she's never asked."

I nod. "So, why is it a secret?"

Another nose wrinkle. "My father would freak if he found out. The only reason he hasn't dragged me into the family business is because I'm a full-time student. Starting side projects is definitely not allowed."

"Allowed?" Oh, I want to say so much more, but maybe it's safest if I just echo that single, loaded word.

She rolls her eyes. "I know. It's stupid. *Totally* stupid."

I was thinking more like disturbingly controlling, but sure, totally stupid works, too. "How do you feel about that?"

"I hate it. But he's my *dad*. And until I decided I didn't want anything to do with his business, we were two peas in a pod."

"That's…real life, though. You don't get everything you want without any consequences for your decisions…" I trail off. Shit. I'm the last person to be giving anyone a lecture on playing Pollyanna. "I'm sorry. It's none of my business."

She just shrugs. "You're not wrong. I know I need to have that come to Jesus conversation with him. Soon."

"Bah. Whatever. Live your life as long as you can, the way you want to."

She lifts one eyebrow in a coolly patrician way I'm sure I couldn't pull off. "That sounds like a hint at your fabulously interesting life I want to know more about."

"Nice try." I wink. "So. Anything more I need to do for the wedding shower?"

We talk about flowers—can't hurt to have lots—and sugar cookie favours—cute in concept, but does anyone really want to take cookies home?—and then we give Violet a quick call to loop her in, too. Everything is coming together nicely, which is good, because we're down to the wire.

Of course, I've been delightfully distracted.

When Sasha excuses herself to the washroom, I check Lachlan's text—and am very glad I waited until I was alone to read it.

Lachlan: Max guessed that we're seeing each other. I'm not very good at keeping you a secret.

My frustration is definitely tempered by the second line. More than I expected. There's a weird, warm sensation blooming in my chest, actually.

Beth: Okay. Thank you for telling me.
Beth: I'm out with Sasha right now. She's on the guessing warpath, too.
Lachlan: Maybe unavoidable.
Beth: But complicated...

He sends a dorky smiling cartoon in response. I don't know how to decode that, but if he's not stressed, then I won't be, either.

I flip to my contacts and click on Hugh's name.

Beth: Hey.

Not the most original opening line, but I don't know how to lead with *So people are starting to assume Lachlan and I are a couple and how do you feel about that when we're both pretty obsessed with getting you naked?*

Hugh: Evening, beautiful. Long day, eh?
Beth: Yeah. I'm out shopping now, though.
Hugh: Buy anything indecent?

We text back and forth about my shopping trip and I promise to send him anonymous lingerie pictures when I get home. Before I can bring up the point of why I started texting him, Sasha returns and I shove the phone back in my bag.

We'll pick that back up again when I get home. And maybe by then I'll have found my backbone.

HUGH

WHEN I MOVED to Ottawa two months ago, I took the first available one-bedroom, short-lease apartment recommended to me.

It's perfectly fine for my purposes, which consist of sleeping, eating, working out, and getting changed.

I don't even have a TV. The guy who sublet my place in Toronto offered me a decent price for all my living room stuff, and it made moving a hell of a lot easier.

Now I'm sitting on my weight bench—the only furniture in the main room of my apartment—and trying not to think about how long it might take Beth to get back to her place from the coffee shop.

I'm way too eager to keep texting with her.

Hell, if she invited me over tonight, I'd be there in a heartbeat, even though we both have to work first thing in the morning. I'm definitely in that early phase of a new relationship where sleep is optional and every encounter leaves me feeling a bit lightheaded and giddy.

Maybe that's why I like dating so much. I'm a perpetual teenager inside, riding the emotional highs like I'm surfing in the

Pacific Ocean. Sure, there's an epic wipeout that's almost always inevitable, but it's worth it for the rush.

But this restlessness, this *eagerness*, is unusual even for me.

When my phone vibrates, I jump. I'm grinning like a fucking idiot as I swipe in to read the message.

Beth: Home. Just tried this one on.

The attached picture is pretty tame, but it gets my blood pumping all the same. Red silk, creamy skin. I shift all the way to the end of the weight bench so I can lie down on it, and I brace myself by spreading my legs wide.

I'm only wearing gym shorts, so reaching in and cupping my thickening dick is easy. Texting back with just my thumb proves a bit harder.

Hugh: Gorgeous. Still wearing it?
Beth: Trying on another.
High: Pic pls.

She readily complies. The next picture is cleavage, with a tantalizing shadow. My mouth waters.

Hugh: That makes me hard. And hungry.
Beth: I'll wear them this weekend.
Hugh: I can't wait. You're crazy hot.
Beth: And you are very kind.
Hugh: I'm jerking off right now. Who's kind?
Beth: I'm blushing!
Hugh: Good.
Beth: Are you in bed?
Hugh: Soon.
Beth: Me too.

I picture her stripping out of the satin and stretching out naked on her bed, and I tighten my grip on myself. Tonight isn't the night for raunchy phone sex.

Fuck, it pains me to say that.

We're both off the clock for a few hours and she bought sexy underthings.

She's practically begging for me to whisper in her ear until she comes with her hand jammed between her soft thighs.

Beth: So... good night, then
Hugh: Wait
Beth: Waiting...
Hugh: Can I call you?
Beth: Sure.

The smiley face she adds is adorable. Fuck it. I'll make it quick.

THE NEXT DAY, the PM's schedule is as expected, but there's a tension simmering on the Hill because we all know he's going to Beaumont at some point. It's like someone's pulled the pin on a logistical grenade, and is just holding the hammer down.

Throw it already.

But that's not how natural disaster visits work. I'm vaguely aware of this from being on the other end of them. The flooding in Manitoba, an ice storm in Quebec.

When the afternoon hits and we're pretty sure it's not going to happen today, I head to the gym to try and shake off my funk, but the punishing workout doesn't help.

Lachlan comes into the change room as I'm getting out of the shower. We're not alone, and he doesn't even glance at the towel slung low around my waist.

As queer men, this is engrained in us from before we understand that we're different than the expected norm. For me, the passing as straight, passing as a bro, is something I still bristle at on the inside. It's flashbacks to high school, to bullying, to sick feelings and worry and distrust.

It's easy right now to pretend we're not looking at each other because it's unprofessional and this is our workplace. That's not a lie.

It's just not the whole truth.

I leave before he gets his stuff in his locker and has a chance to turn around.

The restless ache gets worse, and when he texts me ten minutes later, I want to ignore it. Maybe show him, show me, that I can master this feeling.

I tell myself it's a choice that I still look at his message anyway.

Lachlan: Want to grab a coffee after work?

The instinct to say no is strong. I shove it down.

Hugh: Yeah. Beth up for it too?
Lachlan: She says not until the weekend. I'm standing at her desk.
Hugh: I thought you were going to work out.
Lachlan: Nah. Just had a quick shower. I'm off the clock until the morning, though. Meet at seven at my place?

Ah. "Coffee".

Hugh: Sure.

LACHLAN PRESSES me up against the wall in his foyer and kisses me like a man dying of thirst and I'm an oasis.

It's hard and demanding, his lips pulling at mine, his tongue thrusting deep without invitation.

"Had a long day?" I ask him roughly as I grab him and spin him around.

"Something like that."

I wrench his shirt out of his dress pants, wanting his hard, muscled core under my touch. I splay my fingers wide across his flexing belly, and cup the back of his neck with my other hand. He stills immediately, my big raging bull.

"Here?"

He nods. "I've got lube in my pocket."

"Gotta be prepared for coffee," I say, a harsh laugh marking the end of my snarky statement, but he doesn't care. I think he wants that verbal sparring just as much as the physical one. He has to be on and polite all day long.

Nice to come home and have someone to be a dick to. Give a dick to, too.

But we haven't fucked yet, and his foyer isn't the place for it. I'm not so in denial that I don't know that's going to be full of fucking feels for me after all this time.

I'll want to hold him afterward, too.

But lube is good for other things. I take the single use packet from him after I strip off my t-shirt.

I rip it open and squeeze some onto my fingers as I watch him undo his shirt buttons.

"All the way off," I growl when he lets the shirt just hang open. That's hot as hell, but I want bare flesh. Big arms, working shoulders I can sink my teeth into. "And then get my jeans open."

He tugs me closer, unzipping me first, then his dress pants. I'm not wearing anything under my jeans, and he groans as the wet tip of my dick slaps against his hand. He circles my straining head with his thumb, then lifts his hand and sucks it off.

Fuck.

I reach between us and circle our cocks with my slicked-up hand. We both hiss at the first slide of skin against skin. I lean my forehead against his, and he wraps his arms around me, his hands low on my waist, his biceps straining as he frames our bodies. Our secret, thrusting, furtive sex inside his front door.

But the restlessness I've felt all week has vanished, and I'm full of a giddy warmth. Our hard breaths, the furrow of his brow as he tosses his head back, the scent of lube and pre-come rising between us…it's hot as hell, and right as fuck.

I say his name, a whispered groan, and he urges me closer. "Come here," he breathes.

I slam into him, our cocks pinned between our bodies, and the slide turns into a grind as we kiss, hard and wet. A kiss that tears at any last pretence of civility as we thrust and rock together.

His hips grind up against mine, and I push back with equal force. I want him to come hard and fast. I want him to paint me with his pent-up need that only I can fix. I'll rub it into my skin as a badge of honour.

He wraps his long, solid fingers around the back of my neck and holds on tight. The harder he grips, the closer I know he is, and the dirtier I get. I slide my hands around from his hips so I can cup his ass. He flexes hard against my invading touch, but I'm having none of it. That tight trench, that smooth pucker.

Mine. All fucking mine.

And when I stroke over his tight hole, he shoots hard, like a fountain in fucking Vegas.

My big, sexy brute.

I slam him back against the wall and reach between us, grabbing his firehose of a cock, trapping it against mine. I point them both to my belly as my own orgasm rips up from my balls.

He lets out a long, satisfied sigh once I let him go. "I needed that."

"I could tell. Want to talk about it?"

He hesitates, then tips his head toward the kitchen. "Yeah. Coffee?"

I grin and wave at my come covered belly. "Sure. Let me just clean up first."

THE NEXT MORNING, as I'm dragging my tired-ass body out of bed before dawn because I stayed at Lachlan's until almost midnight, the pieces of the puzzle finally click into place and I realize what the problem is.

Even though I see them every day, I think I miss Lachlan and Beth. I miss them together. I saw Lachlan last night, and Beth is talking about the weekend…and yet, that's what the weird feeling in my chest is.

Longing.

Fuck me.

I try to tell myself I'm just *missing* them. No *longing*. No big feelings. Because I see them behind masks of propriety that make me want to strip them bare. Because I gorged myself on them, naked and honest, for four days straight over the long weekend.

Because as the seconds tick by, minutes passing and turning into days, I can see last weekend better than when we were in it, and it was perfect.

Obviously, one misses perfection. That's not a big deal.

Perfection is fleeting, in that desperate, holy fuck kind of way that makes you think all the stars have aligned and you're having a once-in-a-lifetime experience.

Yeah, we'd talked about it happening again, but there was a solid part of me that wasn't sure that wasn't wishful thinking. That we'd slide back into the love triangle thing again, instead of the unexpectedly right triad.

So I miss them—us—together.

And so I'm lying in bed, lazily stroking another pile-of-bodies-inspired hard-on.

What I need to do is to stop moping, and lock down a plan if I want to quell the nerves inside me.

I don't like being nervous about a relationship.

I like to be in control, and that usually means clear definition of what a thing is—and isn't—before we get too deep.

That didn't happen this time.

It didn't happen the first time with Lachlan, either.

But that was foolishness I won't repeat. No falling in love this time. I've learned my lesson.

29

LACHLAN

THURSDAY COMES AND GOES. Gavin snaps at a reporter in a scrum when he's asked about the clean-up in Beaumont. It's going slowly and there's some fuckery going on between the municipal, provincial, and federal levels of government. But the meat of his response—that it's an exceptional tragedy which requires an exceptional response, and "good enough" is, in fact, *not*—gets lost and what gets looped all day on the news is his flash of anger instead.

By the end of the day, he's laid down the law—tomorrow he's going to the Beaumont Elementary School and he's going to be fucking helpful.

I'm not sure it's going to go like that at all, but we pull together a functional travel plan. We'll drive, because it's only two hours away, and we can bring our own security so we aren't a drag on local resources. I send an advance party with a two-fold assignment: find a place for the prime minister to meet with displaced residents and hear directly from them what they need in the next seventy-two hours; and report back the early intel on that question so he can bring something with him.

It's a decent plan.

It gets derailed before it can even get off the ground by three drunk, entitled young bucks in suits who decide to piss their frustration with the government literally onto the Parliament buildings.

So Friday begins a few hours after Thursday ends. I'm dragged out of bed at three in the morning with an apologetic call from Corinne Smith, my former partner at RCMP HQ—and our hockey team's goalie, when we actually get a chance to play. The Ottawa police made the decision to hand the suspects over to us, and she's giving me the heads up. One of the guys under arrest is too stupid to shut up about how much he hates Gavin, and it starts to sound like he's threatening the prime minister.

That jams up my plans to accompany the prime minister's convoy today, so on my way in to question the drunken idiots, I wake some people up.

"What's up?" Hugh answers the phone with gruff sleep dripping off his greeting. I shouldn't be thinking about how good his voice sounds or how much I'd like to have woken him up by rolling over instead of hitting the call button.

I fill him in. "I need you to shift over to the PM's detail this morning."

"On it."

I hesitate. So much I want to say, but it's easier to keep it professional in moments like this. "Thanks."

There's a beat on his end, too. "Yeah, of course. Later."

At the RCMP headquarters, I head to the interview rooms and talk to Corinne first. She apologizes for the early morning wake-up, but I agree with her that it's better to be safe than sorry.

And once I get into the first interview room, I realize two things pretty quickly.

One, these jackasses are no threat to national security.

But two, I don't give a fuck, because they're jackasses who think the world should be served to them on a platter.

So if they need to think they're being investigated as national security threats to make them quake with fear...that's just fine with me.

The guy I talk to first is the one the investigator feels was more of a follower. Weak, and easily flippable, although I'm not in the mood to give him that carrot just yet because I don't like the garbage spewing out of his mouth. I don't spend much time with him before I leave him to sweat and move on to the next.

Craig, douchebag number two's name is, and he's *pissed*.

When I walk in, his face shifts into forced politeness, but it takes effort on his part. "Bro," he says. "I have *rights*. I've been waiting forever to call my lawyer."

Bro.

I grab the chair across from him and spin it around so I can straddle it. The stupidest shit disarms idiots. "The way I understand it, you've all had a chance to make a call and they're on their way in."

"That bit—the other cop won't let me talk to my attorney."

"It's four in the morning, man." I give him an easy shrug and ignore the fact he was about to call Corinne a bitch. Rising to that bait wouldn't get me anywhere. "It takes some time for people to put on pants. But I didn't see any lawyers on my way through the building. Although maybe this is good for us. We can clear this up before they come in and make you stay quiet."

"Make me?"

"You don't want to be turned into a free speech martyr, do you? Have this come back on you at work?" There's a fine line here. I can't threaten him, even though I want to. "The investigation into your threats is going to take some time. Better for you if it stays quiet."

"I didn't make any threats."

"You said..." I flip open the folder Corinne gave me. "*Someone needs to teach that treehugger a lesson he won't forget.*"

"That was a joke."

"Do I look like I'm laughing?"

He scowls and slumps lower in his chair.

"I'm going to talk to your friend next door. Think about what kind of attitude you want me to ask your boss about when I go in and tell them you're not going to be coming to work today."

"We just—"

I stand up. "We take threats seriously. Excuse me."

The third guy is still too drunk to talk. I don't think this is going to court in a serious way, but just in case it did, I wouldn't want to risk questioning someone whose words might get tossed.

Instead, I head to the break room and grab a cup of coffee from the machine. It's hot, and that's all that I can say about it.

Corinne finds me there and jerks her head back to the interview rooms. "Lawyers have arrived."

"Good." I drain my cup and toss it into the recycling bin. "Let's get this show on the road."

The defense attorneys they've hired aren't that familiar to me. In the year that I've been at Parliament Hill, I've only had to come down and do this twice. But one of them recognizes me, and knows that I'm the PM's chief of security.

It helps if they know we're taking this seriously.

"What do you want here, Ross? You don't really think this is a security risk, do you?"

I give the lawyer a bland shrug. "I don't presume to know anything more than what the evidence tells me. Your client's words were inflammatory and dangerous. So far I've heard a whole lot of excuses and not a lot of self-reflection or comprehension of the severity—"

"Okay. Give us twenty minutes to talk in private."

"Sure. We'll use that time to draft warrant requests for their social media accounts."

Nineteen minutes later, we've got carefully coached apologies and a plan to get them back to the city cops, who will process them for indecent acts.

"You understand we'll still be monitoring your behaviour

going forward? We're not going to close this case until we're confident it was a one-off nuisance event."

We get a round of chagrined nods.

Corinne's mouth is twitching as we walk back to her desk. "What?"

"I was expecting you to be harder on them."

"Spending the day shitting themselves that their bosses will find out they almost were arrested for uttering threats is punishment enough. Ideally, I'd like them to learn something from this."

"You think that's going to happen?"

I shake my head. "Probably not. But I don't want to harden their hatred for the prime minister, either."

"You've gotten soft up on the Hill." But she winks, softening what otherwise would be a stinging indictment.

I laugh. "If they were an actual threat, I wouldn't have hesitated to take them down, don't worry."

"I wasn't that concerned. Sorry to drag you out of bed."

"Nope. That's my job."

MY PHONE IS full of messages when I hit the parking lot, so I head straight to the Hill. The convoy is underway, and the advance team has reported in. The town is being inundated with stuff— donations of clothing, toys, food that will likely spoil, unfortunately. What they need is shelter.

Gavin's chief of staff, Stew, is waiting for me when I get back to the office. He waves me into the conference room. "Looks like we've got a good plan," he says. "The army's got mod tents that aren't bad. Big enough for a family of eight. No privacy, but spacious and heavy duty."

I nod. "Yeah. I've seen those on bases."

He introduces me to a team from the Department of National Defence, who go over the rapid deployment option Gavin can offer the town today, so people can move out of the school gymnasium.

It shouldn't have taken four days, but it's a solid plan, and the prime minister will like it.

I stop in at Beth's desk to say good morning when the meeting breaks up.

"I heard you didn't get much sleep last night," she says quietly.

I shrug. "Happens sometimes."

"Will you want to hit the hay early tonight?" She asks it innocently, but the small smile tugging at the corners of her mouth is asking a lot more. *Are we still on for the weekend?*

"I'll be fine," I say under my breath. "I'll catch a second wind. Hugh should be back in time for dinner. We can cook at my place."

"Sounds perfect."

I steal one of her pencils and wave it goodbye at her before I take my leave.

Downstairs in my office, I turn on the news and watch my team do their job. The coverage is more glowing than earlier in the week, and Gavin—as he always does—comes off as genuinely concerned about the situation on the ground, and the long-term impact it will have on the residents of Beaumont.

He's got his jacket off and his shirt sleeves rolled up, and the cameras catch part of a conversation he has with a teary single mother. She leans into his side as he gravely tells her he'll make sure the insurance companies live up to their obligations.

And just like that, he's taken back the news cycle.

AFTER LUNCH, I get a visitor. Ellie knocks on the door to my office, then pokes her head in when it swings open a bit.

"Is this a good time?"

I wave her in. I don't miss that she's got one of Beth's purple file folders in her hand. "Wedding stuff?"

She nods. "I've got the final guest RSVPs here. Beth is going to email them to you, but I had a couple of notes you should be aware of…"

On her side, she has an uncle who had a bad run-in with the RCMP as a teenager, and forty years hasn't tempered his dislike for us. That makes me laugh. Sure, we can handle some dirty looks.

The other notes were just as easily dealt with. This wedding coordinator gig has proven easier than I expected. "You getting excited?"

She beams. "Yes. And thank you for your email outlining the precautions about paparazzi. That made me feel a lot better."

"Any time."

We spend another twenty minutes going over the last of the to-do list items. It's pretty short now, but all of that added work pushes my day longer than I would have liked. When I look up from lunch, I realize it's already four in the afternoon.

Even though my day started thirteen hours ago, I want tonight to be good. I swear under my breath. I haven't been shopping all week, and I still have at least an hour or two of work to do.

I grab my keys and jog upstairs. Gavin should be back soon, but right now the office is quiet. Beth's not at her desk, but I hear the photocopier working in the room around the corner, so I look for her there.

She's wearing a pencil skirt today and a buttoned-down blouse. The skirt is dark grey and the blouse is light blue. It's an entirely appropriate work outfit, so I blame my lack of sleep for immediately jumping to a filthy librarian fantasy as she leans over to pick up her papers from the side basket.

I shake my head to clear the lusty haze, then clear my throat to get her attention. "Hey."

She twists around and gives me a warm smile. "Hey."

A now-familiar spark leaps between us. I want to kiss her so much it hurts. I glance at her mouth and she presses her lips together. No, I know we can't, even before I drag my gaze back up to her sparkling eyes. "Tonight," I promise instead.

She presses her fingertips to her lips. "Definitely."

My heart hammers in my chest. "Uh…" I tighten my hand into a fist, and the sharp edges of my keys cut into my palm. Right. I hold them out. "I need to do some shopping for dinner. Feel free to let yourself in."

She steps closer and wraps her fingers around the keys. "Okay."

"And pack an overnight bag."

"Will I need clothes?" she whispers conspiratorially.

"The weather's going to be amazing. Maybe we'll go out at some point."

She winks, and yeah, it's more likely that we'll keep her totally naked, just as she expects. "Anything can happen."

From the main room of the office suite comes a flurry of noise. The prime minster has returned. She brushes past me, and I take a deep breath.

Probably a bad idea for me to follow with the makings of a hard-on.

30

BETH

BEFORE I LEFT THE OFFICE, I found a quiet moment to tell Hugh that I was heading home to pack a bag, then going to Lachlan's. So I'm not surprised when I pull into the driveway and find Hugh leaning against the corner of the house, a lazy grin on his face.

He's also been home and changed. He's wearing a dark grey dress shirt over jeans, and he's got a pair of aviator sunglasses on, too.

He looks every inch the irresistible bad boy Lachlan and I adore, and I'm so glad the week is done and we can do this for a night or two.

I grab my backpack, which he takes from me as soon as I reach him. He tangles his fingers in mine as we walk to the front door, but he doesn't kiss me until we're inside. I set Lachlan's keys on the table once Hugh's done making me breathless, and we make ourselves at home.

I really love Lachlan's place. It's small, but he's done some smart things to make it seem bigger, more spacious than it would otherwise look. And he hasn't been afraid to update it and bring a modern aesthetic to the inside.

The living room is awesome, the kitchen is amazing...but by

far, my favourite space is the giant master bath he's put in just off his bedroom. I stop in the doorway after tucking my backpack next to Lachlan's dresser.

Hugh presses his big, warm body against my back and tugs on the still-damp ends of my hair. I didn't bother to straighten my bob like I usually do for work. They'll just muss it up anyway. So I let it air dry and the ends are probably flipping out this way and that.

"Want another shower?"

I grin. "With company?"

"Can never be too squeaky clean."

"Mmm." I twist around and run my hands over his shirt, enjoying the tight ridges beneath. "When Lachlan gets home? We can scrub him head to toe."

"Yes. Excellent plan." He covers my hand with his and brings my fingers to his buttons. Daring me to unwrap him. "Want a drink while we wait?"

I swallow hard as I undo the first button. His skin is warm and tan, begging for me to stroke him as I reveal each delicious slice. "Yeah. Wine, maybe?"

"We should go get that," he says huskily.

I undo another button. "Yes."

"Beth…"

"I missed you."

He takes my hands with a groan and pulls them up his body before he lets me go and drives his hands into my hair. He holds me still as he kisses me ruthlessly. "I missed you, too," he says roughly. "I wanted to be there Tuesday night when you came in my ear. That was so fucking hot. It's kind of killing me only doing this once a week."

Once a week for an entire depraved weekend. But I know what he means. It doesn't feel like enough.

If we were dating publicly, we'd see each other a lot more.

If we were dating publicly, we wouldn't be able to keep our hands off each other.

And Lachlan.

I ease back and pat his chest. "Let's...get that wine."

He drags in a breath. "Yeah."

"He'll be home soon."

"And we have all weekend."

"Mmm."

We find a bottle of wine and glasses, and lean against the counter as we toast to a night off.

The minutes tick by, and our resolve to wait for Lachlan remains steadfast, but filthy thoughts manage to intrude into the conversation anyway. As he finishes his glass of wine, Hugh gives me a dirty look. "You could tell Daddy all about your day."

I laugh, but the look in his eyes—fierce, hungry, feral—takes my breath away. Interesting. But I'm not in the mood to play games. Not that game, anyway. I cup his cheek and soften my voice, making it sultry and terribly inappropriate. "Or you could tell Mummy about yours."

He grunts, and I glance down his body. He lets me check out his growing erection before chucking me gently under the chin. "I'll take you over my lap."

I wink at him. "I'll take you on your knees."

He raises his eyebrows, and I mimic his *oh yeah?* expression. Our stand-off is interrupted by the front door opening, and we're laughing hysterically when Lachlan joins us in the kitchen. He wraps his arms around me from behind and drops a kiss on the side of my neck. "What's so funny?"

"Hugh's trying to play sex games instead of telling me how his day was."

"That's because his day was shit. Sex would be my choice, too."

"I'm dating teenagers," I mutter, but I spin around to squeeze Lachlan. "And it was a long week for you guys. I'm sorry."

"I need to grab a shower," he says. "But I bought a whack of stuff for dinner. Let me get that heating up, and then—"

"We can do that." Hugh says. He grabs the bag from Lachlan. "What all did you get?"

"Marinated chicken tenders, a couple kinds of salads, a baguette, and chocolate cake for dessert."

"Amazing." Hugh unpacks. "How do I cook the chicken?"

Lachlan crosses to him, takes the bag out of his hands, and kisses him hard on the mouth. "*You* don't."

I take a big sip of wine. Good lord, it's hot when they touch each other. "Kiss him again," I urge. "Show him who's boss."

Lachlan laughs. "He's the boss." But he pulls Hugh in, exaggerating the kiss this time, slowing it down and making it super dirty for my benefit.

I. So. Appreciate. That. Effort.

A weak moan slips out of my mouth as I brace myself back against the counter. "We'll join you in the shower." I drain my glass and set it down firmly. "Actually, I'll get it started."

I peel off my top and drop it on the kitchen floor.

Then I turn and let them watch me walk away. There's a scuffle, then the fridge door opens and closes quickly.

By the time I've got the shower going, they're right behind me, stripping down to their birthday suits.

Excellent.

AFTER OUR SHOWER, which uses up all of Lachlan's hot water and three condoms, we get dressed again—sort of. The guys put on jeans. I pull on one of Lachlan's t-shirts, and underwear because I don't want to distract him from the task of cooking me dinner.

Once it's ready, he doesn't set the table. Instead he stacks three plates next to the stove. "Let's watch a game while we eat."

I don't bother to repeat my gripe about dating teenagers.

They won't care. And really, it's his house. If he's comfortable with us eating in his living room, so be it.

Except two shower orgasms have weakened my usually decent poker face, and Lachlan catches on to me as we settle on the couch. He gives me a grin. "You want us to go back to the kitchen with our plates, don't you?"

"I…" I try to relax my spine. "No. It's all good."

Hugh guffaws. Like, out loud, no way does he believe me, hilarious laughter. "Are you uptight about food messes?"

Lachlan gives him an incredulous look. "How have you not noticed this about her?"

"I think I was distracted by how addictive her pussy is. Fuck off."

I blush. "I'm not that uptight. Or I didn't think I was. It's just… the two of you are a lot of testosterone in a small space. And you both piled a lot of food on your plates. I'll just watch the game and try not to think about food particles flying around, staining the couch and the—"

Lachlan sets his plate down and reaches for me, hauling me into his lap. "Did you by any chance have a bad day, too?"

I shake my head, but yeah, maybe. I dunno. "It's been a long week."

"You're stressed."

Hot, unexpected tears prick behind my eyelids and I nod. "Maybe."

He rubs his thumb along my jaw and eases me in for a kiss. His lips are soft, coaxing, but beneath my bottom I feel him getting hard again. "What can I do to make that go away for a bit?"

The possibilities are endless. Sex by itself didn't take the edge off, clearly. I slide a look over at Hugh, who waves his hand. *Your call*, he's saying.

My mind starts whirring.

"But you need to eat your dinner first," Hugh says, still clearly amused. "Here on the couch. Particles flying and everything."

"Meanie," I say softly, but it's hard to care about anything when Lachlan's thumb is slowly working its way across the top of my shoulder.

"You heard the man," Lachlan murmurs in my ear. "Go be a good girl."

I snort. It's not going to be a *Beth is a good girl* kind of night. Hugh already got that message earlier. Lachlan might be in for a surprise.

I'm feeling bossy.

But I eat my dinner, like a good girl.

And when they're cleaning up the kitchen, I head upstairs and start poking around, because I'm also a delightfully bad woman. Newly so and eager to explore more ways to be naughty.

But I don't want to tie Lachlan up, exactly. At least, I don't want to suspend him. I pick through the bag of cuffs and grab the ones I recognize for his wrists.

Then I turn my attention to the rope. I don't need the heavy duty stuff Hugh used last time. Instead, I pick a blue bundle that'll look fun against Lachlan's skin.

Yes, I have a plan.

I skip down the stairs, hitting the bottom landing as they come out of the kitchen.

"What were you up to?" Hugh asks, his eyes lighting up.

I hold up the rope. "I have a stress-relief plan."

Lachlan groans, but he's grinning, too.

I swish past them and head straight to the bedroom.

"Just what exactly did you have in mind?" Lachlan asks as I hop onto his bed. It really is the perfect size for all three of us. I'm so looking forward to curling up between them tonight.

But I have an idea to use it for something a little more active first. "I want your hands behind your back, if that's okay?"

"Sure."

"And maybe tied…"

Lachlan laughs. "Okay. We don't need both the cuffs and the rope." He glances at Hugh. "Do you know how to do a dragonfly sleeve?"

"I do."

Lachlan swings his arms loosely, then brings them together behind his back. "Then I'm yours to bind for the lady."

Hugh gives me a grin. "Remember our safewords?"

I point at Lachlan. "Liquorice." Then I tap my chest. "Olives. And you're cabbage. And if anyone wants to slow down, we say cupcake."

"Excellent memory." Hugh holds out his hand.

I hand him the rope and watch with rapt attention as he finds the mid-point and makes an exaggerated bowtie. Each loop goes over an arm and up onto Lachlan's shoulders, like he's wearing a rope backpack. Then Hugh makes a new knot in the long hanging tails, a new bowtie, and those loops go up Lachlan's arms, too, sitting just above his biceps. The third bowtie goes below the bulging curve of his muscles, the fourth, fifth and sixth on his forearms, so his arms have an elaborate ladder between them.

Hugh tugs Lachlan back, reaches around to palm his impressive bulge, and whispers in his ear. "Step out of your jeans." Hugh helps with that, getting in some good gropes along the way.

Once Lachlan is naked and trussed up, I wordlessly point for him to come to the edge of the bed.

I wrap my hand around his very hard cock and stroke him gently.

"I want…"

His eyes hood as his erection grows in my hand, pulses against my fingers as I jerk him off. "Anything."

"Anything?"

"Yes." A single syllable, guttural and honest.

"I want your mouth," I whisper as I glance up at him. "And I want Hugh to have…whatever he wants."

He jerks, his arms straining at the rope binds. "He might want to fuck me."

"No might about it," Hugh says as he joins us, now naked as well. "Is that what you want? Lachlan's head between your legs, and me behind him?"

That image floods me with heat and I nod.

"You *are* a good girl," he says, winking as he saunters to the bedside table. He lazily tosses lube and a couple of condoms onto the bed. "Get naked, or it's hard for Lachlan to lick you up. He doesn't have any hands to use, you see."

I grin and turn my attention back to my tied-up lover. "I do see that. That's quite the situation you've gotten yourself into, baby."

Lachlan flexes, pumping his cock through my hand. "I'll survive."

I sigh and let go of him, falling back onto one elbow as I ruck his t-shirt up my body. "I didn't realize I could tie you up and demand you go down on me. I feel like I've been missing out."

"Any time you want, beautiful. You don't even need to tie me up."

"But that's part of the fun." I pause in my stripping, with just the bottom curve of my breasts showing. "Will you teach me how to do it?"

"Sure. Not now, though. Show me your breasts."

"I'm busy learning about knot work."

"Don't make me beg," he groans.

I wiggled out of my shirt, because I don't need begging, not tonight.

"Come and kneel in front of me as you take off your panties," he says hoarsely.

It's kind of awkward at first, trying to take off underwear while kneeling and being kissed and nuzzled by a bound man, but as his lips brush over my neck and onto my collarbone, heat skitters over my skin. I bend backward a bit as I lift one knee, then the other, and somehow it works.

It's actually crazy erotic, that he can only use his mouth to touch me, and when I tumble backward, he bends at the hips, following me with his mouth.

Hugh moves around the bed, propping me up with pillows and shifting around as Lachlan kisses and sucks at my breasts, my belly. I think he gives me a hickey on the curve just above my mound, and when I lift my head to see, Hugh sticks another pillow behind me.

"You don't want to miss anything," he says softly as he leans in to kiss me.

No, no I don't.

My legs fall open as Lachlan kisses down the crease from my hip to my thigh, firm enough not to tickle me, and onto the soft skin right at the top of my leg. He rolls his head to the side, pressing his cheek there as Hugh finally gets into position behind him.

Every muscle in Lachlan's body is straining, and Hugh taps him on the hip, urging him to relax.

Lachlan laughs. "Not happening."

Hugh winks at me. "Nah, you like it when it's a bit of a fight."

That's the second time he's said that, and it makes me squirm in a delicious way.

But when Hugh settles his hands on Lachlan's hips, then his ass, there is a change in his body. The tension shifts, maybe, and when Hugh strokes down the crease between his cheeks, Lachlan doesn't resist.

"Been a while," he mutters, his breath hot against me. I slide my attention back to him. His head is still pillowed on my thigh and his eyes are closed. His mouth is right next to my labia, and his next inhale is long and slow.

I flush with embarrassed heat as I realize he's breathing in the scent of me.

And I'm crazy turned on, so…

Ah. His tongue darts around and licks lightly at my outer lips, then he lifts his head and licks again, finding my wetness this time.

I spread my legs shamelessly, opening myself wider for him, and I realize I'm going to have to work here, because he can't adjust his position that much.

Except then Hugh does something, and Lachlan rocks forward, his open mouth sliding up my sex until his tongue curls around clit.

I jerk my gaze back to Hugh. He's got a finger or two inside Lachlan.

Prepping him.

And with each slow thrust of his hand, Lachlan licks me.

"Can you take another?" Hugh asks, and Lachlan groans. I feel the vibration right to my soul. When he nods, Hugh steps back and grabs more lube.

My eyes must be like saucers as I watch breathlessly. I know the mechanics of it from last weekend, but he's using more lube than he did for the plug, and I hadn't actually *seen* that.

"That's so hot," I whisper as Hugh wrings a grunt out of Lachlan.

This time when they start shifting back and forth, I match their pattern, rolling my hips and holding myself open so Lachlan can tease my clit better. I'm aching for something more, like his mouth sucking on me, but there's no point in asking for that until Hugh is actually inside him.

I glance at the condom and Hugh follows my gaze.

"Not long now," he promises. "I can't wait to get inside him."

Lachlan freezes, and I run my fingers over his hair. "Shhh."

"Yeah, pet him, that's good." Hugh grabs the wrapper and rips it open, the tear of plastic making Lachlan strain against the rope. He surges forward, his forehead rolling up onto my hip.

I softly rub Lachlan's head, pressing him against my body as I watch Hugh sheath himself. He takes his time, getting good and hard, then he strokes himself a few times once he's covered up, spreading the lube around.

"He's all slicked up," I murmur, then I make a soothing sound as Lachlan trembles. "You okay?"

He nods. "Want it."

"Good. I want to watch."

He makes a strangled sound in his throat at that. Ooh, a nerve. "Have you ever… been watched?"

He shakes his head in my lap.

That's heady. Heat swells my breasts, pulls my nipples tight, as I think about what a gift this is. "I can't wait. This is crazy hot."

He exhales roughly, hot breath wafting over my bare skin. "Yeah?"

"Oh, absolutely." I shift restlessly as Hugh taps his erection against Lachlan's backside. "I'll shut up now."

He laughs, then groans as Hugh spreads his cheeks and rubs the fat head of his cock right there.

"Keep talking, Beth." Hugh hisses in a breath. "Yeah. Fuck. Tell him what you see."

I'm squirming now. "You're pushing into him."

"Slow," Lachlan says, his voice strained.

"I know." Hugh pauses, then his hips flex again, just a hair. "Lemme in."

"It's going to feel so good," I whisper as I tug on Lachlan's hair. Time for him to be distracted. I pull his face to my pussy and roll my hips, no longer nervous about him breathing in the scent of me. Breath it in? I want to rub it all over him, to cover him with sex so he forgets to be nervous about me watching Hugh take him like this.

And it works.

He dives right in, his lips and tongue moving urgently over my swollen flesh. Each lick and thrust is electric, and the guttural cries he lets out in between are erotic as hell, too.

Behind him, Hugh rolls his head, tipping his face to the ceiling. I gaze through glassy eyes at the way his muscles strain, too. Two raging beasts rutting in front of me, at my command.

"Is this what it was like when it was just the two of you?" I ask. A remarkably coherent question for how sex-muddled I feel.

Lachlan groans and Hugh nods slowly. "Yeah. Sort of. You're a delicious addition. You love her, don't you, Lachlan?"

He means my taste, that's all.

But as Lachlan sucks my clit into his mouth, suddenly hard and demanding, a wave of intense emotion slams into me. I jerk my gaze back to Hugh's face and he gives me a crooked, knowing smile.

I drop my gaze to the rope ladder holding Lachlan's arms behind his back. Further back, to the spot where Hugh is now seated fully inside him.

Sex.

Focus on the sex.

"Are you ready to get fucked, baby?" I tug on his hair. "That's so good, just like that. Keep sucking on my clit. And Hugh's going to blow your mind."

I don't even know what I'm talking about, but it sounds hot, and frankly, I can't imagine he'd consent to it if it wasn't going to blow his mind.

It's blowing mine, and I'm a body removed from the intrusion.

But I know what it's like when Hugh slides into me, taking up a breathtaking amount of space where there's normally nothing but longing. And I've imagined taking him—taking either of them—in my ass.

It makes me clench tight, but it also makes me hot and achy.

"You're so lucky," I whisper. "Hugh's good, isn't he? I can tell he's taking his time. Letting you adjust to how big he is. How thick and hard."

"I've gotta go slow," the intruder says, his eyelids heavy and his lips swollen as he gazes lovingly at where Lachlan is stretched around him. "He's tight."

Big, thick, hard. Tight.

Such dirty words. I like them all. "He feels good?"

"Fucking amazing. I've missed this." He rocks forward, and Lachlan curls his tongue around my clit, greedily sucking at me.

"Do that again," I breathe, and Hugh does, and Lachlan does, and it's so decadently sinful I want to scream.

Hugh shifts his hold on Lachlan, his big, thick fingers tangling in the ropes, and I lose myself in the rhythm of our bodies, the push and pull of sex. Heat swirls beneath the surface of my skin, and from the soft sheen of sweat coating Lachlan's bulging arms, he feels it too.

Hugh looks cool as a cucumber, the dirty man that he is. But the look in his eyes betrays that this is unusually hot for him, too. He's wild for it, deep down. Wild for us, together, spread out on the bed in front of him.

I cup my breasts, pulling on my nipples. Put on a bit of a show. Touching myself, touching Lachlan, too. Hugh likes it best when I hold Lachlan's head between my legs and get myself off, pulling my thighs up and then spreading them wide.

"He's driving me wild," I tell Hugh, my voice cracking. "His mouth is so good."

"Your pussy tastes like magic, that's why. I want a taste myself when we're done."

"I'll be dead when we're done."

"I'll bring you back to life with my tongue."

"Is that magic, too?"

"You know it." He growls and bucks his hips.

Lachlan lifts his head and gives me a sex-drunk look. "You're an evil, wonderful woman," he says, his words slurring a bit.

"You like that."

"God, yes."

"You okay?"

"Uh huh." He licks his lips. "You can be harder. Get yourself off on my face."

Wild disbelief wars with hungry arousal as I reach for his hair again. My fingers tangle through the short strands, then I just spread my fingers wide, instead. I hold his head still as I rock against his mouth, tiny little movements now, so close...Climbing, climbing...My clit throbs as I rub it back and forth against his lips. It's not enough, but it's so good, and I'm still climbing. I think maybe this way I could just keep winding up forever.

I tug his head to the side, and he keeps licking and sucking there. My thigh, the curve of my hip, the top of my mound. Hugh's moving him all over the place now, and I let him go.

I need my hand to stroke myself over the edge.

And I want to release him from his duty of pleasuring me, to release him into his own pleasure.

I flex my leg beneath his face. His eyes are closed, his brow pulled tight, and his lips are parted. He's a sculpted Greek statue, tipped forward, being ravaged. "Come for him, Lachlan."

A ragged groan slides over those lips, and my eyelids flutter as that sexy, lurid sound pulls on something inside me. I roll my head and look to Hugh. His face is twisted, too.

We're all close.

I think Lachlan goes first. He shudders, then seizes up, all of his muscles flexed hard against the rope confines, and then Hugh's swearing and holding himself deep inside our lover. I wonder what that feels like. Is it a fight to stay inside? Does it hurt so good as he clamps down?

Heat twists fast in my belly, deep and low inside me. I want to feel that. I want Hugh to take me there, some day. Maybe soon.

My face flames as I rub my clit faster, my pussy and ass both clenching to be filled.

Soon.

And for now, I've got the heavy weight of Lachlan on my leg, and Hugh's gaze locked on my fingers as I frig myself over the edge.

One of them tells me I'm beautiful as I twist in freefall, the climax ricocheting through me.

Then Hugh falls forward, bracing one hand against the bed as the other fumbles with the ropes. I scramble out from under Lachlan and help him loose, then I rub his shoulders as he sits up and leans back against Hugh.

They both give me lazy, happy grins.

"That was good, right?" My heart is hammering in my chest.

Lachlan holds out his arms. "Come here."

I fall into him, and he kisses the top of my head, then I bury my face in his chest. I hear them kiss above me, and I'm so fully of happiness I wonder if I might burst.

After a few minutes, Hugh disappears to get a washcloth. Lachlan gasps when it's not as warm as he expected, and Hugh just shrugs.

"Beth gets it extra warm. You get what you get."

"Jerk." But Lachlan pulls him close and kisses him again, and I want to take a picture of the way they're looking at each other.

I love you both.

It's the craziest, most dangerous thought. But it's true.

I can't say it out loud, though. I'm going to bury it deep, my little secret.

We crawl into bed, me in the middle, and Lachlan strokes my cheek. "Was that better stress relief?"

"That was perfect."

"After the wedding, everything is going to quiet down. Then we'll have the summer to explore this thing between the three of us in detail."

"Detail?" Hugh asks, delight dancing in his voice.

Lachlan winks. "Great detail. Intimate, careful, close-up…detail."

I twist my arms around so I'm hugging them both. "I can't wait."

"And I have another surprise for you both," Lachlan says.

"What?"

"I finalized the travel schedule this afternoon. Without any inappropriate manipulations on my part, Hugh and I are both off the rotation schedule for the prime minister's honeymoon."

"Oh." My eyes go big and round, and hope leaps in my chest. "So we can have some down time together?"

He nods. "I think we should rent a cabin for a few days after the wedding, don't you think?"

I throw my arms around his neck. "You're a genius." I kiss his mouth with a loud smack, then spin around and kiss Hugh, who's laughing at me. "Just the three of us, surrounded by nature. Mountains, maybe?"

"You want mountains?"

"Yes."

"Then you'll have them."

31

HUGH

June

I'VE NEVER BEEN a fan of weddings. Maybe I've been going to the wrong ones, but the promised easy bridesmaids or curious groomsmen thing never panned out for me.

This wedding, however, might just change my mind. For one thing, while Beth and Lachlan aren't officially a bridesmaid and a groomsman, I'm definitely getting lucky with both of them. And for another, the setting is fucking magical.

Enough to win over even the least romantic of souls.

Gavin and Ellie are getting married at a lodge high on a summit above Squamish, a picturesque former logging town halfway between Vancouver and Whistler.

And despite the fact that I'm working, implementing our security measures, I'm able enjoy the beauty more this time around.

Two days ago, I was here with the advance team assessing the site and establishing a security protocol and my attention was focused on finding all the security holes and coming up with ways to plug them.

There are a lot of trails around the venue that are easily accessible without the aid of the gondola for anyone who's willing to do some serious uphill hiking.

And Squamish has no shortage of people into that, so cutting public access, even for a day is a no-go. As an avid hiker himself, Gavin wouldn't even consider the notion.

Instead, we opt to restrict access to the lodge where the wedding and reception are being held and set up a secondary perimeter of remote cameras which will be monitored from a mobile command centre.

Fortunately, paparazzi are our biggest security concern. We've managed to arrange a no-fly zone around the venue, and secure access to the suspension bridge and viewing area, so it would take a mighty intrepid photographer lugging one of those over-sized telephoto lenses to get any kind of shot, let alone one worth selling.

I meet Stew and Adrienne's three boys on the suspension bridge as I head back to the lodge.

"Where are you guys headed?"

"Dad said we could explore the trails today, and if we're well behaved at the wedding tomorrow, we can go zip-lining up in Whistler before we go back to Ottawa," Alan says in a rush of words. I feel kind of smug for being able to tell the twins apart. It's not hard if you're paying attention. Alan has a tiny scar above his right eye. Eric doesn't. Sadly, some people can't be bothered. I did laugh when I heard a kid call Eric 'the other Alan', though.

"Sounds like a fair deal. Try not to get lost."

"Oh, Daniel has a map," Eric says, pointing at his big brother. "He's in Venturers. That's where you go when you're too old to be a scout anymore."

"In that case, have fun exploring."

Such a nice family.

My phone vibrates before my jacket pocket emits Lachlan's

ringtone. I'm a little startled at the sound—especially in the quiet of the forest.

Most of the time, my phone is set to vibrate only, but being surrounded by people for three full days and virtually no privacy, Lachlan, Beth, and I set up ringtones to make it easier for us to talk privately.

"Hey Lachlan, what's up?"

"Are you nearly done? Things are good to go on this end. We're just waiting on Ellie."

I give a small chuckle. He's worried I'm going to upstage the bride and arrive after she does, interrupting the rehearsal proper. "Relax, I'm only a few minutes out."

"Is that you half-way along the footbridge?"

"You know it is."

He lets out a long sigh. "Hurry up. You look like you're out for a Sunday stroll."

I suppress my urge to shoot him the finger, but I do pick up the pace.

When I get back to the lodge, Beth is having a glass of champagne with Gavin while they wait for his bride-to-be to arrive for the rehearsal.

She's radiant. I want to walk over there, pull her into my arms, and kiss her senseless. Two things keep me from doing exactly that.

I'm on duty. And our affair is a secret.

A dirty big secret.

Lachlan is only a few steps away. His eyes are constantly moving, searching the area for the slightest thing out of place. I love that look. It may have been what first attracted me to him all those years ago.

Another dirty big secret.

Normally, I love secrets. I revel in them. Especially when they're deliciously filthy. The forbidden can be so irresistibly tantalising.

But not this time.

All this sneaking around doesn't feel right. It eats at my gut.

Usually, I love shit that doesn't feel right. That's my wheel-house. But after two months of deliciousness, today has been full of weird and unfamiliar feelings.

Guilt, maybe. It feels disrespectful to be the reason why Lachlan and Beth have to hide their feelings.

If it weren't for me…

My thoughts trail off as Ellie appears.

She looks stunning in a floaty ivory floral print dress that comes to her knees. It's a bit more formal than a sundress, but she looks comfortable.

Gavin's eyes light up as soon as he spots her. He crosses the floor to meet her, then pulls her into his arms and kisses her like nobody's watching.

I steal a glance at Beth, then Lachlan. Am I standing in their way?

BETH

ONE OF SASHA'S many wedding gifts to Ellie was arranging for a team of beauty professionals to pamper us on the morning of the wedding.

They show up at quarter to six carrying trays of Starbucks coffee, so I love them.

"We were waiting when the baristas opened the door," the makeup girl says.

"You are goddesses," I whisper as I curl my hands around a steaming latte and wonder if maybe I can just grab a few more minutes of sleep while I sit here and breath it in.

I think Hugh and Lachlan slipped out of my room sometime around three. Not nearly enough sleep, but totally worth it.

Hair is the first order of business. It's a treat to have someone else straighten my hair, and once my bob is sleek as can be, the stylist twists in some delicate rhinestone details that catch the light when I turn.

Breakfast arrives at seven, and in the middle of the room service carts is an ice bucket with two bottles of champagne that look like they cost an obscene amount of money.

"Sasha, this is incredible," Ellie says as she pops a strawberry in her mouth.

The maid of honour shakes her head. "Wasn't me. Must have been your husband-to-be."

Violet—who got out of the five-thirty wake-up call on account of growing a human being, and having a protective doctor for a husband, so she's just joined us—picks up a bottle of bubbly fruit juice. "And he thought of me, too."

Gavin's mother—an insanely elegant woman who intimidates everyone, including the prime minister—stands up and peers at the tray, then snaps up a small white card folded in the corner. Eagle eyes, that woman. But she probably got a full night's sleep last night. "Game day. Fuel up!" She reads from the card, then glances up and frowns at Ellie. "Who is Tate Nilsson?"

"A friend of Gavin's. A hockey player," Ellie adds, surprise all over her face. "That was really nice of him. He's coming today, so we'll need to remember to thank him." She waves her fingers at Sasha. "Maybe you can say something in your speech?"

"Uh…" Sasha wrinkles her nose. "Really?"

"Yes, really. Be nice."

"He's a—" She cuts herself off and glances toward Gavin's mother, and Ellie's mother, and then presses her lips together and nods. "Fine."

I'm not sure how exactly Tate's rubbed Sasha the wrong way. He's a total playboy, which may have been what she was going to say, but *jerk* or *pompous asshole* could have been just as likely. He's the captain of the Ottawa Senators and a friend of Lachlan and Gavin's. He even plays hockey with them in the off-season for fun.

And he was at the holiday play party I went to at Max's—with Sasha.

But I don't think they had any run-ins that night.

It's curious, but I don't care right now. He bought us fancy champagne, and I want some.

Breakfast of wedding champions.

The next hour spins by in a whirlwind of make-up instructions. At one point I head down the hallway to get more ice and find Hugh guarding the elevator entrance to our floor. He's got an ear piece in, and while I've seen them wear those before, of course, there's something about bubbly first thing in the morning that makes it seem extra-hot.

He takes one look at my probably-really-pink face and laughs. "Having a good time?"

"I. Love. Weddings."

"Yeah? I couldn't tell."

I twirl in my pretty dress. "We'll dance later, right? This dress was made for dancing."

"It sure was." His voice slides lower. "Can't wait to peel you out of it, too."

"Mmm, naughty man." I stop and tap my finger against my lip. "I was on a mission here."

He points to the bucket in my other hand. "Ice?"

"Yes!"

"Do you guys have any food in that suite?" he calls after me as I skip away.

"Yes!"

"Eat some of it?"

"Maybe!" But he's right, so when I get back to the room I carefully nibble on a bagel.

It's not that I'm drunk. It's that…now that today is here, I'm really excited for my boss. And his beautiful bride. The love in the air is palpable. Gavin's speech at the rehearsal last night made me weepy in the best way.

Okay, I might be a little drunk.

I spread some cream cheese on my bagel and slide my champagne flute away. Thanks, Tate, but that's enough of that for now.

Since we flew across the country for this wedding, this is the first time Ellie's had a chance to meet the make-up artist, and it takes some back and forth until she's happy with her look. It's important to her that she still look like herself, and when they finally spin her around, she totally does.

A magical fairy version of herself.

Her dress is stunning, a V-neck, wide-skirted swirl of blush chiffon, a warm, glowing paleness that's definitely not white—because that's Ellie, non-traditional to the core—but still completely bridal. Like the inside of a shell, and she's the pearl in the centre.

Her hair is up in loose curls spilling out of a twist, and she has the most amazing not-quite-a-tiara worked into the do. It's a spray of rhinestone and pearl flowers on a branch, delicate and ethereal looking.

She gleefully spins around, her fingers tucked into secret pockets she's quite proud of.

Pockets are a big deal. I get it.

"Do you have something blue?" Her mother frets.

Ellie takes her hand and replies in quiet French. *"I don't need superstitions to bring luck to my marriage, Mama."*

"It's the way to do things."

She just smiles. *"It's time to go, yes?"*

In a nod to tradition, Ellie's going to travel to the wedding site with her parents. Over the last two days I've seen them be polite to each other, but they're not close. Her parents are sweet, but very traditional.

I wonder how many times over the next hour the something old, something new worry is going to come up again.

Sasha and Ellie exchange a wordless look, then we head down to the lobby, Hugh escorting us before he goes back up to get Ellie. He doesn't need to do this, but today there are exceptions being made. Chivalrous ones, really, not for security reasons.

Romance is in the air.

He waves for our car. Max is already at the wedding venue

with Gavin, so we have a hired car to drive us. Violet sits in the front, and Sasha and I pile into the back.

When we arrive at the parking lot for the Sea to Sky Gondola, we're stopped by an RCMP guard, who checks our names against a guest list before allowing us in. Most of the wedding guests are coming up to Squamish from Vancouver on a couple of hired coaches, mainly to avoid an annoying and totally unromantic choke point here as they check credentials. According to Lachlan's carefully timed out schedule, that convoy would have departed Vancouver at quarter to nine this morning, and should already be here, with guests on their way up to the lodge at the top of the mountain.

Our driver pulls up to the front doors of the striking wood and glass structure called Base Camp. He helps Violet out first, then opens my door. Sasha is about to open her own door when a bright red sports car—something flashy and low slung, totally impractical—tears into the lot.

It didn't actually come close to our car, but she scoots away from her door and slides across to get out the passenger side all the same.

"I didn't realize Ellie had invited any jackasses," she mutters, and I cover my mouth, trying to stifle a laugh as I peer past her to check out who it is—and gauge just how awkward this is about to become, because whoever it is, we're probably riding up the gondola with them.

A silver pickup pulls in, too, and I try to run through the guest list in my head, figuring out who would be driving themselves. Gavin's family and other guests who live somewhat locally. But even people in Vancouver would meet the buses at the Fairmont Vancouver, so they can hitch a tipsy ride back at the end of the afternoon.

The identities of both mystery drivers soon becomes clear as they get out of their respective vehicles and meet in the middle of the parking lot to shake hands.

The speed demon is none other than Tate Nilsson.

I glance sideways at Sasha and she's rolling her eyes. "Of course, why am I not surprised?" She takes a deep breath. "Do you know who that bearded hottie he's talking to is?"

Violet shakes her head. "No clue."

I know who it is, though. "That's Jack Benton. He's the owner of the Vancouver Lumberjacks. He's a long time friend of Gavin's." I don't bother to give them his full bio. It's not the time, nor is it my place.

Sasha snaps her fingers. "Right. I met him when I was a kid."

I choke on the reminder that she's younger than me by enough to have been a kid who met Jack as an adult. "He's not that much older than Gavin." I think he's just barely in his early forties.

"My dad had him over for dinner at one point. He called me cute."

Violet laughs. "And you're going to bring that up today, aren't you?"

Sasha gives us an innocent look. "We'll see where the day goes."

"Maybe let's wait to tear through the hot guests until after the ceremony. Come on." I nod toward the building that we need to go through to get on the gondola that will take us up the mountain.

Inside, we find a short queue of guests and we get in line. Signs posted explain the gondolas can take up eight people at a time, and sure enough, Tate and Jack saunter into line right behind us before we get to the loading point.

"Hello, ladies." Tate holds out his hand to Violet first. "Violet, you look stunning. Did you have a good breakfast?"

"We did, thank you." She takes his hand and instead of shaking it, he lifts it and brushes his lips against her knuckles.

Then he winks. "How's that giant-ass teddy bear? Did you find a spot for him in the nursery?"

She laughs out loud. "We did. He actually takes up the entire nursery, but that's okay."

"Giant teddy bear? I haven't heard this story." Sasha looks at Violet, then Tate, but only for a split-second before she spins toward Jack. "Sasha Brewster, by the way."

"Jack Benton," he says, holding out his hand. He moves like Lachlan does, tight, controlled movements of a big, broad body. His voice is slow and deep, and his expression is solidly neutral.

"We've met once," she says. "A number of years ago."

He rocks back on his heels. "Brewster Automotive."

Her mouth twists in a wry smile. "Yeah. And today, I'm the maid of honour."

He nods. "Sounds like fun." He shifts his attention to me. "Miss Evans."

Ms., usually, but Jack Benton can call me whatever he wants. "Nice to see you again."

"How are things in the PMO?"

"Crazy."

"You still have me on Gavin's schedule next week?"

"As long as you promise not to talk shop today."

"I wouldn't dream of it."

"Then yes, we'll see you next week."

He laughs out loud at that, his eyes crinkling. "He should give you a raise."

I grin. "I'm a public servant, Mr. Benton. My salary is fixed to a grid, but I appreciate the thought."

He winks. "Maybe I should hire you away from him. I can offer you all the raises you want."

"That's not even tempting a little bit, but thank you for the kind offer." I twist toward Violet. "Violet, have you met Jack?"

She laughs. "No, I haven't had the pleasure, although I think Max has mentioned your name. Violet Roberts. I'm Max Donovan's wife."

"I heard about the wedding. Congratulations. Where is your husband?"

She points at the gondola. "With the groom, up top."

He holds out his arm. "Then may I escort you up?"

"That would be lovely, thank you." The gondola attendant waves them forward, and they step into the sleek carriage first. Sasha follows, and Tate and I take up the rear. There's nobody waiting behind us, so we're alone as we begin our ascent.

Jack and Violet are sitting on one side. Sasha and I are on the other, and Tate is standing in the middle, legs wide, and the swing of the gondola doesn't even faze him.

It bothers Sasha, though. "I didn't like this yesterday," she mutters, glancing out the window before blinking her eyes shut and swivelling her head toward the floor. "And I like it even less today."

I feel for her—it's a long ride, about ten minutes, and as we rise above Howe Sound, the water glitters up at us as if to say, *yeah, wow, you're really high up there in a swinging tin can.*

On the other hand, it's the most breathtaking view. "I'd love to come back in the winter to ski," I say.

Jack waves his hand towards someplace off in the distance. "I've got a chalet in Whistler you're welcome to use."

I wink at him. "I'm pretty sure I'd be fired if I accepted gifts from someone who wants to do business with the Government of Canada."

"You know what I like about you, Ms. Evans?" He gets it right this time, and I know it's deliberate.

"What's that, Mr. Benton?"

"You're a stickler for honesty."

Oh, if only he knew the secrets I'm currently keeping. "I try," I murmur.

The gondola sways side to side as the cable curves higher up the mountain, and Sasha groans.

"You okay?" Tate asks.

"Fine." She shoots a quick, sharp look up at him. "You could sit."

He grins. "I didn't want to crowd you."

Another sway, and this time his perfect balance slips a bit. He's not at risk of actually falling on her—but like his tear into the parking lot, she doesn't like the way he jams his hand against the side of the gondola to brace himself. "Just sit," she snaps.

As soon as we get up to the summit, I'm shoving a glass of champagne in her hand. And making sure that Tate sits on Gavin's side, near the back, maybe.

He leans in, curling his hand over the back of the seat right beside her, and pivots onto the bench. "There, I'm sitting." His grin is too cocky by half, and he knows it.

At least one of them is enjoying this.

I sneak a look over at Violet, who is innocently gazing out the window, but I'm pretty sure she's biting the inside of her cheek to keep from laughing.

Okay, so we're all enjoying this a little.

Just as long as Sasha doesn't murder the NHL player by the end of the day.

33

LACHLAN

I'M WALKING across the lobby of Summit Lodge when I hear Beth's laugh. Guests are still milling around inside, as we've got fifteen minutes or so until the bride arrives and the wedding can begin—and Jesus, I sound like a wedding coordinator.

One more hour, and the PM will be happily hitched, and then it'll just be like any other formal reception he's hosted.

So I can spare a moment to stop and search for my woman. To sweep my gaze over her modern take on a flapper dress and appreciate just how stunning she is.

She's with Ellie's best friend and Violet, and Tate is lagging just behind her with Jack Benton, who I don't know well, but recognize at a glance.

Sasha makes a beeline for me, so I only get a quick chance to wave at Beth before she heads for the viewing platform where the outdoor ceremony will take place.

"Lachlan," the maid of honour says, looking a little piqued.

"Ms. Brewster, what can I do for you?"

She rolls her eyes. "You guys are way too formal. Beth was doing that *Ms. Evans, Mr. Benton* thing with Jack in the gondola, too."

I grin. "It's in our nature. So, sorry, *Sasha*, what can I do for you?"

"Ellie's on her way."

I nod. I don't need the update, I have a team of eight Mounties accompanying her from the inn. "Thanks."

"And…"

Ah, there's more. "Yes?"

"Keep an eye on Tate."

Don't laugh at her, don't laugh at her… "Okay."

She gives me a suspicious look. "Are you on his side?"

"There are sides?"

"Were you involved with the breakfast stunt?"

"No?"

"I'm on to him. He's playing some kind of game."

"I couldn't even begin to imagine what that might be," I say dryly, but if Tate's annoying Sasha with breakfast food, I actually can imagine.

Oh, Tate. You have no idea what you're getting into with this one.

I like Sasha Brewster just fine, but sometimes she's spoiling for fight. I remember when Gavin and I showed up at her apartment so he could win Ellie back, and she went toe-to-toe with him. She has zero qualms about staring down the prime minister and accusing him of inappropriate behaviour with his interns.

A manslut like Tate Nilsson doesn't stand a chance with her.

And I say that with enormous affection for his manslutty ways. Tate's a great guy. I'll have to find out what the breakfast thing was all about.

Sasha takes a deep breath, then nods sharply. "Fine. But seriously, watch him today. He may have driven here drunk."

This time I can't keep my laugh inside. "I doubt that very much."

She glares at me, and I right my face again.

"Yes, noted, thank you. We'll take him out back immediately for a breathalyzer."

She rolls her eyes and spins out of my orbit.

I take a deep breath and continue with my slow circle of the lodge.

Stew and Adrienne arrive with their boys all dressed up and hair combed. I'm always impressed how well behaved those kids are—because Stewart's told more than a few stories. Mostly about the twins switching places.

It takes another fifteen minutes for everyone to take their seats. Ellie gets on the gondola at Base Camp at ten minutes to eleven, and when she steps off, it's exactly the top of the hour.

"Everyone's pretty much seated," I tell them. I extend a hand toward Ellie's parents. "Could I show you the way?"

Hugh stays with Ellie, and I guide them outside. Sasha's talking to Gavin's niece, who was handing out programs, and I nod for her to join Ellie around the corner, where they'll wait for the music to change before proceeding down the aisle.

Once Mr. and Mrs. Montague are seated, I take up a position on an elevated step near the entrance to the lodge, where I can see everything but still hear communications over my ear piece clearly.

The guitarist starts playing *Jesu, Joy of Man's Desiring*, and everyone stands, chairs shifting and feet shuffling. Sasha walks down the aisle first, looking every inch the beautiful socialite she pretends to be most of the time. As she curves to her designated maid-of-honour spot, Gavin moves to the top of the aisle, naked anticipation on his face.

I've seen this man in every way possible. Diplomatic and every inch a world leader. Under pressure to get the job done, no matter what. And more personally, too. Literally naked and horny for his woman. Before that, lusty and distracted, desperate to not want her as much as he did.

I've even seen him head over heels in love with her, day in, day out, and still, none of that holds a candle to the earnestness of his expression now.

The cellist joins in, the music soaring now, and Ellie turns the corner.

Behind her, I can see the curve of Hugh's arm as he waits in the shadows.

The music is effective at setting a romantic, significant tone, clearly, because I find myself longing for him to appear before me.

And when he does, relief flutters bright. I always feel better when Hugh and Beth are close at hand.

"Friends and family, we are gathered today to mark the most special of occasions, the marriage of Gavin and Ellie. Together, we will witness the joining in the legal state of matrimony of this couple, according to the order and the custom prevailing, and under the authority given and provided by the Province of British Columbia.

"This couple has given serious and careful thought to this tradition, of binding themselves to one another, as allowed by the law of the land. They come to this union freely, equally, and with common rights. Their marriage will continue thusly, as a life-long companionship."

My chest tightens as her words sail all the way to the back of the gathering. I've been to easily a dozen weddings, maybe more. I've never heard these words spoken this way.

Out of the corner of my eye, I see Hugh doing a scan of the crowd. His gaze stops on Beth for a second, and the tightness gets worse.

I step silently, moving slowly around to the right, so I can have both of my lovers in my line of sight as the ceremony continues.

"They've spoken to me about their desires to raise a family together, to support and encourage each other in their work and personal endeavours. And they understand that to commit to one another in marriage is to share all that comes hence. Sickness, health, joy, sorrow, prosperity, and challenges."

Each word is a weird prick against my skin. Nothing new, of course. You don't get to be a forty-one-year-old bisexual man without realizing that your path to white picket fences is more convoluted than most, and who actually knows what the hell is at the end of the winding way, anyhow?

But there's something in the officiant's solemn reverence that slices unexpectedly deep, and I'm looking at Hugh, and looking at Beth, and it hurts.

A single skin prick is no big deal. A few are annoying. But too many, too close together, and you get a real wound.

And I don't want to hurt today.

So I shake it off. Words have meaning, so I can toss back some pretty healthy words of my own. Freedom. Decadence. Private ecstasy. Twice as much love to share, double the arms to be held in.

As Gavin's sister joins them at the front to read a poem that doesn't rhyme, Beth looks over at me. Her hair sparkles in the late morning sun.

A soft cloud floats overhead, softening the brightness from the sky, but nothing can touch the brilliance of Beth's smile. Her eyes are wet.

I love you so much. The promise reverberates inside me.

I don't know if we'll ever have a chance to say it in front of people like this, but tonight, I'm going to make sure she knows it to her core.

"Do either of you know of any legal impediment to this marriage?"

The officiant has returned to the ceremony script, and in unison, Gavin and Ellie respond with a practiced, "We do not."

"There having been no reason given why this couple may not be married, I ask you to give answer to these questions."

Beth winks at me, and I can practically hear her impersonating the stiffness of the language. *I ask you to give answer to this most important question. My place or yours?* My lips twitch.

"Do you, Gavin, commit to Eleanor the love of your person, the comfort of your companionship, and the patience of your understanding; and to share equally in the responsibilities of your life together?"

His mouth curls up in a soft smile, and his eyes are locked on his bride's face. "I do."

"Do you, Eleanor, commit to Gavin the love of your person, the comfort of your companionship, and the patience of your understanding; and to share equally in the responsibilities of your life together?"

"I do," Ellie breaths, nodding as she says it.

I do another scan of the crowd, letting my gaze settle on Hugh next as they begin their exchange of vows. What would it be like to share equally in the responsibilities of life with him? Not boring, that's for sure. Ache explodes inside me. No, there's no making light here.

Fuck me. Now is not the time to have an emotional break-through. Six more hours and they're all mine. And I'm all theirs. But right now, I'm on the clock.

Watching your boss get hitched—there are worse jobs. I need to keep that in mind.

"Please join your right hands, and once you're settled, Gavin, please repeat after me." Ellie passes her bouquet to Sasha, then the officiant lowers her voice to a murmur, so the vows ring out in the groom's voice only.

"I, Gavin, take thee, Ellie, to be my lawful wedded spouse, to have and to hold, from this day forward, in whatever life may hold for us." A light wind picks up and he reaches across to tuck an errant strand of hair behind Ellie's ear before she repeats the same vows back.

"I, Ellie, take thee, Gavin, to be my lawful wedded spouse, to have and to hold, from this day forward, in whatever life may hold for us."

Max remembers his cue at this point and is already holding

out the pouch with the wedding rings when the officiant turns to him.

"Inasmuch as you have made this declaration of your vows concerning one another, and have set these rings before me, we all recognize these rings as a seal and a confirmation and acceptance of the vows you have made."

Gavin and Ellie exchange their rings quietly, without the officiant prompting from the script.

After he slides her ring on, he reaches up and brushes a tear off her cheek. I sneak another look at Beth, and at the same moment, she turns to catch my gaze. This time there are no smiles, but the look we share is warm and understanding.

The official photographer scurries backwards down the aisle, breaking our private moment, and then officiant raises her voice again. "Upon the authority vested in me by the Province of British Columbia, I pronounce you duly married."

Gavin and Ellie look at each other, smiles spreading wide across their faces. He cups her cheeks in his hands and kisses her thoroughly. I think he was supposed to wait for instruction, but it doesn't matter.

Her hands come up to curl around his arms, and when he eases back, she chases him for another quick kiss of her own. It's adorable and I hope the photographer caught that moment. That's the kind of moment they'll want to remember.

When they turn to their guests, they're holding hands, fingers entwined, and everyone who wasn't already on their feet now stands, cheering loudly.

34

BETH

After the ceremony, Gavin and Ellie sit for a few formal family portraits with the wedding photographer, then carefully make their way onto the footbridge that sways high above the valley below, and runs from the lodge to a hiking trail beyond.

Most of the guests, myself included, stay on the viewing platform and cheer them on, champagne in hand, as Gavin kisses Ellie over and over again so the photographer can capture that one image that they'll send out to the world in a few hours.

When they return to the lodge, we make our way inside for a wedding luncheon. Quebec cheese, at the bride's request, and B.C. salmon at the groom's.

The food, like every other element of the day, is incredible. Even though a lot of wedding details crossed my desk over the last four months, seeing it all come together is something else. The dogwood blooms that decorated the invitation were echoed across the top of the program, and now they're in front of us again on the printed menu. And that gorgeous lavender colour I'd teased Lachlan about is everywhere, with purple hydrangeas and sea holly tucked into urns overflowing with white flowers, most of which I can't name, but I love them all.

Ellie's bouquet is drawn from the same flowers, and framed in green leaves.

The same musicians who played during the ceremony, a guitarist and a cellist duo, have come inside, and continue to play during lunch. I have a clever app on my phone that recognizes music so I can buy it, but I don't want to pull out my phone lest Gavin and Ellie think I'm taking pictures of them.

They didn't go so far as to confiscate phones at the door, although it was discussed—but they decided they trusted their friends and family not to tweet about their private moments.

I'm not going to risk them questioning that when they're having such a good time, so instead I get up and head over to the musicians. They have some business cards, and I pick one up.

The cellist smiles at me. "We play weddings, corporate events, whatever you need."

"I live in Ottawa," I explain. "But I love that song your partner is playing."

"That's Beethoven's *Pathetique*, the second movement."

I nod my thanks and make a mental note.

Then I take a spin past the wedding cake, because I swear there is nothing in this world that smells better than ten pounds of buttercream icing spread out over three layers of sponge cake.

It's like breathing in sugar-laced air.

"Enjoying yourself?" Hugh asks in my ear, and the sound of his low, rich voice takes the moment from sinfully enjoyable to delectable foreplay.

"Doesn't that icing smell amazing?" I ask quietly, keeping my gaze on the cake.

"It does. We'll have to smuggle a piece to the cabin tonight. Eat it off your body."

"You'd take turns?"

"Hell no, we'll lick it up at the same time, jockeying for position." He moves around me, his arm brushing mine in a completely innocent way.

The casual brush of his suit jacket against my bare arm makes me burn from the inside out.

"Dancing will start soon," I murmur.

"It's been on my mind since you twirled away from me this morning."

His radio crackles then, and he moves away with a regretful smile. Soon, though. Soon we'll dance, and later we'll claim each other again at a cabin in the woods.

Gavin catches my eye as I head back to my table, and swing past where he's standing to give him a hug.

"Congratulations," I say, meaning it so hard. He looks more youthful today than he has in the last three years that I've worked for him. For all the distractions and problems that wedding planning caused, I'm reminded that this day, marrying Ellie, is incredibly important to him, and I'm so glad to have been a part of making it happen just the way he wanted it.

I'd never have thought Gavin as needing this public spectacle—and it's not *public*, because he and Ellie have gone out of their way to ensure there's no unauthorized media coverage.

But it's a statement in front of the people who matter.

He needed to do this in front of her parents, with all their traditional concerns. In front of his parents, more urbane, of course, but still worried about how their son wound up shacking up with an intern. To declare before all that Ellie was his other half, his love.

As someone else comes up to speak with him, I turn back to look at Hugh, and see Lachlan just behind him.

My heart catches at the raw expression on his face.

Gah. Weddings are supposed to be happy occasions, but I get that for them, this might be weirdly bittersweet. And they need to stay locked down, too, because they're working.

When Lachlan notices me, he smiles, his gaze warming immediately. I return his smile, and he heads toward me, clapping Hugh on the shoulder as he passes.

He reaches my side as Max taps a spoon against the side of his champagne flute to get everyone's attention, so we stand next to each other as the best man gives his speech.

Sasha's next, with a brief maid of honour toast, and a totally heartfelt thank you for everyone that made the wedding special—Violet and myself for our help with the bridal shower, Ellie's and Gavin's parents for being lovely hosts the night before at the rehearsal dinner, and Tate for surprising the bride et al with breakfast this morning.

"She makes that sound so sincere," Lachlan says under his breath.

"Right?" I glance sideways at him. "What do you think is going on there?"

He snorts. "She's not interested in him at all."

"But he is?"

"Maybe." We both look at the brawny hockey player at the same time. He's leaning against the wall, his tie tugged loose, and he's staring at Sasha. Lachlan grins. "More than maybe."

"Oh my."

"It's none of our business," he says.

"Right."

A beat of hesitation, then he lowers his voice. "You'll ask her about it and report back?"

"Oh, heck yeah. She's been totally nosy about you and me. I get to turn some of that around as soon as we get back to Ottawa."

"But don't push. She's prickly."

I shake my head. "Not really. She's more misunderstood than anything, and besides, girl talk is different. Plus it doesn't look like Tate minds a bit. Maybe he's into the chase."

"They'll sort it out." He does a slow circle as he looks around the room. Ever vigilant. "Time to dance soon."

"That's what I just said to Hugh."

"We'll trade you back and forth all afternoon."

And all night. I shiver in anticipation. "I'm going to get a new glass of bubbly before the official first dance. I guess you can't have any?"

He shakes his head. "But I'll come find you as soon as the dance floor opens up to everyone."

We share a quick smile, then I make my way to the bar, where the bartender is filling an entire tray of champagne flutes. I snag one, then find a good spot on the edge of the dance floor.

A DJ has taken over from the classical musicians, and the speakers crackle as he begins to play Blue Rodeo, "Lost Together."

The bride and groom keep it simple, stepping and turning a bit, but just as often simply swaying in each other's arms.

For the next song, the DJ invites their parents to join them on the dance floor, but Gavin doesn't switch off partners. He shakes hands briefly with her father, than sweeps Ellie back into his arms, and their parents dance coupled up. I'm not sure he's going to let her go all night.

The couple next to me move, and the gap they leave is quickly filled by a lumberjack who sat on the other side of the room from me during lunch.

"Mr. Benton," I say.

"Ms. Evans."

"Are you enjoying yourself?"

"As much as anyone can in a suit." He's got a glass of something that looks like serious alcohol in his hand. "Would you like to dance?"

I glance across the room and catch Lachlan's eye. He was talking to someone, but he's cut that conversation off now and is striding toward us.

"My first dance is already spoken for," I murmur. This is a bit reckless, really, but it's not like people don't wonder about us. And it's just a dance.

"Ah." Jack takes a sip of his drink, unperturbed. "I'll watch, then."

I laugh, and hold out my hand as Lachlan stops next to me. I brush my fingers against the back of his upper arm, just a glance, but it's enough to ground me. "Lachlan Ross, you remember Jack Benton."

"I do indeed. Good to see you again, sir."

"I'll be in Ottawa next week. Beth's got me on the schedule to see your boss. Maybe you'll join us for a drink."

"Absolutely."

"Well…" Jack nods. "Enjoy your dance with the lady."

And with that, he's gone.

Lachlan gestures to the dance floor as the DJ invites everyone to join the families. Gavin's love of Canadian music is going to affect the playlist heavily tonight. Right now it's Spirit of the West, "And If Venice is Sinking."

It's an upbeat, sexy song, but Lachlan still pulls me into his arms, one hand firm in the small of my back, the other holding my fingers close to his chest as he spins me around. A thrill twirls inside me. Only at a wedding could we dance in front of everyone we know, and nobody clue in to how special this feels for us.

Maybe not nobody. When the song ends, Lachlan hands me off to Hugh, whose gaze is bright.

"Were you watching us dance?" I ask as he squeezes my hip.

"I was. You two look good together."

"He can dance, eh? I wasn't sure…"

"Yeah." Hugh dips his head, closing the space between us. His breath brushes my temple. "Our boy likes to move his hips."

"Did you used to go dancing?" I don't want to be too curious about their relationship, because there's still a lot of unresolved stuff there, but I can't help it. I adore them both and want to know everything.

"Not anywhere like a club. But he likes to listen to music when he's cooking, and sometimes we'd dance in the kitchen."

"That's adorable. I want to see you dance at the cabin." He

doesn't say anything, and I turn my head just enough press against his jaw. "Please?"

"Yeah."

I take a deep breath as he turns me around the dance floor, then I let my question spill out, fast and without overthinking it. "What else did you do? Back then, when you were together?"

He laughs roughly. "Not much, really. We spent a lot of time in bed. There wasn't that much to do, and we had a lot of chemistry."

I smile. "I bet."

Hugh strokes his hand up my back, and for a second I think he's going to change the subject, but he surprises me by opening up—all the way open. "When I met Lachlan, he was dating someone. A woman. It was casual, and there wasn't any chemistry really, but it was Moose Lake. It's not like there were a ton of single twenty-somethings to choose from.

"But he was off-limits, technically. And from the second I laid eyes on him, I wanted him. It was actually terrible." Another laugh, this one dry. "Maybe that's why we didn't work out, because it started in a weird place."

"Oh."

"He didn't cheat on her. They broke up a few weeks before we did anything. I don't even think he...He didn't get it then. He'd get it now, though. He'd understand. But back then, he didn't, and that meant that we fought at first."

Hugh's all tense, and I squeeze his shoulder. "He wouldn't get what?"

He shakes his head. "I dunno. How I felt, I guess."

"Why do you think he'd get it now?"

"Because how I felt about him ten years ago...that's how he feels about you."

"Us."

He gives me a tight smile.

"Hugh…"

"Tonight," he says. "At the cabin. We'll dance and we'll talk."

THE PRIME MINISTER TIES THE KNOT

June 24, 2017 / Squamish, B.C.

At eleven in the morning, Prime Minister Gavin Strong married Eleanor Montague, a PhD candidate at the University of Ottawa.

The wedding was attended by friends and family, and took place at the Summit Lodge at the top of the Sea to Sky Gondola. The groom's family has hiked in the area for generations and the location is said to have been chosen for sentimental reasons.

No formal wedding photographs have been released, but the prime minister posted a single picture to his official social media accounts.

The couple will honeymoon in an undisclosed location for a week. The prime minister and his new wife will return to Ottawa after the Canada Day weekend.

35

—————

LACHLAN

THE RECEPTION ENDS at five in the afternoon with a final toast to the bride and groom. Gavin and Ellie take the first gondola down, and from there, a fresh security detail will accompany them to their honeymoon on Tree Top Island, a private property in the Salish Sea owned by Gavin's parents.

As soon as the PM and his bride are gone, I dispatch Hugh to check himself out of the hotel and head up the highway and get us checked in to the cabin I've rented for our retreat from the world.

Beth and I wait until everyone is gone, and the catering staff are almost done cleaning up, then we make our departure, too.

We swing past the hotel to collect our bags and quietly check out a night early. We change out of our fancy clothes, too, since we can.

The cabin is part of a low-key resort further up the highway toward Whistler that appealed to me because the cabins were rustic but also modern and comfortable, and one in particular was promised to be private, at the end of a gravel lane.

But there are some amenities, including a cafe near the

246

entrance to the resort, and this is where we meet Hugh, in the parking lot.

He's leaning back against the trunk of his rental when I pull up beside him. Beth leaps out and wraps herself around him, and the sight of his strong arms hauling her close gets my blood pumping.

Yes.

Mine.

I slide my phone out of my pocket and take a picture of them, their foreheads pressed together as he whispers something wicked. The look on his face tugs hard at my heart.

I grab our bags, then he points the way past the cafe and down the lane. Our cabin is, as promised, private, and when Hugh opens the door, Beth gasps.

From the outside, it's a quaint, shingled cottage.

Inside, it's newly renovated. Whitewashed walls, a window seat surrounded by bookshelves, flowers on the old steamer trunk that doubles as a coffee table. It's a spartan but stunning living space that blends seamlessly into a modern kitchen at the back. And through an open door to the only sleeping space, we see a king-sized bed, covered in a white duvet.

A one-bedroom cottage, perfect for three lovers.

I carry our bags in there and set them on a wide bench in front of the window, which is open, letting the breeze in through the screen. Outside, it's still light out, but it's getting late. The shadows are long and the forest is starting to come alive with the faint sounds of bugs and birds and small animals.

In the near distance, a rushing river adds to the soundtrack.

"Amazing place," Beth says as she winds her arms around my waist.

I tip her head up and kiss her. "Amazing company."

Hugh joins, his hands behind his back. "What should we do first?"

Beth twists around to kiss him, too. "Me. Tonight, I want you both."

Heat rockets through me. "At the same time?"

She nods.

"I was hoping you'd say that. I came prepared." Hugh holds out a box, neatly tied with a fat satin bow. Beth takes it from him, but he covers her hands with his. "But you need to wait until we finish unpacking."

"But..." Her fingers flutter at the ribbon. "Is it what I think it is?"

"Put it down, beautiful."

"Is it lube?"

He laughs. I think that's a yes. "Let's go to the kitchen."

"Because I think lube is a fantastic present," she says pertly as she scampers ahead of us.

He'd already unloaded a lot of groceries into the fridge, so it doesn't take long to get the rest stowed away.

"Mmm, did you get a cherry pie?" Beth makes a groan in the back of her throat that makes me hard.

"You like?"

"Cherry is the pinnacle of pie, so yes, I like. Good job."

"Would you like some now?"

She shakes her head. "Later." Her cheeks turn pink. "We should work up an appetite first. Unless *you* want pie now?"

And we're done in the kitchen. I pick her up and toss her, shrieking, over my shoulder. "We want you now, since that wasn't clear. Questioning our priorities..."

"I'm not," she cries out, laughing as I carry her into the bedroom. I dump her on the bed and she grabs her present again. "But Hugh made me wait, so I wasn't sure. Can I open this now?"

I turn around to ask Hugh, and he's right there. He bumps into me, softly, his chest brushing mine. "Very soon," he says to Beth but his attention doesn't leave my face. "But first I want you to put on some music."

"What are you doing?" I ask him, my gaze caught on the curve of his mouth.

"We didn't get a chance to dance earlier."

Behind me, Beth makes an approving sound. "Yes, dance. I downloaded the Spirit of the West album with that song we danced to on it…" She scoots around me and darts into the living room, returning with her phone in one hand, and a decorative ceramic bowl in the other. "Want to see a magic trick?"

She selects a song I recognize, "Slow Learner", then puts her phone in the bowl, and the sound amplifies enough to fill the room.

"Excellent trick," Hugh says, catching her and drawing her against us. He kisses her hard on the mouth. "Good girls get presents. Go investigate."

She squeaks and he pats her on the bottom, then holds his hands out to me.

"It's been a while," I say, trying to remember how we did this, but as soon as he sets his hand on my hip, I remember.

Ten years disappears in a flash.

"Of course I'm going to lead."

"But I'm taller."

"Uh huh. Whatever. I'm in charge."

"I don't know how to follow."

He smirked. "Sure you do."

He'd been right then, and it's still true now. With a shift of his weight, his left thigh presses into mine, and I step back, making room for him to move forward. Brush, press, hold. Step, step, slow. His body is hard and warm as he fits us together, legs and hips. Cocks, hardening behind denim. Chests and arms.

But it all comes back to the sway of our hips, and the foot-work that keeps brushing our dicks together.

Slow learner.

It's a strangely fitting song. Nothing slow about how we

learned to dance together. We fit from the very beginning. But the rest of this has been a decade in the making.

I mouth the lyrics at him as he spins me around. His hands crawl up my body, pressing and twisting me against him, until the song ends and his hands are on my neck, the back of my head, and he's kissing me.

Hugh always takes my mouth hard, but this is different. It's fierce possession and I give myself to him without hesitation. He kisses me until my thighs burn and my head is cloudy with want.

"Beth, did you open your present?" His words are gravelly and rough in my ear as he holds me close.

"I got distracted watching you make out," she breathes. "Hang on."

I turn around in the circle of Hugh's arms as she tugs on the ribbon. The lid of the box tumbles off as the red satin falls to the bed, and she gasps.

"Oh, you shouldn't have," she teases, reaching inside to pull out a brand-new silver butt plug. "Is this for me?"

"It is."

She makes an excited-but-nervous face and sets the plug down before pulling out a few more gifts from the box. Lube and condoms, but not just any condoms. The first one looks like it's gold. The second is hot pink. The third is... "Strawberry flavoured!" she exclaims. "Fun?"

I laugh because the question mark is definitely valid there. Hugh murmurs a warning in my ear, then rubs his mouth against my neck, making my head woozy again.

"Lachlan hates novelty condoms," he says gruffly. "I thought we could convince him they weren't so bad."

"Is it wrong I like my dick to just look...like a dick?"

Beth wiggles the gold condom at me. "I think this one is yours, then. Hugh can put it on you and we can say he has the Midas touch."

"Well, if Hugh's touching me, I'm fine with whatever," I say, my words slurring a bit. "But just on principle."

She winks. "Of course. Come here, Mr. There's A Right Way to Condom."

Hugh pushes me towards her and I tumble onto the bed, hauling her against me as I roll onto my back. She kisses me softly, still laughing, but I take the fire Hugh's started inside me and I brush her with those flames, too. We're all going to to burn tonight.

I trace her curves, over her t-shirt at first, then under. Need overcomes grace. I ruthlessly shove my hands under the fabric to get at her skin. More, I want more, and she gives it to me, wriggling free of her clothing.

Hugh joins us on the bed. He touches her with master strokes, warming her up before he reaches for the lube.

She's taken fingers a few times, and a smaller plug last weekend.

But this is going to be big. Literally, figuratively. I cup her face and kiss her as he spreads her legs, getting her to straddle me and present her gorgeous bottom to him at the same time.

"Breathe through it," I tell her as she tenses up. "You know what to do."

"I take everything back," she whispers, but her eyes are bright.

"That's what safewords are for." I wink at her. "You know the drill."

"Mmm." She closes her eyes and does her best to welcome Hugh's thick finger.

"Good girl," I murmur, brushing my mouth against hers. She parts for me and I pull her close, deepening the kiss until the space where I end and she begins is questionable at best. She squirms closer, trying to escape Hugh's relentless prep. I keep kissing her. Tongue and teeth, but not too hard. And then distractingly soft as he reaches for the plug.

She groans into me as he presses the steel against her hole, then gasps, losing control of her breathing as it gets wider. "Slow, slow…" Her breath hitches as she begs Hugh to take his time, and I'm sure he is.

I stroke her hair as she buries her face in my neck. Her back is arched, a gorgeous pale curve to the flare of her hips. Hugh's got one of his hands spread wide over the rise of her ass, and I following the corded line of his muscled arm up to his face. He grins at me, wicked filth incarnate.

"We're just getting started, beautiful. We're gonna go as slow as you want us to go, because we've got all night." He licks his lips as he holds my gaze and shifts his words to me now. "What should we do first with our stuffed little Beth?"

She whimpers against me and I pet her hair. "Is one of us going to end up in your ass tonight?"

She nods gamely, a bob of her head, even as it's still buried against me.

"You're going to need to stretch nicely around that plug, then. Up you get."

She gingerly peels herself off me, rising until she's straddling me.

A naked prize caught between two dressed men.

That gives me an idea.

"Let's dance again," I say roughly as I stroke my fingertips over her breasts and her belly. I love the way she trembles beneath my touch.

Hugh nestles in behind her, his arms wrapping around her waist. I touch his hands where they splay across her belly and he catches my fingers in his.

"You need to let me go so I can put music back on," she whispers, but we don't release her.

Not yet.

I curl my body up so I'm sitting, and she's on my lap, and Hugh's behind her. I hold them both tight.

This is everything I've ever wanted. I had no idea. My whole life, I was waiting for these two, and the universe tried to fucking show me.

I was blind, but I'm trying to make up for lost time now.

I kiss Beth, then Hugh, dragging him around her, and she wriggles free. When the music starts playing, we get off the bed and join her.

All we can manage is a slow, pulsing sway, but it's enough. We dance together, twisting Beth between us. The music seeps under our skin, makes us restless and wild.

On the next song, Beth cups my heavy bulge through my jeans and whispers that I should be naked, too. I strip down as Hugh pulls her into his arms.

They're stunning together. His rugged dark tan a stark contrast to her creamy paleness. His muscles heavy and carved next to her willowy curves.

As soon as my dick pops free, heavy and horny, I take myself in hand and stroke. Watching them move together is dirty and perfect, the best porn of my life.

Hugh notices first and whispers to Beth that I'm jerking off. I watch his lips move and curl my lips into a filthy smile. Yeah I am.

She murmurs something back, maybe another instruction to get naked, then slides to her knees in front of me. "May I?" she asks, so fucking polite.

"Yeah," I grunt. "Lick me up."

Her tongue darts out, pink and eager.

Behind her, Hugh's gaze is locked on her ass, and he's stroking himself, too.

"Come here," I say, gesturing for him, and she turns on her knees.

We jostle a bit for position, our cocks bumping as we rub them against her mouth. Her wet, swiping tongue is a crazy tease, and I want to push deeper, shove past her lips and into her throat, but we've got a plan tonight.

Double penetration.

She wants to take us both.

I sling my arm around Hugh's neck and pull him close. We're both going to be inside her, together. Cocks rubbing back and forth.

He looks at me, his eyelids hooded, and I groan. We kiss, a hard crash together, then we look back at Beth, playing with our engorged cocks.

She smiles up at us and Hugh growls. "Dirty girl."

"Your dirty girl," she purrs, and he laughs weakly as he leans against me. His mouth is on my neck again, his stubble scratching, and I press into the sensations. His tongue, his teeth—

"Fuck!" I jerk away and he holds on tight as he laughs against my skin.

"Did you just bite me?" My dick throbs and my neck howls in protest.

He kisses the flesh he just abused. "Yeah."

"Fuck." I'm panting now, but… "Do it again."

He makes a satisfied sound in the back of his throat. "You like that?"

Jesus, who the fuck knows. "Like is relative."

He pulls back, frowning. He grips me by the back of the neck and presses his forehead against mine. "No."

"What?"

"Say it. Say you like it. Don't hide behind some love-hate bullshit."

I blink at him, my mouth dry. "I… Yeah. Fuck. I like it. Bite me."

Beth stands, and Hugh pulls her in close. "You bit him?" she asks him, her voice all breathy.

"Hard," he answers, his eyes glittering.

My balls pull tight.

"Can I bite him?"

She's asked him, not me. A long, pregnant pause stretches out as I stand there, dick getting wetter by the second as my body proves it's fully on board with any fucked-up shenanigans Hugh has in mind.

"Can you?" He tugs on her hair, tipping her face up to his so he can kiss her. "You better. Our boy needs it."

We fall onto the bed, Beth decorating my chest with a gentle line of love bites that make me thrust my hips in the air.

"Harder," I whisper. "You could suck, too. Mark me up."

Hugh nudges into me, rolling me onto my side, and I wrap Beth in my arms. Her legs slide through mine, my cock tapping against her belly.

Hugh licks a line from my neck to my shoulder, then covers that flesh with his mouth and sucks—hard. He pulls on my skin until I'm groaning, and then he sinks his teeth into that hickey and leaves his mark.

I swear under my breath, a long chain of filthy words as he kisses the hurt away, and then I roll onto my back.

"Beth," I growl. "Get the fuck on top of me."

She swings her leg over me, but instead of guiding her down to my cock, I pull her up to my face.

I trace her folds with one hand as I use the other to press against the plug in her bottom. She jerks against me.

"Hold on tight, beautiful."

I'm not going to make her come. I want to feel that on my cock. But I need a quick taste of her tangy goodness. Just a quick swipe of my tongue, a little suckle against her clit.

Fuck, I could die and go to heaven right now.

As the tremors fade from the shock of my tongue and the plug moving inside her, she begins to rock against me face.

Yeah, baby. I bet that feels good. Her moans rise, soft and sweet, and I lick up the juices sliding freely from her swollen pussy.

The bed shifts, Hugh moving, then again as he returns.

I feel him rolling a condom onto my straining cock, then he pulls Beth off my face.

She's flushed and grinning, and he gives her a mock stern look. "You were going to come like that, weren't you?"

She shrugs. "Can't blame a girl for trying."

He taps her bottom. "Lean forward."

She stretches out on top of me like a cat, bottom high in the air. We're both breathing hard as Hugh tells her he's removing the plug. He wipes away the excess lube with a washcloth, then takes them both to the washroom.

I'm sinking her sweet, tight pussy onto my cock as he returns. She's already close, the soft ridges of her cunt fluttering around me as Hugh preps her for him. A finger makes her squirm, and two—fuck, that feels good for me, too.

And then he's behind her, condom on.

"Ready for me?" he asks, and he's grinning because he knows the answer is no-yes-no-oh-God.

As long as it's not olives, we're good.

"I'm ready," she whispers.

36

BETH

LACHLAN PRESSES INTO ME, a deep, urgent thrust, before easing back and holding himself almost all the way out of me.

Just the tip of his erection, thick and hard, presses against my entrance. My pussy contracts around him, wanting him back.

"Wait, wait…" he says under his breath, watching me as I try to fuck down on him. He holds my hips firm and doesn't let me move. "He needs space inside you."

A tremor of fear ripples through me. They won't both fit. That's what he's saying. This is a terrible idea and as much as I love, love, love how their fingers make me feel, I've now officially asked for more than is humanly possible and we need a new plan.

I open my mouth and a breathy whimper comes out, because Hugh is rubbing his cock against my back hole and oh my God, the feels.

Good ones, bad ones, crazy ones I don't fully understand.

So. Much. Feeling.

Thanks to the plug, I've already had this violation tonight, and my body knows how to push against him, to bloom and welcome him inside me.

It still burns, but it's a familiar ache that brings with it heart-stopping pleasure.

And he's so much bigger than the plug or their fingers. He's a blunt weapon of mass destruction, it feels like at first, so thick I'm not sure he's going to actually get inside me, but he does.

I don't bother begging him to go slow—I'm not sure I could talk, for one thing, and for another, he couldn't go any slower.

For all his dirty, torturous ways, he's a crazy careful lover, especially with my ass.

He holds himself just inside me as my muscles spasm around him, then he squeezes his hands into the fleshy curve of my hips and pushes all the way inside me.

Beneath me, Lachlan groans. "Jesus, I can feel you fucking her."

"That's the idea," Hugh says, his voice cracking. "God, Beth. You're so fucking tight."

Here is where I should tell him it's because he's so big. Big and hard. But all that comes out is more of those feeble, whimpering moans, because he's inside my ass—and he is big, and hard—and feelings have replaced language in my brain.

Like Lachlan did, he holds himself deep inside me, then eases almost all the way out.

And Lachlan thrusts into my pussy.

Mother of— "Ah!"

He nails every sweet spot on the way in, and on the way out, Hugh's filling me from behind.

A disorientingly good push-pull slide of hard flesh against soft begins. Hugh, then Lachlan, and back again. Slow, sure pumps of their hips, driving their cocks into my body from two different places, but oh so close together.

My skin feels hot and tight, my breasts heavy as they rub against Lachlan's chest. Between my legs, my clit is hard, throbbing, and Lachlan's making sure to rub against it, too.

I want to do something, but all I can do is hang on tight as they plunge in and out of my body, filling me completely. Over and over again.

And then Lachlan says, "Can we both fit inside her at the same time?"

What the fuck do they think they've been doing? But Hugh understands, even if I don't, and he holds himself inside me at the end of his next thrust.

Lachlan tries to press into me, and it feels like he might actually be cleaving me in two—delightfully, orgasmically so, but still, tearing me apart. And he can't get in.

"Up you get, beautiful," he whispers. "I need you up."

He presses my upper body off of his chest and passes me to Hugh, who wraps his arms around me, cupping my breasts in his hand.

My vision swims as I gaze down at Lachlan. Big, rangy muscles. Hot, turned-on expression. And where our legs are tangled up, where I'm spread wide for him, his cock, wrapped in his fist.

He wants to put that monster inside me, while Hugh is buried in my ass.

"No…" I breathe.

"Cupcake?" Hugh asks in my ear, and I shake my head. Not that kind of no. The good kind of no. The holy-fuck-are-you-fucking-sure kind of no.

Behind me, Hugh flexes his body, driving his cock deeper into my ass and lifting my pussy so it's more on display for Lachlan.

"Look at how pretty you are," Lachlan says, his voice kind of breathy too. "You can take us both, I know you can."

I shake my head. "I can't."

"Yes…" He hisses as he rocks his cock against my clit, then lower, between my slick labia. "Oh, you're so wet for me. So good. Ready?"

I don't bother to answer. Either it's going to work or it's not, and either way, I'm like ten seconds away from spontaneously combusting.

This time he gets inside me, and it feels impossible, but he's still pressing, still stretching my body around him. Making a permanent space for himself.

Laying claim.

My breath is shaky now, and spots dance at the edges of my vision. Another inch, and the thickest part of him will be inside my body, up against Hugh's cock.

"I'm going to…" I toss my head. "Yes, please. God, *please*."

"You're doing it. Are you ready to come? We want to feel you fucking milk us at the same time," Hugh growls. "I want to feel Lachlan spurt deep inside your pussy, you got that? Pull it out of him."

"Ah…" I swallow hard and flutter my hands towards my belly.

Hugh pinches my nipples, tugging them.

I press against my skin, my hands shaking. Yes, yes, that.

Lachlan drifts his hands up my thighs as he pulses in the last inch, in tiny little movements. Not taking no for an answer.

Claiming what's his.

When he's fully seated inside me, his hands settle on my hips, his thumbs teasing the creases where my legs meet my pelvis.

All I need is for them to move, just a little, and I think I'll come.

Behind me, Hugh pumps his hips.

Below me, Lachlan grinds up as he shifts his hand over and rocks against my clit with his thumb.

Between them, I close my eyes and scream as something deep inside snaps, something bright and explosive.

Like a tripwire connected to a thousand tons of pleasure, overwhelming all my circuits. I shudder in Hugh's arms, a spasm that triggers another and another, as they push and grind against me, stringing out my orgasm and triggering their own.

When they slip out of me, it's a weird shock, and my body feels permanently changed. Or maybe that's just my heart.

Hugh disappears to clean up first, then Lachlan rolls off the bed as our lover rejoins us.

I don't move a muscle because I'm dead.

Hugh's having none of that.

"Time for pie," he says breathlessly as he slaps my ass. "Then a shower before round two."

Round two of Kill Beth With Pleasure? And pie?

I roll over and snag his hand, pulling him close. "You're crazy," I whisper, kissing his fingers. "And amazing."

He crouches beside the bed and brushes my hair off my face. His expression is hard to read, but my brain is too scattered to try and decipher weird boy feelings right now. "You enjoyed that?"

"Oh, yeah."

"I think he needed that, too." He glances over his shoulder toward the bathroom.

"He's just—" I cut myself off as Lachlan returns. "Pie time?"

I get two satisfied, hungry grins in response.

But we're definitely coming back to that conversation at some point this weekend.

3 7

———

H U G H

I DON'T FALL ASLEEP.

I couldn't even if I hadn't already made the decision that I'm not staying.

I've changed my flight. I did it earlier today, and even after what we've shared tonight, I don't regret it.

Well, that's a fucking lie.

I already regret it.

But it's what needs to be done, and I know it.

I stroke Beth's hair. Lachlan's arm is wrapped around her, as it always is when we sleep together, and I rest my hand on his forearm next. I love his strength. The size of him. My big ox.

Hers now.

My gut churns and my heart slams against my chest as I slip silently out of our cabin. The gravel road will be too noisy for me to make a speedy departure, so I dash along the grass between the cabins and the river towards the cafe where my rental is parked.

The first call comes shortly after I leave the resort. Lachlan's ringtone. I ignore it as I turn onto the highway towards Vancouver.

Moments later, I get a voicemail notification, followed immediately after by a text. Then comes Beth's ringtone. It kills me hit reject—because I'm not rejecting her. But I'm in no headspace to handle a conversation with either of them. I just need to get home.

I flip my phone to airplane mode. I'm off duty for a couple more days, so being unavailable for a few extra hours won't affect the PM's security.

Traffic is pretty much non-existent this time of the morning, and I make it to the airport in under two hours.

38

BETH

Lachlan's not sleeping.

Neither am I, though.

Hugh's missing, in more ways than one. There's a two-hundred-pound hole on his side of the bed, and we slept through his decision to leave.

He left a note with a single line on it.

I need some space.

He's been gone for at least three hours. Lachlan tore out the door when we woke up and found the note, but it's anyone's guess where he headed, and he's not replying to our text messages. After our first attempts to call him were ignored, he turned off his phone.

So now we lie here.

"Go to sleep," I whisper against his back.

He rolls over, spreading his arms wide, and I tuck in beside him. My heart aches, because I know Hugh didn't head out into the night for some alone time.

I replay the conversation Hugh and I had while dancing at the wedding. I should have picked up on it sooner.

"I want to be up in case he comes back and needs to talk," he says.

"He's not coming back," I whisper, my voice cracking.

"Don't say that," he says roughly. I bite my lip and he squeezes me tight. "Shit. Fuck."

Hot tears press against my eyelids and I burrow tighter. This is all my fault.

"He's a big boy. He'll be fine." There's so much grit in Lachlan's voice, it scrapes against my skin. He might not be able to cry, but I can. I'll cry for both of us.

***

My phone wakes me up a few hours later, and I scramble for it, heart pounding because in my sleep-deprived state, I think it might be Hugh texting back.

It's just my alarm, telling me to take my pill.

I roll out of bed and go to my bag. I press my thumb against the bubble pack and pop the little pill out. Four days until my period arrives. I'd been so stoked about the perfect timing, that I wouldn't need to take two packs back-to-back to make sure sexy times could continue unaffected.

Turns out I only had the one night to worry about.

I tuck the pack away and drag myself into the bathroom for some water.

The giant claw foot tub calls to me, so I nudge the door shut so as not to wake Lachlan, and turn on the water. I take my pill, then dump some shampoo under the tap.

Emergency bubble bath.

It'll do.

A quiet knock on the door tells me I did a shit job of not waking up Lachlan. "Come in."

He pokes his head around the door. "Morning."

He looks as miserable as I feel. "Want to take a bubble bath with me?"

"How about I make coffee instead?"

I nod. "Okay."

He comes back ten minutes later with a tray of food and a wooden stand to put it on, and we eat breakfast like that, me in the tub, him leaning back against the sink, sipping his coffee.

"I could get someone to run a search on his credit cards," he finally mutters.

Yes, do that, I want to say. Track him down and we'll go toss a net over his sorry ass and drag him back here so we can tell him we love him. Instead I sink lower in the tub and blow a raspberry at a pile of bubbles near my mouth.

"Probably a bad idea, career wise."

I nod. Probably.

"I saw some board games," he offers next. "On the book-shelves."

So after my breakfast-in-the-bath, we play Scrabble, and it's fine.

So is the cuddle we have in the window seat. Fine.

And the nap that follows, because we're exhausted. That's perfectly adequate. I love Lachlan, and he's being careful and attentive, but this isn't how we were supposed to be spending these few days together.

We're missing our third, and it fucking hurts.

By mid-day, I'm pissed off at Hugh.

And since he's not here, I'm kind of grumpy with Lachlan, too, which *so* isn't fair.

So I grab Hugh's note, which we haven't really touched again, and I scrawl across it, **We've gone for a hike because you're dumb. Love you. Stay put if you come back.** And I hand it to Lachlan, who laughs for the first time all day.

He nods. "Okay, let's get outside."

And hopefully, out of our heads a bit, too.

I thought we'd just go for a quick walk, but Lachlan packs a bag with water and snacks, and goes over a hiking trail map left by the cabin rental people.

He's taking my *hike* statement seriously. I packed running shoes, but I don't have a pair of long pants, and I tell him that.

"We'll keep it easy," he promises.

Famous last words.

We head out the back of the cabin, cutting across long grass towards a rail bridge that's marked as safe for crossing. The sun is bright today, and it's nicely warm as we cross the bridge, the river rushing beneath us. We stop on the other side and Lachlan points out the path he's picked for us. Ahead about a kilometre, to a rise that's marked on the hiking map, then back again. Easy.

Except then he says, "And of course, we'll be bear aware."

I freeze. "Pardon?"

He waves ahead of us. "Solid chance of seeing a black bear out here. There's lots of food around this time of year, so they won't do us any harm. We just don't want to surprise them, or get between mama and cubs."

Uh huh. I glance back in the direction of the cabin.

"Hey," he says softly, weaving his fingers through mine and tugging me close. "You wanted to get out of there. The sun is shining, it's a beautiful day. Let's do this."

"With bears."

"With me. And we'll sing to keep the bears away."

"You're crazy."

"I'm the most boring, responsible person you've ever met. Would I let anything happen to you?"

I shake my head. No, he wouldn't. "Okay."

He brushes his lips against mine, softly at first, but the spark is there—like always, although it takes us both by surprise right now. He deepens the kiss, sliding his tongue against mine.

He turns my sadness into something else. Anticipation. I

chase him for another kiss, and when we finish, he picks me up and spins me around. "We just have to be loud. That's all. We're sharing their space with them, it's only fair to give them a heads up that we're coming."

We head off, singing camp songs at first, then just talking. We play a couple of rounds of twenty questions, too. It's easy to make noise with him, it turns out, and before I know it we're nearly back at the rail bridge again.

We can see it just ahead, but Lachlan holds up his hand for me to stop as we cross under hydro lines. Their path is carved out of the woods, and the clearing to our left is a meandering hill down to the river.

"You want to go down there and check it out?" he asks.

Heck yeah.

He reminds me to go slow over the uneven ground, and it takes us half an hour to pick our way down to the rushing water.

It was totally worth the detour.

"Wow," I say as we come to a stop at the river's edge. The river bed is wider than the actual flow of water right now. It must get wider and deeper in the winter and spring. Right now we can walk a ways across rocks and logs before we reach the crystal clear water.

I kneel and dangle my fingers in it. It's cool, but not as cold as I expected. I stand and glance across the river. Then I look back at Lachlan.

"What are you thinking?" he asks, but his smile tells me he has a good idea.

And it *is* a good idea, too. "Is it safe to cross?"

He shrugs. "Yeah. Should be."

"Shoes off or on?" I narrow my eyes at the water ahead of us. Lots of rocks. Some sand and logs, but…

Lachlan makes the call easy. "Shoes on. Easier to climb the bank on the other side."

"Fair enough." I take a deep breath, and step into the water. Oh, God. That's colder on my ankle than it was on my fingertips.

I take another two steps, then I can get out of the water and onto a dry log. Then another, and pretty soon I'm in the middle of the river, Lachlan right behind me.

I laugh and hoot, throwing my hands in the air. This is amazing.

This is what I needed today.

We're almost at the other side of the river, the cabin side, when Lachlan taps my arm.

"Don't freak out," he says quietly. "But there's a bear on the other side of the river, about a hundred metres away."

I freeze.

"Keep going," he prods. "We're almost there."

Bear. Bear. Bear.

"Beth!"

I squeak and force my legs forward, splashing a bit. My pulse is going a mile a minute, and if I have a heart attack in the middle of this river, that will ruin the whole this-day-is-getting-better thing I was rocking a few minutes earlier.

"We're good, don't worry, keep moving." His voice is even and steady in my ear, and when we step out of the water, he takes my shoulders and forces me to turn around. "See?"

Bear. Bear. *Bear.*

I gasp at the black furry butt ambling back into the woods on the opposite side.

Bear.

"Oh my God," I whisper.

"See? Nothing to worry about."

"I shared a river with a bear…"

"You did." He strokes a finger along my cheek, then kisses my nose. "Want to go make some celebratory dinner together?"

"Steaks?"

"You know it."

39

LACHLAN

THERE ARE ONLY TWO STEAKS.

Motherfucker.

I stare at the trays of meat Hugh bought, and had already stashed in the fridge before we arrived yesterday.

Two steaks.

Two giant chicken breasts.

A single tray of brats, when I know if he was planning on eating them, there'd be a second tray, too.

He wasn't planning on sticking around.

At some point, he decided to ditch us here. A slow, angry burn crawls up my neck.

He took my God damned shopping list and used it to set us up in a love nest. Then he dirtied it up but good before skipping out.

Why in hell wouldn't he know that we'd fucking miss him when he did that?

"What is it?" Beth asks.

I jerk my attention to where she's sitting in the living room. She'd been reading a book, but now she's staring at me.

"You opened the fridge and then just stood there," she says, standing up.

I close the door. "Yeah."

"Do you want help with dinner?"

I shake my head. "No." I pull the fridge door open again. "I want a beer. You?"

"Sure."

I grab two bottles and take the caps off before I join her. Dinner can wait.

I set the bottles on the steamer trunk turned coffee table and pick up her foot, now bare, because her only pair of socks are drip drying on a rack in the bathroom. "Are you cold?"

She shakes her head. "I'm fine."

"I've got extra socks. Big manly ones. Wool. You could—"

"Lachlan, what's wrong?"

"Hugh only bought food for the two of us. Two steaks. Two chicken breasts."

Her face falls. "Oh."

"Wherever he is, he planned this." That's hard to say. I thought after the last two months we were all in the same place, on the same page, but I'm realizing with bitter distaste that I had no clue what was going on his head.

Not the first time I've been blindsided by him, though.

I'm a sucker for thinking this time would be different.

It was different, though. We had Beth.

Have.

We have Beth.

She hasn't said anything. She's peeling the label off the beer bottle tiny piece by tiny piece. I take a drink and look at her anew, too.

"This isn't what you wanted, is it?" God, those words feel clumsy and wrong in my mouth.

She jerks her head up, her eyes wide and alarmed. "No."

"I think we need to do a better job of saying things."

She laughs weakly. "Yeah. Probably."

"What are you thinking?"

She presses her lips together and shakes her head.

I lean forward and brace my forearms on my thighs. "I want you both. Maybe we need to start there. Was that not clear? Is that not okay?"

"It's more than okay," she whispers. "But I don't know how clear it was."

"Not even after last night?" Or any of the nights that came before it? All my muscles tense and flex as the heat under my collar slides down my spine.

"It was the wedding." She tips her bottle of beer back and drains it. Then she stands and starts pacing. "We had a conversation while we were dancing. And I didn't get it at the time…"

"Get what? Damn it, spit it out."

She holds up her hand, her forehead tight. "Please don't push. I'm not sure what I'm trying to say. Okay? I don't know your entire history. You two have been super cagey about that. So don't expect me to hand you the answer on a platter. I don't have it."

Shit. I nod. "Right. I'm sorry."

She shrugs. "I freaked out earlier. I'm glad we're taking turns." She does another pace of the living room, then stops and gives another small shrug. "Okay. So Hugh told me a little about how you first hooked up. How you'd just broken up with a woman…?"

I nod. Even after all these years, the hot, weird mix of guilt and excitement in my veins is a feeling I'll always associate with those early days before Hugh kissed me.

"I think he thinks that meant more to him than it did to you." She says it softly, but the words are fists, fast like lightning.

He's not wrong.

And he's completely wrong, but that's a secret I've buried deep, and I thought…

Well, I'd thought wrong. Turns out it's not that easy to move forward as if the past weren't ugly.

"And the wedding stirred that up. We may have given him the impression that…" She groans and tips her head back. "Fuck. This is so weird to talk about when we've only been dating for a little while." She looks at me and winces. "Don't read too much into this, but I'd been thinking about you and me—and Hugh and me, and Hugh and you—yesterday. And he saw that. It was hard to hide."

There's a side-note of insecurity that we're going to have to come back to in a minute. *Don't read too much into it.* Jesus. But I want to get to the bottom of this first. "Sure. It's hard to go to something like that and think, I want that, and it's out of reach."

"Do you want that?"

"Yeah, in an abstract way."

"And with a woman? Or a man?"

I don't know. "Either, I guess. I mean, until I met you—" The words die on my tongue. Meeting Beth had changed everything. But that had its own ugly tinge, too.

I've made a mess of the two relationships that mean the world to me.

She gives me a hopeless look. "I think this conversation is supposed to be a lot happier than this."

I take a deep breath. "Yeah."

She moves closer, until her knees brush mine. "He loves you, you know. He loves you so much it hurts him that you don't notice."

"I…I don't notice? I can't keep my hands off him."

"He thinks it's different," she says softly.

"From what?"

"From how you feel about me."

It is different. But…not more or less. Just, they're not the same people.

I reach out and take her hand. She resists for a beat, but then I tug her into my lap. "I love you," I whisper against her temple. "So much that I've fucked everything up."

She presses her skin against mine. A breath, in and out. "And how do you feel about Hugh?"

A painful hurt unfurls in my chest. "I love him, too."

"But you haven't said it to him." Her voice cracks and she pulls her knees up to her chest, squeezing them tight. I wrap my arms around the ball of her body. "And he needs to hear it."

"He won't believe me."

"We'll need to convince him, then." Her voice is sure and confident, and the tension in her body ebbs as she relaxes against me and presses her face into my neck. "I need you both. This is crazy. We've just begun, the three of us. We can't be over yet."

"I don't know…"

Her fingers dance over the pulse point by my collarbone, then up the tendons on the side of my neck. Gentle, loving touches. "Can you tell me about your breakup the first time?"

I squeeze my eyes shut. No. Yes. I don't know. "I left him. That's the short answer. An opportunity came up, a posting, and I applied for it. I didn't tell him until I had the job."

"How did he react?"

"We fought. We fucked, too. That didn't stop until I left." And then the night before I left, he finally asked me if he should visit.

"Might be too complicated," I'd said.

"You sure?"

He'd not only asked, but he'd doubled down on his hope.

And I'd dashed it.

Because we were getting too intense, too much, for two guys fucking around.

It took me another year to admit had been the first man I'd wanted to have a real relationship with, and that had scared me. And by then, the regret had faded to a bittersweet *what if* level.

"He asked if we could keep seeing each other," I say faintly. "I shot him down."

"He told me we'd talk last night. And then we didn't. Maybe he couldn't?"

I nod, my insides twisting. "Easier said than done when he had every right to expect me to shut him down again."

She growls under her breath. "This is not a mature way to break up with people."

That makes me smile. "He's not breaking up with us. We won't let that happen."

"Promise?"

With every fibre of my being. "Yes."

"I should tell you something else. He said…how you feel about me—and I guess he sees that as different from how you feel about him—that's how he felt about you back then."

That makes my head spin. "No. We had feelings for each other, but it wasn't like that."

"Like what?"

There's no way I can tell Beth how I felt about her from that first moment I laid eyes on her. It makes me sound like a stalker. But holding back is what got us into this mess in the first place.

"You are my North Star," I whisper. "Everywhere I am, no matter what I'm doing, I gravitate towards you. You hold still in the swirling chaos so I can find my way to you. You are bright and constant in my sky."

"Maybe Hugh—"

I kiss her to stave off the questions and doubt. I can't handle the guesswork any more. We'll figure this out. We'll get him back. But I kiss her because she's my Beth, too.

Our Beth.

Fucking Hugh.

But he's running scared because I hurt him a long time ago, when he was a brash young man, and maybe we need to start there to fix this.

I can't do that right now.

But I can kiss her. I can make her dinner and hold her tight, make love to her and show her how much it means to me that she embraces not only me, but my crazy love for another lover, too.

SHE FALLS ASLEEP AFTER DINNER. We're talking on the bed, about bears and hiking, and I'm lazily stroking the bare skin of her back under her shirt.

And then all of a sudden, I realize she's not awake, and she's so sweetly konked out I don't even try to rouse her for sex.

We have all the time in the world for sex later, and a good night's sleep has been in short supply.

I grab a paperback from the living room, then tuck her under the blankets. I turn out all the lights but the small one beside me, and start reading.

Four hours later, I'm almost done the book. My eyes have gone gritty, but the story is compelling, and it's not that late still. I glance at my phone.

How did it get to be almost one in the morning?

I set my book aside and close my eyes, but despite the tired lids, I'm wide awake. My pulse is jacked up from an emotional couple of days and a thrilling spy book.

And on my shoulder, I can feel Hugh's mark. He left it and ran.

I try counting backwards, and thinking about the drill for cleaning a pistol, a machine gun. Packing lists for an overnight hiking trip I could take Beth on.

Hugh would be all over that.

My eyelids flutter open.

Fucking hell.

I shove out of bed and grab my phone. Time to try to get ahold of him again. And if he's still on radio silence, my next text is going to be filled with motherfucking expletives.

40

HUGH

IT'S NEARLY four in the morning and I officially give up on sleep.

The flight back to Ottawa was torturous.

I tried hard to ignore all the tangled-up feelings I'm reluctant —terrified, more like—to name. But there was nothing life or death going on to distract me, and the hole in my heart kept getting bigger and more jagged with each passing hour.

It's impossible to keep from replaying in my mind how Lachlan and Beth gazed at each other all weekend—like they're deeply in love.

Then there was the dancing.

It was a fucking mistake to try and make up for not dancing together at the wedding with a private dance at the cabin. That just jabbed a stake in my heart in a different way, reminding me that I've re-closeted myself in a whole new way with this relationship.

It's one thing to want to dance with Lachlan. It's another to wish the three of us could dance together.

But, there's nothing that could provide enough cover for any of that.

A real relationship between three people close to the prime minister? That's a pipe dream. A huge, unnecessary complication.

Lachlan would never hear of it. Because the reality of the world is, three's an unacceptable crowd as far as marriage and society are concerned. And it's this truth that erases any reservations I have about my decision to leave.

Even with my emotional turmoil, I can at least admit to myself, marriage is where things are heading for Lachlan and Beth, one way or another.

It's what they both want, and this weekend underlined that in an undeniable way.

When I finally got home, I hit the sack ridiculously early because I'm heavy in denial and avoidance, and sleep seemed like the best option.

Despite the physical exhaustion from the last twenty-four hours, my mind refuses to rest.

I wander out to the kitchen to make coffee, and I look around my apartment.

It's fucking stark.

It didn't bother me before. Probably since I haven't spent much time here.

I let myself get too comfortable in the fantasy of something else. In the fantasy that this place might be temporary and it didn't matter if I have a couch or a TV

I should have known better. Should have kept my distance from temptation.

It was all a colossal mistake.

My phone sits on the kitchen counter, right where I tossed it when I got home last night. I eye it like it's a rattle snake ready to strike, but I can't put off the inevitable any longer.

I switch the phone from airplane mode and set it back down while I brew a cup of coffee.

Notifications start to pop up everywhere.

Voicemail, missed calls, text messages, E-mail. Hell, if I had a Facebook account, I'm sure that would be screaming at me, too.

The guilt slams back into me like a freight train.

I decide to start with the text messages because I know I can't handle hearing their voices.

Lachlan: WTF man?
Beth: Are you okay?
Lachlan: Damn it, Hugh. Call me.
Beth: We're worried about you.
Beth: Please let me know you're okay.
Lachlan: Hugh. I don't know what's going on with you, but I'm going to kick your ass for making Beth cry.
Lachlan: She thinks she did something wrong. You need to fix this.

A rock-hard knot lodges deep in my chest as I stare at Lachlan's last two texts.

Then my phone vibrates and Lachlan's ringtone comes through the speaker.

Shit. I'm still not ready to talk to him, but I need to suck it up. We still have to work together.

And it's the middle of the night there. If he's calling me at one in the morning, I'm an asshole if I don't pick up, no matter how much I don't want to yet.

I take a deep breath and answer before the call has a chance to flip to voicemail. "I'm here."

"Jesus, Hugh." I can almost see his hand sliding over his head, his fingers sifting through his hair as he says it.

He sounds more relieved than angry and I'm a little surprised.

There's silence, and I don't know what to say, so I continue to gather my thoughts and wait.

"Where are you?"

"Ottawa."

"You knew you were leaving, didn't you? It wasn't a spur of the moment thing. It was planned."

There's no point in denying that. "Yeah."

"I don't get it. How could you spend the night fucking and sucking Beth and me like we are the most important people in your life if you were going to sneak out afterwards?"

I want to be flip. I want to tell him I needed one more fabulous memory for the spank bank. I want to make it easy for them to let go. But they deserve the truth, at least.

"You are the most important people in my life. And I needed to show you that one last time."

"Damn it, Hugh—"

"Go to bed, Lachlan. I said I needed space, and I meant it." I end the call. I can't talk about this yet. Somewhere along the way, I lost control of what I was doing.

I need to find that control again. And when I do, I'm never letting go again.

41

LACHLAN

WHEN I RETURN to the cabin, there's a lamp on and Beth is sitting up in bed. I was sure she was sleeping when I got up. How much did she overhear?

"Well?" she asks, her eyes bright with hope.

Fuck. I'd hoped to have some time to calm down and process that call. My heart is pounding and I don't want Beth to pick up on my agitation.

"You should be asleep," I say, gently.

"So should you." She pats my side of the bed. "Right here."

And Hugh should be on the other side of her.

There are so many other things that he should be right now.

My chest squeezes tight and I just nod as I try to swallow the lump in my throat.

Crossing the floor, I keep my breathing slow and steady in an effort to calm my heart rate before climbing in beside Beth.

She snuggles in close, and as I pull her into my arms, she twirls a finger in my chest hair. "What did he say?" she asks.

Jesus. I can't tell her what she wants to hear and she's already cried an ocean of tears.

"He's in Ottawa. And he needs space."

Her finger stops moving. "He isn't coming back."

"No, but that doesn't necessarily mean anything for when we get home," I say, trying to sound more optimistic than I feel.

"We could go to him now."

If only it were that simple. "Not yet. I can't see either of us being able to stay away from him while we're all in Ottawa—even for just a few days. It'll be easier for us to give him what he thinks he needs from here."

She lets out a long sigh. "I suppose you're right."

Hugging her tighter, I lean down and kiss the top of her head. "We should try and get some sleep," I tell her.

She doesn't respond. Instead, she slips her hand behind my neck and pulls me down for a kiss.

A gentle brush at first, then more insistent. I open and she teases her way in, her tongue gliding against mine as she slips her leg over me and grinds herself against my thigh.

I groan into her mouth and roll us over until I'm on top of her.

She spreads her legs wider. The invitation is clear. She's wet, and I'm hard.

There's no foreplay this time.

We're both swirling in a maelstrom of hurt and confusion and sometimes a good hard fuck is all there is to keep your head above water.

I take control of the kiss, plunging my tongue deep as I bury my cock inside her.

She wraps her legs around my waist, and I slip an arm under her knee and lift it higher, desperate to get as far inside her as I can.

All the pain and anger I've been desperately trying to keep down come spewing out.

My hips jerk and pump wildly. I'm a savage. No finesse at all. Just an overwhelming need to rut.

I'm not going to last long, but even in my frenzied state, I'm not so selfish as to leave her hanging, so I reach between us and use my fingers on her clit.

When the last spasms of my orgasm subside, I reach down to hold the condom in place as I pull out.

I hit bare flesh instead.

No condom.

Fuck. I'm a complete idiot.

I roll over onto my back and drag my fingers through my hair.

She slowly follows me, pressing her fingers to my chest.

Can she feel my heart pounding?

"I'm sorry."

"It happens."

"Not to me." I drag in a much-needed breath. "I wasn't thinking."

She turns to her side and slides a finger down my cheek. "It's okay. I think, or at least I hope, this where we've been heading? We just hadn't had the conversation yet."

"That's not the point. I didn't give you the choice. I was irresponsible."

"Oh please. If you're irresponsible, then so am I. I still had more than enough functioning brain cells to tell you to suit up, and I know damn good and well, you'd have complied."

She's not wrong. But the guilt of unprotected sex weighs heavy. I haven't gone without a condom in over ten years. Long before Hugh.

Fucking Hugh.

42

B E T H

WE GET BACK to Ottawa Tuesday night and Lachlan takes me to my apartment.

"Do you want to stay tonight?" I ask as I open my front door.

He exhales roughly. "I should go find Hugh."

"I thought we were going to give him some space." I set my keys on the hall table. Lachlan sets my bag by my bedroom door, then sets his hands on my shoulders. "We are. About us. But I need to make sure that we are okay about work, too."

Right. I flush. "Of course, I wasn't thinking."

"It can wait until tomorrow if you'd rather."

I shake my head. It's better if Lachlan lets Hugh know as soon as possible that we want to see him at work, as friends, whatever he wants, however he wants it. And I'm planning on going to work tomorrow, too. Gavin won't be back for another week, so I could take the rest of the week as vacation.

If I did that, I'd be hiding.

And how can we go about secretly seducing him back into our fold if we don't see him?

"Go and talk to him, then. You're right. He needs to be reassured this won't blow back on him."

He kisses me quickly. "I'll call you once I'm home."

That call comes just forty-five minutes later.

"Hey," I say as I answer the phone.

"He didn't even let me into his apartment."

"I'm sorry." I sit heavily on my bed. "What did he say? How did he look?"

"He looked good." Lachlan huffs a frustrated laugh. "I wanted him to look like shit, but no such luck. And he didn't say much. He apologized again, but it was like he was just trying to shut down the conversation. He relaxed a bit when I told him I just wanted to talk about work. He's back on the schedule tomorrow, but at the residence, and he's there until the PM gets back."

I nod to myself, absorbing that. So I likely won't see Hugh until next week. That...makes me sad. I thought I'd be relieved, because it'll be awkward, but this doesn't feel right at all. "Is it just me, or does this feel wrong?"

"It's not just you. But I don't know how to make it right until he relaxes a bit."

"We need to tell him how we feel about him."

"He doesn't want to hear it right now."

I frown. I know we're at the end of a long travel day, and now is not the time to push this, but I think Lachlan's wrong.

I think Hugh very much *wants* to hear that we love him. I'd just bet anything he doesn't believe that's what we'd say.

"And..." Lachlan sighs. "I've decided to fly back to Vancouver to meet up with the prime minister. The team out there is stretched tight."

I blink at the phone. This was supposed to be our time. At the cabin, but also this week as we eased back into work.

A rare chance to be together, far from the spotlight that follows the PM around.

And now that Hugh's not interested, for whatever misguided reason, Lachlan's checking out, too?

"Fine," I say, because what else is there to say? And it is fine.

It's not good, acceptable, ideal or any other adjective I like, but it is *fine*. "I should hit the hay."

"Beth…"

"Good night, Lachlan." I take a deep breath. "I love you."

He makes a happy exhaling noise, between a sigh and a laugh. "I love you, too."

THE NEXT MORNING, Lachlan is waiting for me outside my apartment building, leaning back against his car. I never drive to work, because it's a quick bus ride and I like those few minutes to read. I guess today I'm getting a drive in.

"This is a surprise," I say, stopping in front of him. "A very nice one, though."

He gives me a soft, lingering kiss, then hands over a cup of coffee from the shop on the corner. "I was thinking."

"Mmm?" I take a sip before following him to his car.

He opens the passenger door for me. "About how you said 'fine' when I told you I was flying out to Vancouver."

"Oh." I stop in the space between him and the car and look up. "Well…ignore that."

"I don't want to ignore that. I want to understand it." He braces his forearm on the roof of the car and frowns down at me. "You think I shouldn't go?"

"I…" I trail off, but he's asking. "I think we'd promised this week to each other, and just because Hugh backed out of that plan, I'm still here."

His face falls. "Shit. No, you're right."

"But I get that work sometimes interferes, and you and I can hang out any time. It's really fine."

"I'm starting to pick up on the nuances of the word." He grimaces. "Why didn't you say that last night?"

"Because it had been a long day and I didn't want to sound like a harridan."

"You'd never."

I shrug. "But I do understand."

"I didn't book a flight."

"You should."

"I might. But I'm talking it out with you first." He gestures for me to get into the car, and I do.

After he's pulled into traffic, he takes my hand, and he holds it the whole way to the Hill.

I feel a little funny getting out of his car and heading into Centre Block with him, but nobody gives us a second look. Upstairs, I log in to my computer as he reads emails on his phone.

We have a visit from the South African President scheduled for next month, and the communications staff have sent me the final invitation list for dinner. I read over the names carefully, comparing them to previous events. Gavin likes to mix up who gets a nod to these kinds of things, and we have a small list of people who behaved badly in the past, and maybe shouldn't get an invite again.

I fire back a response, nixing two names, and suggesting four others.

Then I look up to find Lachlan watching me. "Yes?" I ask with a smile.

"It's been a while since I've just sat here and watched you work. I like it."

I roll my eyes. For the past year, Lachlan's spent a lot of time at the security desk across from mine, but when he rejigged the teams after Hugh arrived, he started spending more time else-where. "I like it too," I whisper, then I sit up a bit straighter. "Now let me get back to work."

Just then an email comes across my screen, and from the way

Lachlan straightens up and goes all serious, I can tell he's reading it, too.

"Our boss never really takes a knee, does he?" I say lightly, glancing across the way. "I guess you're going to Vancouver after all."

4 3

HUGH

LACHLAN DOES EXACTLY what I asked him to do, and he leaves me alone for the rest of the week.

It makes me feel like shit.

I owe them both more than this cowardly, silent break-up, but every time I reach for the phone, I freeze up.

But when he emails on Thursday night, giving me the heads up that the PM and Ellie have decided to attend a public Canada Day celebration, and he's heading out to Vancouver to lead up the security team, I email back.

From: Hugh Evans
To: Lachlan Ross
Subject: Re: Did you see the PM itinerary change?

I did see that, and I wondered. Makes sense.

Email is safe. There's some distance there, and conversations about work are fine.

Except the bastard takes advantage of that and calls me when he lands. I answer because I can't ignore him, and it might be about work.

It's not.

"I know it's late there," he says quietly, and despite myself, I find myself growing hard.

Would he know if I stroked off to the sound of his voice?

He probably would.

I shouldn't.

I probably won't.

"No worries," I say, pacing around my quiet and still-empty apartment. "I was up. You at the hotel now?"

"Just got in, yeah."

"Good."

"Hugh, we gotta talk."

"No we don't."

"Yes we fucking do. For six weeks, we built something special, and you just blew it to smithereens without a single word."

Not true. I left a note. I don't say that, though. I grit my teeth instead and let him keep pummelling me.

"You don't fuck and run. That is not how you show the people in your life that they're important. You communicate. You talk things through. You've been involved in the D/s side of life long enough that I shouldn't have to fucking tell you this shit."

He's right. Deep down, I know better than to make and act on hasty decisions. I know better than to make decisions that affect other people without their input. But I did it anyway.

Even though I'd planned to leave, that decision had still been spur of the moment—about halfway through the wedding cere-mony, although in hindsight, it had started brewing at the rehearsal dinner. I'd changed my flight between leaving the reception and heading to the cabin.

I squeeze my eyes shut and bang my head against the wall. "I may have made a mess of this."

"Ya think?"

But I was coming from a good place, and he's gotta know that. "It boils down to this." I suck in a big shaky breath and let it out slowly. "The wedding brought into focus something I'd been ignoring. Something I didn't want to see."

"What the hell do you think you saw?"

"You and Beth. You've got a forever kind of love."

"And what about you?"

"I'm not really built for long-term relationships."

"What the fuck are you talking about, Hugh?"

"The three of us, together, is something that can never happen. You and Beth had feelings for each other long before I showed up. And while it's been a lot of fun, it's time for me to bow out and leave the two of you work your way towards happily ever after."

"I'm going to stop you right there, dick-for-brains. It's clear you need some space. But you don't know what the hell we want, or how we want it."

I smile at his trash talking, but it's a weak, passing happiness. The truth is, I know what *I* want, and I know it's not possible. "Fair point," I admit. "I shouldn't have put this on you guys. I'm the one who can't…"

"Can't what?"

I don't know how to answer that right now. "I just can't."

He huffs in frustration, then growls. "Fine. You should do something with Beth this weekend. Grab a coffee."

"Yeah." But we both know I won't.

He might think it's because I'm scared, but I know better.

I walked away while I still could. I won't be able to do it again. If I go back to them, it'll be until they're done with me.

"I'll let you get to sleep," he finally says, quietly. "I'm going to text you something after we hang up, so don't turn your phone off."

"I couldn't even if I wanted to, I've gotta work in the morning."

He laughs and we say goodbye.

The text is a photo. It's a sucker punch to the gut, because it's a picture he must have taken that day at the cabin. Beth in my arms, and we're both laughing and...

Damn him.

We look like we're in love.

Another text comes in. This one is a threat, and completely justified.

Lachlan: Remember, you made her cry. Don't do it again.

Direct hit. If she calls me for coffee, or anything else, I won't be able to say no now.

Well played, Ross. Well played.

BETH

July

I SPEND Canada Day by myself, doing a month's worth of meal prep. Living the damn life, I am. In the end, Lachlan flew out to Vancouver, and I don't blame him. Gavin and Ellie are going to to a public parade today, and the turnout is going to be crazy.

His first priority has to be to keep the PM safe, and while he trusts his team, it's not the same as if he's walking six feet behind the man himself.

So I've got the first weekend of July to myself, and by Sunday, I'm going squirrelly.

Sasha calls and when she picks up on the fact I'm in the dumps, she suggests retail therapy.

I can't afford retail therapy, Sasha-style, so I beg off and tear my closet apart instead. I ask myself if each piece brings me joy, and pretty soon I have a massive pile of stuff to donate.

Maybe when one of your boyfriends has shut you out for stupid, makes-no-sense reasons isn't the best time to do a joy-test on clothing.

But I'm on a roll, so I go to my dresser next.

The first thing I see is that bra and panties set I bought last month. That I took pictures of and sent to Hugh.

Damn him.

Without overthinking it, I reach for my phone.

BETH: **I miss you.**

OF COURSE he doesn't reply. So, hands shaking, I take a picture.

No lingerie. Just me, bare and wanting him. My arm across my breasts, the curve of my neck, the side of my lip caught in my teeth.

I hit send.

HE SHOWS UP forty-five minutes later, freshly showered. His eyes are dark and haunted.

"This is a bad idea," he says roughly as he follows me down the hallway and into my living room.

I put on a robe to answer the door, just in case, but he came in. He let that door shut behind him.

I drop the robe. "Is it?"

"Beth…"

"I miss you. That's all." I swallow hard. That's a lie. "This doesn't have to mean anything."

"Of course it means something." He's closer now.

I want to glare at him, to jut my chin and tell him I know. *It means everything.* But something scared him off. We need to walk *us* back to a place he can handle.

A place where we're naked and laughing and love is a hazy threat still in the future.

He throws himself onto my couch and spreads his arms wide.

"Do you have an itch you need to scratch, beautiful? Because I can do that. But there can't be any strings attached."

"No strings," I whisper, even as my heart drops.

"And you tell Lachlan about this." His eyes go bright at that.

"I'll tell him everything," I promise. "Every hot, delicious detail. And he'll do the same if you visit him."

He watches me through guarded eyes as I crawl into his lap, his big hands squeezing my thighs. "That's not going to happen."

"Okay." I don't argue the point. Of course it's going to happen. We've already learned once that willpower is no match for the chemistry between the three of us, or any combination therein.

"Show me what you want," he says hoarsely.

Without hesitation, I cup my breasts, teasing my nipples with my fingers. My eyelids flutter as I feel his gaze sweeping over my body. His attention is just as potent as my touch, and I want more of it. "Tell me what to do next."

"Show me that you're wet already." His voice hardens as he takes over.

I reach one hand between my legs and swipe at the ready moisture there. It strings between my fingers, clear and slippery.

"Feed it to me."

I gasp as heat enflames me, but I do as I'm told, lifting my fingers to his mouth. He licks them clean, his tongue flat and broad.

He takes his time.

He makes it dirtier than I thought possible. "Delicious," he whispers as his tongue slides off the tip of my ring finger. "More."

I stroke myself again, then offer him my hand.

Back and forth we go, until I'm squirming and he's rock hard beneath me.

Then he picks me up without a word and carries me into the bedroom. I watch, every muscle in my body screaming to be used and abused, as he strips out of his jeans and t-shirt.

I don't miss that he came over commando.

He wanted this just as much as I do.

When he's naked, he crowds against me, pushing me up on the bed. I tangle my fingers in his hair and search for his lips with mine.

He stops me. "No kissing."

"What?" I laugh as I lean in again, my mouth brushing his. "Come on. I promise I'll make it dirty."

He jerks under my touch and his voice cracks. "I need some limits."

There's something there that touches me and reminds me that deep down, even brashy, cocky Hugh has a sensitive, wounded soul inside. One we haven't spent enough time thinking about, clearly.

"Fair enough." I drift my lips over his cheek and trace the curve of his ear with the tip of my tongue. "This is better anyway. Keeps my mouth free to be sassy."

"I can find something to keep your mouth occupied if need be."

"Mmm. Don't make promises you can't keep…"

The taunt works. He flips me over and slides up my body, fast as lightning. He kneels beside me, half-straddling my upper body, his hips canted toward my face. His cock bounces against my mouth before I get my act together, but when he fists himself, I'm ready.

I part my lips and he slides in roughly. I tamp down the rush of adrenaline and exhale as I swallow him. Jesus, he's thick. But he tastes good, and I'm so greedy for this I'll take it however I get it.

He pumps his hips, fucking my face until I'm groaning around him. Then he pulls out and reaches for my condom drawer.

Okay, so this is going to be a quickie.

I can handle that.

He kneels between my legs, staring at my pussy as he rolls the condom on. Before he presses the crown of his cock against me, he touches me first, and it's an unexpected gentleness that cracks my heart.

I roll my hips, trying to keep us on the no-feelings, just-fucking track. He doesn't have any idea how he affects me. Protecting my heart is going to have to be my job alone.

I'm a grown up. I can do that.

I can pretend this is just sex.

Amazing, incredible, dirty sex.

"Now," I tell him breathlessly.

"Not gonna be gentle," he warns.

"Good." No sooner is the word out of my mouth than he's there, at my entrance, and then inside me in the next beat. A thick, hard intrusion that takes my breath away.

And it is good. I curl my legs up, opening for him, welcoming the brutal pummelling. I want him to do this, to lose himself in me, to work out in our physical connection what he can't find in words.

He takes me with him, too. Wraps me in his arms as he moves his powerful body above me, into me. He finds all the spots that light me up and rubs against them, hard. Fucking come, his body says to mine. Come apart, come for me, come, come, come.

And I do, because I'm his. I'm so easy for him, so open, that all it takes is his mouth on my tits, his cock in my pussy, and I'm pulled apart at the seams.

After he deals with the condom, he pulls me into his side and I press my cheek against his chest.

I listen to the pounding of his heart and wish I understood.

We lie there, together, long enough for me to foolishly get my hopes up that maybe we can talk. "Hugh?"

"Mmm."

"We miss you."

"No." He swings his arm out from under my head and sits up.

"What?"

"Don't do this."

I sigh. "Is this really your plan?"

He gives me a warning look, but I might not get another chance. I press on.

"Every time we reach out you'll turn it into just sex, nothing more? Pretend that's all we have?"

"You weren't complaining a minute ago. And you summoned me."

That's true. But he came. "I know…"

He kisses the spot where my neck meets my back, then lower, down my spine. All the way until his hands are on my hips, and he's urging me up.

Onto my knees, so he can take me again.

And I let him. I let him fuck me until I'm gripping him in another shuddering orgasm, until he pours himself into me, because I'll take it.

Then I don't say anything more, not even when he rolls onto his back beside me and stares at the ceiling.

And when he gets up and silently pulls on his jeans, I hold my breath. I hold it until he leaves, until the too-loud click of the lock promises he's gone—tauntingly, because what was I expecting?

That's when I let my breath out, and the tears follow.

45

LACHLAN

ONCE AGAIN, I'm across the country from Beth—and Hugh, the grumpy ass—and I'm antsy to get back to Ottawa.

Gavin, however, is enjoying his Sunday afternoon at home. His real home, in Vancouver, in the heart of his riding. His father bought him a new charcoal grill as a wedding gift, and he's got it fired up.

Ellie opens the slider and steps onto the deck. She's got a yoga mat bag slung over her shoulder, and one of my men trailing behind her. "I'm off," she says, pressing up on her tiptoes to give Gavin a kiss.

"Have fun at yoga, wife."

She grins. "Will do, husband."

Yeah, I'm definitely ready to head home.

Ten minutes later, another member of my team comes to the backyard. "Excuse me, sir, but there's a visitor here to see you. Jack Benton."

Gavin frowns and rubs his jaw. "Sure, send him back."

The owner of the Vancouver Lumberjacks strides onto the deck a minute later, and Gavin extends his hand. "Jack, good to see you again, and so soon."

Benton grins. "Had a fantastic time at your wedding."

"Was our scotch up to snuff?"

"Decent enough, thank you."

Gavin glances at me. "Have you met Lachlan Ross, my chief of security? He'll be sticking around for this conversation."

"Yes, a few times." He shakes my hand, then glances back at Gavin. "I've never known you to need a chaperone."

Jack says it with a laugh, but Gavin's not kidding around.

"Just keeping this strictly friendly. I am glad to see you again, but the timing is curious given my upcoming trade agenda and your scheduled visit to my office. When the press asks me about your impromptu visit to my house—and they will—I want to be crystal clear we didn't talk business out of turn."

"Ah." Jack clears his throat. "Right. That's going to make what I say next kind of awkward."

"Don't do it." Gavin frowns. "Come on, man. You know I'm being raked over the coals about pay-to-play politics. Just because we go back nearly twenty years doesn't mean I can make an exception for you."

"I'm selling the team."

My eyebrows hit the roof. Whoa. I'm a die-hard hockey fan, and I didn't see that coming.

Apparently, neither did Gavin. "Wow."

"So I am here to lobby you. But not about sports."

Gavin groaned. "You know I wasn't worried about that. How about a beer? Tell me more about the sale."

"I've put the lumber yards in a blind trust, too."

Gavin gives me a pained look. "You've heard me trying to tell him to shut up, right?"

I step forward. "You want me to toss him out?"

Jack just laughs. "I definitely want a beer. Unless that would be too awkward for an informal job interview."

Gavin snorts. "This will be good. Follow me."

We head into the kitchen and he rifles through the fridge for three bottles of beer. I'm curious as hell, but my role here isn't to ask any questions.

Luckily Gavin asks them for me. "So what's going on? You think my poll numbers are going to slide into oblivion and I'm going to need to be rescued after the next election? What's your plan, Jack? Start a new environmental law firm, Strong & Benton?"

"It would be Benton & Strong, if we ever did, and that's not a bad retirement plan." Jack holds out his beer. "But I'm not planning to retire for a few decades yet. I'm actually here to ask you for a job, prime minister."

Gavin silently holds out his own beer and they clink the glass necks together. His face pulls tight into a frown.

I'm not following.

Frowns are, generally speaking, not something to toast.

"You want to get into government. Foreign Affairs or International Trade?"

Jack shrugs. "Wherever you'll have me."

"You don't want to run? I'd put you in my cabinet in a heartbeat."

He shakes his head. "Nah. The limelight has never been for me. I want to get my hands messy with policy."

"Oh, fuck me," Gavin groans. "You want to fix softwood lumber."

"We never got it right, and you know it. There was only so much I could do when I was running my own businesses. Now I want to make it my sole focus. And you know we owe it to them."

"Yeah." Gavin scrubs his hand over his face, then groans again. "Okay." He shoots me a quick look. "Give us a few minutes alone, Lachlan."

I take my beer and head outside.

I don't know what this means politically. But Jack Benton is moving to Ottawa—and he flirts with Beth like he wants to lick her up for dessert.

That's my fucking job.

Hugh's, too.

Things on Parliament Hill are going to get awkward this summer. And just when I thought getting past the wedding would mean things got easy for a while.

46

BETH

SOMETHING IS up with the prime minister. He arrived back in Ottawa late last night, but I got an email alert from Lachlan that he was on the move at half past five this morning. I'm not needed in the office when he goes in that early, but I drag myself out of bed just in case.

I stop at the coffee place on the corner just as its opening.

"Early Monday?" the barista asks.

I nod, and I must look weary, because he gives me an extra espresso shot for free.

I tip well.

Stew is already in Gavin's office when I poke my head in and wave.

"Morning," I say to them both. And then to the PM, "Did you eat breakfast?"

He grimaces at me.

"I'll get you coffee. And a muffin?" He nods. "How about you, Stew?"

"I'm good, thanks." He waves a thermos in the air, but doesn't look up from the report he's poring over.

An hour later, the morning briefing is extra short, just the bare necessities, and Stew and Gavin stay holed up once the senior staff disperse.

My job, when they get like this, is to hold down the fort—sometimes pretend that nothing is going on, and sometimes carefully walk that line between denial and distraction, because something *is* going on, and it'll break soon.

I never care what it is. I'm vaguely political in the way anyone who lasts in Ottawa has to be. We want to know that tax dollars aren't being wasted, and good policy is being enacted. But most of the time, we're too cynical to get upset or excited when something new is announced. My attitude makes me a great executive assistant, because I care about keeping Gavin on schedule and on task, and couldn't care less about the details of what he's working on.

So I spend the morning doing what I usually do, but I'm also keeping an eye on the schedule. Gavin pops out for the two can't-miss events on his calendar, but on his way back in, he asks me to organize dinner for six people.

Okay, long day it is.

LACHLAN RE-APPEARS AT DINNER TIME, and frowns when he sees me sitting at my desk.

"How long have you been here?"

"All day."

"That's—"

I hold up my hand and smile. "My business."

"I'm just saying, I got some downtime in the middle of my crazy split day."

"But you were up earlier and will be out later than I will tonight. And you do long shifts regularly. For me, this is a rare thing, but when he needs me, I'm here." I point to my desk. "And

I'm currently writing a list of pieces I want to add to my wardrobe, so I'm hardly working at all."

"Clothes?"

"I did a big closet purge yesterday. It's a long story."

He glances at his watch. "I've got time."

We're alone in the outer office, but Gavin could pull the door open at any time. And Lachlan thinks he's asking politely about my wardrobe overhaul when really, my yesterday story is explosive and is liable to just piss him off.

Or turn him on.

Maybe both.

"Not now," I murmur. "Not here."

He lowers his voice and leans in, his eyes searching my face. "Is it a scandalous shopping list?"

I smile. "No. It's the story that followed the closet purge that isn't work appropriate."

"Now you have me hooked." He sits on the edge of my desk. "Give me a hint."

"Call me tonight when you get home."

"Let me drag you into the copier room and you can spill all your dirty secrets right now." He winks and stands up. "Or not. But I am calling you tonight."

And I will tell him what happened with Hugh.

So that gives me two, maybe three hours to figure out just what exactly did happen, and how I want to frame it so Lachlan doesn't lose his mind.

47

———

LACHLAN

I CHEAT and call her from the car after I drop the prime minister at 24 Sussex. It's later than I thought, but I'm still taking the chance.

"You're driving," she says.

"I am."

"Then you'll have to wait until you get home to hear my story."

I decide to just ask for what I want. "Or I could come to your place?"

"I'm already in bed."

"That sounds perfect."

"We both have to up early tomorrow."

"I've got a change of clothes with me." There's a long pause before she answers, but I'm already driving back towards downtown.

"Okay," she finally says. "Let yourself up."

———

SHE ANSWERS the door in a robe and nothing else. The primal

306

man inside me appreciates the long slice of soft, bare skin I can see, but I don't miss the fatigue tugging at her eyes.

Focus on what matters, I remind myself, and we head straight to bed.

Naked, because why give up the opportunity to be skin-to-skin? But something tells me Beth isn't in the mood for sex.

I'm not wrong.

She walks her fingers across my chest once we're tucked in. "Okay, so…"

I chuckle. "Yes?"

"I was purging my closet. And then I came across some lingerie I'd bought when we started dating. A set I'd taken pictures of, and sent to Hugh—nothing identifying or revealing, don't freak out."

"I'm wondering why I didn't get the same pictures," I grumble, and she kisses my skin.

"How often is the PM in eyeball range to your phone screen?"

"Good point." Although the same could maybe said about Hugh, but I'm not going to argue the issue. "So did he like the pictures? Did he say anything?"

"Oh, that was back in May. The photos. But finding the lingerie reminded me of them…so I sent him another one." She presses against me. "Like this. Naked. But still…classy."

"You're killing me. Classily. Go on."

"So he came over yesterday afternoon. Which feels like a lifetime ago now."

My heartbeat speeds up. "Yeah?"

Instead of the good update I want to hear, though, I get a heavy sigh.

"I think I messed things up," she says softly. "We…had sex. And it was intense, and good, but full of rules. And then he just left at the end."

Shit. "I'm sorry."

"I thought it was a good idea."

"Yeah." I press my lips against her forehead, ignoring the way my dick is thickening at the thought of Hugh here, being bossy and intense with Beth. But my flash of arousal doesn't last long, because he left her again.

"I should go kick his ass," I say. I mean it, too. He needs an attitude adjustment for using her.

She pokes me in the side. "I invited him over. I knew what I was getting into once he was here."

"He hurt you."

"He hurt himself, more. I really think that somehow along the way, he's convinced himself that he's only temporary for you. For us. And he went into our relationship eyes wide open, convinced that was the case, but it got to be too much."

"That's crazy." I pull back and frown down at her when she doesn't say anything. "Isn't it?"

"I don't know. I think…maybe not crazy. Not true, of course. We love him." Her voice drifts on a sigh. "But somehow I don't think telling him that will be enough."

I THINK about what Beth said all the next day. And when I get off work, instead of going to my house, where Beth headed an hour earlier, I find myself at Hugh's apartment building.

It's nothing like Beth's lovely place. It's a giant concrete building, probably twenty apartments on each floor. The front door doesn't close all the way, so even though there is a buzzer system, I don't need to call up and announce myself.

This is good, because I don't want him to have any advance warning that I'm here. I'd been prepared to wait until someone came out, but now I don't need to.

I make my way to the fifth floor and find his unit easily.

I don't even know if he's home, but I knock anyway.

There's a long stretch of nothing, so I knock again. Official-like, so he thinks maybe it's the landlord. Wonders if there's a gas leak or something.

I'm not sure it works, and I'm about to take a step back when the door swings open.

We stare at each other for a long beat.

Then I push my way past him, into his apartment, because I'm not taking no for an answer.

"Hey," he starts to say, but I'm not listening.

I stalk down the short hallway and into the... what should be the living room.

Except it's empty, save for a weight bench.

Behind me, I hear him sigh. "Sure, come on in."

"You don't have any furniture," I say as I turn back to look at him. This is not how I meant to open the conversation.

"I have a bed," he says, his words clipped. "Want to bend over it?"

I ignore the jab and wave at a cardboard box in the corner. "You haven't unpacked."

"I haven't spent much time here. And it doesn't really matter —this place might be temporary."

I give him an incredulous stare. "Temporary? You already have one foot out of the city?"

"Can you blame me?"

"You can't fucking leave."

"Why the hell not?"

I'm yelling now. I can't dial it back. "Because we need you."

"You have each other."

I storm towards him, stopping myself just before I slam into him. "Is this the wedding bullshit again?"

"It's not bullshit. You have no idea what it was like to watch you *longing* for her. And her right back at you. You have no idea what was going through my mind as I realized I was just a... means to an end."

Oh, he's got it so fucking wrong. I bump up against his chest.

"Is that so? Is that what was going through your mind at a wedding between two people who love each other? That I must be using you?"

"That's not what I mean."

"That's what I hear." I lick my lips. "What the hell do you think was going through *my* mind at the wedding?"

He shoves back against my chest. "I don't need to guess. It was written all over your face. You love Beth."

"Yeah. With my whole heart. But that doesn't crowd you out. I love you, too."

Hugh shakes his head. "It's not the same."

I nod. "No, you're right. It's not *exactly* the same. You complete me in different ways."

"We can't share you."

"You don't…it's not like that." I rub my hand against my chest. Why does this fucking hurt so much? This is supposed to be the happy, easy part. I'd decided to come and confess just how much I want him, how much *we* want him. But now the conversation's twisted.

His jaw flexes and his eyes glint. Hard and unyielding. "A lot has changed in the last ten years. I've changed. I'm more experienced now, but smarter, too. And I know what I want." He shakes his head. "And what I don't want."

No. "Don't try and pretend you don't want us."

"Maybe you have no clue what I want. Or what I wanted back then."

"You were never shy about making that known."

"I wanted you."

I know what he means and it makes me shake. "You wanted —" Sex. An affair. Excitement.

Not me without all of that.

Except that's exactly what he means.

He gives me a wounded look. "I wanted *you*. And you left me."

My mouth is dry and my heart is pounding so fast it might

just explode. "I'm not leaving you now. I'm asking you to come back. I'm asking you to give me a chance."

"I did. I gave you a chance."

He can't dig his heels in like this. It's not fair. "Ten years ago? Fuck you. I didn't know who I was then. And we didn't have Beth."

"Does she need to be a part of us, for there to be an us?"

I stare at him, dumbstruck. I don't know how to answer that. "Do you not want..." No, I can't finish that thought.

His face twists. "Of course I do. But you still can't imagine just being with me. Even if it's only hypothetical."

It's not until he stalks out, slamming the door behind him, that I realize I never got a chance to tell him that I was thinking the same shit as he was during Gavin's wedding ceremony.

Fuck.

No, this isn't how this ends. And I'm sure as shit not waiting for him in this sad, depressing shell of an apartment. I grab my keys and head after him.

48

HUGH

I DON'T KNOW where I'm going. I get as far as the alley behind my building before the adrenaline crash slams into me and I stop.

I just…stop.

Footsteps race up behind me, then slow.

"Don't run away," Lachlan says, his voice cracking.

I can't turn around.

But I'm not running.

"I love you."

I'm really not running now. Stupid hope. I straighten my back.

"Talk to me." He's close now. Almost right behind me. "Tell me what's going through your head. Help me understand what's got you scared."

"I'm not scared." It's a knee-jerk lie that takes me right back to high school.

I pace into the alley, then turn around.

He spreads his arms wide, his hands turned up. "What can I say?"

I shake my head. "Nothing. I'm fucked up. There. That's the truth of it. Happy now? I'm so broken inside it doesn't matter what you say, because the words get garbled in my head. There will always be a piece of me that is primed for flight."

"Sure, okay. So now that we know that, we can cope." His lips twist into an almost-smile. "Beth can practice her rope skills and tie you down."

"It's not funny. I…Something inside me…"

"You're a hard-ass man now, for a very good reason. I should have seen it sooner." He exhales roughly, then turns and leans his back against the brick wall behind him.

"What are you doing?"

"Getting comfortable."

"In an alley."

He looks around, lazily, like this is no big deal. "This is where you led me. Next time, freak out in the direction of a park."

"There won't be a next time."

"Sure there will. And maybe I'll lose my cool sometime, and Beth might snap at us for getting food on the couch. "

"What are you doing?"

"You already asked me that." His voice is smooth, and I suddenly realize what's going on.

He's interrogating me. Good cop. If I don't give him the information he wants, he'll try the bad cop. Get in my face. Get loud.

I laugh, because what the fuck else can I do?

And the twisted thing is, I like this good cop, bad cop routine. It gets under my skin, gets me going.

It's hot.

I'm so fucked up.

"I can't tell you that there would be an us without Beth," he says quietly. "Because I refuse to consider that possibility. But I can tell you that not once in the last week did we consider the possibility that we—" He gestures in the general direction of wherever he thinks Beth is. "Could be an us without *you*. This whole time, we've been giving you space, not that it looks like you've used that wisely to do any thinking."

I can't think. I'm stuck in survival mode. I didn't even see it coming.

"Beth told me about Sunday afternoon." He gives me a hard look. "That was a dick move."

"Yeah."

"She's fine, by the way. But I think you made her cry again, and I told you not to do that."

Fuck. "Is she pissed at me?"

"What do you think?"

There are a lot of ways I can justify what I did. She invited me over, I made sure it was good for her. But the truth is, she deserved better. "She ought to be."

"She should cane your ass. But that doesn't seem to be in her nature. She's been extraordinarily understanding, in fact. She seems to be under the impression you have a deep-seated fear of rejection."

I jerk as if he'd just poked me with a live wire.

He grimaces. "So I need to apologize for my part in that." He steps away from the wall and moves towards me, slow and steady. "I pushed you away ten years ago. I'm sorry. I shouldn't have done that. I wanted you, too. In every way. I loved you, then, and I love you now. I never stopped loving you, and I'm so fucking sorry I hid that from you."

It's everything I've secretly wanted to hear. My mouth runs dry. If I let my guard down here, if I let him in, I'm never going to be able to let him go. "It took a long time to get over you."

"For me, too. Get over you. I'm not sure I ever did."

"I love Beth, too."

He smiles. "I know. Come on. She's waiting for us."

My heart stutters in my chest. "Where?"

"Home."

49

BETH

I'm three trays of cookies into stress baking when Lachlan texts that he's bringing Hugh back to his place.

Lachlan: Got him to listen. Told him I love him. Bringing him home.

The relief that washes over me is strong enough to buckle my knees. Heart thumping, I lean against the granite countertop and take a deep breath.

When Lachlan told me he was going to see Hugh, I packed enough clothes to stay here for a week. If it worked, I wouldn't want to be away from them. And if it didn't, I knew we'd need to cling to each other to deal.

Lachlan's key in the front door jump starts my anxiety again. Before I can coordinate moving my feet, Hugh's in the kitchen doorway, then across the room.

I sink into his embrace. His lips brush my cheek, my temple, then press into my hair as I squeeze him tight.

I don't even realize I'm crying until he's easing me up onto the counter and wiping my face.

"I'm sorry," he whispers.

I shake my head. "We didn't notice you pulling away."

"I've learned to hide my feelings pretty well." He grimaces, and I touch his face. He's so tough. Too tough.

"Do you want a cookie?" I ask, my voice catching.

He nods roughly and I pull him close again, wrapping my arms around his neck this time.

"I made peanut butter chocolate chip, and regular chocolate chip, and I've got a batch of oatmeal raisin if you want to pretend to be healthy."

"Gimme a chocolate one."

Lachlan's beside us, cookies on a small plate, before I can even move. Hugh takes one, and I shift my hug to Lachlan.

He runs his hand up and down my back soothingly. "May I have a cookie as well?" he teases.

I laugh. "Maybe we should make some coffee to have with them instead of just gobbling them here at the counter."

Hugh winks at me mid-bite. "Watch out for crumbs."

I swipe the rest of his cookie and shove it in my mouth.

He gasps and I raise one eyebrow in challenge. *What are you going to do about that?*

Lifting his hand slowly, he reaches up and brushes the corner of my mouth with the pad of his thumb. "Crumbs," he whispers, and leans in.

Then he licks me.

A big, wet, cheeky swipe of his tongue on my face.

I shove him in the chest, and he doesn't move an inch. By now I'm laughing so hard my sides hurt, and he's leaning in to do it again.

"Uncle, uncle!" I cry.

"Uncle by marriage and we meet the day after your eighteenth birthday. The marriage is a sham and when I see you it's love at first sight?"

"Gross," I whisper, but I let him kiss me anyway. I've missed his dirty ways.

"Or are you begging for mercy?" he asks silkily. "I'm generally not a fan, but I'd make an exception for you."

He's such a liar. A soft-hearted, sensitive soul trapped in an alpha male's body.

And as much as I can't wait to get dirty and teasing and raunchy with him…I want to find out more about that secret side of Hugh he managed to keep hidden from us while distracting us with sex.

"I'm calling a timeout on welcome back sex," I say with a sigh, patting his delightfully hard chest through his shirt. "Just a short one. So we can have milk and cookies and talk."

He rolls his head to the side and gives Lachlan a pained look. "She wants to talk."

Lachlan gives me an indulgent smile as he moves to the coffee maker and pulls out three mugs from the cupboard. "She's smart that way."

I scoot off the counter and plate up some of the cookies, and put the rest in a resealable container for later.

Hugh watches me work for a minute or two, then crosses his arms and shrugs his shoulders. "Okay. What do you want to talk about?"

"I don't know exactly. I guess I want to know why you ran, and what we can do to ensure you won't feel pushed to that again in the future."

He groans. "Because I'm an idiot? And I won't?"

Not good enough. "You aren't, and you might. Any of us could get cold feet about this relationship. Regular relationships fail all the time for stupid reasons, and they don't have the pressure of not being able to…talk to their friends, for example."

He frowns at me. "You could talk to your friends about us. We trust your friends. Don't we? Do you need better friends?"

"I'm not looking to confide in anyone about you guys, so

that's not really the point. I'm just saying, two hot heads and a bossy woman…we're liable to run into conflict again. I want us to agree that we talk stuff out, even if it's uncomfortable."

More talking. I'm not surprised that suggestion is met with uncomfortable silence—from both of them.

I turn my attention to Lachlan, and he shrugs. "You're not wrong. But maybe Hugh needed some time to process, too? It's all worked out in the end, hasn't it?"

I want to point out that's incredibly naive, but I don't know that Lachlan's wrong. I *think* he is, but time will tell.

He hands me a cup of coffee and gives me a soft kiss. "We'll figure it out. What we know for sure is that we're all in this, right? We're a…couple. A triad. We are in a relationship, the three of us."

Right. "We love each other," I say, turning to Hugh.

The look on his face is everything. Happiness and disbelief and eagerness all rolled up together. "I'm yours," he says, his voice full of desire. "Completely."

I take a cookie and hold it out. "Okay. Talking part of the evening is now concluded. Come here and be mine."

5 0

———

HUGH

It's back to regular hockey with the PM on the Sunday after Canada Day, and for the first time, I'm invited along. They haven't played in over a month due to the aftermath of the tornado and the prime minister's wedding.

The PM's not-so-secret pick-up team has become a thing of national pride. And when I joined the security detail, Lachlan made it clear without saying a word that it was a closed hockey team, no new members needed.

Especially not someone who had a hard time not causing trouble.

But he's finally come around to loving my brand of trouble, and I've promised to be on my best behaviour.

"You still play in goal?" he asks as I toss my hockey bag in the back of his vehicle.

"That a problem?"

"You might need to play up today." His mouth turns up at the corners, an unconscious half-smile. "But we could use a back-up goalie."

"Who's your regular?"

"My former partner." His eyes twinkle as I rear back in jealousy. "Work partner. Have you met Corinne Smith yet? She's our goalie."

"Maybe. She works at RCMP HQ?"

"Yeah."

"No worries. I'm flexible." I wink. "As you know."

We get in the car, and he turns on the radio, but after getting on the highway, he turns it off again. "You'll understand why I didn't invite you sooner once you meet the rest of the team. Actually, I owe you an apology for not filling you in sooner."

"About what?"

He gives me a rueful, goofy look. "The entire team is kinky. It's a long story, but Gavin needed a safe space when he met Ellie. He asked me to pull together a hockey game or two. I couldn't ask him if he needed more than an actual game, so I put together a safe community for him. Other than the one time I was with him and Ellie, they haven't yet utilized it, but..."

"You created a private kink space for the PM. Just in case he'd need it."

He shrugs. "Yeah."

"How many favours did that take?"

"Not many. I needed to tap some professional guys to get enough players on the team."

"Like Tate Nilsson."

Lachlan laughs. "Exactly."

"Who else knows?"

"It's a pretty tight secret. The guy you replaced, Tim, he knew, because he swapped off with me for being Gavin's point man during the whole Ellie thing. When Tim left to work at the National Childhood Exploitation Coordination Centre, it wasn't necessary to loop anyone else in immediately because 24 Sussex is pretty locked down and officially vanilla these days."

"Unofficially?"

"There might be a time when the PM and his wife-to-be want

to play discreetly. And it'll be our job to protect their right to do that."

"Understood."

"I'd have told you eventually."

I know he would have. But we've arrived at the rink, so we don't need to re-hash the hostility of my return to his life and how that sent him into a tailspin.

What matters is he pulled up, hard, and now we're here. In more ways than one.

I HAVEN'T PLAYED since leaving Toronto and it feels like it.

It's not like I'm out of shape. I still managed to work out regularly in that time, but my stick handling isn't as elegant as I'd like to believe it usually is.

Lachlan, on the other hand, doesn't look like he's skipped a game ever.

I spend a little too long watching his sexy legs glide down the ice and I miss an easy pass.

Fortunately, Tate manages to snag the puck and race toward the other team's goal. The goalie blocks the shot, but Gavin scores on the rebound.

My error didn't hurt us, but I spend the rest of the game trying to keep my eye on the puck instead of my lover. Mostly, I succeed.

At the end of the game, I skate up to Lachlan and jerk my head towards the stands where Ellie and Violet are packing up ready to leave. "Maybe Beth should come to the next game," I tell him.

It's just a passing thought, but his reaction surprises me. He just grunts and heads off to the locker room.

I know we're still in the early days of our relationship, but at some point… Looking back up at the stands, my chest gets tight.

Ellie and Violet are wearing dorky beaver hats, an unofficial uniform of their cheering squad. Beth would look adorable in a matching toque.

I give my head a small shake, then follow Lachlan off the ice.

After the game, most of the team meets up at a nearby pub.

Lachlan claps Max on the shoulder as we walk in. "I figured you'd have gone straight home."

"Not tonight. Violet told me she'll be going to sleep early anyway, so I may as well enjoy an evening at the pub while I still can, because once baby Donovan shows up, it'll be all hands on deck. So, Gavin and Ellie dropped her off home and here I am."

His face lights up when he mentions the baby. Impending parenthood looks good on him.

We sprawl out around two tables pushed together and order a disgusting amount of food. Nachos, poutine, wings. The conversation is light and easy. Sports and weather, home renovation and travel. For a group of pretty diverse income levels—Max and Tate at one extreme, and the public servants at the other—they've got a lot in common.

And then there's the one thing they all share, but don't talk about in a pub. So really, this is just like any kink munch I've attended in the past.

By the time my belly is full of poutine, I feel like I'm fitting right in.

While we're waiting at the bar for another round of drinks, Corinne walks up to Lachlan. "Pool table's free. How about a rematch?"

Lachlan smiles. "Sure, I'll be right there."

"Rematch?" I ask after she heads to the back corner.

"Yeah. She challenges me to one every time we're somewhere with a table. She's convinced one day she'll beat me."

Once we have our drinks, we join her. I sit on a tall stool against the wall that gives me a good vantage point of both Lachlan in action, and the balls on the table.

Ha. Balls.

I blame that dirty thought for the inappropriate chain reaction that follows as I watch Lachlan bend over the pool table to take his next shot—one leg on the ground, the other along the edge. The view is mouthwatering. He banks the shot, and the cue ball ends up kissing the fourteen between the cushion and the ten ball. While Corrine walks around the table, figuring out her shot, Lachlan settles against the wall a few feet from me.

I want him to lean against me while he waits for his next turn. I want to kiss him and tell him what a great shot he made.

And if he were any other man—or woman—I was dating, I wouldn't hesitate to do exactly that.

But our relationship isn't public yet.

And on top of that, tonight his whole demeanour screams *don't touch*.

He's going out of his way to avoid being physically close to me.

And as the night goes on, that begins to really irk me.

"It's about time you got your long-lost bestie on the ice, Ross," Corinne says after she misses sinking the three ball in the corner pocket.

Lachlan just shrugs and lines up his next shot.

I know that's all he can really do, but there's a part of me that's thinking what the fuck?

Is this what every hockey night is going to be like? We're best buds from way back?

All that talk about wanting to be with me, dragging me back in…Does he only mean within the four walls of his house?

I jam those thoughts down, take a long swig of my beer, and survey the room.

Tate is busy chatting up a couple of hot women at the bar.

Lachlan wins a few minutes later, but only because he was the first to sink the eight ball. He plays Max next and gets his ass handed to him in short order.

"Hey Donovan, if you ever get tired or doctoring, you could always hustle pool."

Max chuckles. "I'm sure Violet would one hundred percent support that as a career change."

"It never hurts to have a back-up plan."

Lachlan's words prick at me, even though I know he's only joking around with Max. Even out of context, I don't like that he hedges his bets. I don't want to be a secret, and I don't want to think about my boyfriend having back-up plans.

I stand up and drain my beer. "Are you just about ready to go?" I ask him.

He gives me a curious look, then shrugs. "Yeah, sure."

He finishes his drink, we settle our tabs, and we say our goodbyes.

Once we're in his car, he turns towards me. "Are you okay?"

"No, I'm not." I take a deep breath and let it all out, because fuck it. "What happened to wanting a relationship that involves me? Tonight, you seemed to go out of your way to make sure I'm known as your best friend."

"But you are my best friend."

I'm a hell of a lot more than that. "I fuck you, Lachlan. Don't distract from that point. I'm not comfortable with being gentleman friends for life."

He nods, his face pulling tight. "I hear that. I just think...they don't need to know the details of our relationship."

No, not right now.

"I thought we were on the same page about that. Beth has been really clear about not wanting anyone to find out."

I don't bother to point out to him that the last time she said anything like that was back in May. A lot has changed since then, and I'm not sure Lachlan's noticed.

BETH

I END up staying at Lachlan's every night for nearly two weeks. By the middle of July, I've taken over a third of his closet with work clothes, and I find myself standing in the middle of his bedroom with a laundry basket of yoga pants and t-shirts, wondering if I'm accidentally moving in, one piece of clothing at a time.

I probably shouldn't do that.

Hugh stays here, too, but his clothes live at his apartment. He brings an overnight bag in from his car every night, and departs with it in the morning.

"Huh," I say to myself as I dump the laundry basket on the bed. "That's interesting."

So is talking out loud when nobody else is home. Interesting, crazy...

I fold my clothes neatly.

Then I look at the dresser.

No.

I dig my bag out from under the bed, where we kicked it a few days ago after I unloaded yet another pile of clothes for my extended love nest stay.

I put all my clean laundry in it.

I don't touch the stuff in the closet, because it's already neatly hung up.

Then I resolve to sleep at my own place tonight. Lachlan has a night shift, the first of four in a row.

Hugh is working days.

If he wants, he can stay at my place, too.

He can bring his duffle bag with him, and take it in the morning, and in between he can give me lessons in appropriate boundaries.

I END up staying at my apartment all week, and by the time Friday rolls around, I miss Lachlan's place.

I miss his king-sized bed and being sandwiched between two big, warm bodies.

I still love my neighbourhood, though, so on my last morning there for the next little while, I decide to walk to work. I leave extra early so I can loop around to my favourite bagel place, and take my time strolling toward the Hill. And I'm glad I do, because on the way I pass a For Sale sign on a house that's way beyond my budget.

But I just happen to know someone who's in the market.

Jack Benton, who came to Ottawa and had a secretive meeting with the prime minister—way more off the record than I was expecting. But then the news broke that he's selling the Lumberjacks, and the pieces started to fall into place.

He's moving to Ottawa to join the government, and he's going to need a place to live.

I take a picture of the stunning modern house, all glass and wood and dark grey panels, and fire off an email from my phone. This place has *billionaire-who-wants-to-be-close-to-everything* written all over it.

From: Beth Evans
To: Jack Benton
Subject: A house I would definitely look at if I were you

This is the nicest house I've seen for sale in The Glebe, fyi.
Unless you want an estate outside the city? And feel free to tell
me to mind my own business, but I like real estate. I helped
Max Donovan find a house when he moved here.

WHEN I GET TO WORK, Lachlan is sitting at my desk.

"What are you still doing here?" I ask with a happy smile, setting my coffee in its spot before I hang up my purse on its hook.

"Thought I'd say good morning before I head home to sleep."

I wink at him. "Good morning."

"Ships passing in the night..." he trails off as my phone rings, and we switch spots.

It's an unknown number, so I answer it with the formal Office of the Prime Minister of Canada spiel.

"That's quite a mouthful," a warm, rich voice says in my ear. "Jack Benton. Is this Beth?"

"It is. Hey Jack," I say as I hold up my finger for Lachlan to wait. He glowers at me, and I mouth, *I love you* before continuing. "Did you get my email? I just happened to see the For Sale sign go up on my walk to work this morning, and I thought of you."

In my ear, Jack laughs. "You walk to work?"

"Of course, it's great exercise. We can walk together, if you'd like." I'm teasing, and mostly for Lachlan's benefit. He looks like steam is going to shoot out of his ears any second.

On the phone, Jack makes a noncommittal noise. "I think your Mountie might object."

"Quite possibly." I press my lips together to keep from smiling.

Lachlan's not going to like that Jack's figured it out. I do, though.

"Would it be presumptuous to ask you to go and do a walk through of the house with a real estate agent? I can't get back to Ottawa for a few weeks. But if you like it…"

"You would buy a house sight unseen?"

"You'd see it for me. And if it doesn't suit my purposes, then it's an investment property."

If Sasha Brewster's shopping habits ever shocked me in the past, this has just blown that out of the water. "Uh…sure? Yes, I could do that for you."

"Great. I'll set something up and have the agent contact you directly."

He hangs up without another word, and I set the phone back in the cradle.

Lachlan crosses his arms and frowns again. "Date with Jack?"

I don't like how he says that. And I don't like that he's said it here. I give him a warning look which he totally ignores, so I get up and gesture for him to follow me into the copier room.

"What are you doing?" I whisper when we're around the corner.

"What was that little smile about?"

Damn it, he didn't miss that. "Well…" Shit. No secrets, and we agreed to talk about things. "Jack guessed that I'm yours. When I said we could walk to work together—which was a joke, by the way—he said my Mountie might object."

"I do," he growls. "But what the fuck is he doing asking about your personal life?"

"It just happened in the course of the conversation. Is it a big deal if he knows we're together?"

Lachlan shakes his head in disbelief. "He doesn't know about Hugh."

Oh. Shit. But… "I get that you're wanting to be protective of Hugh—I do, too—but deniability only goes so far."

"Deniability? You didn't even try. You were too busy flirting with Jack Benton to think about the impact of this."

Oh, he didn't just say that. Fuming, I twist away from him.

He catches my arm and spins me around, pressing me against the wall. "That was a jerky thing to say," he says quietly, then takes a deep breath. "I just…"

I nod. Yeah. "Lots of minefields to navigate in a secret relationship."

He touches my cheek, a light brush of his fingertips that still lights me up inside. His gaze drops to my mouth.

"Not here," I whisper.

"I know," he says, leaning in. He hovers there, not quite kissing me, for agonizing seconds before stepping back.

From around the corner—dangerously close—Gavin calls out my name. "Beth?"

We leap apart and I stride back in the direction of my desk, bumping right into the PM as he rounds the corner.

He looks at me with a frown, then slides his gaze past me and his frown deepens. "Lachlan?"

"Yes, sir."

"I thought you left a while ago."

I clear my throat. "We were just discussing Violet's baby shower. Lachlan was under the mistaken impression he wasn't coming, but of course he is."

Gavin nods slowly. "Okay. Maybe not the most pressing conversation?"

"Right. I should get back to work."

I slide past my boss. From behind me, I hear him awkwardly tell Lachlan that of course he should come to the shower.

And now I've made another complication.

Fantastic.

I'M STILL WOUND up about this by the time lunch comes around, so I use the excuse that Gavin didn't bring anything either to run out to a sandwich shop. I need fresh air.

I need perspective.

I get a sandwich, but no perspective.

I feel all tight and confused inside, and I think I've got that mostly locked down until Hugh shows up at my desk at three and finds me furiously blinking back hot, stupid tears.

I will not cry, I will not cry... But then I take one look at his worried face and know that's a losing battle.

I jump up and head to the copier room again, this time with a fistful of work because I need an excuse to be hiding back there lest I'm caught again.

Hugh is hot on my heels.

"You don't need to follow me," I mutter. "I'm fine."

"You just burst into tears at your desk."

"Burst is an overstatement. I got momentarily overwhelmed. I'm fine now, and I have work to do."

"That can wait a minute." His hand comes down on top of the photocopier lid. "Look at me. What's going on?"

"Lachlan and I had a weird fight this morning." I sniffle and Hugh grabs a box of tissues off the supply shelf. He rips it open and hands me one. "Thanks."

"What was the fight about?"

"Jack Benton guessed that we're together."

"The three of us?"

"No. Just Lachlan and me. I mean, he..." I huff out a breath. "He called Lachlan 'my Mountie'. And I didn't deny it. Lachlan was furious."

"Aw, beautiful." Hugh pulls me into his chest. "He is your Mountie. I get it. I wouldn't want to deny that, either."

"I'm sorry," I say, weeping into his chest. "I don't know what language to use here."

"I know. It's a steep learning curve, this poly thing. We'll figure it out."

He cups my cheek and leans in, brushing my mouth with his.

And because I have the worst luck in the world today, that's when the door opens.

We freeze.

Someone clears their throat, and I just want to die. I can't even hide behind Hugh because we're standing sideways to the door. Whoever is right there just got an eyeful of an undeniable embrace.

"I was wondering if you had the Stats Can report," Gavin says dryly.

This is isn't happening.

"It's copying." I spin around, not making eye contact with the PM. "Or it will be when I hit this button." I slam my hand down on the copier display and with an ugly whine, it comes to life.

Ch-chunk. Whirrr. Whoosh. Slide.

The noises of a photocopier make the most surreal soundtrack to one's personal life being painfully revealed to one's boss.

Gavin's not going away, either. "Beth, can I talk to you for a minute?"

I close my eyes. This isn't happening. "No."

It comes out in a harsh snap. Oops. When I open my eyes again, Gavin's giving me an incredulous look. "Excuse me?"

And I've officially had it with men. "No. You can't speak to me." I gesture away from the copier room. I'm not sure if I'm pointing to his office or not, but the shoo-ing is clear. "Unless you want to fire me for kissing my boyfriend, this is none of your business. With all due respect."

He swings his head to Hugh, who's had the very good sense to stay quiet. Then Gavin looks back at me. "Uh..."

On second thought, maybe we should do this in his office. Or not at all.

Yes, not at all would be my first choice.

"Your boyfriend?" The door closes, but Gavin's still on the wrong side of it. This side. And the photocopier room is not big enough for the three of us. He gives Hugh a pointed look. "May I?"

Hugh, bless his heart, doesn't move. "May you what? Sir?"

Gavin shakes his head. "I don't even know. Have a moment alone with my assistant, maybe?"

Would this be less awkward if Hugh gave us some space? Yes, I think so. I nod at him and he ducks outside.

Gavin scrubs his hand over his face. "I can't believe I'm asking this, but...what about Lachlan?"

"It's complicated."

"I'm getting that."

"Today has been a weird confluence of events that dragged some personal stuff into work, but I swear we haven't done anything here, ever, and—"

"Ever? How long have you..." He holds up his hand and shakes his head. "Never mind. I don't want to know. Are you okay?"

I nod. "I'm fine."

"You know we love you."

"Yeah." I give him a weak smile. "Thank you."

"And...you know I understand a thing or two about love trumping propriety. Right?"

Another nod. "Uh huh."

"All right. We can stop talking about this now." He stops and looks at the door, where Hugh is, I'm sure, standing very stiffly on the other side. "Is Hugh coming to the baby shower, too?"

My eyes go wide. "Yes. Maybe."

He nods. "Okay. Good. They should both be there. That's... good. If you're happy."

"I'm happy."

"Excellent." He points to the copier. "When that's done, I'd like to read it."

"Definitely."

We bobble our heads in nervous nods at each other, and then he leaves.

Hugh steps back inside and closes the door. "Well?"

"Oh my God. I think he knows about us. All of us. And I think it's fine."

He swears under his breath. "It's not going to be fine for Lachlan."

"But…"

He shakes his head. "We need to think about how we're going to tell him."

Oh, for fuck's sake. I'm so over this emotional rollercoaster. I grab my photocopies of the Stats Can report. "Fine. Can you pick up something for dinner tonight?"

"Sure."

"Great." I stomp back to my desk. Domestic bliss, triangle-style, is some complicated shit.

LACHLAN

I WAKE up at six in the evening to an empty house and a terrible mood.

I look at my phone, but there's no message from Beth. Nothing from Hugh, either. And my mood is just weird enough that I don't want to reach out to them, either.

I throw myself in the shower, hoping to steam the prickly feelings away, but they persist.

Doubts slam around in my head, and my fucked up sleep this week isn't helping, either.

When Beth lets herself in, I'm surprised to see her. "Hey," I say quietly, joining her in the front hall.

She gives me a tight hug. "I'm sorry about earlier."

"Me too." I take a deep breath. "But the thing is—"

She holds up her hand. "Hang on to that thought. Hugh's on his way over and we can talk once he gets here. He's picking up dinner."

"Okay."

She licks her lips, and I suddenly realize she's nervous. "What's going on?"

She shakes her head. "Nothing."

"Nothing?"

"It can wait."

"It can wait isn't the same as nothing."

"Right."

"Beth." I growl a warning, and she slips past me, heading for our bedroom.

Our room. When had I started thinking about it like that?

I follow her and lean against the door as she strips down. Maybe we should fuck. Hard and fast. I'd bend her over the bed and stroke between her legs until she was wet for me, and then I'd bottom out. Fill her up and make her forget whatever the not-nothing-shit-that-can-wait.

She pulls on shorts and a tank top that apparently live in my dresser.

I head to the kitchen and put on the kettle. I feel like tea.

Ten minutes later, I've made tea that I'm not drinking, and she's in the living room holding a book she's not really reading.

Fantastic.

The front door opens and in strides Hugh, carrying takeout.

Beth leaps up and gets in front of him.

He gives her a lazy grin. "What's going on? Did you start talking before I got here?"

The tension in my brain snaps. "You talked about this already together, but she can't bring it up until you're here?"

"Whoa." He sets down the takeout bag and reaches for me. "Come on, that's uncalled for."

"No." I jerk away from him and grab my keys. "I'm not ready for whatever emotional intervention you two have planned."

"Lachlan!" Beth sounds shocked, but really, did I not project clearly that I wasn't up for this?

Fuck.

I mumble something about needing space—and no, the irony isn't lost on me, even as I see red—and I head outside.

I'd parked on the street so Beth could have the garage. Maybe deep down I'd known I'd want to be able to escape.

Fuck.

I jump in my car and just start driving.

This is not how I react, ever. Storming out is impulsive. And stupid when you do it from your own house, and realize you've got no idea where to go…or who to talk to about an unorthodox love life.

Gavin's not an option. Our professional relationship has already been on rocky ground..

If he gets even the slightest whiff I've upset Beth, I can kiss my career goodbye. Probably worse than that, even.

Besides, he's freshly married and the last thing he needs is his lovelorn chief of security on his doorstep intruding on marital bliss.

I briefly consider Tate. Sure, he's a total player and probably the least qualified person I know to give relationship advice. But he's kinky, and not committed to the over-romanticized notion of Team Beth-and-Lachlan. Or if I fuck this up, Team Beth-and-Screw-Lachlan. Then I remember he's away.

After aimlessly driving Ottawa's streets, I find myself at Max and Violet's.

It's twilight and their lights are on, so I assume someone is home and awake, but can't seem to get my ass out of the car.

I should leave. Dropping by unannounced is rude.

Particularly so when they're in the final countdown days to a baby arriving.

But Max at least knows something about how I feel about Beth. And like Tate, he's also seriously kinky, so he's not likely to balk at Hugh being part of the relationship equation.

I'm still having a heated debate with myself when there's a knock on my window.

I look over to see Max standing there, gesturing for me to open it.

"You've been sitting there with the engine running for the last ten minutes and you look like shit."

Jesus. I'm a fucking planet killer on top of everything else. "Sorry, I should go," I say as I reach for the gear shifter, ready to put it in reverse and back out of the driveway.

He shakes his head. "Not in the state you're in. Get your sorry ass inside. Violet's asleep and I need a distraction. You're it." He crosses his arms and stands there. Waiting.

I'm not going to win this one, and deep down, I don't really want to, so I close the window, turn off the ignition, and follow him.

He leads me through the house to the kitchen. "Have a seat," he says, pointing towards the table. "Beer?"

I pull out a chair and nod. "Yeah, thanks."

He grabs a couple of bottles from the fridge and sets one in front of me, then sits in the spot adjacent as he twists the cap off. "So, what have you done to fuck things up with Beth?"

I twist the cap off my own beer and stare for a minute. "It's complicated."

He chuckles. "It usually is."

"And unconventional."

Max's head perks up and he leans forward. "Oh, really?"

Part of me is screaming to get the fuck out, this is a mistake. The rest of me knows I have to suck it up, to accept Max's help—however much he needs to make me uncomfortable in the process.

But that screaming fear is familiar. It's the same thing I ran scared from a decade earlier.

And if I'm going to sort this out, we're going to have to start being honest with people we trust. Hugh deserves that much. He deserves the moon, but this is what I can control.

"It's not just Beth I've fucked things up with."

Max doesn't even blink. "Hugh?"

I do a double-take. As much as he's not shocked, I am doubly so that he's figured it out. "How did you guess?"

He gives me a bland look. "I had an inkling right from the start. I was there the day he arrived for a meeting with Gavin, remember?"

Yeah. I remember that day only too well. I hadn't realized how transparent I was at the time.

"But it was really a combination of things over time. Some glances at the wedding, and then that tension after hockey last week."

Shit.

If Max has guessed… Does the prime minister know? *If he does, then he hasn't said anything, has he?*

Max leans back in his chair. "Are you getting serious with one of them?"

"Both."

"Oh."

I take a long swig of my beer. "It's not what you think. There's no cheating involved."

"Oh? Is it kinky?" He asks that with a joyful wiggle of his eyebrows, and to my surprise, it helps.

Kinky sandwiched between bi and poly, in the crazy layers that make up my sexual identity. And as I think about that question, all the pieces fall into place.

It took an affair with Hugh for me to fully realize myself as bisexual. But I'd run scared. That taste of insanity—too addictive, too perfect—was more than I could handle.

But I'd had that taste. And I couldn't ignore it. Pretending I hadn't been changed was impossible, so instead of retreating, I'd forged ahead in the only way I could find that matched my rule-and-order identity. Kink, with all its protocol and agreed upon boundaries.

And now I've got Hugh again, this time with Beth.

There is no order to loving Hugh.

No rules for how wild and hot Beth makes me.

Zero protocol that addresses how to carry on as if falling for them both hasn't altered me on a cellular level.

I nod slowly. "Yeah, it's kinky. And so much more."

Before I know it, the whole sordid mess is spilling out. From Moose Lake through to me walking out on them this evening.

Credit where it's due, Max hasn't said a word. Not so much as a judge-y expression.

When I finally finish, my bottle is empty and I've been spinning it around it my hands for a few minutes. I tap it against the tabletop and lift my hands in the air. "So that's it. That's where we're at. I thought I could handle it, but then I blow up at Beth about Benton being on to us—and only half of us."

"You didn't blow up just now at me, though. Maybe cut yourself some slack? Because, yeah. I'd say that definitely qualifies as complicated and unconventional." He goes to the fridge and grabs another beer and holds it up. "Are you good for another, or...?"

I am fine to have a second, but I shake my head. "No, thanks. I'm fine."

"Can I get you something else, then? Pop, juice, water?"

"Actually, water would be good."

Max opens his beer and sets the bottle on the table, then brings me a glass of water.

"Don't think about it, just spit out the first thing that comes to mind. What do you want? Or maybe I should ask, who do you want?" he asks.

"I'm greedy. I want them both."

"Then, what's stopping you?"

Shit. When he says it like that, I can't believe it's that simple. "I gotta go."

"No shit. I mean, good luck."

"Thanks." I'm going to need it. I have some world class grovelling to do.

53

HUGH

Lachlan's been gone for a few hours. Officially, I'm not worried. I understand a man needing some space. I've been that man more than once.

Unofficially, I don't like this. It's not a good sign that every time we hit a speed bump, we break a little bit.

Beside me on the couch, Beth sighs. Okay, *we* don't break. Lachlan and I are struggling with the dynamics here way more than she is. Even with her teary frustration earlier, she's unwavering in her knowledge that she wants this relationship, complicated dynamics and all.

"What are you thinking?" she asks without looking up from her book.

"That you're tough, and amazing, and we probably don't deserve you."

She closes her book and gives me a solemn look. "How do we make this work?"

I gesture for her to climb into my lap. Time for some tough love, with love.

I slide a strand of her hair between my fingers, then tuck it behind her ear. "Maybe we don't."

"No. That's not an acceptable answer." I love the way she says it. Like she'd take on a million-man army to defend our love.

"You can't force him to be something he's not."

"He's not *not* anything."

That's where she's wrong. "He's a private guy. He's never going to be one for public displays of affection. He's always going to want to be a homebody, open and honest with us here, but closed to everyone else out there."

"The world at large, sure, maybe. But our friends? That's just not feasible."

"Which loops us back to, maybe this won't work in the long run."

"No!" she snaps, and I reel back from the intensity of it. "We just went through this bullshit a few weeks ago with you." She growls and throws her hands in the air, and I'm not sure if I should laugh or hide. She's *fierce*. "Fuck, Hugh. This is not cool."

Yelling, cursing, wild eyes…I've never seen this side of Beth before.

I love it. A lot, but now's probably not the best time to tell her that. "You're right."

"*I'm going to kick his ass*," she says mockingly. "That's what he said about you. And yet here he is, needing his own ass kicked."

"No, what he needs is…a dinner party. We need to have someone over who won't even blink at the three of us being in a relationship. Then we can do a bigger group event, maybe something kinky—or we could go dancing at a gay club."

"Yes," she says, her voice lifting with hope. "He'd love to go dancing, I think. And we have the baby shower, too. That'll be a safe space. The guest list is all friends from the hockey team."

"Baby shower?"

"Max and Violet's. Gavin asked if you'll both be there."

A baby shower as a coming out party for a polyamorous triad. The PM's social circle definitely is kinkier than I'd ever suspected. "Sounds like a plan."

Outside, a familiar sounding engine rumbles to a stop.

Beth gets up and moves into the hallway, wringing her hands.

The front door opens and Lachlan stalks in.

"You're back," Beth says.

He gives her an intense look. "Yeah."

"Are you okay?"

"No."

"Lachlan…"

"I'm here. I'm not okay, but I'm here, because I want to be with you. Both of you."

I hang my fingers off the top of the door frame to keep from grabbing him and throttling him to within an inch of his life. The wild look in his eye tells me that he's come around, even though he's still shaken.

He sets his keys on the hall table and falls to his knees in front of Beth. "I've loved you from the day we met, with my entire heart, even when it fucking hurts. Even when I thought it was doomed, I've never wavered in how much I love you. But that scares me, too, I'm not gonna lie." His voice cracks, and he looks at me.

I stay where I am, stretching off the door.

He holds my gaze as he continues. "I've loved this fierce once before. Never stopped, not for ten long years. And I wasn't smart enough to get my shit together back then. Might not be fearless enough now, but I trust you'll push me into the light."

I drop my arms and squeeze my hands into fists. He's the most fearless man I've ever known. "You're honest with yourself," I say hoarsely. "That's more important than anything. Just because you want to keep things private doesn't mean you're living in fear. Take it from one who knows."

"I don't want to keep things private," he says roughly. "I ended up at Max's house. He'd already guessed, in a way. Although he thought I was just torn between the two of you. But I told him everything. And he didn't even blink."

"Oh good," Beth breathes, and sinks to the floor in front of him. "Because…"

She trails off and looks at me. Okay, apparently we're doing this on the floor in the front hallway.

I join them, sitting with my back against the wall, and I take Lachlan's hand. "The prime minister may have stumbled across Beth and me making out in the copier room today."

"What?" He tries to jerk back, and I hold on tight.

"Not making out," she adds hastily. "A kiss. A sweet, chaste, make-me-feel-better kiss."

"I said making out to soften the truth," I tell her.

She rolls her eyes. "That's not how healthy communication works."

"Well, I'm a newbie at this. Sue me."

She kisses me instead, rising on her knees to press her lips first against my mouth, then Lachlan's. Then she crawls into his lap. My hold-him-down strategy, taken to the next level. "Here's the thing," she whispers, giving him her sweetest look. "He kind of guessed, too. Although he jumped right over being torn and just assumed I was happy dating you both. I didn't tell him every-thing, though. That's not the kind of relationship we have."

He blinks at her, then laughs under his breath. "So Max knows. And Gavin knows. Which means Violet and Ellie know by now."

I take a deep breath. "I guess we should invite Tate over for dinner then."

"And Sasha," Beth says. "But not the same night."

"God, no," Lachlan says, brushing his lips against her temple. "Are you okay with this? For real? You're basically coming out as polyamorous. We can't be pushy about that."

"No, it's okay," she says. "I'm not ashamed of loving you both. I don't want Sasha to grill me six ways from Sunday about how we have sex, because that's personal, but I want to call you my boyfriends."

"Partners," Lachlan says swiftly. "I'm too old to be anyone's boyfriend."

A slow, happy smile crawls up my face. "Partners."

Beth makes a happy sigh and bites her lip as she nods. "Yeah," she whispers. "That's exactly what we are."

54

BETH

WHILE 24 SUSSEX is being transformed by caterers for what has probably turned into the most elaborate baby brunch ever, we're at the arena watching the guys play an early Sunday morning game of hockey.

I'm wearing a toque that Ellie has knit me for the occasion.

Even though Ottawa is suffering through an end-of-July heat wave, inside the hockey arena it's positively chilly, and the hat is appreciated.

It's a beaver, just like Ellie's and Violet's hats.

But my beaver is holding two…sticks.

Sure, let's call them sticks.

I'm only wearing this hat for hockey, and only because we're carefully under RCMP guard that ensures nobody will ever take a picture of it.

Except Ellie, who's got her phone out.

"Am I blushing?" I mutter to Violet.

"Yes," she says, making a wincing face. "Okay, I think my uterus has officially run out of space."

Ellie swivels towards her with the phone and Violet winks at me.

I'm glad I got her an extra-awesome baby present. She deserves it. They've both been really awesome about welcoming me to their Frisky Beavers club.

And since Sasha has been in Greece on a research trip, I've avoided having to answer any nosy questions about sex.

Ellie's phone vibrates while she's trying to take a video of Violet's belly. Speak of the devil... "Sasha!" she says as she stands up, the phone pressed to her ear. "Are you here?"

She waves her hand in the air as a polished blonde head bobs into view beside the player's bench on our side.

Sasha climbs up to us. She looks suspiciously tan for someone who was on a research trip. She squees over Violet's belly first, then hugs Ellie, and finally me.

Then she stops, her hands on my shoulders, and she does a slow scan up to my hat. "Wait a second," she says, and I hate how smart she is.

There's no need to explain my relationship to her. Sasha figures it out from the hat.

"You're a Frisky Beaver now too, eh?" Her eyes light up. "Two players? You dirty, dirty girl. Lachlan and... Hugh?"

I don't even get a chance to answer before she plops onto the bench beside me and claps her hands together. "I want to know everything."

"No."

"But—"

"I love you, but no."

She's undeterred. "I brought ouzo back from Greece."

I giggle at the reminder that Lachlan hates liquorice. "That would make it hard for me to kiss—" I groan as she cackles and rubs her hands together.

"Excellent. Keep going. I'm in such a dry spell lately, I need to live vicariously."

"No. Tell us about your research trip. Was it on a beach?"

It turns out it was, and her tan is a justified fringe benefit of learning about micro businesses that pop up in depressed economies.

And by the time she's done filling us in, the game is over and there are sweaty men to kiss.

Sasha watches me kiss Hugh, then tips her head to the side. "Are you the one that doesn't like liquorice?"

He howls and points at Lachlan. "Nah. That's all him."

"Good." She nods at him. "I brought back some ouzo. We can celebrate you making my friend happy with some shots at brunch."

He throws his arm around her and kisses her cheek. "We're going to be best friends, aren't we?"

That makes Corinne and Max guffaw, and Lachlan growls something that I miss, so Hugh kisses him, too. It's a quick peck, but it still makes my heart skip a beat, because it feels so right.

"And now back to our place," Ellie announces. "We have parents-to-be to toast."

"With ouzo!" Sasha and Hugh cheer at the same time.

We do toast them with ouzo, as well as champagne and some rye that won the world's best whiskey competition last year.

By mid-afternoon, everyone is pretty giggly, even the mom-to-be who has been indulging in chocolate covered strawberries instead of champagne.

Violet and Max are surrounded by a sea of pastel tissue paper and at least three gifts from each person in attendance.

Just as Max starts to muse about loading up the back of their vehicle, the catering staff sweep in and do that for him.

Ellie winks at me. That was my idea, and it's a good one.

"To the shower planning committee." Max raises his glass. "Excellent job. And I'm sure Lachlan's thrilled at the lack of dildos."

Beside me, Lachlan snorts. "This way we could take pictures."

Max winks. "Right. Speaking of dildos..." He smiles indulgently at Violet and I try hard not to blush. "I've decided to—

temporarily—close my basement dungeon. Well, it's permanently closing in my basement. But I've decided to look for a safe and secure separate location. So while we're naming our baby, maybe you could all put your heads together and think of a good name for a private sex club. Because as my gift to you all today…I'm extending lifetime memberships. If you'd like, of course."

My mouth drops open, then I look at Lachlan. "Yeah?"

Oh, yeah.

I can't wait.

55

HUGH

August

I BLAME the continued heat wave for my genius idea go dancing. Lachlan immediately frowns when I stop by his office to suggest it, which just turns me on.

I'm incorrigible.

And because he secretly wants to go out, by the end of the day he's got the name of a club Oliver recommends.

When we get home that night, we find Beth in the bedroom, talking to Sasha on her iPad. Beth is wearing leather leggings and a lace bra. I approve, but I'm guessing that's not her complete outfit.

I lean against the doorway to the bedroom and watch as she tears into the closet. She's taken over most of it. Lachlan's moved most of his clothes upstairs to the smallest, previously empty bedroom. Mine are slowly migrating here as well.

We haven't formally talked about moving in together, but it's happening in an organic way.

Case in point: Beth is so comfortable here that the bedroom looks like a bomb's gone off in it.

She holds up a bright blue shirt and Sasha shakes her head. "What about a skirt and boots?"

"You're showing your age, Sasha," Beth groans. "There is no way I'm wearing a mini skirt. I don't even own one."

"Do you want me to bring you some clothes?"

Beth glances over at me and flashes a quick smile. "No, they're already home. It's time to go. This is fine. I feel good in these leggings."

She pulls out a slinky red top and holds it against her body. "Hot?"

Hell yes, I want to say, but I won't interrupt. I do catch her eye as she spins, though. *Hot*, I mouth. She grins.

But apparently Sasha disagrees. "Yeah, it's sexy, but it's also literally hot. And then sweaty."

I laugh out loud and Sasha peers around. "Is that a man?"

Beth grins. "That's Hugh."

I walk into the camera view. "Sweaty? Gay men have *never* been known to like sweat."

Lachlan saunters in and joins us on screen. "Sweat? Yeah, we like that. Reminds us of sex."

Beth laughs and throws the red shirt at me. "I might still wear a dress. Okay, Sash, we're going. You can meet us there later if you finish your work."

"Later!" And the screen goes dark.

Beth puts her hands on her hips. "Leggings? Or a dress?"

Lachlan shrugs. "Up to you. We like dresses. Reminds us of sex, too."

He has a point. "You can wear whatever you want, beautiful."

"I need more warning next time," she says, her voice shaking as she grabs a black dress off her bed and tugs it over her head. Once she smooths it over her hips, she reaches under and pulls off the leggings. "I fail at being cool." She grabs a pair of boots from the floor and shoves them at Lachlan's chest as she stops in front of us. "Plus we have to clean this disaster up before we go, because when we get back, I want sex. Lots of sex."

We exchange an amused look over her head. "Yeah," Lachlan says. "We're good with this plan."

"Okay." She bounces on her toes. "I am excited. This is an awesome idea. It's just kind of sudden. I wasn't expecting this." She reaches for Lachlan's hand and squeezes his fingers.

"Oliver wouldn't have suggested this place if it wasn't safe for us to cut loose." Lachlan lifts her fingers to his mouth and kisses her hand gently. "And Hugh's obviously not straight, so he'll be popular with the cool kids."

I howl in mock outrage. "Although that's true. I can't play it straight like you can."

"This is just my natural uptight Gaelic nature," he says gruffly. "I'm not playing at anything."

I wink at him. "You're right. I help you put the *gay* in Gaelic."

"I don't need any help with that," he says stiffly, proving my point.

Beth rubs up against him. "You can both help me put the gay in something tonight."

I grab her wrist and spin her around, until she's wrapped in my arms and I can move against her, slinky hips to curvy bottom. "Like you?"

"Is that gay? I think not."

"It's not straight. Not the way I want to do it." I lick the curve of her ear. I'm fucking pumped to go dancing tonight. And to bring them home again. "I want us both inside you tonight. After dancing. Would you like that again? Lachlan in your ass, me in your pussy? Our cocks sliding back and forth against each other as we pump into you?"

"Maybe." She licks her lips. "Or...you could fuck Lachlan. It's been a while."

That's definitely gay. And hot. I want that, too.

"That's up to him," I say roughly.

He turns away, but I don't miss the hitch in his step. "I thought we were going dancing," he tosses back over his shoulder.

I look at Beth. Her gaze, like mine just was, is locked on his high, tight ass. And she's grinning like a Cheshire Cat. She didn't miss his reaction, either.

"You'll get your wish," I whisper to her. "And then we'll get you between us. The best of both worlds."

Instead of answering, she spins around in my arms and kisses me, eager and horny.

Through the front door window, there's a flash that interrupts us. Headlights sweep across the front of the house. Our taxi has arrived.

I squeeze her tight. Tonight's going to be something else.

THE BOUNCER *LOVES* BETH. He takes one look at her, then at us, and gives her a *you go girl* high-five. So the attitude is great. Not sure about their security standards, but that's what she's got us for.

Lachlan clears his throat. "Ross. My name should be on the list, party of three."

"Oh honey, it's all good. You could come here any night and get to the front of the line. Come on in." He pulls the door open and we head inside.

It's packed, which explains the line stretched down the block.

Excellent pick, Oliver. There's anonymity in crowds. And the music is great.

"Shall we get a drink?" I say, pointing toward the bar. "It might take a few minutes to get to the front of the pack."

Beth nods, and she's already dancing.

This was a good call. It'll be fun for Lachlan, but I think maybe she's the one who needs it most of all.

As for me, I've got them together. That's all I wanted. I'm a happy boy now.

By the time we get to the edge of the long bar, Lachlan's been eye-fucked three times and Beth is giggly over how it's affecting him.

"You're not jealous?" I murmur against her ear as the DJ slides between songs.

She shakes her head. "He only has eyes for us. It's all good. And he's *blushing*. He didn't blush when he helped rescue someone from nipple clamps at the play party."

Because that was service, and familiar. This is a stretch for him, even on his own, and we're making it that much more complicated and personal with the three of us being here together.

We need drinks, stat.

Beth bumps into the woman next to her, and swiftly apologizes. And somehow ends up making a new friend. "I'm Beth," she says sweetly. "And this is Lachlan. That's Hugh."

The other woman waves and introduces her girlfriend, but I don't catch their names as the music gets louder.

It doesn't matter, shots have arrived, and we tip them back.

"You three are adorable together," the lesbian on the right shouts. "Alpha male book ends." And Beth gets another *you go girl* high five.

Lachlan winks at them and tips back his shot. Then he kisses me, takes Beth's hand, and heads for the dance floor.

Our boy likes to dance after all. And we've got all night.

BETH

WE TUMBLE in the door just after three in the morning. We're sticky, and sweaty, and so turned on it hurts.

And I'm not tired in the least.

I start to unbutton Hugh's shirt because he's taking too damn long. He laughs and tries to help me, but I shoo him away. "Let me," I breathe. I bare his chest, and step back to admire him. "So hot."

He flexes for me, and I whimper.

"Shower?"

He shakes his head. "We've got big plans for you tonight, remember? Better to shower afterwards."

I shiver. "Right."

He goes to the dresser and pulls out a brown paper bag that he's put a bow on. "Present time."

Lachlan chuckles and sets his hands on my hips, bracketing me from behind as I reach for the dirty gift. The bag is surprisingly heavy for the size. "You're going to condition her to get wet every time she sees a ribbon."

Hugh's eyes light up. "That's genius. I'll increase the frequency of the presents."

My thighs ache at the thought—in a good way. I open the bag and pull out a large tub of lube. And there's nothing classy about it, either. **Anal Lube! Extra Slick!** it advertises. It's even got a pump top built in.

My cheeks must be scarlet. Lachlan brushes his lips over my flaming skin. "Still so sweet and vanilla at times, our Beth."

"This one is silicone," Hugh says. "I've been wanting to try it for a while. Tonight seemed like a good opportunity to give it a whirl."

Whirl. I can only imagine.

And when I do, I get pretty slick all on my own.

Lachlan pulls all the blankets and pillows off the bed as Hugh closes in on me, a wolfish predator on the prowl. He strips me down, then boosts me into his arms, wrapping my legs around his waist before he carries me to the bed's edge.

"Tonight is all about you," he says roughly as we tumble onto the mattress.

Lachlan joins us, crowding against me from the other side. Hugh cups my face, then turns me away from him, towards Lachlan. Presenting me to our lover for a kiss.

Our tongues tangle in a hot, wet slide as Hugh kisses the back of my neck and across my shoulder. He reaches around and cups my breasts, then eases me back so Lachlan can work down my body.

My nipples ache for his mouth, and when he moves from one to the other, I whimper at the loss. Before I can say I want his fingers there, Hugh's shifting out from behind me. I fall gently onto my back, arms flailing wide, and Hugh covers the peak that Lachlan just left.

Together they lick and pull and suck at my breasts until I'm writhing between them. Hugh breaks away long enough to grab the lube, then he returns his mouth to my chest. Blindly, he pumps some lube into his hand, then spreads that slickness into mine.

I reach for their cocks, and the lube really is extra something. Hugh goes back for more, and then he's sliding lube through my labia. I hardly need that, but as he strokes my folds, it feels... different. Like this lube might last a while. Like he has plans to fuck me until dawn, to take his time and keep me on the edge.

"Are you going to take turns inside me?" I'm all breathless. It would be embarrassing if, as I asked that, their cocks didn't flex together as if they share a dirty brain.

"Now we are," Lachlan says, kissing me hard. He rolls me towards Hugh, so I'm on my side, and I kiss the instigator of all this slippery fun.

Lachlan lifts my top thigh and nudges his erection up against my entrance. "Me first."

Heat flares through me. Okay. The first thrust is so slick, it's almost too much. I gasp at the unforgiving stretch, but as he rocks all the way into me, it feels too good to not beg for him more. "Again."

His hand tightens on my hip and he pumps his hips, three more ruthless thrusts before he slides out.

Oh, God. That's cruel. I practically crawl onto Hugh, pulling him inside me to replace that empty ache. He's thicker than Lachlan, so I get another squirmy press of male flesh inside me. Taking up space and laying down a claim.

Theirs.

Forever.

He takes his time, pressing in, then out. Grinding against my clit at the bottom of each thrust, and teasing my entrance when he pulls back.

Then it's Lachlan's turn again.

Then Hugh.

I'm dizzy by the time Lachlan bottoms out in my pussy again, and when I reach for Hugh, Lachlan is still inside me.

"Easy there," he whispers in my ear. "One at a time."

Hugh throbs in my hand. Then he takes his place inside me,

and when he's balls deep, he leans in and kisses me. Hard, demanding, and turned on. "Feels so good, rubbing up against Lachlan. Jockeying for position inside our woman. Sharing you like this. We're going to do this all night."

I whimper, and he eases out. We keep kissing as Lachlan takes me again.

Then Hugh again.

I'm shaking and so wet for them. I don't need lube at all, but it doesn't stop Hugh from reaching for the tub.

More lube.

More fucking.

In.

Out.

Lachlan.

Hugh.

And then Lachlan again, and Hugh doesn't get all the way gone.

My eyes go wide.

Lachlan's rubbing the crown of his erection against the bottom of Hugh's cock. And Hugh is still halfway inside me.

I try to roll my hips, but I'm trapped between them.

"You want that, beautiful?" His eyes are glazed over. I bet mine are, too. Lust hangs heavy in the air as he reaches between my legs and—

Ah.

Oh.

Lachlan lets out a strangle groan from behind me as Hugh coats them both with more lube, and then Lachlan presses in.

Past Hugh, and into me, stretching me wide.

I can't breath.

"You were built to take us both," Hugh says.

That's probably not true, but oh God, I want to believe him. Lachlan groans from behind me. He wants to believe it, too.

And as they work in and out of me, I realize I'm going to come.

Maybe it is true. Maybe I was made for them, to take me like this.

I need— "Clit," I manage to say, and Hugh gets his thumb there as they slowly pulse back and forth together.

Inside me, together.

Heat swirls and everything fades to a glossy, fantastic bright white as my climax begins. It's long and heady, sustained and wild. It rocks through my entire body and shatters my brain, my heart.

It destroys me, and it's perfect.

LACHLAN

I STOP at the grocery store on my way home to pick up celebratory foodstuff. Hugh and Tate are at Hugh's apartment right now, loading up his bed and his weight bench.

He's moving in. There's no reason for him to keep paying rent on his apartment, and he doesn't have that much stuff.

Beth's clothes have mostly moved in, but she owns her condo, and has a lot more furniture than we have space for. That process is going to take longer, but it doesn't matter. Maybe she'll keep her condo as an income property.

What matters is that all her pretty dresses are hanging in my closet, and she sleeps in my bed each night.

When I get home, Hugh's not back yet, but Beth is. She's out on the deck reading.

I stand at the back door and just watch her. She's stretched out on the lounge chair, her legs bare, and her skirt hiked up high on her thighs.

That's an invitation too tempting to pass up. I quickly put away the groceries, then pour myself a glass of the lemonade she's made, and head out to say hello.

She twists around when she hears the door. "How was shopping?"

"Quick. I got a watermelon for dessert."

"Mmm." She smiles and tips her face up to the sun. "Lemonade, watermelon, and a deck to read on. I love summer."

I lean down and cover her mouth with mine. "I love you," I whisper after I kiss her thoroughly.

I move around the chair and lift her legs so I can sit under them. I slide my hand up her thigh, and her eyes go wide.

"Your neighbours…"

"Our neighbours. And they can't see anything."

"Tate…"

"Isn't here yet. Let me make you feel good. Please?"

The sweet request always works on her. She sighs and relaxes into my touch. I stroke my fingers back and forth over the soft skin of her inner thighs, then higher. I hook the elastic edge of her panties and tug them aside.

She's wet for me already, soft and warm and slick. I revel in the plump, swollen feel of her flesh. I could touch her for hours, but we don't have time for that right now.

"Wider," I murmur, and she drops her far leg to the ground. My forearm slides against her close leg as I ease two fingers into her and roll over her clit with my thumb. "How fast can you come?"

She closes her eyes and arches her back. "Keep doing that and I'll come pretty fast."

My cock swells, making my pants tight as I fuck her with my hand. I watch with greedy eyes as her lips part, her cheeks flush, and her eyelids flutter.

Our beautiful woman.

Our Beth.

Ten years ago, I went to a tattoo parlour with Hugh and on a whim, got a compass tattoo.

"I love your ink," I told him. I meant, I love you, but I couldn't bring myself to say that.

"You should get something the next time I go in."

"Yeah." My mind started to spin.

And later, when I went with him to his favourite place for a touch up, I pulled out a sketch I had in my wallet.

"Could you do something like this?" I asked the artist.

"I can do exactly that."

"Man, that's awesome," Hugh said, leaning over me. His hip pressed against mine, his arm looped lazily around my shoulders.

"You should get the same one. We're both on the same path, after all. Searching for our true north."

"Yeah, yeah. Love it."

It took us ten years to find her.

As she trembles down from her orgasm, as I lick my fingers and watch her smile at me like a queen who has just been well served, I get an idea.

"Have you ever thought about getting a tattoo?" I ask.

Her eyes light up, then her gaze drops to my hip. She licks her lips. "Maybe."

"I have an idea…"

BETH

I STARE at the black ink sketch on the translucent paper in front of me.

"It's perfect," I breathe.

The North Star rising over the curve of the Earth.

The tattoo artist holds it up to my hip. "It'll sit right there, with the lines ending here and here." He points to my hip bone and lower down on my pelvis "Should take me a bit more than an hour. We can do it now, or you can book an appointment for next week."

I glance at Hugh, then Lachlan. We stopped in here on a whim, but we have the afternoon free. They're both grinning.

"I'll do it now," I say, my pulse fluttering.

"Sounds good. Have you eaten in the last few hours?"

I nod. "Just had lunch."

"Perfect. Fill out these forms while I get the sketch onto transfer paper, and then we'll get going."

That doesn't take long, and the next thing I know, he's prepping my skin. Then he presses on the transfer to outline the tattoo he'll copy in permanent ink. Oh wow, this is really happening.

He hands me a mirror. "Check that positioning for me."

I love it, and Lachlan and Hugh nod along.

The artist grins. "Okay. Time to take a deep breath and let's do this. Why don't you tell me about the sketch idea. Does this have a special meaning?"

Before I can answer, Lachlan takes my hand. "It sure does."

Hugh grabs a wheeled stool and takes up a position on the other side of me. "She's our North Star."

Okay, then. We're telling this stranger the whole story. I blush. "What they said."

The artist bobs his head. "Cool."

I blink. It is, but...no reaction? And then the tattoo machine touch my skin, dragging a dull, unforgiving slice of pain across my nerves, and I forget everything else. "Ahhhh..."

"You okay?"

"Uh..huh." I exhale roughly. "That's not what I was expecting."

"I'm working on the star first. It'll hurt more when I get to your hip bone."

Oh, goodie. But the next press isn't as bad, or it's exactly the same, and I know what to expect now. I breathe through it, and we fall into a pattern. Every few minutes, he wipes my skin before proceeding again. It doesn't that long at all for him to declare the star completed, and he shifts lower, right above my yoga pants now for the curve of the Earth's shell.

"My sister's in a polyamorous relationship," he says casually as he makes short, painful strokes for the islands that dot Northern Canada. I regret not going with the ocean there.

"Yeah? Cool," I grind out. It is, but my brain is pretty fuzzy right now.

He laughs. "Endorphins kicking in?"

"Uh huh."

Lachlan's phone vibrates in his pocket. He ignores it and keeps rubbing circles on my arm. It stops, then starts again.

"You can answer it," I whisper, and the tattoo artist lifts the tattoo gun off my skin.

"Do you need a minute?" he asks.

Lachlan shakes his head. "We're good. Whatever it is, it can wait."

But then on the other side of me, Hugh's phone vibrates—and then starts playing music.

"Oh shit," he says, his eyes going wide. "I mean, it's fine, keep going, dude, but…" He pulls out his phone and shows me the screen. Max's number. "I gave Max a ringtone because there's only one reason he'd call me."

"Oh my God." I gasp and wave my hand at him. "Answer the phone."

"Hey, Max," Hugh says, grinning at me. "What's up? No way. Cool news. Okay, well, we're in the middle of something, but we can be there in an hour or so."

"We can go now," I say, pushing myself up.

Lachlan presses my shoulder back to the table. "The baby will wait," he says, gesturing for the artist to continue.

Hugh hangs up and sits down again. "Baby's not here yet. We've got some time, but they're at the hospital, and Max thought we might want to do the classic hang out in the waiting room thing."

"I do!" I realize my voice has carried clear across the tattoo parlour, and I drop it back to a whisper. "Yes, I want to do exactly that. Let's go now."

The tattoo artist laughs. "Give me ten more minutes and you can leave with a finished tattoo, how does that sound?"

"Like torture," I moan, but I close my eyes and smile.

HUGH DROPS us at the front doors of the hospital and goes to find a parking spot. Lachlan and I head straight to the new mom and baby ward, and run into Sasha in the hallway. She's got a big bouquet of flowers.

"Oh, we didn't bring anything," I say. I don't know where my head is at, that's normally something I'd think of.

"On it," he says, pulling out his phone. He texts Hugh.

Lachlan: SOS need a teddy bear. And chocolate. From the gift shop?
Hugh: On it.

I giggle at the accidental echo of my men sounding so similar.

"Where do we go?" Sasha asks, and Lachlan is apparently a master at reading the confusing hospital signs, because he glances around and then points us unerringly toward the waiting room. We find an RCMP officer standing outside, and inside, Gavin and Ellie are relaxing in the plastic bucket seats. They jump up as we come in. Ellie and Sasha hug, Gavin shakes Lachlan's hand, and then they turn to me. I gingerly offer Ellie my non-bandaged side for a one-arm hug.

"I was getting a tattoo when we got the call. Have you had any further updates from Max?"

Ellie shakes her head. "But apparently Violet's contractions were right on top of each other when they came in. That's either a good sign, or excellent birth control."

I laugh again. Tattoos make me super giggly, because I'm pretty sure that any other time, talk of contractions would have me squirming in a not-at-all good way.

"Where's Hugh?" Gavin asks, and it blows me away that he's just so accepting of our relationship. Although I'm not sure why…but I appreciate it.

"Parking the car."

The next person to walk in the door is Violet's best friend Matthew, who we met at the baby shower, and his boyfriend, who he introduces but I miss the name.

Then Hugh arrives with a cute little teddy bear and an entire basket of chocolate options.

He sits on the other side of Lachlan from me, and Lachlan slings his arm across the back of Hugh's chair, squeezing his shoulder. "Find a spot okay?"

"The garage was mayhem, but someone pulled out just as I turned a corner, so we're right next to the elevator."

"Score."

Matthew's boyfriend leans in and the conversation veers into a parking garage construction debate.

I lean into Lachlan's arm and close my eyes.

"How's the tattoo?" he murmurs.

"Achy." I take a deep breath. I'm still spinning from the experience. How crazy that we walked in on a whim and now I'm branded like this.

As theirs.

I smile to myself, then glance up at my lover. "I can't wait to take the bandages off when we get home." And carefully get between my men, and their tattoos that will both point to mine.

"We'll have to be gentle," he says under his breath as he laces his fingers through mine.

My smile grows.

MAX APPEARS in the doorway an hour later. His eyes are bright, his hair is standing on end, and he's sporting the world's biggest shit-eating grin. "I'm a dad," he announces as we all stand up and crowd around him. "Violet's holding our son. My boy. I have a boy! His name is Noah. And I'm his dad."

Gavin throws his arms around his best friend, and there's a lot of back thumping. We all take turns congratulating him, then he tells us he'll be back in a few minutes with Noah—and we're allowed to look at him, but probably not touch, because while he likes us, that's his son and he doesn't care if that's paranoid.

It's the sweetest, most overwhelming thing I've ever seen.

My eyes are wet when he disappears again.

"A boy," Ellie says, wiping tears off her cheeks too. "How amazing."

Sasha's beaming. Her smile slips when Lachlan mentions that Tate isn't responding to messages to get his ass to the hospital, but then Max returns with a tiny, perfect baby wrapped in blue and white striped flannel, and nothing else matters.

Unlike Max and Violet, Noah's fuzzy head is fair. "I was blond as a kid," Max says, his voice full of marvel. "But I never thought…he's just so perfect."

I gently rub Noah's tiny foot. "And tiny."

"Do you want to hold him? I didn't think I could let him go, but maybe I could. For a second."

My heart explodes. "Could I?"

He nods, and carefully hands me the most precious eight-pound bundle in the world.

"Oh, my…" I press my lips together to try and keep from crying. "He's gorgeous, Max."

"That was all Violet's doing." He glances toward the door.

I gaze down at the baby, then carefully hand him to Ellie. She has the same here-take-my-ovaries expression on her face that I'm sure is painted all over mine. Sasha takes a quick cuddle, then it's Gavin's turn.

"Hey, little man," says the prime minister. "Ready to take on the world?"

I turn to smile at Lachlan, but the look on his face steals my breath, my smile, my entire heart. Then he tosses his arm around Hugh and hugs him tight. Both of their gazes are full of emotion.

One day soon, we'll talk about a baby of our own.

And she will be the luckiest baby in the world, to have three parents who love her to the moon and back.

TATE

I'M STANDING in the middle of the empty Senators locker room when my phone pings again.

Another text message, to go with the dozen others I haven't been able to reply to.

I pull the phone out and scroll through the last few updates.

Everyone is leaving the hospital now, letting the new mom and baby have some much needed rest.

I missed the gathering.

I head out to my truck. Damn it.

I drive back into the city. Instead of heading straight home, I park just off of Bank Street and head for my favourite coffee shop.

Any minute now, the news is going to break. This might be my last chance to soak up some adoring fan attention. Take some selfies, get some numbers of hot, easy hockey fans.

Can't wait to see you in nothing but my jersey, babe.

Works every time.

A couple of co-eds recognize me in line, and the attention soothes my soul like a sex balm. Yeah, honeys. Room for both of you in that jersey if you squeeze tight enough. Tits together. Cuddle up on my lap. That would make me feel better.

After we take a couple of good shots for Instagram and Snap-Chat and whatever else they know about and I don't because I'm old and broken and too damn expensive for my team—okay, now I'm reeling, the shock is wearing off—I excuse myself to order the coffee I came in for.

Might be my last in this city. Until I come back as just another guy who used to be famous here.

Didn't you use to play for the Senators?

Sure did. You'd look good in my Vancouver jersey, though.

Doesn't have the same ring to it, even if the Lumberjacks are heading into next year with a solid chance at the playoffs.

"So, like...throwing down with some barely legal puck bunnies is more important than celebrating your friend's new baby?"

I brace myself against the coffee bar and count backwards from ten.

I get to seven before I spin around and give Sasha Brewster my best don't-give-a-fuck-so-fuck-off smirk. "Bustin' balls as usual, I see."

She flips her perfect blonde hair and smirks right back. "Baby's adorable, by the way. A boy. They've named him Noah. And we all agreed you can't be left unsupervised with him until he's thirty-five."

"I'm a fine influence on children."

"You're a public menace." She flicks her wrist. "Go hang out with your afternoon bedmates. You're in my way and I have studying to do tonight. I need coffee."

"All work and no play makes Sasha a b—" I cut myself off, even though her expression doesn't change. "You know what? I was just meeting some fans. It's a free country and I wasn't doing anything wrong."

"I'm sure their parents will be thrilled to see a man old enough to be their father hanging on them."

"I'm not—" Shit. Quick math says that I am.

She taps her tongue against the top of her mouth and makes a sound like she's telling a horse to get going.

I see red. I move to the side, but I don't go bloody far.

I wait, patiently, quietly, until she's got her coffee, and then I follow her outside.

"What are you doing?"

"Following you home like a creeper," I say mildly, because the length of time it took for her to get her coffee was just enough time for my rage to simmer and re-focus.

She smirks again. We're smirk twins today.

But there's something else I recognize in her expression. She's fearless.

And for the first time in nearly a decade, I'm flooded with fear. I recognize that epic feeling of righteousness in her, and I want some of it back.

"You can't come up," she says confidently. "I don't entertain assholes."

"Entertain." I snort. "Is that what you call it when you have guys over to fuck?"

"I…" Only Sasha could turn a stumble over lewdness into an elegant pause. "Yes."

"Well I wasn't offering to bang you, but if you manage not to call me an asshole again, I'd be open to—"

"Tate." She stops in the middle of the sidewalk and does a quick glance around before continuing. "What the hell is going on?"

Two more things I like about Sasha Brewster.

No matter how much she doesn't like me, she does a quick check for curious onlookers, paparazzi, and recording devices before laying into me.

And secondly, her eyes lit up, just for a second, at the idea of fucking me.

I shrug. Then I take a deep breath and spill what's not going to be a secret for much longer. "I was traded an hour ago to the Vancouver Lumberjacks."

Her eyes go wide, then she does another quick surroundings check. Then she grabs my hand and starts walking.

She doesn't say anything, and neither do I.

It doesn't take long to get to a nice walk-up apartment, and we head upstairs.

I'm just enough of a pervert to hope this means I might get my dick wet. And enough of a realist to know she's taking serious pity on me.

A pity fuck…Jesus, I haven't had one of those since…ever.

That would be new and interesting.

No. Not where my head should be.

And it's not where she's going with this spontaneous coffee talk in her apartment, either. She opens the door and plunks herself into an armchair not really big enough for two.

Shame. I don't see a point in having furniture that's not big enough to get freaky on.

I take the couch.

"The Lumberjacks?" Her brain is clearly spinning. "That's Jack Benton's team. Did you know this was coming at the wedding?"

I shake my head. "No clue. And he's in the processing of selling the team. This decision was made quite recently, too. It's a long, complicated, stupid story."

About how I chose money over stability, and waived my no-trade clause because I thought I was safe.

There's a big lesson there, but I'm not feeling it yet.

"When do you go?"

"Soon. I need to find a place to stay, because I won't like whatever hotel the team has arranged. I have aless than a month before training starts, but I want to find a house."

"Do you need help with that? Maybe you could stay at Gavin's place." She snaps her fingers together. "No, you'll want to be closer to the arena, right?"

"Sasha."

"Of course, you won't want to buy right away, so maybe we can find you a sublet."

"Sasha."

"And—"

"Hey, Hot Stuff, settle down for a second. I don't need you to play real estate agent for me, but I appreciate the offer of help."

Her lips pull together in a surprised O.

I give her a weak smile. "What I really needed was someone to hear it from me first. To say it out loud. I'm being traded. Now that I've done that, I can move forward. It'll be fine."

She nods weakly. "Right."

We sit in silence for a bit. Then I give her a half-smile. "Sorry for calling you Hot Stuff."

"It's better than calling me a bitch."

Ah, so she hadn't missed that. "I stopped myself."

"It was in your head, though."

"Not really. No, seriously, I don't think you're…Jesus, Sasha, I promise you I don't think you're a bitch, not in a bad way. I think you're made of steel and you fucking turn me on like crazy when you pop your claws out."

Her eyes are huge now, and I do a quick mental replay of what I just said. Aw, shit.

"Ignore me," I say after clearing my throat. "I tend to just say shit like that."

"One night."

"Pardon?"

She looks outside, then back at me. "One afternoon."

"I don't follow." Except I think I do, and I think I'm in, but Sasha moves faster than I do.

"Never mind."

"You're talking about sex? I'm in."

She holds up her index finger. "I want it officially noted that I still don't like you."

"Noted."

"And you're okay with that?"

I grin. "Hot Stuff, I'm more than okay with that. If you want to tell me that you hate me while I'm balls deep inside you, you'll feel just how much I don't mind that kind of smack talk."

"This is a terrible idea," she whispers.

I stand up and peel off my t-shirt.

She nods, a wobbly, disbelieving, am-I-really-doing-this-with-him head bob. Then she points to the bedroom.

One afternoon.

Then I'm moving across the country.

What could go wrong?

———

———

Thank you so much for reading *Full Mountie*! **There are two epilogues for Beth and her men, so keep reading for those— they start on the next page!**

Tate's book is scheduled for August 2017! Keep in touch with us via our website to hear all about *Mr. Hat Trick*: www. friskybeavers.com

We invite you to sign up for our exclusive VIP mailing list there. Jack's book is coming, too…we have a lot of kinky men in power that need happy ever after endings.

~ Ainsley & Sadie

EPILOGUE 1

BETH

Two years later

IT'S BEEN ALMOST EXACTLY a year since I last walked out of Centre Block as an employee. And I'll be back soon.

But today, I'm sporting a visitor's badge, and because the security guards think my daughters are cute, they hung two badges on my double stroller, too.

"Ready to go visit Daddy?" I ask, but the rice crackers I gave them for the walk are still occupying their primary attention.

That'll change when we get to Lachlan's office.

I check my phone to see if Hugh has arrived, but there's no text yet. Right around the time the girls were born, he transferred off the PM's detail and now works on financial crimes out of RCMP HQ. It's a straight Monday to Friday job, with little overtime. Perfect for a new father, even if he gets to share that load with another dad.

Today we're going to sit in the House of Commons gallery and watch the PM introduce a bill legalizing polyamorous marriages.

I don't know if it will pass. I hope it does. I'd love to have a civil recognition of the fact that I've married two men. But the truth is, they're already my husbands in spirit and practice.

When we get to Lachlan's office, I park the stroller against the wall and unbuckle the girls.

Megan isn't walking yet, but she'll cruise for miles if she can hold on to something. I get her out first and stand her next to the stroller, putting her pudgy little hand on the side. "Here you go, my Meg. Hold on to that."

Ally waves her hands as I unbuckle her next. She's our little daredevil, and she's already taking some unsteady steps. Smaller than her sister, and fairer too, she looks like an innocent angel, too young to climb and tear things apart. I know better, and I make sure she's holding my hand firmly before I wiggle my fingers for Meg. "Let's go."

Before we can knock on Daddy's door, though, footsteps sound on the staircase from above. Fast ones, running, and that gets the girls' attention.

"Pah!" cries Meg as Hugh comes into view. "Pah! Pah!"

He gives us a blinding smile as he reaches us, and after giving me the world's fastest kiss on the mouth, he drops to his knees and picks up his daughters. "Papa's here."

Lachlan must have heard the commotion, because his door swings open and he spots us. "There you are."

Since Hugh has the girls, Lachlan hugs me.

"We've got half an hour or so before it's time to head to the gallery," he says, holding me tight as he reaches out so Ally can grab his finger. "Should we go upstairs and say hi to your godfather, girls?"

I DON'T RECOGNIZE the young man sitting at my desk, but he knows me. "Mrs. Ross-Evans! I'm Sanjit. So nice to meet you."

"The pleasure is all mine. Are you my replacement's replacement?"

"Only for the lunch hour. I'm an intern here. Mr. Strong told me you'd be arriving, and he said you can go right in."

"Thank you." I wink at Lachlan.

"He's a good kid," he murmurs under the cover of the girls squealing.

"And so polite!"

He chuckles as I tap on Gavin's door, then push it open.

He's on the phone, but he waves us in. Hugh sets the girls down on the couch, standing and holding on to the back. They immediately start bouncing. When Meg stops, Ally stops, then they both laugh and start again. Rinse and repeat.

I look at Hugh, then to Lachlan. We're all smiling. Like, cheeks-aching, eyes-crinkling, holy-shit-our-kids-are-adorable smiles.

I take a deep breath. Even though the media won't use our names, we're going to be made a little public today. And that's okay.

As the PM has said forcefully in interviews leading up to this moment, love is love. There's no asterisk on that.

Gavin hangs up the phone and claps his hands together. "How are my favourite almost-one-year-olds?"

He and Ellie have an almost two-year-old at home, a little girl named Chandler, and Ellie recently found out she's expecting again.

Babies everywhere.

He looks at me. "You ready for this afternoon?"

I take a deep breath and nod. "You bet."

"I'm going to do my best for you."

"I know you will."

"And you're coming back to work soon, right?"

I laugh. "In three weeks."

"Thank God."

IT'S A SURREAL THING, watching your personal life influence a piece of legislation.

After Gavin introduces the bill, there are a lot of speakers for and against. It's hard to sit there and hear people say that my family is immoral. But others stand up and talk about the benefits of formalizing loving relationships, and that makes my heart swell.

Then an aide leads us to a press room.

I was totally against the girls coming with us, but the press corps agreed not to take any pictures, and Hugh made a persuasive argument for how seeing the three of us interacting with our kids—just like any other family—would show in a single moment, what an entire speech couldn't convey.

He's exactly right.

My babies win over the press with a single shared giggle. My handsome husbands help, too.

My life. My family.

Mine.

I'm full of pride as I nod at the communications director. "We're ready for questions now."

EPILOGUE 2

HUGH

When I come downstairs from putting the girls to bed, I find Beth in the kitchen.

"Where's…" I trail off as she points to the master bedroom.

I cross the hall and push the door open. I find Lachlan on his knees, waiting for us.

Beth follows me in.

"Hands behind your back," she tells him.

His grin is slow and easy as he obeys.

The position pushes his chest out. His hard nipples, front and centre. I itch to tug on them with my teeth.

She circles him slowly.

Then again, this time, trailing a finger down his cheek to his lips. "Open."

He moans quietly as his lips close around it.

That moan of his sends ripples low in my belly.

Beth looks over at me. "I want you to fuck him," she says. "I want to see him take every inch of you." It's not a big ask at all. But, the gleam in her eye along with that sultry smile of hers could convince me to go along with pretty much anything she can come up with.

"As you like."

She presses her hand between Lachlan's shoulders. "Hands and knees," she demands.

He leans forward and presents his ass to me.

I lube up and kneel behind him. When was the last time we did this? Months ago? Blow jobs and Beth keep us more than satisfied, but this…this is special.

He groans as he slowly opens for me.

With both my hands on his hips, I press deeper, until I'm all the way in. I hold still, savouring the moment. It's been so long. I've missed him like this more than I care to admit.

I pull partway out and Beth crouches by his ear. "Shall I give you a hand job while Hugh rams your ass?" she asks.

Our wife has a filthy tongue now. It's crazy fucking hot.

I plunge hard and deep.

"Yes please," Lachlan groans, nodding enthusiastically.

Beth kneels on the floor next to him and strokes her hand up and down his cock, falling into rhythm with my thrusts.

Lachlan's hips rock into me. Beth smacks his ass and he stops moving. "Do you want to come," she asks him.

"Oh, God, yes."

"Then you should probably stay still and let us help you with that. Otherwise, I might tie you up and make you watch while Hugh fucks me, instead."

Lachlan's head drops, his breathing ragged.

His submission is always beautiful to me, but never more so than when he gives it to Beth.

I can't hold on much longer. Lachlan's so tight, and the whole scene has been the perfect fantasy. I give Beth a nod and she kisses his back as she pumps her hand faster.

"I'm going to come," Lachlan grinds out.

"Give it to us," she murmurs against his skin.

I glory in the first few spasms around my cock. Then I pull out, rip off the condom, and shoot over his back.

Each spurt, marking him as ours.

THE END

Turn the page for some bonus Ross-Evans family photos and more information about other books by Sadie Haller and Ainsley Booth

FOUR PHOTOS THAT HANG ON THE WALL IN THE ROSS-EVANS LIVING ROOM

Beth and the girls, home from the hospital

Lachlan (Daddy) and Hugh (Papa)

Where's my sister? Meg and Ally out for a stroller walk

Meg and Ally at a preschool picnic

ACKNOWLEDGEMENTS

By the third book in a series, acknowledgements start to feel a bit repetitious. So first of all, thank you again to our partners for being supportive and cooking meals, etc. We love you and appreciate all the patience as we buried our heads in our computers.

We finished this book exactly a year to the day that we started *Prime Minister*, so we need to also thank Maria Rose again, who inadvertently inspired a series from that planned-standalone novel. For the same reason, we should probably also thank Frisky Beavers wine. If you live in Ontario, grab a bottle. It's delicious!

Jessica Alcazar gave us the #FuckingHugh hashtag after he showed up at the end of Dr. Bad Boy. That hashtag informed more of this book than we expected! We love it, thank you. She also leads the cheerleading in Ainsley's reader group, where other hashtags for the books came about. #SluttyBeth, #FilthyLachlan, and our favourites, #LachlanInTheMiddle and #Lachlan-Sandwich.

We wrote the first third of this book at the Fun in the Sun Conference. We are blessed to be a part of such an amazing writing community that fosters such events. If you are an aspiring author, look for a regional RWA conference. It's a wonderful way to get your toes wet. Or drag a friend along and start writing together. Magic can happen!

Until the next book!
~ Ainsley & Sadie